ANOTHER SHORE

Sarah Ansbacher

CASA MOCHA BOOKS

A glossary of Hebrew and German terms can be found at the back of this book.

First edition 2026

ISBN 978-1-83828-246-2

This novel is dedicated to the memory of
Michael Adler, my dear uncle.
A lover of books and an avid reader,
he championed my writing from the very first book.

Chapter 1

24 November 1940
SS Atlantic, Haifa Bay

The land stretched before them like a promise, holding their hopes in its hand. Close enough to see. Too far to reach.

Lilly rose on her tiptoes, straining for a better view of the shore over the heads of the passengers on the crowded deck.

'Can you see anyone?' her cousin, Hannah, asked.

Lilly caught the real meaning. They had already spotted Hannah's fiancé's ship in the harbour – empty now. The question was not whether he had arrived, but what had become of him.

Hannah craned her neck. 'Where have they all gone?'

Lilly wondered too about her brother. Had he and his wife come from their kibbutz to meet them? Did he even know their ship had finally arrived?

She searched for signs of a welcoming party, but they were too far away to make out any movement. 'I can't see from this distance.'

Lilly's eyes scanned past the port's sloping warehouse roofs to the city beyond where commercial buildings and modern apartment blocks fanned around Haifa Bay and neat stone-clad villas climbed up the slopes.

Their epic voyage lasting eleven weeks and five days was fraught with danger and filled with moments when they had feared they might not survive at all. Now, looking at the city unfolding before her, Lilly could not wait to set foot on the land. Her new home. For the first time since losing her husband, she felt ready to start over.

Three hours had passed since their ship, the SS *Atlantic*, made its euphoric entrance into Haifa Bay at sunrise as its passengers sang Hatikva amid tears of joy. After hugs all around, their friend Stefan, whom they had met during the journey, brought out his camera and a precious roll of film saved especially for the occasion. He snapped several pictures of the city's panorama framed by Mount Carmel's slopes before angling his lens towards the passengers gathered on deck.

His wife, Jenny, shook her head in mock disbelief. 'Why would you want to remember the awful conditions on the *Atlantic*?'

'As a record,' Stefan said. 'If I don't take pictures, I don't think anyone would believe what we endured to reach Eretz Israel. And once we have settled in a beautiful new home, we will appreciate it all the more.' He pointed the camera in her direction. 'Smile!'

Jenny posed by the railings, Haifa in the background, with the first relaxed, genuine smile Lilly had seen on her face since the start of their journey.

'Let's have one with all the girls,' Stefan said, his voice alight with the thrill of the moment.

Lilly, Hannah and their friends, Erika and Janka, gathered on either side of Jenny.

'You too, Alma.' Stefan gestured.

Alma passed their baby to her husband, Max, and joined the group.

'And you, Gisela.'

The older woman chuckled. 'I'm hardly a girl.'

'I see nothing but beautiful ladies here,' Stefan said with a slight bow of his head.

Gisela blew him a kiss. 'Bless you, *Schatzi*.'

She squeezed in beside Lilly, everyone pressed close together. The friends put their arms around each other, their faces beaming with joy. Their journey was at its end.

'Wonderful!' Stefan looked up from the viewfinder. 'Now, how about one with the whole Lifeboat Chevra?'

The Lifeboat Chevra was the name coined by Janka's brother, Alexander, for their little group who had slept in and around a wooden lifeboat on deck. After the captain disposed of most of their coal, they had to chop up the lifeboat for fuel, together with almost everything else on board made of wood, including two of the masts.

Stefan looked around until he spotted an acquaintance from his native Danzig. He handed him his camera with brief instructions and crammed in behind Jenny.

He beckoned the men. 'Come on!'

Max handed the baby back to Alma and positioned himself behind her, his arms around both of them. Alexander wedged in behind Janka, with their cousin Isaak beside him.

Their new photographer peered through the viewfinder. 'Everyone smile and say Eretz!'

Laughter bubbled up as they called out, 'Eretz!'

The shutter clicked, the group broke formation, and Stefan went to retrieve his camera. 'I'll send you all a copy once we're settled and I've had a chance to develop the film.'

Lilly, like the rest of the Lifeboat Chevra, had expected to sail straight into the harbour and disembark, anticipating emotional goodbyes before going their separate ways. But three hours later they remained in the bay. Waiting. The *Atlantic* had moved no further.

There had been no announcement about their disembarkation. No information at all.

Relief and elation had given way to growing unease.

For the past hour, Alexander, impatient to realise his dream of living on a kibbutz – perhaps already dreaming of orange groves and afternoon sunshine – had roamed the ship seeking out leaders and friends from his Prague group, attempting to find out when they could go ashore. Now he had gone off to try his luck among the platoon of British soldiers who had accompanied them on the last leg of their journey from Cyprus.

'What is taking so long?' Hannah said, her gaze still fixed on the SS *Pacific*, her fiancé Karl's ship, moored inside the harbour beside the SS *Milos*. The *Atlantic* and the two other ships had carried over three thousand Jewish refugees escaping Nazi-occupied Europe. The *Pacific* and *Milos* must have reached Haifa some time earlier. Both vessels looked dark and deserted.

'Why won't they let us enter the harbour too?' It was Erika, standing beside Hannah, her voice carrying the same quiet frustration. Erika's boyfriend had also sailed on the *Pacific*.

Lilly sensed something was wrong. A glance at Isaak told her he felt it too. They exchanged a look but said nothing.

There seemed to be no obvious reason for the port authorities to deny their entry. The harbour appeared to have enough room to admit the *Atlantic*. Apart from the two ships from their transport, most of the vessels were small, the notable exceptions being a cargo ship and a sleek white ocean liner. Smoke billowed from its funnels, and Lilly could see the movement of passengers on its upper deck. The liner had either arrived ahead of them or it was preparing to leave. She could not decide.

Leaden clouds gathered over the Carmel slopes, eclipsing the sunlight that had greeted them at dawn. Rain hung in the air. From the solitary mast of their motionless ship, the Union Jack snapped and strained in the rising wind.

Lilly shivered and bent to retrieve the coat draped over her suitcase. Her mother had given her this coat right before they parted in Vienna. She nestled her face into the fur collar and inhaled, hoping for a lingering scent of Mama's perfume, but it had long since faded. Instead, she smelled sea brine and the mustiness of the hold where the coat had been stored for most of the journey.

'I wonder how much longer it will be,' Gisela said, pressing a hand into the hollow of her back. 'Ow.' She let out a little moan.

'Why don't you sit down while we wait for an announcement?' Lilly said to Gisela. 'My suitcase is sturdy enough to double as a seat.'

'If you're sure?'

Lilly offered her arm for support as Gisela lowered herself onto the case with a sigh of relief. 'That's better. Thank you.' Gisela looked up at the fine drizzle beginning to fall. 'What if my family are waiting in the port to meet me? I wouldn't want the grandchildren standing out in this weather and catching a chill.'

'What's causing the delay?' Hannah said.

Lilly looked out at the harbour again, casting about for a rational explanation to reassure Hannah. She noticed a motor launch circling the *Atlantic*, as relentless as a shark shadowing its prey. Then again, perhaps this was no reason for concern: the British were simply protecting their ship. After all, they were at war.

'What do you think?' Hannah pressed.

'I ... er ...'

'Oh look!' Isaak said, his timely interruption sparing Lilly the need to reply. 'Here comes Alexander. Perhaps he can tell us more.'

The Lifeboat Chevra gathered around him.

'Well?' Janka said, 'What did you find out?'

'Not much.' Alexander's brow furrowed, hazel eyes uncertain. 'Not much at all.'

'Did you manage to speak to any of the soldiers?' Isaak said.

'I tried. The first two were very dismissive and wouldn't answer me.' He pointed across the deck. 'The third one, that one with the ruddy cheeks over there, was friendly enough. But I couldn't understand what he was saying.'

'Did you ask him when we'll get off the ship?' Janka said.

'I did.'

'And what did he reply?'

'That's just it,' Alexander said. 'I barely understood a word. I don't know if he was even speaking English.'

'*Ach quatsch*!' Janka waved a dismissive hand, her fatigue expressing itself as irritation. 'Of course he speaks English. He's a British soldier!'

'Well ... it wasn't like any English I've ever heard.' Alexander mumbled, his shoulders drooping at the chastisement.

'Lilly,' he said, his attention shifting to her without warning. 'Maybe you could try speaking to him? You also speak English well. You may have more luck than I did.'

'Me?' Lilly said, uneasy at the suggestion.

'You'll find he's very friendly,' Alexander said. 'Not like most of them.'

'Oh, please try.' Isaak gave her an encouraging smile. 'There's nothing to lose. Do you want me to come along for moral support?'

'It's all right,' she said, hiding her discomfort from her friends. 'I can do it.'

Lilly wove her way across the crowded deck, still reluctant to approach him, unsure of what to say. As soon as the soldier noticed Lilly, he greeted her with an amiable smile. At least Alexander was right about him being friendly.

'Ey up, lass!' he said.

Alexander had not been exaggerating about the soldier's unusual dialect. Lilly assumed it was a form of greeting.

'Excuse me,' she said. 'Do you know when we will go into the harbour and can get off?'

'Fraid I dunno just yet.' He shrugged. 'No need to fret, lass. There's nowt to worry about. Worse things happen at sea.'

His eyes crinkled, and a chuckle escaped. Whether at the irony of his words, given the setting, or laughing at her, she could not tell.

'Sorry, lass. Just meant it as a joke.'

She hesitated, unsure how to respond.

He dipped his head in a gesture of apology. 'Not t'worry. I'm sure it shouldn't be too long now.'

'Thank you.' Lilly took a step back.

She threaded her way back to her expectant friends.

'Any luck?' Alexander said.

'I asked him—'

'And what did he say?' Hannah asked.

'Alexander's right,' Lilly said. 'His English is very hard to understand.'

'There!' he said to his sister, a triumphant glint in his eye. 'What did I tell you?'

'I think he said we won't have to wait much longer,' Lilly said. 'But I can't be certain.'

'Thank you for trying anyway,' Alexander said.

'So now what?' Janka said.

'I suppose we'll just have to wait,' Alexander said. 'Unless ...' He trailed off as the sound of a sputtering engine broke the calm and a launch drew up alongside the *Atlantic*. The passengers fell silent. Two British policemen boarded their ship.

'I think our welcoming party might have arrived,' Alexander said.

Chapter 2

Transfer. The word rose among the passengers like a rising tide, swelling with whispered translations and sharp intakes of breath.

Lilly's gaze shifted to the *Patria*, the white liner in the harbour where they would all transfer. Mothers with young children and older women first. Quarantine, they'd said.

Officials in shirts and ties, having followed the two policemen onto the *Atlantic*, set about organising the transfer with brisk authority. They cleared a path through the crowd, hauled a table to the bow for registration, and marshalled women with their young children into a line, ready to board the first passenger lighter bound for the *Patria*.

The Lifeboat Chevra pressed closer together, stunned – all except Hannah, who stood apart, eyes fixed on the *Patria*'s upper deck, no doubt scanning the crowd for her fiancé, Karl. The *Pacific* and *Milos* passengers were already on board.

'Are the policemen telling the truth?' Alexander asked.

'Well, we've had a typhoid outbreak,' Erika said. 'And cases of other illnesses.' As a volunteer nurse she had tended to many of the patients during the voyage.

'But why on a ship?' Alexander said. 'Do they not have enough room on land?' He gestured towards the shoreline, at the green open spaces beyond the city and the slopes of Mount Carmel. 'I find that hard to believe.'

So did Lilly.

'Historically, it was common practice to isolate ship passengers before allowing them ashore,' said Stefan, sounding like the history teacher he used to be. 'It's been going on since the Great Plague. In fact, the word quarantine comes from the Italian *quaranta giorni*, meaning forty days.'

'Forty days!' Alexander said, his voice rising.

'That's just where the word comes from,' Stefan added. 'That doesn't mean they will keep us there for as long as that.'

Alexander folded his arms. 'They had better not.'

'And I was so looking forward to reuniting with my family this afternoon,' Gisela said, tracing the edge of the peacock silk scarf at her neck. 'This isn't how I pictured our arrival.'

'None of us did,' Lilly said. 'I wish I could at least get a message to my brother, to let him know what's happening.'

'Maybe you can.' Alexander gestured towards the officials dotted around the deck. 'Why don't you ask one of them if they'd take a letter to shore for you? And while you're at it, see what you can learn. Worth a try, no?'

Lilly agreed. If she had found the nerve to speak to the soldier earlier, she could manage a word with one of these officials now. She skirted the line snaking down the centre of the deck and made her way to one standing off to the side, observing the proceedings near the stern. His suntanned skin and dark, curly hair set him apart from the others.

'Excuse me,' she said in English.

'How can I help you?' he replied in halting, careful German.

'Oh!' She gave him a warm smile. 'You speak very good German for an Englishman.'

His expression remained neutral. 'I appreciate the compliment. But I'm not English. I work for them, yes, but I was born here, in Haifa.'

Lilly looked at him with renewed curiosity. 'You're Jewish?' Her voice lifted with excitement. 'You're the first Jew I've ever met from Eretz Israel!'

He gave the barest hint of a smile before glancing around. Whatever he saw made his smile disappear. Was he being watched?

'I'm so happy that we have finally reached Eretz Israel,' Lilly continued. 'We had such a long and difficult journey, but now we're home.'

'Indeed.'

'Do you know how long we will have to remain in quarantine on the *Patria*?'

The official looked down and straightened his tie. He fussed with the cuffs of his shirt next. Was he trying to avoid eye contact? 'I don't have that information.'

'You see, my brother must be waiting for me at the port. It's already several hours since we arrived. He might be worried.'

The man made no comment.

'Would it be possible for me to write a short note which you could pass to him? I could give you his name and—'

'I am unable to do that,' he broke in. 'And I'm busy right now.'

The rebuff stung. 'Sorry to have troubled you.' Lilly turned to walk away.

'Listen, I'm sorry,' the official called after her. Lilly looked back. 'If I could help, I would. But I can't.'

Was that remorse she saw in his expression? Did he know more than he was letting on?

'Thank you anyway,' she managed.

Lilly made her way back to Alexander and the others, mulling over the Jewish official's perplexing attitude. What a contrast with the Jewish communities in Istanbul, Crete and Limassol who had gone out of their way to help them continue their journey: bringing food, posting letters, even finding coal despite wartime shortages. She would have expected the welcome in Haifa to be the warmest of all. Not this evasiveness from the policemen and indifference from the officials.

'Well?' Alexander prompted.

'I couldn't get much out of him. He refused outright to take a note to my brother.'

'At least you tried.'

'Here's something interesting, though,' Lilly said. 'When I spoke to him in English, he answered in stilted German. Turns out he's Jewish, born right here in Haifa.'

'*Ach so*!' Alexander raised a finger. 'That could explain it. His German probably isn't strong. I might have better luck speaking to him in Hebrew.'

Alexander crossed the deck with an air of certainty, but his exchange with the official was even shorter than Lilly's. He sloped back, shoulders sagging. 'I spoke to him in Hebrew, but he would only reply in German. I didn't think my Hebrew was that bad.'

'Did he tell you anything?'

'It's like speaking to a brick wall!' Alexander threw up his hands. 'He told me we'll be advised in due course.'

Lilly glanced at the Patria. 'Do you feel something isn't right?'

Alexander nodded slowly. 'Perhaps there's something to Stefan's theory after all. They don't want to admit we'll have to stay on the *Patria* for forty days.'

Isaak studied the vessel. 'Do you think it's suspicious that there's smoke coming out of the ship's funnels?'

'It's because they have the electricity running,' Alexander said. 'That's nothing to worry about.'

'You don't think that once we're on board ... they'll send us back?' Isaak said.

'No!' Alexander shook his head. 'The British wouldn't do that. Especially not after they gave us official permission to land in Haifa. If that had been their intention, they would have done so in Cyprus.' He focused on the policeman registering the first passengers at the bow. 'The British may act rather cold and formal, but they are honourable. I doubt they would do anything so underhand. Remember, they made us pay for the fuel before they'd let us sail here. Every single passenger contributed, down to their last coins and jewellery. They can't break their word now.'

Lilly's hand went to her pocket, surreptitiously feeling for the wedding ring from her late husband, Salo – the last item of value she possessed. She had surrendered it as her contribution and, if not for Isaak, she would have lost it forever. Isaak had substituted the brass pedals and castors from the piano Lilly had helped to demolish for her ring. Along with their lifeboat, the cabin partitions, and all but one of the masts, the passengers had fed the wooden piano fragments to the ship's furnace.

'What do you think we should do?' Isaak said.

Alexander raised his hands, palms up. 'We have no choice but to follow their instructions, disappointing as it is not to step onto land today. The last thing we want is to make trouble and give them a reason to bar us from Eretz, especially when we're so close we can see the land and smell the air.' He closed his eyes and inhaled deeply. 'And the *Patria* is in the harbour, unlike our ship. That's a step closer, at least.'

'I agree,' Hannah said, a little too eagerly. 'The passengers on the *Patria* just seem to be milling around on deck. It doesn't look like there's a problem.'

Lilly wanted to say that they were too far away to see much at all, but she held her tongue.

'I think Alexander is right,' Max said, looking at his wife and son. Alma had tucked the baby inside her coat to protect him from the stiff wind and relentless drizzle. 'You ought to join the line.'

'But I don't want to leave without you. I'd rather wait until we can go together,' Alma said.

'The men won't transfer until tomorrow, and you need a proper night's sleep in a decent bed.'

For the past few days, ever since their wooden cabin had been dismantled for fuel, they had all crammed together to sleep on the lower deck. The dark circles beneath Alma's eyes attested to her exhaustion.

Chaim coughed. Alma patted his back and rocked him back and forth.

'I can manage one more night.'

Max stroked Alma's cheek. 'If not for you, we must consider Chaim. It's not good for him to be out in this weather or to sleep in a draughty passageway. He's already coughing. We don't want him to get ill.'

Alma nestled her face against his hand. 'I know you're right. But still. I'd much prefer to go with you.'

'It's only one night. I'll be with you tomorrow. And on the *Patria* you'll have a nice warm cabin to sleep in.'

Max gathered Alma's case and Chaim's Moses basket. 'I'll stay with you until you board the lighter.'

'Gisela, what about you?' Hannah asked. 'You're also eligible to transfer now.'

Gisela's hand moved towards her suitcase. She hesitated and pulled back.

'We could go with you and help you across.' Hannah bent to grab Gisela's suitcase, fingers tightening around the handle as if ready to move. 'I'm sure they'd allow it if we say we're "family" and you need the assistance. Lilly, you'll come too, won't you?'

CHAPTER 3

The rain drummed harder. Water soaked through Lilly's coat and pooled on the bare deck. Her shoes were sodden. Gisela and Hannah hunched beside her, all three inching towards the registration table at the bow.

Alma was already warm and dry on the *Patria*, having boarded the earlier lighter. After a lengthy discussion and farewells, the rest of the Lifeboat Chevra went below deck for shelter. Janka decided to wait and cross with Alexander and Isaak; she felt it unfair to leave them behind. Jenny dithered about joining but, nervous to go without Stefan, chose to remain on the *Atlantic* for one more evening. Erika had wanted to come, eager to see her boyfriend Marcus again, but could not abandon her nursing duties. She gave Hannah a long letter to deliver instead.

Lilly would not be sorry to get off the *Atlantic* and out of the rain. Since they could not go ashore, at least the new ship promised comfort. Yet abandoning the others troubled her. She was using Gisela as justification to push ahead in the queue, while Hannah's desire to reunite with Karl was the main reason they were boarding early. Still, Hannah was not wrong. Gisela was eligible and did need help. Why should Gisela spend another night sleeping on the floor because of Lilly's qualms?

They were not the only women in the queue who hardly qualified as vulnerable. Lilly looked back to see that plenty of other young women – without children or elderly relatives – were waiting to board the next lighter, no doubt tempted by the promise of more space, better conditions, and a bed.

Two places behind, under an umbrella, stood the blonde woman in her trademark pink silk dress and a companion. Though comparing herself to that vile woman offered no reassurance. When they had first boarded the *Atlantic*, the blonde, her husband, and friends had taken a cabin meant for more needy passengers. Hannah, looking for a place to sleep and not realising the cabin was already occupied, had tried the door, only for it to be slammed in her face. She never knew that later, the same woman invited Isaak to sleep on their floor, and he innocently accepted. Alexander had confided to Lilly that the woman's true motivations became apparent the following night when she sidled up to Isaak as he slept, just a few feet away from her husband. Isaak had fled, mortified. Alexander intervened and had the woman and her roommates ejected. Gisela, Alma, and Jenny were among those reassigned to the cabin. Sworn to secrecy, Lilly never told Hannah any of this, and the blonde woman knew nothing of Lilly's role. The woman blamed Hannah for her unceremonious eviction and slapped her across the face. Lilly carried such guilt after witnessing the confrontation, knowing she should have been the target of the blonde woman's anger.

Lilly averted her gaze before the woman noticed her, and they shuffled along with the queue. Only three people remained ahead of them. Hannah brimmed with excitement. Her joy at seeing Karl again outweighed any disappointment over their delayed disembarkation. Lilly could not blame her. Seven weeks had passed since Hannah had last seen Karl when the three ships prepared to depart Tulcea, Romania. His ship, the *Pacific*, had sailed past their own. Hannah caught a quick glimpse of him and gave a wave before his ship headed down the Danube channel towards the sea. The *At-*

lantic had followed, but only managed a few metres before it broke down and had to be towed to Sulina for repairs. And so it began, the litany of disasters that had marked their voyage – which, it appeared, had not quite reached its conclusion.

Lilly was not sure how she felt after her emotional rise and fall. Today she was supposed to start a new life in Eretz Israel and see her brother again for the first time in over two years. But it was more than that. The prospect of the transfer still did not sit right. True, several passengers aboard had contagious diseases. She understood the need for quarantine. So why hadn't the British warned them from the start? Why did she get the impression the Jewish official was withholding a secret? And what would have been the harm in him delivering a note to her brother?

'Why are you frowning?' Hannah said.

'Aren't you worried about transferring to the *Patria*?' Lilly said.

'Why should I be worried?' She smiled. 'It's only for a short time, and Karl is there waiting for me. I'm so excited to see him again.' She cast a glance down as if assessing herself. 'What a shame I didn't have time to change my dress or ask Erika to style my hair.'

Gisela patted Lilly's hand. '*Schatzi*, it's going to be fine. We've waited this long, we can manage a few more days.' Gisela did not refer to her own disappointment. Instead of the longed-for reunion with her two sons and meeting her daughter-in-law and grandchildren for the first time, she would spend an indefinite stay on another ship. 'The others will join us tomorrow. And won't it be nice to sleep in a proper bed tonight?'

'It's just ... well, it feels a little strange, secretive perhaps, the way they are transferring us.'

'Lilly, you worry too much,' Hannah said. 'They explained the reason. Do you remember how you reacted when I first told you I had gone to the Central Office for Jewish Emigration and signed up for this transport? You begged me not to go. You were convinced it was a malevolent plot.' Hannah winked. 'But here we are, standing on the deck of a ship looking at the beautiful sight of Mount Carmel. In a few minutes I'll see my fiancé again. And in another few days, after this quarantine period, we will enter Eretz Israel. What would have happened if I had listened to you?'

The thought unsettled her. If not for Hannah's persistence, they might have remained trapped in Vienna. Her mother, and Hannah's, were still stuck there. They had not heard from them in many weeks. How were they faring under the oppressive conditions? Was there still a chance they could find a way to join them in Eretz? As soon as they were released from quarantine, Lilly would send a letter. Better yet, a telegram.

'I suppose you are right,' Lilly said.

It was too late to turn back anyway; they had reached the front of the queue.

The policeman noted their names and particulars in his ledger and waved them towards the gangway. He stood up and called out to the remaining queue, 'The lighter is now full. This is the last one for today. Transfers will continue tomorrow morning at seven-thirty.'

'That was lucky!' Hannah said, setting off with Gisela.

Lilly bent to pick up her suitcase in one hand and Gisela's in the other. But as she straightened, a sharp point jabbed her in the back and threw her off balance. She pitched forward, and the suitcases slipped from her grasp. She landed hard on her hands and knees on the grimy deck.

'Lilly!' Gisela gasped, rushing back with Hannah.

Mortified, Lilly struggled to get up.

'Miss, let me help you,' an official said, taking her arm. As she got to her feet, she caught a flash of pink heading down the gangway. 'Careful there, the deck is very slippery.'

'Are you hurt?' Hannah said.

'I'll be fine.' Lilly brushed her hands together in short sharp strokes to shake off the dirt, anger simmering below her composure. The front of her mama's beautiful coat was filthy. She bent to retrieve the cases.

'Here, let me take one of those for you,' the official said, lifting Gisela's suitcase as Lilly retrieved her own. He led the way down the narrow, water-slicked gangway that descended steeply to the lighter below. 'Careful how you go.' He looked back at Lilly. She held onto the handrail as she followed him, with Gisela and Hannah behind.

At the foot of the gangway, the official helped Lilly onto the swaying lighter, where a guard on deck marked off a tally. Passengers sat shoulder to shoulder on the benches. A newborn baby let out a tiny wail. At least the rain had stopped.

The official added Gisela's suitcase to the pile of luggage at the bow, and Lilly stacked hers beside it. 'You'll be all right from here, miss?'

'Yes,' Lilly said. 'Thank you for your help.'

He inclined his head before returning to the gangway. Once he had passed, Hannah and Gisela moved to board, but the guard raised a hand to stop them. 'The lighter is full.' He spoke slowly, his voice raised, as if speaking to someone hard of hearing.

'What?' Hannah's voice rose. 'That's impossible. The policeman took our details. He allowed us to board.'

The guard hesitated. He checked his list and scratched his jaw. Pencil in hand, he made a quick headcount of the forty or so passengers. 'No, we're definitely full.'

'There has to be a mistake!' Hannah edged forward, but the guard's gesture held her back.

'There might have been an accidental miscount on deck.' The guard shrugged. 'All those people there. You know how it is.'

'Can't you squeeze us on?'

'Sorry,' he said. 'The rules is the rules.'

'But then we'll have to wait until tomorrow.' Desperation crept into Hannah's voice.

'Orders is orders.'

Lilly read the resolve in his stance; the guard would not relent. He would leave Hannah and Gisela on the gangway, and she was now bound for the *Patria*. Alone.

'Wait!' Lilly said. 'There has been a mistake.'

The guard angled his head towards her, his eyebrows raised.

'The three of us registered for this lighter, but before we reached the gangway, two women pushed past and boarded ahead of us without registration.' Lilly fixed her gaze on the blonde woman and her companion. They refused to meet her eyes.

The guard scrutinised Lilly for a moment, then addressed the rest of the passengers. 'Right, you lot. Did any of you board without registering first?'

No one responded. Of course the woman was not about to admit her actions.

The guard shifted his attention back to Lilly. 'A likely story,' he said. 'Looks to me like your two friends over there who are trying to board without prior registration.'

'I'm telling the truth.' Her words came out firmer than before. She pointed at the blonde woman. 'She pushed me over and slipped past in the confusion when the official helped me to my feet. He can confirm my story.' She looked up the gangway, but the official was long gone.

The guard huffed out an impatient breath. 'Look, we haven't got time for this. We need to cast off. We're already running late.'

The woman simpered with self-satisfaction and smoothed her pink silk dress.

The guard motioned Gisela and Hannah back the way they had come. 'Off you go.'

'If that's the case,' Lilly called to the guard. 'I want to get off and swap places!'

'You can't do that,' he said.

Lilly pushed through to the bow to retrieve her suitcase and Gisela's. 'I can and I will,' she said and stepped off the lighter.

Lilly looked from Gisela to Hannah, saw the longing in her cousin's eyes.

'You go,' Gisela said and nudged Hannah's arm. 'Before they leave without you.'

'Are you sure?'

'Lilly and I will be fine for one more night,' Gisela said. 'Go and be with Karl.'

'Thank you so much.' Hannah gave them each a fleeting hug. She picked up her suitcase under the guard's frown and boarded the lighter in Lilly's place.

From the deck of the Atlantic, Lilly and Gisela waved to Hannah as the lighter pulled away. Lilly felt satisfaction mixed with fury. She had helped Hannah reach Karl, but the blonde woman had stolen their rightful places. If Lilly had been reluctant to transfer to the Patria before, now she was determined. Tomorrow morning, she and Gisela would be the first aboard.

Chapter 4

24 November 1940
SS Patria, Haifa Harbour

Hannah gave a stiff wave in reply to Lilly and Gisela's enthusiastic ones from the railings of the *Atlantic*. She felt the blonde woman's hostile stare fixed on the back of her head. Hannah did not dare turn around.

The distance widened between them. Hannah's conscience pricked that she had taken her cousin's place, even though the choice to swap was Lilly's and she seemed more than willing – maybe slightly relieved. She had voiced reservations about transferring to the *Patria*, but all the *Atlantic* passengers would follow soon enough.

Perhaps it was better this way. Hannah would have time for a private reunion with Karl before the others arrived. And Lilly would not be alone; she would be with Gisela and the rest of the Lifeboat Chevra.

Hannah only wished that Lilly had someone of her own. She was too young to remain a widow. Hannah still thought Alexander would be good for her cousin. True, there were differences in their upbringing, lifestyle, and outlook, but surely if they cared enough for one another, those could be overcome. He was a kind, honest, charismatic man – and it did not hurt that he was also tall and rather handsome. Clearly, he came from a respectable family. Janka, his sister, thoughtful, sincere, and a fellow book-lover, had become one of Hannah's dearest friends. Isaak, their younger cousin, was warm-hearted and funny. Resourceful too. It was impossible not to love him. And the way Alexander and Janka looked out for him was admirable. They treated him more like their sibling than a cousin. Hannah appreciated that. She felt the same about Lilly.

Lilly had come a long way in the two years since losing Salo, but the loss had taken its toll. What a shame she was not yet open to starting a new relationship. She had gently turned down Alexander and Hannah did not want to pressure her. Hannah suspected Alexander still cared for Lilly and hoped in time Lilly might feel ready to love again.

The lighter entered the harbour, and Hannah could no longer make out Lilly and Gisela. Her thoughts shifted to Karl. Apart from a quick glimpse as his ship sailed past theirs in Tulcea, they had spent almost three months apart. Now they would be together again, this time for good. And soon they would be married. Thinking about their wedding made her stomach flutter.

The lighter moored alongside the *Patria*. Up close, the sleek white liner was even more imposing than she had expected. The ship towered above them. Before they were allowed to disembark, the crew had to unload the luggage. Passengers from the *Patria* descended the gangway and formed a human chain to transfer the suitcases from the lighter to the deck. Hannah recognised a few as Karl's friends. Her eyes travelled up the line of men on the gangway. At the very top, a pair of glasses shimmered as they caught the light. Karl. He paused and set down a valise. He had noticed her too. Karl looked thinner, his face more gaunt than she remembered, but when he smiled his same beautiful smile, Hannah felt a rush of love. She wished she could run up the stairs, straight into his arms. Karl waved and placed a hand to his heart; the sign they had used in the past to express their love from a distance. Then he stooped to retrieve the valise and continue his work. Hannah would have to wait a few more impatient minutes for a proper reunion.

At last they could leave the lighter. Hannah headed towards the gangway, only to find her way blocked by the blonde woman and her brunette companion. The woman gave Hannah a look of undisguised contempt. Hannah hung back, chiding herself for letting the woman intimidate her, but unwilling to risk another altercation. The woman snapped her gaze away, smoothed down her pink silk dress, and, taking her companion by the arm, pushed between the other passengers to be the first ones up the gangway.

Hannah still didn't understand the woman's irrational behaviour. Aside from an accidental collision on deck after they boarded the *Atlantic*, what had Hannah ever done to deserve such hostility? For some inexplicable reason, the woman blamed Hannah for arranging her eviction from the cabin, though she had done nothing of the sort.

Hannah waited until the women were out of sight before joining the orderly queue of passengers filing off the lighter onto the gangway. She looked to her right, where the *Atlantic* was anchored in the bay on the other side of the breakwater. Strange to see it from this distance. Despite their gruelling journey, that ramshackle ship had managed to transport them all the way from Tulcea to Haifa.

Time to leave the past behind. Ahead lay her future. Hannah took a deep breath to calm her racing heart and ascended the gangway. This was the moment she had longed for. Throughout every trial and tribulation, the thought of seeing Karl again had fortified her. Now each step brought her closer to her fiancé.

Hannah reached the deck of the *Patria*. Karl was waiting for her. He extended his hand, but a policeman blocked his path. 'You'll see her later.'

Armed guards separated Hannah and the other women from her lighter to a corner of the deck. A nurse waited with a hand-pump duster. 'Close your eyes and raise your arms,' she said.

Hannah complied. They were on board this ship for quarantine, after all. Once this was over, she could be with Karl. The nurse pumped clouds of DDT over each passenger, white powder settling on their hair, skin, and clothing.

No sooner had the disinfection process ended than guards ordered them to collect their luggage and line up for customs inspection. The women were called to one of two policemen standing behind a table, their cases opened and contents scattered across the surface in a frenzied disarray. Karl watched from across the deck, a concerned expression on his face, but when Hannah caught his eye, he gave her a nod of reassurance. He must have seen this disorganised procedure several times before.

'Next!' The policeman on the right stared at her with a piercing gaze. Everything about him was sharp: his narrowed eyes, angular cheekbones, the thin hawkish nose. Hannah hurried forward to the table. He motioned for her to open her luggage. He plunged his hands in, his strong fingers rifling through her suitcase and rucksack, flinging her clothes and underwear over the surface. The policeman's lips flattened, less a smile, more a smirk, as he lifted out her copy of *Around the World in Eighty Days*. He examined the front and back covers, flipped the pages, and tossed it onto a growing pile of confiscated items behind him.

'It's just a novel,' Hannah said. Lilly had given Hannah the book as a gift right before she left Vienna. The policeman raised an eyebrow at Hannah, and she felt an odd, criminal sort of guilt despite having done nothing wrong. He delved further until he retrieved a bundle of letters from Karl, her mother, and Lilly and held it up like a prize. He untied the blue silk ribbon that held them together, rifled through the first few, then let them fall like confetti onto the growing pile.

'Those are personal letters from my family. Can I please have them back?'

The policeman scanned the deck. 'Mrs Hoyle!' he called with a beckoning gesture.

A solidly built woman in her middle years, wearing a straw hat and khaki skirt, strode to the table.

'Attend to this one,' he said.

'Yes, Sergeant Tait,' she said in a clipped, nasal tone, her stance firm, gloved hands poised.

She fixed Hannah with a steady look. 'Arms out. Keep still.'

Hannah hesitated. 'Why?'

Mrs Hoyle moved in closer. 'Arms out.'

Hannah raised her arms, hands shaking.

Mrs Hoyle ran her hands along Hannah's sleeves, frisked her sides, and stopped at the pocket of her dress. She plunged her hand in, pulled out an envelope, and raised it in triumph. Erika's letter to Marcus.

Mrs Hoyle read the name on the front, her voice rising: 'Marcus Levy.' She scrutinised Hannah. 'So you were trying to smuggle this message?'

'It's just a letter from my friend to her boyfriend who is on the *Patria*,' Hannah said. 'I'm not smuggling anything.'

Mrs Hoyle passed the letter to Sergeant Tait. They exchanged a brief look, edged with satisfaction.

'Pack your suitcase and come with me,' she said, as if relishing the task.

There was no room for protest. Hannah stuffed her belongings into her suitcase in a clumsy rush and followed Mrs Hoyle who marched ahead without a backward glance.

Mrs Hoyle led her to a small cabin inside the ship.

'Right,' she said and shut the door behind them. 'Clothes off. Down to your underclothes.'

'My clothes?'

'Do I have to keep repeating myself?' Mrs Hoyle said. 'Yes, your clothes. And be quick about it.'

Hannah would have liked to complain, to tell Mrs Hoyle that she had never been treated this way before. Not even in Vienna. She submitted without resistance and closed her eyes against the shame as Mrs Hoyle swept her hands across her body from head to toe.

'All right, you can dress now,' Mrs Hoyle said, her voice dull. Was she disappointed not to have found another trophy to present to Sergeant Tait?

Hannah dressed in haste and grabbed her bags, desperate to leave. 'Can I go now?'

Mrs Hoyle opened the door. Hannah lifted her chin and walked out without so much as a glance at the woman, holding on to what dignity she had left.

Karl was waiting for Hannah when she returned to the deck. He hugged her, pulling the case from her grip. Less romantic, more comforting.

'They treated me as if I were a spy,' Hannah said, her voice tight as she pressed her head against his chest.

'It's over now.'

'But they confiscated my book, which was a gift from Lilly. And all my letters, including all the ones you wrote to me when we were stuck in Tulcea.'

'It's all right. I can write you many more.'

'And they took a letter that Erika asked me to pass to Marcus.'

Karl stiffened and did not meet her gaze.

'She'll be arriving tomorrow with the rest of the Lifeboat Chevra. I suppose she can just tell him everything in person when she sees him.'

Karl hitched his shoulders. 'Let's go somewhere more private where we can talk.'

'This isn't how I pictured our reunion would be.'

'We don't have to let them ruin it.' He entwined his fingers with hers and led her away from the crowds, along the side of the ship to where stairs led up to a quieter spot on the deck above, hidden behind piles of wooden boards and mattresses. The murmur of voices drifted up from below. Behind them, waves broke against the nearby breakwater in a steady rhythm.

He set down her suitcase, slid his arms around her, and kissed her tenderly. 'We're together now, and that's all that matters,' he said, drawing her closer in a more passionate embrace.

She smiled at him, catching her breath. 'I do have some good news. As we arrived in Haifa this morning, Lilly told me she's interested in joining us on the kibbutz. But, she says, she'll only come after we're married, so we shouldn't take too long about it. So we don't have to delay our wedding until we have helped Lilly get settled. Isn't that wonderful?'

'That would be perfect,' Karl said, but his delight sounded forced, his eyes mournful.

Hannah pulled away. 'You don't seem as happy as I thought you'd be.' She was nervous to continue. 'Have you changed your mind about us?'

'No, not at all.' He reached for her hands. 'I want to marry you more than ever.'

He sat, resting his back against a pile of boards, and Hannah followed. He placed his arm around her. 'Do you remember the last time we saw each other before we left Tulcea?'

'As if I would forget.'

'As our ship sailed by and we quickly waved to each other, you looked full of joy. So beautiful.' His gaze seemed wistful. 'I held that image of you in my mind, like a photograph, throughout our difficult voyage. There were times I feared that I might never see you again. But I prayed you would have a safe journey, a smoother one than ours, and that nothing would happen to dull your optimism.'

Hannah could not help her little chuckle. 'Do you know what happened moments after we exchanged waves?'

Karl shook his head.

'Our ship followed yours, but we only got a few metres before the engine broke down and we nearly ran aground. After spending the night right there on the river, a tugboat hauled us to Sulina, where we had to wait another day until mechanics assessed the damage. During the tense wait for repairs, I kept scanning the horizon for your ship, but you were long gone.'

'Not quite. The day you left Sulina and sailed across the Black Sea, we fell behind you.'

'How is that even possible?'

'Our compass failed, and the captain lost his way. He didn't even have binoculars. Instead of going south, we had shifted north. We had to anchor in Varna, Bulgaria to have it fixed. We were meant to leave on *erev* Yom Kippur but were delayed there for six days.'

She winced in recognition. 'And all that time I'd assumed you were far ahead. By Yom Kippur we had already passed Istanbul. When you left Varna, we would have been doing our tour of the Greek islands.'

Karl cast her a curious glance. 'Tour?'

'We didn't have enough coal. The plan was to load more in Istanbul, but our captain was a crook. He extorted extra money from our Transport Committee but didn't buy any. We left Istanbul and he proceeded to sail us around several Greek islands - Lesbos, Samos, and Ios - apparently intending to purchase fuel, but we left each port empty-handed.'

Karl stared at her in disbelief.

'Finally, we stopped in Crete,' Hannah continued, 'having run out of food, water and almost all our coal. We waited there for three weeks. If not for the kindness of the Jewish community in Crete who provided us with food and water and helped us to purchase the coal, we might never have left at all.'

'We too stopped at the island of Crete—'

'So you *were* in the area!' Hannah said. 'We heard a rumour that the *Pacific* was close by. I watched for your ship among every vessel that approached the harbour. Do you remember the dates you were there?'

'Towards the end of October. Let me see ... we were there for a week and left on 28th October. While there, representatives from the Athens Jewish community flew to Crete especially to help us. They too gave us supplies for the rest of our journey.'

'Then we were there at the same time. But you weren't in Heraklion, otherwise we would have seen you?'

'We anchored next to a little town called Agios Nikolaos. A beautiful place. The locals were so welcoming. They brought us gifts and even came out on small boats to play music and sing for us. When we left, a few boats accompanied us for a short distance with the men playing the Greek national anthem. For the first and only time on our journey, we met friendly people who treated us like human beings.'

'Did you say Agios Nikolaos?' Hannah said.

'That's right.'

'Unbelievable! We stopped there a week after you, but under very different circumstances. We did not get a warm welcome. Quite the opposite. The harbourmaster boarded our ship and told us we had to leave immediately.'

Karl leaned in, his expression intent. 'Why?'

'On 28th October, the day you left Crete, Italy declared war on Greece. We feared being trapped in Crete for good. But perhaps, for once, the war worked in our favour. Because the Greeks and the Royal Air Force wanted us to leave as quickly as possible, Mr Sevilla and Mr Cohen, the representatives of the Crete Jewish community, secured coal for us at last. Once they had loaded the ship with coal, we had to depart from Crete. But that night, Captain Spiro deceived us. Instead of sailing east towards Eretz Israel, he sailed south, around the island, and under the cover of darkness, he and his crew dumped most of our coal overboard.'

Karl pressed a hand to his mouth, eyes wide as he listened.

'Then Spiro anchored the ship and tried to escape over the side with one of his crew. Lilly and our friend, Isaak, kept him from escaping until our Haganah could apprehend him. The place where all this happened was just off Agios Nikolaos.'

'What did you do after your captain had dumped the coal?'

'Several Haganah members locked Spiro in his cabin. Two of the passengers took over the captain's role. We burned furniture, wall panels, flooring, anything made of wood that could fuel the boilers. It ran out before we reached the coast of Cyprus. We were spotted by the Royal Navy who later sent a boat to tow us to the port of Limassol.'

Karl pulled her closer. 'Something similar happened to us. Before we left Crete we were told that on the second day of sailing we would see Cyprus. But we sailed the whole day with no land in sight. On the third day, we still didn't spot land or any ships. Just the endless sea. Rumours spread that our compass had broken once more and the captain had lost his way. Our coal was running out. We had to use all the wooden bunks and doors, even the lifeboats, for fuel.'

'Someone on your ship must have also read *Around the World in Eighty Days*.'

'Sorry? I'm not sure what you mean.'

'It's a novel Lilly gave me as a parting gift before I left Vienna. In the story, they too run out of coal and they have to cut up all the wooden furniture to burn for fuel.'

'Really?' A subtle smile played on Karl's lips. 'How funny. Yet appropriate. I'd like to read that book.'

'I would have lent it to you. But that was the book the policeman just confiscated from me.'

His smile faded into a grim line.

'So,' Hannah said. 'I take it you made it to the coast of Cyprus in the end?'

'Not exactly,' he said. 'We spent a fraught night burning all the furniture. Then, on the fourth day, when the sun rose, we spotted land. But we didn't know where we were. Was it Cyprus or Lebanon? No one was sure.' Karl looked up at the rose-gold sky and the tip of Mount Carmel in the softening light, his expression dreamy yet sad. 'We came closer and closer. We saw a magnificent town and hills in the distance. Then someone shouted: this is Eretz Israel!'

'Wait a minute.' The dates tumbled through her mind. Her breath caught as the pieces fell into place with sudden, terrible clarity. 'But that means you already arrived in Haifa—'

'Yes.' His eyes held hers. 'Over three weeks ago.'

Hannah stared at him. 'What haven't you told me yet?'

Chapter 5

1 November 1940
SS Pacific, Haifa Bay

The passengers erupted in celebration, laughter mingling with tears of happiness. Karl and Marcus pressed forward on the *Pacific*'s crowded deck to lay eyes on the Promised Land. When his turn came, Karl gazed at Haifa curving around the bay, the city's modern stone homes climbing the verdant slopes of Mount Carmel.

Karl's heart lifted as they sang *Hatikva*. He remembered the last time they had sung the anthem together: a convoy of four paddle steamers setting off from Bratislava down the Danube on an uncertain journey. His beloved Hannah on the boat right behind. Then, a Swastika flag fluttered from each mast. Now he had reached his homeland, and flying from their mast was a blue and white flag.

'Can you believe it?' Marcus said. 'We've reached Eretz Israel.'

Karl felt a tangle of emotions he could not name. 'Yes. We've come home.'

'I wonder where the *Atlantic* is?'

Karl scanned the harbour but saw no sign of the ship. 'Hopefully not too far behind. I can't wait to see Hannah again.'

'Nor I, to see Erika.' Marcus spoke louder to make himself heard over the exuberant passengers who had begun another song. 'I've missed her more than I could have imagined. There is so much I want to tell her ... and a question I would like to ask.'

Karl raised an eyebrow, grinning. 'The big question?'

Marcus gave a small, self-conscious smile. 'If she'll have me.'

Karl beamed and gripped his friend's shoulder. 'I'm sure she will. She'll be lucky to have you, my friend.'

'Can you imagine us living beside each other on the kibbutz, raising our families together?'

'I could not think of anything more wonderful.'

The singing fell away as a small British patrol boat approached their ship. Karl's smile dimmed, his gaze narrowing. Perhaps they had been naïve to imagine they could slip through the British blockade. Of course, that was not possible when they had sailed right into Haifa Bay. Three officers boarded the ship. Their pristine white uniforms stood out starkly against the passengers' worn, travel-stained clothes. An officer, carrying a folded piece of fabric, strode up to the mast. He lowered their flag with the blue Magen David at its centre and hoisted the Union Jack in its place.

A few passengers clapped at what they viewed as a positive gesture: confirmation that the policemen had accepted them into British territory and the refugees were now under their protection.

Karl was less sure.

The officers offered no explanation, only asked about the whereabouts of the *Milos* and the *Atlantic*. By name. The British had been expecting them.

A pilot boat followed and towed the *Pacific* towards the port's entrance.

Would the British grant them permission to enter? Surely they understood the refugees had fled for their lives.

The arrest of their captain and crew suggested otherwise. A pang of guilt tugged at Karl as he watched him wave to the passengers from the British patrol boat heading into the harbour. His new friend, Hans – known to everyone as HW – did his best to reassure Karl.

'Don't worry about the captain,' HW said, leaning closer. 'He's made the journey before and knew the risks in advance.' He winked. 'And rumour has it the captain has saved a tidy amount of money from these voyages.'

All the same, Karl felt sorry that the captain would serve time in jail on their account.

Later that afternoon, a medical committee came on board to examine conditions. There were several cases of typhoid. The police also brought food for the passengers. Each person received a green apple and a ration of bread.

Karl cradled the apple in his hand and rotated it, studying the fruit from all sides. He inhaled its crisp, sweet scent. The first fruit from the Land.

Karl, like most passengers on board, wondered when officials from the *Yishuv* would arrive to welcome them. But, as HW pointed out, it was Friday afternoon and they were more likely to come after Shabbat.

As the sun set, ushering in their first Shabbat in Eretz Israel, Karl made the blessing over his bread rations: *Hamotzi lechem min ha'aretz* – blessed are You who brings forth bread from the Land. Never had that blessing seemed more meaningful as he savoured each bite. He and Marcus stood on the deck drinking in the view with an unquenchable thirst. They watched the city until darkness fell and the wartime blackout erased it from view. Only a sliver of crescent moon remained visible in the night sky.

Karl was too wound up and too cramped to fall asleep. He had to lie on his side; there was no space to lie on his back. Waves lapped against the hull, but soon he noticed another noise: a boat circling the *Pacific*. The engine's roar grew louder, faded to a distant hum, then rose again. A cold raindrop stung his cheek. Another trickled down his forehead. He sat up. Rain pelted the deck like scattered pebbles, drenching him in seconds. Karl and Marcus snatched up their blankets and rucksacks, joining the crush of passengers below deck. Since they had dismantled the bunk beds and cabin partitions for fuel during the journey, there was less room than before. They had to spend the rest of the night standing in the passageway.

By first light, the rain had cleared. Karl and Marcus returned to the deck. Though bleary-eyed after a sleepless night, the sight of Haifa spread out before them raised their spirits.

The patrol boat traced a constant loop around their ship. Would today be the day they found out when the British would allow them to disembark?

Lunchtime came, still no news. But fresh water and more rations arrived: an apple, a piece of bread, a triangle of cheese, and their first taste of halva: a teaspoon-sized portion of the sweet, sesame confection. Karl let the piece dissolve on his tongue; it melted too soon.

'I feel bad to complain,' Karl said, sitting crushed beside Marcus. 'Especially since we're in Eretz. But I'm still hungry.'

'So am I,' Marcus admitted, contemplating the apple core in his hand. Barely a core. More a stalk and a few seeds. 'I think I'm hungrier now than I was the entire journey. Maybe they didn't have time to arrange the food before Shabbat, and we'll get a proper delivery tomorrow.'

'Yes, I'm sure you're right.' Karl was quick to agree. Marcus's theory offered reassurance in their continuing limbo. 'Unless we go ashore first.'

'Apparently, the British are transferring us tomorrow,' said HW sitting close by, having overheard their conversation.

'What?' Karl's voice rose. 'Transferred to where?'

HW stood up and pointed. 'The *Patria*, that large white liner standing in the harbour.'

Karl jumped to his feet to look. The ship was far bigger than theirs and appeared empty. 'Why would they move us to another ship?'

'Quarantine purposes. When the other two ships arrive, they too will be transferred to the *Patria*. I know it's not what we hoped for, but it's supposedly only three weeks at most since the ship sails for Australia at month's end. After that, those who have relatives in Eretz Israel will be allowed to join them, and those who don't will first be sent to the camp in Atlit.'

'How do you know all this?' Marcus said.

'Rumours.'

Somehow, HW was always first with the news. Perhaps on account of his friendship with members of the *va'ad* from his Berlin group.

By evening, the ship buzzed with rumours. Word spread that the *Patria* had proper cabins for everyone to sleep in, showers with hot running water, and enough toilets without the need to queue.

After the lack of space and terrible sanitary conditions on the *Pacific*, it sounded too good to be true. Karl and Marcus agreed that if they had to wait three more weeks until they could go ashore, a more comfortable ship was preferable. Especially if Hannah and Erika joined them on arrival.

HW was almost never wrong, but the following morning brought no official word about the transfer to the *Patria*. The day brought another surprise, though. At noon, a ship appeared on the horizon. As it drew closer, Karl noticed the severe list, even worse than when the vessel left Tulcea. The *Milos*. The ship looked as if it might sink at any moment. A wonder it remained afloat. The *Milos* kept sailing regardless until the British directed it to drop anchor close to the

Pacific. Though too far to communicate, the sight gave Karl cautious optimism. If the *Milos* had made it, the *Atlantic* could not be too far behind.

Monday found them still aboard the *Pacific*. The crowding and poor hygiene were growing more unbearable, but no confirmation arrived about a transfer. Nor had anyone from the *Yishuv* paid them a visit. Karl understood why they might not have come on Friday or Shabbat. Even Sunday made sense. Since it was a rest day and the British weren't working, they wouldn't have issued permits for members of the *Yishuv* to board. But why had no one appeared by Monday? When their ship docked in Crete, the Jewish representatives had reached them quicker, after flying all the way from Athens.

Still, that afternoon the local community sent them a gift of chocolate. That was a thoughtful gesture, at least, Karl thought as he unwrapped the foil, broke off a chunk and popped it into his mouth.

It was not until Wednesday that the announcement finally came. The transfer of passengers to the *Patria* would begin that afternoon, starting with mothers, their young children, and older women.

Karl and Marcus watched from the deck as policemen ushered the first passengers down the gangway, and onto the lighter.

'You over there!' shouted a policeman from the top of the gangway. He had a dark moustache, trimmed with military precision, that stood out against his pale skin. He pointed in Karl's general direction.

Karl looked around, then back at the policeman, who stared at him with an intense, unblinking gaze. Karl pointed uncertainly to himself.

'Yes, you in the glasses and cap,' the policeman answered. 'And your friend next to you in the cap. We need some volunteers to help carry the passengers' luggage across to the *Patria*. Fetch your belongings and then start carrying suitcases down to the lighter.'

Karl glanced at Marcus.

'Come on,' the policeman said, growing impatient. 'Chop-chop. I haven't got all day.'

With their friends and fellow passengers lining the railings and waving in high spirits, Karl, Marcus, and four other men left the *Pacific*. Everyone believed this move was the first step to improved conditions before their eventual settlement in Eretz. But the mood changed as soon as they boarded the *Patria*.

Chapter 6

24 November 1940
SS Patria, Haifa Harbour

'After we boarded the *Patria*, they assigned the six of us to unload the luggage from the lighter as each new group of passengers arrived,' Karl said. 'We formed a human chain, passing the luggage from person to person up the gangway and onto the deck—'

'Just like I saw you doing when I arrived,' Hannah said.

'Yes. Exactly like that,' Karl said. 'First came the mothers with children and elderly women, then the other women and finally the men. It took three days to transfer all the passengers from the *Pacific*. It was hard ...'

Karl swallowed and drew a breath. He had been rambling. Delaying. Postponing the inevitable. The sky had deepened to purple, almost dark. He could not put it off any longer. Hannah's gaze held steady, waiting. This was the moment he had dreaded.

'I don't just mean the physical work ... I witnessed some disturbing sights. Cruelty. This may not shock you entirely. To my regret, you experienced a taste of that earlier.'

Hannah's expression tightened as if bracing herself, but Karl could not stop now.

'Once the passengers boarded, the policemen instructed them to retrieve their luggage from the pile and join the queue for customs inspection at a long table. Like you did. But if I tell you, those first few days were even worse. Policemen drove the passengers into line like cattle, prodding them with batons, hurrying them along with blows if they did not move fast enough. When they reached the table, two policemen sifted through their belongings, strewed the contents, and confiscated any items they decided were contraband. Books and letters written in German, just as they took yours, or inconsequential items like cigarettes, lighters, a Thermos. But I also watched as they took the medication from a woman with a heart problem. She was already unwell and distraught from the journey. Several times she begged for them to return her medication, but they ignored her.'

'Did they return it?' Hannah asked.

Karl shook his head. 'After a few days, it no longer mattered,' he paused. 'Because she was no more.'

Hannah's hand went to her throat. 'It sounds as bad, I don't know, perhaps worse, than the searches we had before leaving Vienna,' she said. 'But they are English. Allies. Why are they behaving like ... like ...'

Karl nodded, knowing the word she couldn't bring herself to say. 'Marcus and I complained and said as much. We told them that the Germans behaved better when they carried out luggage inspections.'

'And what did they say?'

'They laughed. They didn't seem to care. So we asked to speak to a superior officer. After that, there was a slight improvement in the way the police conducted the inspections.'

'But why treat us like that in the first place?'

'Because they can,' Karl said. 'Some may not understand that we're Jewish. What we have endured. Why we had to flee our homes in Czechoslovakia, Austria, Germany. Perhaps they mistake us for Germans and regard us as the enemy. Or maybe because we're their prisoners, they think they can do whatever they want.'

'But we're not their prisoners,' Hannah said. 'We're only here for a few weeks of quarantine.'

'We thought the same at the beginning.'

'What are you trying to say?'

Karl's hands trembled as he took hers in his. 'The British have not transferred us onto this ship for quarantine. They won't allow us to remain in Eretz. They are planning to transport us elsewhere.'

'No.' Hannah's voice rose. 'No. You must be mistaken.'

'At first it was only rumours,' Karl continued. 'But a few days later, someone on land smuggled a message to a person on board and confirmed it.'

'It's not true,' Hannah insisted. 'When the British towed our ship into the port of Limassol, they said they would give us permission to land in Haifa if we paid for the fuel. And we did: with our most valuable possessions.' Hannah drew back her hands. 'I surrendered my silver watch, a present from my mama for my eighteenth birthday.' She pointed to her empty wrist. 'A platoon of British soldiers even accompanied us on the crossing from Limassol to Haifa.'

'They said they would take you to Haifa.' Karl spoke slowly, waiting for her to absorb the awful truth, just as he had. 'But they never said they would let you stay.'

Hannah got to her feet. 'It can't be. They wouldn't betray us like that. Not after they gave us their word. Not after they made us pay for the crossing. They must let us stay. They must.'

Karl rose and pulled Hannah into his arms. 'I'm sorry, Hannah. After all our plans and dreams of settling in Eretz. To marry here. To start our lives on a kibbutz. I'm so very sorry.'

'How could they do this to us?' Her voice caught on the words. 'After everything we have been through.'

'I wish there had been a way to stop you from transferring to this ship.'

'Where are they planning to send us?'

'We're still not sure. But the rumours say Australia—'

'Australia!' Hannah gasped. 'That's on the other side of the world. Who do we have in Australia? What will we do there?'

'We may not—'

'When?' she said. 'When does the ship sail?'

'Most likely tomorrow. As soon as they finish transferring all the passengers from the *Atlantic*.'

'*Mein Gott*!' Hannah pulled back and pressed a hand to her forehead. 'Lilly. Gisela. Erika. All the others. None of them know.' She faced the direction of the *Atlantic*, now shrouded in darkness. 'We have to get a message to them and tell them not to transfer to the *Patria*.'

'There's nothing we can do.' Karl understood the stages of shock and desperation she was going through. He had experienced them too. 'As much as I wanted to warn you, I couldn't. Even if you had known, they still would have forced you onto this ship.'

'Is there really nothing else? What about a protest?'

'We already tried that,' Karl said. 'Last week, after we found out the truth. A policeman named Arthur, a friendly chap sympathetic to us, showed us his newspaper. It had an article stating we were to be sent to a British colony until the end of the war. Even after the war, they won't let us return to Eretz Israel. In despair, all of us *Chalutzim* held a protest on deck. Facing the shore, we chanted as loud as we could: "We don't want Australia, we want Israel. Friends, brothers, help us!" But I doubt they heard us. We also held a communal *tefillah* service and a twenty-four-hour hunger strike. We found out later that people throughout the country joined the strike in solidarity. But so far nothing has swayed the British government.'

'Maybe we can escape,' Hannah said in growing desperation.

'We tried that too,' Karl whispered. 'Last Thursday night.' He glanced around, checking no one would overhear them. 'Next to the ship's kitchen there's a passageway with a window. A waste barge sits in the water directly below. We planned to jump from the window onto the boat. From there we could reach the oil tanker anchored in front of the *Patria*. Then, using that vessel for cover, we'd swim to shore.'

'And? Did you go ahead with your plan?'

'Almost,' Karl said. 'We waited for nightfall and a change of guard when the passageway was clear. But we discovered we weren't the only ones who had that idea. We reached the passage to find several others trying the same route. The first few made it off the ship. Marcus followed.' Karl sighed. 'I was right behind him. But the guards must have heard a noise in the water. Just as I was about to jump, they raised the alarm. Searchlights blazed, and motorboats went out to fish the swimmers from the water. Policemen ordered everyone into their cabins. I hid and slipped back to our sleeping quarters without detection.'

'Did any of the swimmers succeed?'

'On previous attempts, one or two got away, but not this time. They caught even those who made it to shore. They've locked them in an airless cell with no natural daylight – only a small porthole facing an inner passageway. Twice a day they get two slices of dried bread. Armed policemen guard them night and day.'

'And Marcus?'

Karl lowered his head. 'He's locked up too.'

Hannah drew in a sharp breath. 'So is that why Sergeant Tait and Mrs Hoyle were so suspicious when they discovered the letter addressed to Marcus in my pocket.'

'That's the reason.'

'When will the police release them?'

'They refuse to say.'

'Are you able to visit Marcus?'

'No,' Karl said. 'But Arthur passes verbal messages between us when he can.'

'So that's it,' Hannah said in a broken voice. 'We're trapped with no way out.'

'Not necessarily.' He squeezed her hand. 'We haven't given up yet. The group leaders have sent appeals to the High Commissioner, Sir Harold MacMichael, the British Prime Minister, Winston Churchill, and to His Majesty, King George, asking them to reverse their deportation decision. We're still waiting for replies. I believe they're also exploring other avenues ... All is not yet lost.' Karl bent to retrieve Hannah's suitcase. 'We should go inside. They'll be serving supper now. And we're not allowed to be outside after nightfall.'

'What happens if they catch you?'

'Sometimes they hit us with their sticks. But not too hard. If they leave a mark, we can complain to the ship's doctor.'

'Well, that makes me feel so much better.'

He couldn't tell whether Hannah was being serious. 'Really?'

'No,' she said. 'Not at all.'

Karl led her down the stairs to Deck D, and they sneaked back inside without incident. Hannah grew quiet, contemplative as they walked down the passageway. She had a lot to absorb and come to terms with. Even so, her eyes darted around, examining her new surroundings with curiosity. Low electric lights cast shadows on the wood-panelled walls, remnants from the *Patria*'s former use as a

Mediterranean cruise ship. The modern, spacious vessel impressed her, as it had him.

In the bustling dining room, observed by guards, private conversation was impossible. The hum of low voices and the scrape of spoons against metal bowls filled the air as they ate bread rations and a small bowl of soup. But Karl felt gratified to have Hannah by his side, sitting with a group of his friends, many of whom Hannah remembered from their months of internment in the Patronka in Bratislava. A member of the *va'ad* read out the order of the day.

'Tomorrow, the 25th of November, the ship will be thoroughly cleaned and accommodation reorganised. All passengers must leave their cabins and sleeping quarters by eight o'clock and come on deck. Luggage is to stay below decks. This order must be followed by all.'

As they were leaving the dining room, they ran into HW. 'So this must be your fiancée?'

'This is Hans Wendel,' Karl said, introducing him to Hannah. 'Or HW as we all call him.'

HW extended his hand to Hannah. 'It's a pleasure meeting you. Karl has spoken about you a lot.' His discreet wink made Karl swell with pride.

'It's nice to meet you too,' Hannah said.

'A shame we have to meet under such circumstances.' HW raised his hands in a helpless gesture. 'But let's hope we'll succeed in entering Eretz soon.'

'Do you really think it's possible?' Hannah's question grasped at the thread of hope.

'Yes, I do believe it.' HW smiled, but his eyes betrayed his concern. 'And once we do, I look forward to your wedding. Karl has already invited me.'

'He has?' She brightened.

'Of course, we haven't set a date yet,' Karl said.

HW patted his shoulder. 'It's been a pleasure,' he said to Hannah, then shifted his attention to Karl. 'Don't forget we need to be on deck by eight o'clock.'

'We'll be up there earlier than that,' Hannah said. 'My cousin is transferring from the *Atlantic* on the first lighter tomorrow morning.'

HW's expression softened. 'Well, until tomorrow, then.'

They walked on. 'He seems very nice,' Hannah remarked. 'Where are we going now?'

'I'm taking you to your cabin.'

'Cabin?' A note of wonder entered Hannah's voice.

'Because I was one of the first on board, I secured a cabin for you to share with Lilly and all your friends. Alma is already there.'

'Our own cabin,' Hannah repeated. 'Thank you so much.'

'It's not big and it only has six beds,' Karl said as they descended to the lower deck. 'So when everyone arrives tomorrow someone will have to sleep on the floor.'

'That's all right. It's still far better than on the *Atlantic*. Perhaps we can find a mattress.' Hannah paused. 'What about those ones stacked on the deck above where we were sitting earlier? What are they for?'

'I think they either came off or are for another ship. The *Libertad*, someone mentioned. I'm not sure. We can borrow a mattress without anyone missing it. I'll fetch one for you tomorrow.'

'What happens to all the other *Atlantic* passengers who arrived today?'

'They'll be sleeping in the dining room for tonight,' Karl said. 'Tomorrow there is to be a whole rearrangement. I suppose that's part of the reason everyone must assemble on deck tomorrow by eight o'clock.' He stopped outside a door. 'Well, this is where you are.'

'Where's your cabin?'

'Sleeping quarters,' Karl said. 'All the men are in the hold.'

'Oh.' She frowned.

'It's quite comfortable,' Karl said. 'Especially after the *Pacific*. We even have straw mattresses.'

'Where shall I find you tomorrow?'

'I'll meet you here,' Karl said. 'Say around quarter to seven? That should give us time to have breakfast before the first lighter arrives.'

'I'll be ready and waiting.'

Karl set her case on the floor. 'Well, then. I suppose we ought to say goodnight.' He placed his arms around her waist and leaned in towards her.

'You over there in the cap!' came the shout.

Karl pulled away. The policeman with the dark moustache was advancing towards them, baton in hand. 'What are you doing loitering around here?'

'She arrived today,' Karl said. 'And I was showing her to her cabin.'

'Is that so?' He gave Hannah a once-over, his eyes lingering on her form.

Hannah shrank back against the door, her eyes cast downward.

'Well, you've shown her now, so you can clear off to your own quarters,' the policeman said.

Karl wished he did not have to leave her so abruptly, but the policeman pointed his baton, drove him away, and left him no choice. He left, hoping she would secure the door behind her.

'Karl,' she called after him. He wheeled around. Hannah said nothing more, just placed her hand on her heart.

Chapter 7

'It's open!' came the reply to Hannah's gentle knock. She opened the door and paused to survey her new, spacious sleeping accommodation. A six-berth cabin with three metal-framed bunks arranged in a U-shape. Each bed with a proper mattress. Pillows. The upper bunks also had a fitted wooden ledge, held in place with sturdy metal brackets, wide enough to store a rucksack and other belongings. Against the left wall stood a washbasin and water jug with a framed mirror above. She set down her suitcase and considered where best to stow it.

How different from the *Atlantic* where, for most of the journey, Hannah had slept in a cramped lifeboat on the open deck. The *Patria* would provide a more comfortable voyage. Small consolation when she had no desire to travel any further.

Alma sat cross-legged on the bottom right bunk, propped against the wall as she held baby Chaim against her shoulder, massaging his back to wind him. She managed a feeble smile, yet her eyes remained doleful. '*Wie geht's*?'

Hannah shrugged. 'You heard the news?'

'What's happened now?'

Hannah hesitated, unsure how to break it to Alma, in case she did not know.

'That we're being ... deported?'

'That,' Alma said. 'We found out the moment we boarded the *Patria*. Before we had even retrieved our luggage. One policeman announced he had a big surprise in store. He told us with obvious glee that they hadn't transferred us for quarantine but because they won't allow us to enter Mandatory Palestine and plan to deport us elsewhere. We just stood there stunned, our mouths hanging open. A few women burst into tears. The policeman just laughed. Apparently, he found our distress amusing.'

'They weren't violent, though?' Hannah searched her friend's face. 'They didn't hit anyone, did they?'

'Oh no! Nothing like that.' Alma shook her head as if Hannah was overreacting. 'I doubt they would be that harsh. They were just abrupt. But the policeman who broke the news, one with hard eyes and a dark moustache, was so cold and callous. On the other hand, your fiancé was kind. He helped us with our luggage and did his best to calm and reassure us. He said the group leaders are still making appeals, so there's a chance we'll be allowed to remain.'

'How did you work out he was my fiancé? I don't think you've ever met before.'

'Because he was asking all the women who came off the lighter if they knew Hannah Rosen, his fiancée. When I told him we were friends, Karl said he would show me to this cabin once we'd been processed. After he boarded, he secured it for you and Lilly. He asked some women from his group to make sure no one else took the cabin before we got here.'

Hannah felt a fresh wave of love and gratitude for Karl's thoughtfulness.

Alma moved the baby to her opposite shoulder. 'In that sense, we are lucky. The others from the *Atlantic* have to sleep in the dining room until tomorrow morning when they rearrange sleeping assignments.'

'Most likely, that's why we all have to be up on deck by eight o'clock in the morning.'

'That probably doesn't apply to us because there's nothing to change in ours. I might not bother going up that early when I have a comfy bed and the chance to sleep in. Between feeds.'

'I'll be on deck even before that. Lilly and Gisela are due to arrive on the first lighter tomorrow morning.'

'They didn't come with you?'

'They were supposed to, but two passengers pushed in ahead.' Hannah waved her hand as if batting the memory away. She was not in the mood to recount the confrontation with the blonde woman and her companion. 'Long story.'

Alma nodded as if realising not to pry further. 'I still can't believe they intend to deport us. Especially after everything we've been through. How can the British do this after they gave us permission to sail to Haifa?'

'I said much the same thing to Karl. Such a betrayal.'

The baby had fallen asleep on her shoulder. Alma carefully laid him in the Moses basket on the floor beside her and tucked the blanket around him. She patted the space on her bed.

Hannah eased off her rucksack, placed it on top of her suitcase, and crossed the cabin. She sat beside Alma. 'Oh!' she said in surprise. 'This is nice and soft.' She bounced up and down feeling the mattress move beneath her. 'I haven't slept in a proper bed for over a year. Not since I left Vienna.'

This time Alma's smile was real

'Which bed is mine?'

'You can choose.'

Hannah eyed the porthole on the back wall above the top bunk. Closed for the nightly blackout, it would offer a view from the bed in the daytime. 'Is it all right if I take the top one?'

'Be my guest.' Alma gestured with an open palm. 'We can figure out the rest tomorrow when the others arrive. We're a bed short, so someone must sleep on the floor.'

'Karl said he'll help me fetch an extra mattress. I don't mind giving Lilly the bed and sleeping on the mattress.' Hannah sighed – the reality of their situation hitting her anew. 'None of them realise they are about to be deported. What are they going to say?'

Alma said nothing.

'How will Max react to the news?'

'Heartbroken.' Alma's gaze dropped. 'He was looking forward to a fresh start in Eretz. After the Nazis arrested him, he spent several months imprisoned in Dachau and suffered. Even I don't know all the details because he still finds it hard to talk about. Max's father was arrested with him, and ... he never came back. So many others did not return. When Max was in Dachau, I was terrified all the time ... I didn't know if I'd ever see him again. They only released him once I could prove I had made arrangements for us to leave the country. The Max who returned was a different man. Although he is better than he was.'

Alma gazed down at Chaim asleep in his basket. 'Becoming a father has brought Max so much joy. He smiles again. Despite everything, we have much to be grateful for. I feared Max might never get to meet his child. But he did. And that's what I will tell him tomorrow when he joins us on the *Patria*. As long as the British don't send us back to Europe, and as long as we are together, that's what matters most in the end.'

Hannah had not known Alma well on the *Atlantic*. They had been friendly, but not close. Alma seemed introverted. She and Max kept to themselves. Hannah only spoke to her more after Alma began sharing a cabin with Gisela and Jenny. But now she saw something in Alma she hadn't noticed before: a quiet strength and resilience.

This woman had coped with her pregnancy alone after the Nazis arrested Max. She was in the advanced stages when she worked for his release and then had to care for her broken husband. She endured terrible conditions during the voyage, gave birth on the ship, and nursed a newborn when she herself was malnourished. Chaim's birth may have had something to do with Max's recovery, but Hannah now saw that Alma's love and resolve had played no small part.

'You have a very positive attitude.'

'I'm trying. What else can I do? But I hope Karl is right and the appeals to the highest levels of the British government will have some effect. They are fighting the Nazis. I would like to believe they are fair-minded. Surely they will understand why we had to escape and allow us to stay in Eretz.' Alma stifled a yawn behind her hand. 'In the meantime, let's try not to worry. We may not be deported. And let's try to enjoy the little blessings: a comfortable bed, a hot shower—'

'Hot shower?' Hannah sat straighter, brightening.

'Yes, I had one earlier.' Alma ran her fingers through her still-damp hair. 'In a bathroom with private cubicles, hot and cold running water. It was like paradise.'

'I could do with a proper shower. I don't suppose I can have one now. That policeman, the one with the moustache and hard eyes you mentioned, is patrolling the passageways and sending everyone to their sleeping quarters. Perhaps I can shower first thing in the morning.' Hannah took a moment to think. 'I've arranged to meet Karl at quarter to seven. If I get up at six o'clock, that should give me enough time. But I no longer have a watch, so how will I know the time?'

'I still have mine.' Alma lifted her sleeve, revealing hers. 'I could wake you.'

'I don't want to disturb you.'

Alma let out a soft chuckle. 'Don't worry, I'll be awake. This little one is like an alarm clock. At quarter to six he's usually crying to be fed.'

'I should let you get to sleep now, while Chaim is sleeping.'

Alma did not protest.

Hannah got up from the bed, rummaged in her rucksack for her toiletry bag and towel, and had a thorough wash. Not as good as a shower, but what a joy to have a basin in their room and fresh water, rather than seawater, to brush her teeth. Hannah changed into a nightdress – she had not worn one for months. On the *Atlantic*, they had slept in their clothes.

She climbed up to her bunk and let her head sink onto the pillow, enjoying its unfamiliar softness. She was too restless to sleep and had no book to read.

Outside, rain pattered against the hull. The robust vessel gave the faintest creak and sway. Hannah could picture the less stable *Atlantic* rocking in the waves. Lilly and the Lifeboat Chevra would be grabbing their belongings and rushing to the lower deck to escape the storm, wishing they were already aboard the *Patria*.

Who were the luckier ones? Hannah, dry and warm in a comfortable bed but knowing they might be back at sea by tomorrow night, heading who knows where? Or her cousin and friends, huddled on the *Atlantic*'s lower deck, still believing the transfer was temporary and soon they would start their new lives in Eretz Israel?

CHAPTER 8

25 November 1940
SS Patria, Haifa Harbour

The narrow bridge stretched endlessly in both directions. Hannah dared not look down. She had stepped too far to retreat, yet stood frozen, afraid to face the unknown.

'Keep going,' her father said.

Hannah had not realised that her father was on the bridge with her. How could he be here? He had died of a sudden heart attack when she was only five years old. She barely remembered him. But now she saw his face and heard his long-forgotten voice.

'Hold tight, keep going,' he encouraged her. 'You are going to be fine.'

'Hannah, it's six o'clock.' The voice pulled her from sleep.

Hannah's eyes flickered open. She tried to cling to the dream, but her father's face and voice were slipping away from memory.

'You asked me to wake you,' Alma said in a hushed voice from her lower bunk where she sat nursing Chaim.

Her heart rose and then plummeted as she remembered where she was. The *Patria*. The ship that was set to deport them to an unknown destination. But Karl was here too, and soon he would come to meet her.

Hannah reached up and unfastened the hinged cover over the porthole. Their cabin faced Haifa's curving bay towards Acco, its low outline silhouetted against the dawn's blue-grey sky. After the night's storm, pale sunlight dappled the bay's choppy ripples a pewter hue. She wondered how Lilly and her friends were faring on the *Atlantic*. The ship was out of sight from this direction. Soon, Lilly and Gisela would arrive and she would have to break the news about their one-way transfer.

'You looked so peaceful, I was sorry to disturb you,' Alma said. 'Did you sleep well?'

Hannah lay back down and stretched out on the mattress, enjoying the sensation of a pillow beneath her head. 'Yes, I did. The sound of the rain lulled me to sleep. I can't remember the last time I slept so deeply.'

It was neither in the three months on the water nor in the months before in Bratislava – in the stifling air and filthy mattresses of the Slobodarna hostel, or the drafty, cavernous warehouses of the Patronka complex where she met Karl.

It was not since the November Pogrom in 1938 when Nazi Brownshirts confiscated their apartment and threw Hannah and her mother out onto the street. They had run to Lilly's home only to find the apartment ransacked, her uncle – Lilly's father – arrested, and Lilly clinging to the body of her murdered husband, Salo. It had taken Hannah, her mother, and her aunt to prise Lilly away. After that, she had hardly slept at all.

It must have been before the Anschluss in March 1938, before the Nazis marched into Vienna, before they found themselves part of the Third Reich, and as Jews became subject to persecution and humiliation. When she was still seeing Gerhard who she thought was the *one*, before he emigrated to America with his family and betrayed her. When Lilly and Salo were newly married and blissfully happy. When life had been good. Perfect, even. The way life can only be when viewed in hindsight.

Two years had passed since then and Hannah's life was just as uncertain. Hannah had not received a letter from her mother in months. She did not know how her mother and Lilly's mother were faring. She did not know if, by the end of the day, they would have permission to remain in Eretz Israel or, without an eleventh-hour reprieve, would be forced to sail away from its shore. Yet, she had slept well. Maybe there came a time when you became numb to your situation. Or exhausted.

'How did you sleep?'

'Quite well, between feeds,' Alma said. 'You didn't hear Chaim's cries during the night?'

Hannah dimly remembered a tiny, insistent wail but it melded into her tangle of dreams. 'I must have heard him, but carried on sleeping,' she said. 'How do you wake up each time?'

'You do when it's your own. You can't sleep through their cries. Even your body reacts and starts producing milk,' Alma smiled down at her sleeping son and then up at Hannah. 'One day, after you and Karl are married, you'll hopefully have a baby of your own and you will see.'

Hannah forced a smile, masking the ache within. She and Karl had planned to marry and settle down on a kibbutz. What would happen to their plans if they set sail on the *Patria*? Could they marry and start a family when cast adrift into the unknown?

But look at Max and Alma. That was exactly what they were doing. They had no choice. And as long as they were together and safe, perhaps that was all that mattered.

If they had to leave Eretz Israel, would Hannah still marry Karl? Of course she would.

Hannah swung her legs off the bed and slid down the ladder. Karl would come in less than an hour and she wanted to have a shower first.

As Hannah gathered her towel, wash bag, and fresh clothes, Alma gave her directions to the shower room.

'Enjoy,' she said, yawning, and climbed back under the covers. 'I'm going to get a little more sleep before Chaim's next feed. See you later.'

The shower room already teemed with activity; Hannah seized the last unoccupied stall. She shut the door, undressed, and stood beneath the sprinkler head. Turning on the tap, she let the water rain down over her. Hannah could have cheered as she lifted her face to the flow. Hannah revelled in the luxury of warm, running water and the chance to shower her full body in privacy rather than the piecemeal attempts behind a blanket as they had done on the *Atlantic*. She washed her hair and body, sloughing off sea salt and accumulated grime. She scrubbed away months of dirt and despair.

By the time she had finished she felt refreshed. Fortified. Ready to face the day no matter what it would bring. As long as she was with Karl, Lilly, and the Lifeboat Chevra, they would confront this problem together, as they had every other challenge. For the meantime, the *Patria* remained anchored in the harbour.

She dried off and slipped on the dress that Lilly had made for her before she left Vienna. Once it had been a vibrant emerald. Now faded and worn, the dress was more of a grey-green, but it was the best item of clothing Hannah owned.

Hannah vacated the cubicle, which was taken by the next woman in line. She jostled beside the others at the row of sinks to study her reflection in the mirror. The unfamiliar face that looked back at her was gaunt after months of inadequate food. Her dress had once hugged her curves, but now it hung off her frame.

Her hair had almost returned to its natural caramel colour. Only at the tips did the dry, peroxide-damaged evidence linger from when she had dyed her hair blonde to pass as a non-Jew in order to walk Vienna's streets to buy supplies for her family without harassment. She vowed to herself that never again would she disguise her identity as a Jew. She took scissors from her wash bag and cut off the straw-coloured ends. Satisfied with the results, she styled her hair in an updo the way Erika had taught her.

Hannah crept back into the cabin to avoid disturbing Alma and stowed her belongings. She appraised herself and, on a whim, changed out of her sensible lace-ups into her one pair of elegant black patent-leather heels. She had only worn them once since leaving Vienna, the evening of her engagement party on the *Helios*. The shoes seemed more fitting on this smarter ship. She left the cabin, closing the door behind her. Karl was already waiting outside.

'Sorry,' she said. 'Did I keep you waiting long?'

'Not at all.' He drew closer, his lips finding hers. 'I'm early. I couldn't wait any longer. But I didn't want to knock in case you were still sleeping.'

'I've been up for a while. I just had a wonderful, refreshing shower.'

'You look really ... beautiful this morning,' he said, with a bashful smile.

Hannah beamed.

They ascended the stairs to the deck above and strolled down the passageway, fingers entwined. For all the world they might have looked like an ordinary couple in love enjoying a holiday on a cruise ship. If you disregarded the armed British guards posted on every corner. A constant reminder that they were Jewish refugees with an uncertain future.

Before they reached the dining room a lanky policeman strode towards them. Hannah hung back, shielding herself behind Karl, but he remained at ease, and the policeman smiled.

'Arthur,' Karl said. 'I'd like you to meet my fiancée, Hannah.'

The policeman gave a polite bow of the head. 'Nice to meet you, miss.'

'Any news?' Karl lowered his voice. 'How is Marcus?'

Arthur shook his head. 'Not much news, I'm afraid. And I haven't seen Marcus yet today.' He rolled his eyes. 'Our *friend* with the moustache is lurking about. You know how he enjoys throwing his weight around. But I'm delivering their food tonight, and when I do, will try to exchange a word with Marcus.'

'If you see him,' Hannah said, 'would you mind telling him that his girlfriend, Erika, is transferring to the ship later. She gave me a letter for him. But they took it during customs inspection.'

'Erika,' Arthur said, as if memorising her name. 'I'll tell Marcus Erika's coming aboard today and she said to send her love.'

'Thank you,' Hannah said, moved by his kindness. 'When will they release him?'

Arthur's face fell. 'I'm afraid I couldn't say. He's a decent fellow. It's a shame, but my hands are tied.'

'It's not your fault,' Karl said. 'You've done more than enough. We really appreciate your help.'

Arthur patted Karl's shoulder. 'I wish I could do more.'

If Karl was nervous about what the day would bring, he did a fine job of disguising it. He walked into the dining room, standing tall with Hannah by his side. The breakfast offering was simple but far better than on the *Atlantic*: fresh bread, butter, marmalade, and a cup of tea.

The dining room was humming. People chatted as they fetched their breakfast, or sat around the wooden tables where once waiters would have served passengers travelling on a cruise. The tables were designed for eight, but at some, ten or twelve squeezed in elbow to elbow. Once the remaining *Atlantic* passengers arrived, the *Patria* would feel as crowded as the ships they had left behind.

With her plate and cup in hand, Hannah followed Karl as he negotiated the tables to find them seats. Focused on Karl, she almost bumped into two women who brushed past.

'Sorry,' Hannah said. A brunette in a smart navy suit, lips painted red, stepped aside. The second tottered on heels and blocked her path. Hannah recognised the flowy pink silk dress, more suited for evening wear. Draped across her shoulders was a silver fox fur stole, legs and tail on one end, a lifeless head on the other. Its glassy eyes glared at her. Hannah stepped back and found herself caught in the blonde woman's vitreous stare. She swayed, gripping her cup tighter.

'Careful there,' the woman said, syrupy sarcasm coating her words. She lunged forward as if to steady Hannah. 'You almost spilled your hot tea on me.'

Hannah tried to remove her hand from the woman's tight grasp. Tea dripped from the cup, over the back of her hand and onto the floor. She felt the sting of a burn.

'Clumsy,' the woman tutted.

Hannah stared down. A brown stain bloomed across the front of her dress. The brunette companion averted her gaze.

'Hannah?' Karl's question cut through her humiliation. 'Is everything all right?'

Hannah could not find her voice.

'Oh,' the woman said. 'Have you found a young man willing to pay you some interest? I'm impressed. I see you're no longer trailing after your sister or that old woman.'

The brunette stepped back and looked from side to side as if searching for a way to slip out unnoticed.

The blonde woman gave her full attention to Karl, evaluating him like a painting on a gallery wall.

'Not bad,' she commented, more to herself. 'Not bad at all.' She half-closed her eyes, emphasising her long lashes, darkened with mascara. 'But if you should get bored …' She simpered at Karl, seized her brunette companion's stiff elbow and sauntered away, hips swaying.

Karl watched her go. 'Who is she?' he said. 'That woman looks like trouble.'

'She is,' Hannah said. 'She's the reason Lilly and Gisela lost their places on the lighter yesterday.'

'They will be here before long,' Karl said. 'And don't pay that woman any mind. She's not worth it.' He took Hannah's plate and cup from her hands and gave her a clean handkerchief.

Sitting beside Karl, Hannah dampened the handkerchief with water from a carafe on the table and scrubbed at the tea stain on her dress. A stubborn mark remained in the middle of the damp patch but there was no time to change. She picked at her bread.

'Not eating?'

Hannah shrugged.

'Shall we go on deck?'

'Yes.' Hannah pushed back her chair. 'Let's do that.'

Outside, sunlight gleamed off the wet deck as the grey rain clouds cleared. It was not even seven-thirty, but already the passengers were congregating.

From the starboard railings they surveyed the *Atlantic*. A lighter was secured alongside.

'It seems the first group will be leaving shortly,' Karl said.

Hannah's stomach twisted. In minutes, Lilly and Gisela would board, expecting temporary quarantine. How could she tell them they might never see Eretz Israel again?

Chapter 9

25 November 1940
SS Atlantic, Haifa Bay

Lilly and Gisela climbed the stairs from the lower deck's gloom into the morning light, accompanied by the Lifeboat Chevra. The heavy grey clouds were drifting apart to reveal hints of blue, but the smell of must lingered about the *Atlantic*.

Last night's downpour drove them to shelter in the packed lower deck. There was no room to sit, let alone lie down. They spent the night crouching or standing – sleep was impossible. Lilly tried to doze upright, but each sway jolted her awake.

Now autumn had taken hold, it had become too cold and wet to sleep on deck. Lilly would not be sorry to leave the *Atlantic*. Especially if the *Patria* offered her a proper bed in a cabin protected from the elements. Lilly and Gisela would have transferred yesterday and spent a more comfortable night, if not for the blonde woman's actions. Lilly still seethed at the woman for pushing her over.

Lilly took Gisela's arm to steady her, with Erika supporting her from the other side, as they picked their way across the slippery deck. Alexander and Isaak followed behind, carrying their suitcases. The rest of their friends walked with them like a farewell parade, looking forward to their own departure later in the day.

Lilly had intended to be first on board that morning, but others were just as eager. They joined the queue for the registration table where eight people waited ahead.

In the harbour, the *Patria* gleamed in the morning light. Figures moved around on the deck. Lilly smiled as they advanced up the line, thinking that in a few minutes she would be with her cousin again. She looked forward to hearing about Hannah's long-awaited reunion with Karl.

'Will you be all right from here?' Erika asked as they reached the front of the queue. 'I need to return to the infirmary to help prepare the most seriously ill patients for hospital transfer.'

'We'll be fine,' Gisela said, indicating the rest of the group waiting at the railings. 'Thanks for your help.'

'Please send Marcus my love,' Erika said. 'And tell him I can't wait to see him later this afternoon.'

Gisela gave an indulgent smile. '*Ach*! Young love.'

'We'll be sure to pass on the message,' Lilly said.

'Names,' the policeman said as they approached the table. He was older than the one yesterday and wore a thin-lipped expression.

'Lilly Simon.'

'Gisela Klein.'

'You already have our names,' Lilly said. 'We were supposed to board the last lighter yesterday evening.'

The policeman furrowed his thick brows, flipped the page of his ledger, and ran his finger down the list. 'Yes, I can see the names have been entered.'

'Should we continue to the gangway ...?'

He lifted his gaze to them. 'If your names are on the list that would mean you boarded yesterday.'

'Well, we didn't. As you can see, we're still here.'

Lilly offered a friendly smile. The policeman did not return the gesture.

'Everyone whose name has been noted would have boarded the lighter. We only record the names of each person as they leave the ship. So that can only mean one thing.' He fixed her with a stony stare. 'Lilly Simon and Gisela Klein are not your real names. You are falsifying your identity and impersonating other passengers.'

'Of course they are our real names.' Gisela straightened her peacock silk scarf. 'Why would we give false ones?'

'I don't know.' He crossed his arms. 'You tell me.'

'Those are our names,' Lilly insisted, taken aback by the unexpected turn of events. 'The reason you already have them is—'

'Look here, miss,' he broke in. 'You're holding up the queue. Either you give me your real names or stand aside.'

'We can't provide you with any other names. Please, will you just let me explain?' she blurted. 'After registering yesterday, another passenger pushed me over. As an official helped me up, she and her companion rushed down the gangway ahead of us and took our places. When we reached the lighter, we were told it was already full.'

The policeman was unmoved. 'That sounds highly improbable.'

Lilly glanced around for the official who had helped her up. He could confirm her account, but she could not spot him. 'It's the truth.' She pointed to her coat. 'See these mud stains? They are from the woman pushing me over. I still can't remove them.'

'Showing me your grubby coat isn't proof of anything,' he said. 'Everyone on this ship looks dirty.'

Alexander caught Lilly's eye from the railings. He raised his palms in a silent question. She beckoned, and he threaded his way through the knots of passengers and joined them at the table.

'What's the matter?'

'The policeman thinks we've given him false names because they are on the list from yesterday when we didn't board,' Lilly said.

'I can confirm their real names,' Alexander said. 'I know them well.'

'And you might also be lying on their behalf.'

Alexander's jaw tightened at the affront. 'I would not lie.'

With a sweep of his hand, the policeman dismissed him.

'The guard!' Lilly's voice was urgent. 'The one directing the passengers onto the lighter. Is he the same one as yesterday? He saw what happened and can tell you.'

'He's busy down there marshalling passengers, and I'm not dragging him up here to prop up your far-fetched story.'

'Officer,' Alexander said, stepping forward again. 'If you're not prepared to confirm their names, but need to transfer all the passengers from the *Atlantic*, how will you do that?'

'Very well!' He huffed. 'Stand aside until I've finished registering the others and I'll send for him.'

Lilly, Gisela, and Alexander backed away from the table and moved to the railings. Gisela stroked her peacock silk scarf.

'What's going on?' Janka said.

Alexander filled them in.

'I hope it is the same guard from yesterday, otherwise what will we do?' Lilly said.

'Don't worry,' Alexander said. 'They are the ones who want to transfer us. They'll have to sort it out.'

'What if you were to give them another, made-up name?' Isaak said. 'The authorities won't know.'

'Perhaps not,' Alexander said. 'But both Gisela and Lilly have family already in Eretz. If the authorities were to do background checks and find out they've given false names, they could get in trouble. It's not worth it. Best to be honest and let them sort out their mistake.'

'You're right. I didn't think of that.'

'You two over there.' The policeman crooked his finger. Standing beside him was the guard from the lighter.

Lilly and Gisela went back to the table.

'Do you recognise these two women?' He asked the guard. 'Did they try to board the lighter yesterday?'

The guard peered at them. 'Oh yes. Yes, they did.' He pointed to Lilly. 'She had just boarded when another young woman came down the gangway with that one.' He nodded at Gisela. 'But I kept a tally of the passengers and the lighter was already full. That other woman begged me to squeeze them on. But I told them the rules is the rules. Then this one here got off. The other woman took her place, and these two remained behind.'

'Hmm ... So two other passengers boarded with the wrong names.'

'I wouldn't rightly know. I just keep a tally.'

'We'll have to send a memo to advise the *Patria* and request they check the names of all passengers who boarded on the last lighter.' He faced the guard. 'Thank you for your confirmation. As you were.'

The policeman licked his finger and flicked to the previous page. He crossed out their names, and put question marks and a note next to them. 'Right,' he said and flipped to a brand new page. 'Names.'

Checking the correct spelling, he entered their details again. But by that time, the first lighter, filled with passengers, had already left the *Atlantic* on its way to the *Patria*.

Chapter 10

25 November 1940
SS Patria, Haifa Harbour

Hannah scanned the faces of the passengers as they disembarked the lighter. Women of all ages, some accompanied by small children, boarded the *Patria*. Lilly and Gisela were not among them.

'Where are they?' Hannah asked when Karl rejoined her after hauling luggage at the gangway. 'Could something have happened to Gisela – or Lilly?'

'I'm sure there's nothing to worry about.' He brushed the dust from his hands. 'They'll probably be on the next one.'

'Is it possible they discovered the real reason for the transfer and refused to board?'

'Unlikely,' he said. 'It doesn't look like any of the others knew.'

Guards herded the women into a corner of the deck for disinfection and customs inspection. Mouths agape, voices rising in confusion.

'Lilly said she would take the first one this morning.' Hannah looked back at the *Atlantic*. 'It doesn't make sense.'

'There must have been a long queue of people boarding. Or perhaps,' he said, his tone too relaxed, 'she overslept and missed it.'

'*Ach quatsch*! Between the heavy rainstorm, having to find shelter below deck where there's little room to sit, never mind lie down, I doubt she slept much at all.' Hannah stopped.

Karl pushed his glasses up the bridge of his nose.

'I'm so sorry.' She pressed a hand to her mouth and lowered her gaze, mortified at how she had snapped at Karl. She had never spoken to him like that before. 'I'm not sure what came over me.'

'I understand,' he said in a quiet voice. He rested his hands on her shoulders. 'You're afraid that Lilly won't come. You're afraid that she will.'

Hannah looked up at him. 'How did you know?'

'Because I felt the same while I waited for you to arrive. For three weeks, with no word of your ship, I worried constantly about you. Then, yesterday morning, when we finally saw the *Atlantic* approaching the harbour, I was relieved.'

She rested her head on his shoulder.

'Part of me wished for your freedom,' Karl continued. 'But another part of me hoped they would transfer you as well because I couldn't bear for us to be separated. Then I felt guilty for being so selfish and dreaded having to tell you the truth about the *Patria*.'

'Yes, that's exactly it,' Hannah said. 'What am I supposed to do?'

'There's nothing you can do,' he said. 'Ultimately, we don't have a choice in the matter, do we?'

'No,' Hannah said, her voice resigned. 'We don't. I only wish things had worked out differently, and they had kept their promise and let us land.'

'We might yet have a reprieve,' Karl said. 'Remember, the transport leaders have sent many letters. By now the High Commissioner, British Prime Minister and the King may have received them. When they read about our situation, they might show mercy and allow us to remain.'

'I do hope so.'

'It's still early. Let's not give up yet. Come,' he said, taking her hand. 'Let's walk to the stern to see if the next lighter has left the *Atlantic*. Maybe Lilly will be on that one.'

It was now well after eight o'clock and almost all the ship's passengers were out on deck. Karl and Hannah threaded their way between the clusters of people.

The stern too was brimming. They edged through the crowd to reach the railings where they could make out the lighter nestled against the *Atlantic*'s hull. It looked as if it was already laden. They watched and waited. The sky had cleared after the overnight rain. The air was mild, freshly washed. It smelled of brine, seaweed, with a hint of disinfectant rising from the cabin cleaning below.

It was another few minutes before the lighter slipped away from the *Atlantic*. Hannah kept her eyes trained on the little vessel moving slow and steady. The lighter lifted and settled with the waves, heading for the *Patria*. Away from the semblance of freedom. Karl squeezed her hand; she squeezed back.

Hannah studied the faces in the lighter as it drew closer. She picked out a woman wearing a red cloche hat and sitting beside her, an older, grey-haired woman. 'I think I see them,' she said, although the vessel was still too far away to make out their features. Other passengers on deck began to call down to family and friends. The woman in the red hat gazed up at the *Patria*.

'Yes. It's Lilly and Gisela.' Hannah cupped her hands around her mouth.

'Lilly!' she called over the din. She raised her arms. Then Lilly spotted her. She spoke to Gisela, pointing upwards. The two of them waved back.

'Save a place for us!' shouted another woman from the lighter.

'I should tell Lilly and Gisela we have a cabin.'

'I doubt they'll hear you over this racket,' Karl said.

'I'll try to signal,' Hannah said, making hand gestures. Lilly nodded and blew her a kiss as the lighter moved past, veering right for the harbour entrance.

'Let's go back to midships to meet them,' Karl said.

They wove their way across the stern to the port side promenade. A crowd was gathering at the railings. The lighter had just entered the harbour, but no one was watching the vessel. Instead, they were pointing at the water, looking towards the ship's bow. Karl shouldered forward for a closer look, drawing Hannah with him. People thrashed in the water, at least ten of them, swimming hard for the shore. Hannah leaned out and angled her head towards the bow as several more jumped from the ship.

'They're escaping.' She looked to Karl for an answer. 'In broad daylight?'

He shook his head, equally confused.

Whistles blew. Voices shouted from the bow. A loud bang.

At first, Hannah thought a shot had been fired at the swimmers, but the boom rumbled through the ship. Vibrated through her feet.

'We're under attack from the air!' A guard ploughed his way through the passengers. 'Italians. Everyone get below deck!'

Passengers screamed, surging towards the stairs. Some ignored the order and began jumping overboard. Others seemed confused, perhaps not having understood the guard's English, and ran without direction. Karl grabbed her hand. The flood of people swept them along as they streamed below deck. Her legs seemed to move of their own accord.

She recalled the time on the *Atlantic*, right before they reached Crete, when the ship's hull scraped against a coral reef. Panic had erupted as everyone feared a German U-boat had struck them.

They descended the next flight.

Hannah remembered another morning a few days later. The ship was anchored outside Heraklion Harbour when the chilling wail of an air raid siren had jolted them awake. That too had later proved to be a false alarm. Hannah and the Lifeboat Chevra had laughed about it afterwards.

This had to be another false alarm.

But why then was the ship tilting?

Chapter 11

25 November 1940
SS Atlantic, Haifa Bay

The lighter cast off from the *Atlantic* carrying Lilly and Gisela.

'Send my love to Alma and a kiss to Chaim,' Max called from the railings, waving with the rest of their friends. 'Tell them I can't wait to see them later.'

'We will,' Lilly said.

The lighter pitched over the waves, the *Atlantic* shrinking behind them.

'Well,' Gisela said. '*Aller guten Dinge sind drei*!'

'Indeed.' Lilly chuckled. Third time lucky. At last they were on their way.

The *Patria* waited ahead, its stern moored to the harbour's breakwater by a series of cables. As they approached, Lilly realised the ship was far larger than she had expected. It dwarfed the *Atlantic*. The stern appeared to be packed with passengers watching their arrival. Lilly wondered whether Hannah was waiting there too. She ran her eyes along the stern's railings, looking for a familiar face.

'Have you found your cousin?' Gisela asked.

'Not yet. There are so many people on deck, it might be difficult to spot her.'

People from the ship called out to passengers on the lighter, sparking a lively exchange. Lilly searched the stern again. She noticed Hannah waving her arms in the air.

'There she is!' Lilly pointed her out. 'And Karl is there too, standing right beside her.'

'Oh yes, I see them,' Gisela said as they raised their hands in greeting.

Hannah began signalling to Lilly in the same way she and Karl used to communicate back when they were on different paddle steamers, waiting to depart from Bratislava, at the outset of their journey down the Danube. She and Karl had developed their own form of sign language. Lilly had never learned their code. She had sailed directly from Vienna, joining her cousin and the convoy in Bratislava. But when Hannah drew the outline of a box, gestured to Lilly and Gisela, and placed her hands together resting her head on them, like a pillow, Lilly thought she grasped the meaning. She nodded and blew Hannah a kiss before the launch headed left, past the *Patria*, following the breakwater to the harbour's entrance.

'What was Hannah trying to tell you?' Gisela asked.

Lilly smiled. 'I believe she has saved us a cabin.'

'A cabin?' Her brows rose. 'I do hope you are right.'

'So do I.' Lilly stifled a yawn, tired after a sleepless night.

The launch swept in a semicircle to enter the harbour. In a few minutes they would board the ship and Lilly would learn whether her guess was right. Lilly shut her eyes, indulging the thought. A sheltered cabin. A bed with clean sheets. She imagined sinking onto the feathery softness of a real pillow.

A muffled boom – a blast – jolted Lilly out of her daydream. Her eyes snapped open.

Several passengers drew in sharp breaths.

'What was that?' asked a woman at the rear.

Lilly scanned the lighter for the source of the reverberation. The boat remained intact. The water surrounding them was calm, protected by the harbour's breakwater. It could not have been a mine or submarine. An enemy fighter plane strafing the harbour, perhaps? She glanced up: the skies were clear.

Then Lilly saw it.

'*Mein Gott*!' Gisela cried. 'The *Patria*!'

Passengers plunged into the water. Screams pierced the air. People swam and thrashed, arms flailing wildly.

Lilly gripped the bench and half-rose.

'Madam, please remain seated!' came the sharp order from the tense-faced guard.

Lilly sank back onto the bench.

From the port came the wail of sirens and whistles. Police patrol vessels, rowing boats, lifeboats – every available craft in the harbour – rushed to the rescue. But their own vessel was reversing as fast as it could. Back the way they had come.

Moments ago, Lilly had been waving to Hannah and Karl on the deck. The *Patria* had been standing tall and upright. Now the ship was tilting to one side.

'Hannah,' she mouthed.

'Why aren't we helping to rescue them?' called a woman from the rear.

'We're already full,' the guard said.

Gisela squeezed closer to Lilly and raised her voice. 'We can make space.'

'Stop the boat!' shouted several passengers.

'We're full, I said.' The guard stared straight ahead. 'The rules is the rules.'

'This is madness!' said the woman at the rear. 'There are people drowning and we're just abandoning them.'

'Others are going to the rescue,' said a woman sitting in the front row. 'You heard what the guard said. We haven't got the space. Do you want them to overwhelm our boat and put us all at risk? We've got our children to think about.'

As if in response, a baby began to cry.

'And what about our relatives?' shouted the woman from the back. 'My brother is on that ship.'

The lighter had reached the open sea, heading back to the *Atlantic*. Behind them, the *Patria* had rolled over on its side, its three tall funnels no longer visible. All she could see above the breakwater was the bottom of the hull and the wall of the stern.

'We need to go back!' Lilly said, finding her voice. 'My cousin is on that ship. We have to rescue her. She can't swim.'

All eyes remained fixed on the *Patria*. No one answered.

'Please! My cousin can't swim.'

Lilly covered her face. Gisela hugged her close.

As soon as the lighter pulled alongside the *Atlantic*, the guard ordered them to retrieve their luggage and ushered them back to the ship.

Lilly stared at the pile of suitcases, her mind too blurred to identify hers.

'This is yours, isn't it?' Gisela said, her voice gentle, cautious. The older woman struggled to lift Lilly's case and her own. Lilly moved to take it from her. Her legs trembled. The suitcase felt as heavy as a boulder. A line of passengers snaked up the gangway. In the reverse direction, three figures clattered past.

Isaak took the suitcases from Lilly and Gisela. He set them down and hugged them both. Janka and Jenny, following behind, embraced them too. They headed back with Isaak carrying the luggage, Jenny supporting Gisela, and Janka with her arm around Lilly. The gangway's incline seemed insurmountable, every foot forward an effort. Lilly couldn't escape the question that tormented her: What if Hannah is gone and I am alone?

Lilly leaned against Janka's shoulder. Janka held her tight, steadying her as she swayed.

They reached the cramped deck. It appeared to have shrunk even smaller in the few minutes since they had left. A knot of passengers pressed towards them, everyone talking at once.

'What did you see?' It was Emil, the man Janka nicknamed Mr Pencil after Hannah accidentally knocked the pencil out of his hand when they first boarded the *Atlantic*. At the thought of Hannah, Lilly began to shiver uncontrollably.

'How did the *Patria* sink?' he continued. 'Anyone injured? Did any passengers drown?'

'Will you please stop,' Janka snapped. 'Lilly and Gisela have had a terrible shock. Stop asking so many questions.'

'*Schon gut*!' Emil looked slighted. 'There's no need to be so rude.'

'Sorry,' Janka said. 'Please give them some time. Maybe they'll feel ready to talk to you later.'

Emil slunk off with the disappointed group trailing behind.

Isaak laid their suitcases flat on the deck, like benches. He helped ease Gisela down and cautiously held on to Lilly's arms, as if wary of making any sudden movement. 'Come sit,' he said.

Jenny brought them water. Lilly's hands were shaking so much, the liquid sloshed down the front of her coat. Jenny placed her hands over Lilly's to steady them.

Lilly lifted her gaze heavenward. What if ...?

'Lilly.' Jenny's voice cut through her spiraling thoughts. Lilly squeezed her eyes shut. 'Look at me.' Sharp. Insistent. Lilly's eyes opened. 'Hannah is going to be all right.'

'H-how d-do you know?'

'Many boats have gone out to save the passengers. They will also rescue Hannah.'

'She c-can't swim.'

'She is with her fiancé. He will take care of her.'

She guided the cup to Lilly's lips. Lilly gulped it down. 'But ... what if ...?'

Jenny's gaze held steady. 'Hannah will make it.'

Lilly studied Jenny's face. Her unwavering pale blue eyes. Her tight, brave smile. Jenny who always seemed so delicate. She'd been traumatised after witnessing one refugee drown in Bratislava, and another on the Danube at Ruse. 'And we are all here for you. You are not alone.'

Lilly's voice broke. 'Thank you.' She grasped Jenny's hand.

'Alma!'

Lilly spun at the hoarse cry. Max gripped the railings, eyes locked on the overturned ship. Alexander held him firm on one side, Stefan on the other.

'Chaim!' He struggled to break from their grip. Alexander and Stefan pulled him back. Isaak joined them, placing a hand on Max's shoulder. He leaned towards Max, said something in his ear, and motioned towards Lilly and Gisela.

'Max attempted to scale the railings,' Jenny said in an undertone with a pitying shake of her head. 'He wanted to dive into the sea and swim to the *Patria*. The men stopped him just before he jumped.'

Erika hovered behind Jenny. Her face had lost its colour, her eyes were red-rimmed. Her expression spoke of their shared dread. She came forward and crouched in front of Lilly and Gisela.

'Oh, Lilly!' Erika said in a choking voice. She pulled Lilly towards her in a crushing hug. Then she embraced Gisela, a sob escaping her throat. Gisela stroked Erika's cheek.

'One minute the ship was there. And the next …' Erika's gaze moved from Gisela to Lilly. 'How?'

Max leaned closer to listen to their conversation. The other men remained by his side, attentive to his movements.

'We're not exactly sure,' Gisela said. 'When we approached the harbour the *Patria* was there, right in front of us. Passengers filled the stern, watching our arrival.'

'I saw Hannah and Karl,' Lilly said. None of it seemed real. Minutes ago she'd blown Hannah a kiss. And in an instant everything changed.

'What about Marcus?' Erika said.

Lilly tried to recall the scene. Had Marcus been standing next to Karl, perhaps?

'I … I don't remember.' She turned to Gisela.

'Neither do I,' Gisela said. 'If Hannah hadn't waved first, I don't know if I would have noticed her among the crowd either.'

'Did you see Alma?' Max said, his voice desperate.

Lilly paused. 'She might have been there. I can't be sure.'

Max clutched his head, pacing in circles. Alexander and Stefan remained close by, blocking a path to the railings.

'Did you hear or notice anything unusual?' Alexander asked.

'After we entered the harbour there was a sound.' Gisela looked at Lilly for confirmation. 'It was like a muffled blast, wasn't it?'

'Yes, a low boom,' Lilly said. 'At first, I thought we might have struck a mine. But the lighter was fine. I looked up to see if it was an air raid but there were no planes in the sky. Then the *Patria* came into view. It was listing to the right. And people were in the water.'

As she pictured the floundering passengers, her chest constricted. Had Hannah been one of them? She struggled for air.

'Breathe, Lilly.' Jenny took Lilly's hands in hers, making Lilly follow her rhythm of inhaling and exhaling until her breathing steadied and her heart rate slowed. 'You must stay calm.' She looked from Lilly to Max and Erika. 'All of you.'

'Let's not jump to conclusions,' Stefan said. 'Yes, there has been a terrible accident, but look at that massive rescue operation in progress. They should be able to save everyone. Once they account for survivors, they'll compile a list and bring us the details. They know many of us had family on board the *Patria*. Jenny's right. We must stay calm.'

Lilly found Stefan's rational advice reassuring.

Until she noticed Alexander glance at Isaak and the doubtful expression that passed between them.

Chapter 12

Later that night, after the others took shelter below, Isaak and Alexander remained on deck, collars turned up against the cold night air and intermittent drizzle. In the hours following the incident, the police provided scant details about the rescue operation. Contrary to Stefan's assumptions, the authorities gave them no list of survivors. Lilly, Max, and Erika were trapped in uncertainty.

'I don't agree with Stefan about this being a terrible accident,' Alexander said. 'Terrible, yes. Accident, no.'

Isaak leaned closer to Alexander, mindful of the patrolling guards. 'You're saying it was deliberate?'

'I'm almost certain.'

'Lilly and Gisela mentioned there was a faint boom just before the *Patria* heeled over,' Isaak said. 'An explosion? But who would target a ship filled with Jewish refugees? Lilly and Gisela didn't believe it was a mine, and there were no aeroplanes overhead. So I doubt it was the Germans or Italians.' Isaak hesitated. 'What about the local Arabs? After all, they've been rioting against Jewish immigration and attacking Jewish communities for the past few years.'

'Possible, but unlikely. The harbour's British-controlled and heavily guarded.'

Isaak studied him in the darkness. 'You're not saying it was the British ...?'

Alexander shook his head. 'They had no reason to destroy their own ship.'

'Then who?'

'The passengers.'

'The passengers?' Isaak stared at him. 'No, you're wrong. That's not possible.'

'Think about it. The British have been acting cagey ever since we arrived. Why didn't they tell us we wouldn't be able to disembark straight away? Why did they want to transfer us to another ship instead of to a quarantine camp on land? There's no space in the whole of Eretz Israel?' He gestured towards Haifa in blackout, faint outlines of its buildings barely visible by the light of the waning half-moon. 'And why won't they even let us send letters to relatives and friends?' Alexander paused, letting the questions hang in the air. 'Do you remember when we first found out that we were to be transferred onto the *Patria,* you expressed fears that the British intended to send us back?'

'And you said the British wouldn't do that.'

'Well ... maybe you were right, and I was wrong. Perhaps some passengers on the *Patria* discovered the same thing. There's something else ...' He stopped, waiting until two guards passed by. 'It didn't seem important at the time, but on reflection, it is troubling. The night we left Cyprus, Erwin Kovac mentioned something after supervising the coal loading in Limassol Port.'

Erwin, from their Prague group, had helped save the voyage after discovering that Captain Spiro had thrown most of their coal overboard. A mechanical engineer, Erwin volunteered to take over Spiro's role, along with his friend Fritz Steiner, another engineer. On their initiative, the passengers chopped up every bit of wood on the ship to use for fuel, which managed to get them as far as the coast of Cyprus.

'Oh?' Isaak tilted his head. 'What did he say?'

'According to Erwin, approximately twenty-eight tons of coal would be required to fuel the ship from Cyprus to Haifa. But they made us pay for forty tons of coal.'

'So they charged us for more coal than we needed?'

'Yes, but for reasons Erwin couldn't explain, they loaded seventy tons onto our ship.'

'That makes no sense at all.'

'No, it doesn't,' Alexander said. 'But it is possible that these details point to one conclusion: they never intended to let us stay in Eretz.'

'That might be the truth. Lilly also had her suspicions.'

'About what?' a voice said behind them.

Isaak and Alexander spun around. Lilly stood before them, wrapped in her fur-collared coat, red cloche hat pulled low over her forehead. How much had she overheard? 'Oh ... hello, Lilly,' Isaak said. 'How are you?'

'I can't sleep.' Lilly's words caught. 'I'm worried about Hannah, and the others. And I can't help feeling guilty.'

'You mustn't.' Alexander touched her arm gently. 'It's not your fault.'

'I was supposed to board the ship with Hannah. If not for that blonde woman in pink, the one from the cabin, pushing me out of the way and boarding the lighter with her brunette companion, I wouldn't have needed to give up my space. Hannah, Gisela, and I would have travelled across together.'

Isaak's jaw tightened at the mention of the woman in pink. He knew first-hand what a manipulative person she was.

'Even if you had not given up your place for Hannah, she would have taken the very first lighter this morning,' Alexander said.

'At least we'd be together.'

'Maybe it was meant to be, you and Gisela staying off that ship,' Isaak said.

'It doesn't make me feel any better.' Lilly put her head in her hands. 'I had reservations about the transfer from the start. I should have persuaded Hannah not to go.'

'She would never have listened to you,' Alexander said.

Her shoulders sagged. 'You're right, she wouldn't. Hannah was too excited to see Karl again.' Lilly sighed. 'I'm sick with worry. So are Max and Erika. And countless others. Why won't the guards at least give us a list of survivors?'

'Let's give them the benefit of the doubt,' Alexander said. 'They might still be overwhelmed tending to the rescued passengers and haven't managed to compile a list. Let's see what tomorrow brings.'

Lilly wedged herself between Isaak and Alexander, resting her forearms on the railings. 'I hope you're right. What will I do if—'

'Don't even think that.' Isaak reached out to touch her arm, pulling back at the last moment. 'Though I know it's hard not to.'

'It keeps preying on my mind.'

For a few minutes, silence settled between them until Lilly said, 'What were you talking about just now?'

'Er ...' Isaak glanced at Alexander for support, but he was staring awkwardly at his feet.

'I heard you say that I had suspicions. About what?'

There was no point in being secretive. It would only make her worry more.

'We were saying,' Isaak began, 'that the way they've treated us since we reached Haifa doesn't seem right. And I had the feeling you thought so too.'

'I sensed it a couple of hours after we arrived when they wouldn't tell us when we could disembark,' Lilly said. 'And then the news that they were transferring us to the *Patria* for quarantine. I also thought it odd that they would not let me send a note to my brother. Now the guards won't give us a proper explanation about what happened to the *Patria*. I'm convinced they are hiding something.'

Isaak and Alexander didn't reply.

'But you have an idea why, don't you?'

'Yes.'

'And?' Lilly prompted.

'It's possible,' Alexander said, 'that the British did not intend to let us remain in Eretz.'

Lilly was quiet for a moment. 'I see.'

Her calm reaction surprised Isaak. Either she was still dazed, or she had already suspected as much.

'But if that's the case,' Lilly said, 'why did they give us permission to leave Cyprus and sail for Haifa?'

'They may have given us permission to sail to Haifa,' Alexander said. 'But they never said they would allow us to land. We assumed we could.'

'Lilly's right, though,' Isaak said. 'Why the whole charade of taking our valuables to pay for the journey? If they had no intention of letting us enter Eretz, why not keep us in Cyprus?'

'Because as long as we were in Cyprus we hadn't broken any laws,' Alexander said.

'But as soon as we reached Haifa ...' Isaak blew out a long breath, comprehending. 'The British made us into "illegal" immigrants.'

'Exactly,' Alexander confirmed. 'Which is why I suspect the *Patria* sinking was no accident. Somehow, the passengers must have got wind that the British would not allow us into Eretz and sabotaged the ship.'

'You're saying they would sink the ship and risk their lives?' Lilly said.

'Perhaps. If they were desperate enough. And if they had warning, they might have devised a plan to save themselves.'

'No, I disagree there,' Lilly said. 'I saw Hannah and Karl just before it happened. They were waving happily to us along with hundreds of others lining the railings. Hannah did not look like someone getting ready to jump off a ship. If she had realised, she would not have appeared that calm. She can't swim.' Her breath hitched. 'We heard screams. We saw people struggling in the water ... Besides, if that was an explosion, the passengers had no means to carry it out.'

'Unless they had outside help,' Alexander said. 'From someone in Eretz.'

'You mean like the Haganah, or the Irgun?' Isaak said.

'*Genau*!'

'That would be difficult,' Lilly said. 'They wouldn't allow us to send letters to our families already in Eretz.'

'Difficult, yes. But not impossible,' Alexander said. 'But whoever or whatever caused it, if the plan was to send us away, they no longer have the means of doing so.

'What's to stop them from loading us onto another one?' Isaak said.

'It won't be so easy to find another spare ship of that size in wartime.'

Lilly gripped the railings. 'I only hope and pray they rescued all the passengers in time.'

'The morning may bring better news,' Isaak said.

The three of them stared out into the dark sea, where the *Patria* rested.

Chapter 13

26 November 1940
SS Atlantic, Haifa Harbour

As the tugboat dragged their ship into Haifa Harbour in the bleak, slate-grey light of morning, they passed the stricken *Patria*. Up close, Isaak could see the full extent of the previous day's disaster. Debris littered the water: planks, mattresses, lifebelts. Rescue craft patrolled the area. Ringed by an oil sheen, the vessel's submerged hull lay like the carcass of a metal whale.

How many of their people had lost their lives? The guards had still not provided any information. They would only confirm that the rescue operation had been conducted efficiently, but unfortunately there were some fatalities among the passengers, police, and crew. They could not provide numbers, survivor lists, or news of family members.

Max gaped at the *Patria*. He seemed to collapse inward. Alexander and Stefan supported him as he swayed on his feet. Erika covered her mouth with her hand. She shut her eyes tight as Janka put her arm around her. Lilly gripped the railings, her knuckles turning white, staring frozen-faced.

Isaak wished he had the words to comfort Lilly. Max and Erika, too. But how could he reassure them when he had no answers? He knew nothing of Hannah's fate or her fiancé's. Nothing of Max's wife, Alma, and baby Chaim. Nothing of Erika's boyfriend.

They must have been rescued. How was it possible that they had survived the entire journey only to drown in the harbour, so close to shore? Yes, he knew there were no guarantees. So many passengers, young and old, had managed to escape the threats of Nazi-occupied Europe only to succumb to disease during the voyage.

And closer to home, what of Isaak's own family? While he was detained in Bratislava, his father, stepmother, and brother had boarded an earlier boat down the Danube, only to be left stranded halfway when the river froze over. He had made it as far as Haifa's shore, while they remained trapped in Kladovo, Yugoslavia.

Life was not fair. He had learned that at nine, standing beside his mother's grave. But for the Jews in Europe, it was downright cruel.

And yet, how could he give up hope? Without hope, he had nothing.

Gisela placed her hand over Lilly's, and Erika grasped her other, squeezing it. Gisela, who had watched the disaster unfold with Lilly from the lighter, and Erika, who shared similar fears for a loved one. Side by side, they comforted each other.

Isaak kept his distance. Right now, it was not his place to intrude.

The tug guided them past the wreckage to their berth. Once docked, the gangway lowered until it touched the quayside, their ship now connected to the land. To Eretz Israel.

Isaak edged closer to the gangway. Guards from the ship descended. Policemen and dock workers ascended. Changing shifts, conferring, carrying crates. Moving with ease: ship to shore, shore to ship. They did not give a thought to the wonder of setting foot on land.

The guards had given no indication when the passengers would be allowed to disembark.

Labourers on the shore continued their work without a second glance at the *Atlantic* and its passengers. Isaak wondered if any of them were fellow Jews. Did they not realise where they had come from and what they had been through to get here? Did they even care?

Set back from the portside and cordoned off behind tall barrier fences, a group of spectators, the tops of their heads bobbing up and down, craning for a glimpse of the *Atlantic*, their calls drowned out by the noise of the bustling harbour. It occurred to him Lilly's brother and Gisela's sons might be among them. But before he could return to share the news, a towering British policeman, a metal-handled baton tucked under his arm, strode up the gangway.

'You, over there!' he barked at Isaak.

Isaak eyed the policeman warily. 'Me?' he pointed to himself.

'Yes, you.' The policeman raised his baton. 'And you. And you.'

Isaak looked back to see his cousin, Alexander, and Efraim, another member of their Prague group, standing behind.

'If you want to eat today, get down here and shift these crates!'

'What did he say?' Efraim looked puzzled.

'He wants us to load crates onto the ship,' Alexander said, translating from English to German.

'I'd be happy to help,' Efraim said.

'Get a move on!' the policeman shouted. 'I haven't got all day.'

Isaak led the way, hurrying down the gangway, eyes set on the point where it met the quay. He was tantalisingly close. Five. four. Just three more steps and his feet would touch the Holy Land.

The policeman's baton swung forward to bar his path. 'That's far enough.' He nodded to the labourer standing on the quayside, holding a crate of potatoes in his outstretched hands. 'Take the crate up to the ship's kitchen, then come straight back to fetch another.'

The crate felt heavier than it looked.

'Is it just me, or are these crates heavy?' Efraim said as they offloaded their crates outside the ship's main kitchen.

'It's not just you,' Isaak said.

'And did you notice how all the port workers barely look at us?' Alexander asked as they returned to the gangway.

'I did,' Isaak said. 'Why is that? It's like they want to pretend we aren't here.'

'What a warm welcome,' Alexander said, his voice dripping with sarcasm.

'Stop that chit-chatting,' the policeman shouted. 'There's plenty more work to be done.'

'What's he saying?' Efraim said.

'He's telling us to stop talking because we have a lot more work to do,' Alexander said.

'It's not like he's paying us,' Efraim said. 'We're volunteers.'

The labourer handed Isaak a new crate. Then he stacked another on top. The weight pulled at his shoulders. He began his ascent, slower this time.

'Stop your dawdling!'

Isaak looked over his shoulder. The policeman was bellowing at Efraim, who was struggling with his crates too.

'Hurry up, you lazy good for nothing.'

'He doesn't speak English,' Isaak blurted out. 'He doesn't understand.'

'It doesn't take a genius to work out what needs to be done. Maybe he'll understand this.' The policeman swung his right foot and aimed a kick at Efraim's calves.

'Ow!' Efraim cried out. The top crate tipped. Potatoes spilled out, rolled down the stairs, and several plopped into the water.

Isaak and Alexander dropped their crates and scrambled to retrieve the potatoes. The policeman continued to berate them. 'Hurry up and clean up this mess. If you people want to eat, you'd better work faster.'

'*Arschloch*,' Alexander muttered under his breath.

'What was that, lad?' the policeman said.

'Er ... ' Alexander floundered. 'Yes, of course, we need to eat.'

'Hmm.' The policeman looked unconvinced. 'I'm keeping an eye on you young troublemakers.' He gestured with his baton toward Alexander and then at the top of the gangway. 'Carry on.'

On reaching the ship's kitchen, Efraim slammed his crate down. 'What did I do wrong? I was only doing my best to help, and he goes and kicks me like he thinks I'm a lowly slave. I thought we had left this treatment behind in Europe.'

Alexander shook his head. 'So did I.' His hands balled into fists before he exhaled sharply and looked away. 'I'm going to ask Dov, or someone else from the Haganah, to find other volunteers to replace us. Why should we have to endure this? And if he's got it in for us, best we stay out of his way.'

Alexander was still cursing as they headed back to join their friends. 'What a nasty piece of work.'

'There was absolutely no need for him to treat Efraim that way,' Isaak agreed. 'Unless ...'

'Unless what?'

'He believes that the *Patria* sinking wasn't an accident. Just as you thought. Perhaps he holds all of us responsible.'

'Yes.' Alexander stopped. 'That would make sense.'

'I'm not sure we should mention this incident to the others.'

'No, probably best not to. There's enough to worry about without upsetting them further.'

Isaak and Alexander exchanged glances. Lilly, Erika and Max had managed to draw aside a fresh-faced, blond-haired British soldier, speaking with him in low tones. Isaak and Alexander huddled closer to listen.

'Some people remain unaccounted for, so I'm afraid we still don't know the number of fatalities,' he was saying.

As soon as he noticed them, he produced a packet of cigarettes and held it out to them. Alexander declined with a wave.

'Thank you,' Isaak said. He took one. They always came in handy for bartering. The soldier withdrew a lighter.

'That's all right,' Isaak said. 'I'll save it for later.'

The soldier gave a slight smile, and Isaak stuffed the cigarette in his pocket.

'But well over one thousand passengers were rescued,' the soldier continued. 'Thanks to the heroic efforts of British forces and some Australian soldiers who were on duty. So there's a good chance your relatives were saved.'

Lilly pressed a hand to her heart. 'Where have they taken the survivors?'

'To a clearance camp nearby.'

'And what happens to us now?' Alexander said. 'Will we be allowed off the ship?'

'I'm afraid I don't yet have that information,' the soldier said. 'But I imagine it's likely they'll send you to that camp too.'

Alexander raised his eyebrows at Isaak. The first encouraging piece of news they had received since arriving in Eretz Israel.

Chapter 14

25 November 1940
Haifa Port

'Try to rest.' The nurse coaxed Hannah to lie down on the narrow cot. For the past hour she had scanned the faces in the warehouse – no sign of Karl, no glimpse of Alma cradling Chaim, no Marcus. She could not rest amongst the groans and cries, the uncertainty. She had to find them. Fear pressed against her chest. She could barely breathe.

A cup touched her lips. 'Here. Drink this.'

Hannah took a sip of water.

'Good girl,' the nurse said as she gently eased her down.

Hannah's strength gave out and she sagged against the cot. But as soon as she shut her eyes, haunting images flashed through Hannah's mind, drawing her back to the *Patria*. The sudden boom.

'We're under attack!' the guard shouted, driving them towards the companionway. Screams rang out. Passengers poured down the stairwell; others jumped overboard. Before Hannah could process what was happening, Karl grabbed her hand and pulled her down the stairs. The chaos swept them along. A surge of people shoved them from behind. Karl led her down one flight, then another.

Hannah felt light-headed. Off-balance.

The stairs appeared to be tilting to her left

No, surely not. She had to be imagining things.

This was another false alarm.

Like the last time.

Except ...

Karl slowed too, moving with new caution.

'Karl,' Hannah began, as they reached the bottom. 'Did you notice—'

Her words were lost in the tumult. They collided with a knot of passengers shoving past them in a panic to get up the stairs.

Karl snatched her out of the crush and they retreated to the opposite wall. His eyes swept the scene. Cold water seeped into Hannah's shoes. She looked down. A stream flowed through the passageway.

'Save yourselves!' A man shouted from the top of the stairs. 'Go back!' He ploughed between passengers, imploring them to turn back. Even so, he forced his way down: tripping and sliding, stumbling and desperate. Only when he reached them did Hannah recognise him as Karl's friend, HW.

'Save yourselves.' HW's breath came in short, staccato bursts, his eyes wide with terror. 'The ship's sinking.'

Hannah's legs went weak. This could not be happening.

He shouted his warning down both sides of the passageway.

'HW!' Karl called as he started down the next flight. 'What about Marcus and the rest of the boys locked up in the hold?'

'I'm going there now.'

'Shall I come—'

HW had already continued his descent. 'Look after Hannah,' he called behind him. 'Get her to safety.'

Karl spun around. 'Let's go back up.'

Hannah's breathing quickened. 'But ... I can't swim.'

Karl took her hand. 'Don't worry. I'll find another way.'

Hannah remained frozen in place. 'What about Alma and Chaim?'

'They must be on deck already. We'll go up and check.'

'Put on lifebelts!' A policeman hurried down the left passageway, carrying a stack, knocking on cabin doors. 'Put on lifebelts!' Karl grabbed two as he passed and slipped one lifebelt over his head. His hands shook as he tied the other around Hannah's waist. He nudged her back towards the stairway which listed at a more noticeable angle. Hannah and Karl joined the line, gripping the handrail as they climbed the slanting stairs. Hannah tripped; her ankle twisted. The patent-leather heels, chosen that morning for elegance rather than escape, now threatened to send her tumbling. Behind them, Asian and Arab crew members in lifebelts pressed forward. Only one person pushed past in the opposite direction.

'Excuse me. Excuse me,' he said as he squeezed his way through the crowd.

'Arthur?' Karl said as they passed. 'Where are you going?'

'To the boiler room,' he shouted over the clamour. 'I need to open the vents and release the steam, otherwise ...' He shook his head.

'Please be careful.'

He managed a grim smile. 'You too,' he said, before he disappeared.

By the time she and Karl reached the next flight, the ship had tilted too sharply to walk normally. Passengers ahead shuffled up the lower banister, gripping the upper handrail for support – now at chest height. Hannah could not follow in heels. She had to abandon her shoes. Kicking them off, she pushed them aside and continued barefoot. She concentrated on her footing, careful not to slip between the banister posts.

From the deck above came a rumble, crashes, clattering, sliding. Terrified screams. Hannah turned to Karl.

'Keep going.'

From below came a sharp crack of splintering wood. More shouts. A staircase collapsing.

'Karl ...?' Hannah cried.

'Keep going. A few more steps.'

Above, a square of sky beckoned. She focused on it, trying to shut out the sounds of destruction. Seawater rained through the companionway. It drenched Hannah as she climbed, making the surfaces treacherous.

Karl pushed her up onto the deck, following behind. Only five minutes had passed since the boom, but they emerged into a terrifying spectacle. The ship was now listing at an angle of at least forty-five degrees, its smoking funnels leaning ever closer towards the water.

'Head for portside!' Karl shouted above the commotion, rescue craft whistles, sirens wailing across the harbour.

The elevated portside loomed steeply above, making it impossible to stand. Hannah and Karl had to scrabble on all fours to scale the deck. They clawed at the narrow grooves between the planks to gain purchase. Karl crawled ahead. He grabbed hold of the railings, extended his hand to Hannah and tugged her the final stretch. Panting, she gripped the railings and pulled herself to her feet. The carnage revealed itself.

Boards and mattresses, lifeboats ripped from their davits, carpeted the water's surface. The reverberations she had heard moments ago must have been the sound of the stacks collapsing. They had torn through the starboard railings and hurtled into the sea. Hannah whimpered as she noticed an arm sticking out from beneath one, a pair of legs from another. Passengers had dived from the lower starboard side, attempting to swim to safety. They had no chance when the wreckage crashed on top of them.

Several people still clung to the starboard railings. A woman lost her grip and fell with a scream. An elderly, white-bearded man raised his face heavenward, shut his eyes and recited the Shema as the railings tilted closer to the water.

Hannah watched helplessly. There was no way to save them. She did not know how she would save herself. Rescue craft and rowing boats swarmed from the harbour and made for the ship's portside. Passengers were climbing over the railings, sliding down the hull, and diving into the water for rescue.

'Over the railings,' Karl said, hauling himself onto the hull. He held on with one hand and extended the other to Hannah. 'Can you manage?'

Hannah swallowed down a wave of nausea. 'I can't jump in.'

'You won't have to. I see another way.'

Her fingers and toes tingled as she followed him onto the near-horizontal hull. Below, arms waved frantically from porthole windows: passengers trapped inside cabins signalling for help.

'Oh no,' Hannah said. 'Where's Alma?'

Holding onto the railings, Karl led her around the ship's hull to the stern where the ship was tethered to the breakwater by a series of three cables. A line of passengers balanced precariously on the lower cable like tightrope walkers, holding onto a second cable at shoulder height.

'I can't do that,' Hannah said.

'Yes, you can.'

Picking each foothold, they moved carefully downward. The surface was almost flat now but crusted with rust. Barnacles on the lower section scraped her feet raw. They joined the line of people waiting to mount the cables.

'I'll watch to make sure you make it safely to the other side,' Karl said. 'If you lose your balance, I'll dive in after you.'

Hannah stared at him, realising what he had just said. 'You're not coming with me?'

'I have to stay here to check that Marcus, Alma and Chaim make it to safety and do what I can to help. Then I'll come and find you.'

'But it's dangerous.' She drew a shaky breath. 'What if ...'

Karl hugged her.

'I can't do this on my own,' she said.

'Yes, you can,' he said. 'I know you can do this.' She rested her head on his shoulder, not wanting him to let go. She wanted to beg him to come. But how could she stop him from remaining behind to save the lives of others?

'Promise me you'll be careful,' Hannah said.

'I will be,' he said.

He helped her mount the cable. It lurched and swayed. Below, she could see people swimming across. 'Hold tight and look ahead to the breakwater.' He steadied her by the waist until she had a firm grip on the upper wire. 'Don't look back. Don't look down. And don't be afraid. I'll be watching you every step of the way.'

He stepped back to let the next passenger climb on. She was on her own.

Hannah inched sideways along the cable. A young man took his place beside her. He seemed around Isaak's age, nineteen or twenty.

Hannah shuffled another few centimetres.

She reminded herself that Karl was watching her. There was so much she should have said to him before they parted. She should have told him she loved him, that she was so proud of him. What if she never got the chance ...

She tried to shake the dark thoughts from her mind. Karl said he would be careful. She had to trust him and believe that he would make it back. Hannah would see him again. They would have a future together.

Another small shift to the right. Another. And another.

The ship was no longer beneath her. Now water stretched below, rippling blue, down into the depths. Don't look down.

Her hands already burned from gripping the cable. How was she going to make it across this stretch of open water to the other side?

'Keep going,' Karl called after her. 'You are going to be fine.'

Hannah kept her gaze forward. She tried not to glance down. She kept her focus straight ahead, edging her way along the line.

A shuffled footstep. Another. And another.

She had reached the midpoint.

The cable was packed with people. It bounced underfoot. Was it strong enough to hold all of them? A terrifying thought struck: what if the cable gave way and snapped? Fear burned from her chest to her head. Her legs trembled.

Don't think about it.

Keep going. Keep going.

Was it Karl's voice? Was it her imagination?

Her papa's voice came back to her from the dream.

Papa was with her. Karl was with her. She could do this.

Keep going. Keep going.

Another step. Then another.

Her stomach dropped as the young man to her left let go of the cable. She gasped as he plunged down into the water. Her left foot slipped. She gripped tight and slid her foot into place. The young man swam to a boat positioned beneath the line. The rowers hauled him in. Hannah trembled all over.

The next passenger shuffled beside her, closing the space between them.

'Are you all right?'

Hannah managed a nod.

She heard an infant's cry. She glanced sideways and from the corner of her eye she saw he had a tiny baby strapped onto his front.

'How old is your baby?'

'Three days old,' he said.

She slid her feet further to the right.

The wire cut into her hands and feet. Her arms and shoulders were growing tired. Hannah felt she might slip at any moment. But unlike the young man, she could not swim. She would sink. She clung on.

'Nearly there,' the man with the baby reassured her. 'You're doing well.'

Hannah kept her eyes on the breakwater.

One small step. Another. And another.

Finally, she dropped her arms and collapsed onto the jagged rocks, exhausted. She winced at the instant sting of pain. She had gashed her leg in the fall.

Hannah looked back at the *Patria*. Karl was still watching her from the hull. He waved. Hannah waved in reply. He placed a hand to his heart. But before Hannah could do likewise, he climbed back over the railings, and was gone.

Chapter 15

The water lapped against the rocks, too close. With her remaining strength, Hannah clambered up to join other *Patria* survivors who had gathered higher on the breakwater.

Her hands were red-raw. Blood from the gash streamed down her leg. Barefoot, her dress torn and stained. She had no possessions. Her luggage – clothes, the few belongings from Vienna – remained on the sinking ship. Reduced and reduced and reduced. But she had made it. She had survived.

Hannah should have been relieved. She had conquered her fear and crossed over the water, but she just felt ... numb.

People lay on the rocks, faces ashen, exhausted. A few were crying. Hannah saw the man who had crossed the cable beside her. He was now rocking his three-day-old baby. He noticed Hannah and gave her a wan smile. A haunted look shadowed his face. Where was the baby's mother? She didn't dare ask.

Men and women traversed the cables from the *Patria*. Other passengers swam across, reaching the breakwater where outstretched arms pulled them onto the rocks. Rescue boats picked up swimmers and ferried them to safety.

The *Patria* now rested on its side, its funnels submerged in the water. Hannah could hear shouts from the overturned ship and saw the arms of people trapped in their cabins waving frantically from portholes.

She kept seeing them again and again. The lifeless bodies floating on the surface; the woman who had slipped to her death; the elderly man reciting the Shema, resigned to his fate.

What of Alma and Chaim? She hadn't seen them since leaving their cabin that morning. What of Marcus, locked in the hold? And her beloved, Karl, who had returned to save their friends and others still trapped in the ship.

How could this have happened so fast? One minute she had been standing on the deck with Karl waiting for Lilly and Gisela. And the next ...

Hannah's breath caught in her throat as she remembered.

Their lighter had already entered the harbour. Did Lilly and Gisela board the *Patria* without her seeing them? Had the falling planks and mattresses hit their vessel as the ship capsized? Please, no!

Her breaths became shallower. She sat on the breakwater between the *Atlantic* and the overturned *Patria* and had never felt more alone. What would become of her?

Survivors continued arriving, bruised, bloodied, a few almost naked. A British soldier, two nurses, and a doctor moved from person to person tending to the seriously injured. Hannah considered asking for a bandage, but they were already overwhelmed. Instead, she tore a ribbon of fabric from her dress and bound her wound.

A woman emerged dripping from the water, her hair hanging limp around her shoulders, carrying a bundle.

'My baby!' She let out a piercing scream. 'Someone help me. My baby – he is dead!'

The British soldier leapt up, his rifle clattering to the ground. He rushed down the rocks, plucked the baby from his mother's arms and massaged his chest.

'My baby!' The mother buried her face in her hands.

The soldier remained focused, shutting out the mother's cries as he rubbed and massaged. Hannah held her breath. He stripped off his jumper and swaddled the infant.

'Your baby is going to be fine,' the soldier said, but the distraught woman did not hear him. He gingerly tapped her on the shoulder. She looked up.

The soldier held the baby out to her to show his wide eyes gazing around.

She gasped, putting a hand to her mouth.

'Your baby is fine,' he reassured her.

Her tears flowed again, but this time, ones of relief. 'Thank you.' With trembling hands she took her baby and embraced him. 'Thank you.'

'I have a little boy back home in England,' he said. 'I understand.'

The woman nodded, as if she did not fully comprehend his English. 'Thank you,' she said again.

Hannah hugged her arms around herself. Even when all had seemed lost, that soldier had not given up. His actions fortified her. She would not give up either.

She continued to wait, watching for Karl, for Alma and Chaim, for Marcus, among new groups of survivors, but neither her fiancé nor friends arrived.

Hannah had lost track of time, but the shifting light suggested early afternoon. The number of passengers swimming to the breakwater or crossing via the mooring lines dwindled to a trickle until there were no more.

Boats arrived to ferry the survivors to shore. A policeman handed her a blanket, which she accepted, but declined each offer to board. She hung back to wait for Karl. At last, only five men and herself remained. The men climbed into the final rescue craft. Hannah lingered.

'Miss, please board the boat,' said the policeman.

'I am waiting for my fiancé,' Hannah replied.

'If he hasn't arrived yet, he may have been taken straight to the harbour.' He regarded her with pity. 'Many of the passengers were taken there. Come along now, miss. This is the last boat-load. You can't stay here.'

Hannah hesitated, though she knew she couldn't stay. The sun had taken on a golden hue. Soon it would set. She shuddered at the thought of sitting here alone in the darkness – beside the open sea. She picked her way down from the rocks and boarded.

Rescue craft still hovered around the *Patria*. She could make out small teams on the hull cutting open the portholes with acetylene torches. Was the policeman correct? Would she find Karl and the others in the harbour?

Their boat reached the quayside, and the policeman was the first to disembark.

'Follow me,' he said, setting a brisk pace. The five men followed, with Hannah trailing behind.

She glanced back at the *Patria*. Its forlorn hull glowed with a coppery sheen in the late afternoon light. How was it possible for the sun to shine on a nightmare?

And then she looked down.

Ground.

She was standing on land for the first time in three months.

Holy Land.

She had waited for this moment for almost a year, ever since leaving her home in Vienna. It should have been monumental. Joyful. Reverential. A time to pause and kiss the ground beneath her feet.

She was not supposed to arrive like this. Alone. Without Karl, Lilly, or her friends from the Lifeboat Chevra. And yet, here she was.

She had endured imprisonment in Bratislava, a perilous sea voyage, and survived the *Patria* capsizing.

She was alive.

Hannah crouched down and pressed her hands to the ground.

'Miss, are you all right?' the policeman said, noticing she had fallen behind.

Self-conscious, Hannah stood up and, limping on her injured leg, caught up with the others.

'I'm sorry, miss,' he said. 'I didn't realise you were injured. Do you require assistance?'

Hannah shook her head and hobbled after him to a portside warehouse, its entrance guarded by a policeman on either side.

The large warehouse was crowded with people. A group surged forward to meet the new arrivals. A wife embraced her husband. Friends welcomed the other four men. The gathering dispersed. Hannah remained on her own.

She began walking the width of the warehouse, searching for Karl on legs she could barely lift. She watched the emotional family reunions and distraught men and women slumped on benches, grain sacks, or on the floor, some staring unfocused, others sobbing. A woman standing alone stared at Hannah. The woman's brunette hair was bedraggled. She had a gash across her cheek and wore an ill-fitting navy cotton dress. Her face looked vaguely familiar. She seemed to recognise Hannah and strode towards her. Then Hannah remembered that morning at breakfast: smart navy suit, brunette hair elegantly piled on her head, lips painted red. The blonde woman's companion.

To her surprise, the woman gave her a stiff hug. She stepped back and looked Hannah up and down. 'Your dress is torn,' she said. 'The people of Haifa have donated clothes. Let's find you something else to wear.'

Without giving her a chance to reply, she looped her arm through Hannah's. She led her past four long wooden tables where volunteers were handing out food and drink, and stopped in front of a large pile of clothes. Hannah stared blankly at the heap while the woman rummaged, holding up items to gauge her size.

'This might fit you,' she said, settling on a pale blue dress. 'Let's go and try it on.'

Leaving no room for discussion, she took Hannah's elbow, steered her to a bench set against the right wall, and removed the blanket around her shoulders.

'I will hold this up while you change.'

With no energy to protest, Hannah unfastened her lifejacket and placed it on the bench. She raised her arms to lift off her dress and groaned from the effort. Her arms and shoulders ached.

'Is everything all right?' the woman said from behind the blanket.

'Yes.' Despite the pain, she slipped on the donated dress. 'I'm done.'

The woman removed the blanket and examined Hannah, tugging at the waist and shoulders. 'Ah yes. Much better,' she declared. 'Now, would you like something to eat?' She pointed to the row of tables where volunteers – Jewish women in white aprons, Catholic nuns, Anglican priests, and Englishwomen in fitted suits – were distributing sandwiches, oranges, and hot drinks.

Hannah's stomach churned. 'No, thank you.'

'A cup of tea.' Before Hannah could reply, she marched towards the volunteers and reappeared a minute later bearing a cup. 'It's tea with sugar. Good after a shock.' She passed it to Hannah. 'You will feel a little better for it. Drink.'

Hannah took a sip. It was sweet. Warm. Soothing.

'You are quite exhausted?' the woman said. 'Perhaps you should rest for a while.' She hovered awkwardly as if uncertain whether to take her leave.

'Thank you for all your help,' Hannah said.

The woman's face brightened, as if grateful for Hannah's acknowledgement, but her lips did not form a smile. She stepped back and wandered off.

As soon as she had gone, Hannah set down the cup and rose from the bench. She walked up and down. Right and left. Over and over. Round and round. She searched every face.

She came across three young men sitting on the floor eating sandwiches. She recognised them from the Patronka. They had been part of the same group as Karl and Marcus. She had once known their names but could not recall them.

'Have you seen Karl?' Hannah asked. 'Or Marcus?'

All three shook their heads.

'Sorry,' said the middle one, the right sleeve missing from his shirt. 'We haven't.'

'When did you arrive?'

'A few hours ago. Late morning or early afternoon. I'm not sure.' He held out his watch to show her its hands pointing to quarter past nine. 'It stopped working after I dived into the water.'

'How did you get here?'

'An Arab fisherman rescued and took us to shore, and a British policeman escorted us here.'

'Is it possible Karl was taken somewhere else?'

He shook his head. 'I think they brought all the survivors here.' He paused. 'But have you checked the temporary hospital yet?'

'No, I haven't. Where is it?'

'It's at the rear, behind the wooden partition,' he said. 'I hope you find him.'

'Thank you,' she said, already setting off.

Hannah peered around the partition at lines of patients on makeshift beds, relatives hovering beside them, other survivors searching for loved ones. Filled with hope and dread, Hannah tiptoed between rows of beds to check if Karl was among them. She averted her gaze to avoid staring at their injuries, the blood-stained bandages around their heads, limbs, torsos. She checked for Alma and Chaim and Marcus too. None of them were among the patients.

'Excuse me,' she said to a white-uniformed nurse. 'Do you know whether Karl Schiff has been brought here?'

'I'll check for you,' the nurse said.

She picked up a clipboard from a bench beside the partition. Hannah braced herself as the nurse consulted the scribbled list. 'Sorry,' she said. 'I can't see his name here.'

'How about Alma Freund or Marcus Levy?'

The nurse checked again before giving Hannah a pitying look. 'I'm so sorry.'

'I see,' Hannah said, backing away from the nurse. She felt drained, her shoulders heavy.

'You're injured,' the nurse said, looking down at her leg. 'Let me bandage that for you.' She took Hannah's hand and led her to an empty cot, where she cleaned and dressed the wounds on her leg and feet.

'Try to rest,' the nurse murmured, coaxing her to lie down. Hannah could not rest. She had to find them. The nurse brought a cup of water to her lips and then eased her down onto the cot.

She was exhausted, but she could not sleep. Her mind raced, replaying the scenes she had witnessed on the *Patria*. The desperate scramble of passengers up the tilted staircase, the screams from above and below, the bodies in the water.

It was all too much. Too enormous to comprehend.

What would happen to her now?

For a year she had been running away. From Vienna, leaving her mother behind. Nine months trapped in Bratislava. Three months on the water. First a paddle steamer down the Danube, then a ship across the Black Sea, Marmara, Aegean, Mediterranean ...

Here she was. She had finally made it to Eretz Israel. But Karl had not returned. She was separated from Lilly, not knowing what had happened. She was alone with nothing and no one left. Hannah longed for escape. She wanted to run away ... from herself. But there was no more running. Fear had caught up with her. A dark fear that had obscured thoughts of the future and threatened her dreams.

Hannah rolled onto her side, closed her eyes and covered her ears, wanting to shut out this place and everything that had happened. But she was haunted by memories of their last moments together and the words she had said to Karl: 'Promise me you'll be careful.'

'Hannah.' She heard his whispered voice in her head. It sounded so real. She wanted to hold onto the sound of his voice, remain in this liminal state and not have to face the wretchedness of her new reality.

'Hannah.'

A hand touched hers.

Dare she look?

Hannah opened her eyes. Karl was crouching beside her. Her breath caught.

She reached out and touched his cheek. 'It's you.'

'It's me.' He managed a sad smile. His face was drawn, his eyes bloodshot behind his glasses. In the past few hours he had aged several years. But it was still Karl. 'I promised I would come back and find you.'

'I thought ... I thought ...' Hannah choked back a sob.

Karl pulled her close. 'It's all right.' He stroked her hair as her tears soaked his shirt. 'I'm here.'

Chapter 16

Karl helped Hannah back to the main section of the warehouse, his arm steady around her waist. She sank onto a grain sack stacked against the left wall while he fetched sandwiches and tea. As they ate in silence, Hannah kept looking at Karl's face, unable to believe he sat beside her. Alive. But his distant stare betrayed the weight of his recent hours. What was he thinking? What had he witnessed? Hannah did not ask. Karl would tell her in his own time.

'Our first meal in Eretz,' she said. A small opening.

A ghost of a smile touched his lips but failed to erase his haunted expression. 'I only wish it could have been under better circumstances,' he said. 'It should have been a cause for celebration. Not like ...' He looked around the warehouse, at the scene of devastation. 'Not like this.'

'What will the British do with us next?'

'Who knows?' He removed his glasses, slipped them into his shirt pocket, and rubbed his bloodshot eyes. 'I'm sure they'll tell us soon.'

He took her hand, leaned his head against the wall, and shut his eyes, exhausted. Soon his grip relaxed and he was fast asleep.

She watched his chest rise and fall, grateful beyond words. Karl was alive. They had nothing but the clothes on their backs, but they had each other.

Hannah rested against Karl's shoulder. Through bleary eyes she saw the brunette woman still wandering aimlessly. Despite their previous encounters, she felt compassion for her and her resentment melted away.

'Can I have your attention, please!'

Hannah stirred. Karl shook himself awake and checked his watch. She glanced at Karl's wrist and noticed it was already eight o'clock. The murmurs around the warehouse fell silent to listen to the guard's announcement.

'Buses are waiting outside to take you to a clearance camp where you'll be staying for the time being. If you can now please all make your way to the entrance. Thank you.'

Hannah and Karl joined the bewildered and weary survivors as they quietly formed a queue. They shuffled out of the warehouse into the cool night air. A fleet of buses waited on the road outside, engines idling, headlights fitted with blue glass for the blackout. Hannah blinked to adjust to the darkness and wrapped the blanket over her thin cotton dress as the cold seeped up from the concrete and stung her bare feet.

A soldier directed them onto the second bus.

Karl nodded to the driver as they boarded. 'Where are we going?'

'Atlit,' he said.

'Where is that?'

Before the driver could answer, a blond-haired British soldier entered the bus followed by four policemen.

The bus was nearly full. Karl and Hannah sat in the last seats, three rows from the front, with Hannah next to the window and Karl on the aisle.

The four policemen did not look like the regular British police. Each one wore a distinctive black woollen hat resembling a tall Turkish fez.

A woman across the aisle held a little girl of about three. She exchanged a worried glance with Hannah and hugged her daughter closer.

'What kind of policemen are those?' Hannah whispered to Karl.

'I'm not sure,' Karl said in an undertone, sliding lower in his seat, which only compounded her growing unease.

When had she become so afraid?

Once, she had been fearless. Boldly defying Nazi restrictions. After Kristallnacht, she had dyed her hair blonde and walked the streets of Vienna, outside the hours permitted for Jews, in order to buy food for her family. Had she ever considered what might have happened if a Nazi had stopped her? Somehow she had acted confident and had never been caught. Maybe she had been naïve, not fully understanding the risks or consequences. But today, she had reached Eretz Israel. She was safe. And yet, the mere sight of policemen in unfamiliar uniforms was enough to send her into a tailspin.

Only hours ago she had barely escaped the disaster. Was it any wonder her nerves and trust had been shattered?

'Excuse me—'

Karl jolted and looked up at the British soldier standing over them. He extended a cigarette packet. 'May I offer you one?'

'No.' Karl's voice caught. 'Thank you.'

He dipped his head and continued down the aisle, offering his cigarettes to the rest of the adult passengers.

'Should we be worried about those other policemen?' Hannah whispered, once the soldier was out of earshot.

'I don't think so,' he said with strained calm.

'Their hats look Turkish. Are they Arab?'

One of the policemen sitting in front swivelled around. He had high cheekbones and a trimmed black moustache. He offered a reassuring smile. 'Don't worry.' He addressed them in German. 'We are Jewish too. We are here to help you.'

On hearing this, Karl seemed to relax. '*Danke*,' he said, the word sounding like a sigh of relief.

The young soldier, who could not have been long out of school, returned to the front of the bus with his shoulders hunched and lips pressed together in disappointment. Though the passengers had been civil, not a single one had accepted his offer of a cigarette. Undeterred, he approached the young mother across the aisle, crouched down and withdrew a small foil package from his pocket. 'Excuse me,' he said. 'Would your little girl like some chocolate?'

The mother looked from the soldier to her daughter whose gaze fixed on the chocolate. 'Thank you,' she said in halting English. 'You are very kind.'

'My pleasure, madam.' He broke the bar in half and handed it to the girl. Her face lit up as she accepted it and took a bite.

He squared his shoulders and took his seat across from the driver.

The bus lurched, rolled forward, and picked up speed. As they wound through the streets of Haifa, Hannah made out the outlines of homes and a few chinks of light escaping blackout curtains. She wished she could see them in more detail. Her first view of Eretz Israel, and she saw almost nothing. Before long, they left the city behind, and darkness surrounded them on either side. A sickle moon lent a faint silvery glow to the palm trees lining the road, and the thin blue headlight beams illuminated the convoy of buses driving south.

Karl stared straight ahead, silent. He still had not mentioned a word about their friends – or Lilly. Is that what was troubling him? Dread settled in her chest. What did he know that he wasn't telling her? Sitting on a bus full of passengers was not the most opportune moment to launch a private conversation, but Hannah could not restrain herself.

'Karl?'

He startled. 'Yes.'

'What do you think happened to Lilly and Gisela after we last saw them?'

'Their boat returned to the *Atlantic*.'

'Are you sure? They didn't board ... just before ...'

'I'm certain. A British guard on the *Patria* told me the lighter had reversed out of the harbour.' He stroked Hannah's hand. 'They're safe.'

Hannah breathed a little easier. But what about the others? She was too afraid to ask.

Karl sank back against the seat and exhaled, ending the conversation. But he reached for her hand, holding onto it like a lifeline. What was preying on his mind?

Ten minutes later the bus drew to a standstill and the soldier marshalled them off the bus. Hannah peered into the darkness. A searchlight atop a watchtower swept back and forth. She glimpsed high wooden fences reinforced with what appeared to be wire mesh. What kind of clearance camp was this? From the little she could make out in the searchlight, it looked more foreboding than the Patronka, the internment camp in Bratislava where Hannah had first met Karl. As far as she could tell, Atlit 'camp' was a euphemism for prison.

'Keep moving,' ordered another British policeman.

A row of policemen wearing the woollen fez-like hats flanked the open gates. Walking in a column, Hannah tried to make sense of the contradiction. Hadn't the Jewish policemen on the bus said that they were there to help them? Yet, they were herding them into prison.

Next they were corralled into a long wooden barrack. Before Hannah knew it, guards had divided the men and women into two lines, separating her from Karl. Around her, several women wept.

A British sergeant and two Jewish policemen sat behind a long table at the front. They processed the new arrivals in groups of five with swift military efficiency. When it was Hannah's turn, they wrote her name in a large ledger, asked her to add her signature, then directed her to another door at the side of the table. Hannah lingered as long as possible, searching for Karl. Before she could find him, she was ushered out into the cold night with nine other women. The door closed behind them.

'Hello, I'm Rachel,' said a soft-spoken voice in the darkness. A sweep of the searchlight revealed a petite young woman in her early twenties. 'I've come to show you to your hut and help you settle in. Please follow me.'

Rachel strode along a path bordered on either side by barbed wire. The rest of the women traipsed after her, struggling on the uneven ground. Hannah winced as stones cut into her bandaged feet, but she picked up her pace to catch up with Rachel.

'Wait,' Hannah said. 'My fiancé hasn't come out yet.'

'He'll be taken to the men's huts. They are in a different section.'

'When can I see him?'

'Tomorrow. They allow us to meet the men each afternoon for an hour.'

'How nice of them.'

Worse than the Patronka, Hannah decided. There, they were allowed to meet as much as they wanted. But at least she could still see him. They would not be completely separated.

'I know this must be overwhelming. Especially after all that you have been through. But we'll look after you. It really isn't so bad once you get used to the routine.'

'How long have you been here?'

'Since July,' Rachel said. 'We arrived on the last ship that reached Haifa. The *Libertad.*'

Hannah was certain she had heard the name before, but could not remember where. 'You've been here for four months already?'

'Yes, but with any luck, not for much longer. There's talk that they will release us from here soon.' Rachel smiled. 'Then we'll be free to start our lives for real.'

She opened the door to a hut. An overhead light revealed barrack-style sleeping quarters. Fifteen wooden-slatted beds lined either side with shuttered windows above. Ten *Patria* passengers were already there, selecting and making their beds. A female guard distributed a pillow, two grey woollen blankets, cutlery and a straw mattress to each of the new arrivals. She also offered them oranges, white bread, and milk.

'You must be tired,' Rachel said to the group. 'I'll let you get to sleep. I'm in the hut to the right if you need anything, and I'll come by tomorrow to see how you are doing.' And to Hannah. 'Have a good night. Things will look better in the morning. You'll see.'

Hannah selected a vacant bed in the middle on the left and hoisted her mattress onto the wooden slats. A shiver ran through her as she remembered the tall pile of wooden boards stacked on the *Patria's* deck where she and Karl had sought privacy the afternoon before. The following morning, as the ship tilted, those same boards had slid across the deck and plummeted into the water, crushing people below.

She pulled the blanket around her shoulders and dropped onto the edge of the bed. They had reached Eretz Israel and survived the disaster, only to find themselves imprisoned and separated once again. What would the British do with them now?

Chapter 17

26 November 1940
Atlit Camp

Lemon-yellow sunlight slanted through the windows. Hannah had slept for ten hours after her ordeal, deep and dreamless. The bed was unyielding and the wooden hut spartan, but it was far better than the cramped conditions she had endured on the *Atlantic*. The hut reminded her of a *Hütte*, the kind she'd stayed in when she, Lilly and Eugen had gone hiking in the Austrian Alps when she was sixteen.

A decent night's sleep afforded her clarity. Much preferable to be imprisoned here in Atlit, even for months like Rachel, rather than face deportation elsewhere. If only the British would let them stay.

Breakfast arrived. Her new roommates drew together at the hut's entrance with the ease of long acquaintance. All of them had travelled on the *Milos* before their *Patria* transfer. She alone was from the *Atlantic* and knew no one. She sat by herself on her bed, drinking a cup of milk as she watched them. A wave of loneliness washed over her.

How she missed Lilly and the Lifeboat Chevra. Lilly most of all, her closest confidante – like a sister. They had grown up together; no one understood her the way Lilly did. But she also missed Erika with whom she started this journey from Vienna. Erika, who dreamed of becoming a qualified nurse, would have fussed over the weeping gash on her leg. Janka, who sometimes appeared brittle, the hardness a shield for her vulnerable heart. Alexander, Janka's brother and natural leader, rallied them all. Hannah still thought he and Lilly would make a good match. Isaak, the youngest, yet often the most worldly wise, with the kindest heart she knew. Stefan, measured and thoughtful, and sweet Jenny. Max ... *Mein Gott*! What had happened to Alma and baby Chaim on the *Patria*? She could not bear to think of them.

Gisela, who nurtured and comforted them in place of a parent. How Hannah needed her wisdom right now. What would Gisela tell her? No doubt Gisela would say she should be grateful that she and Karl had escaped with their lives. And she was. Though apart, they were both here, and in another four hours she would be allowed to see him. Perhaps Gisela would remind Hannah she had started this journey alone too, leaving Vienna knowing no one. Yet she had made all these dear friends along the way. Hannah edged closer to the group. A young woman about her own age, also barefoot, gave a friendly smile despite a swollen black eye and shifted over to make space for Hannah.

Hannah peeled a juicy orange, releasing its citrus fragrance, and listened to the women's conversation. They were recounting how they had escaped the *Patria*.

'I was trapped in the dining room,' said a woman with a deep cut across her cheek, her arms and legs covered in bruises. The ship listed so quickly. Within minutes the door was above our heads. Water rushed in through the portholes. The electric lights went out. Tables and chairs tumbled around, hitting and crushing people in the darkness. At first, people were screaming and then ... ' She shuddered. 'I can't even begin to describe the terror. I thought it was the end for me. Then several men called to us from the opening above. Someone threw a rope. I grabbed onto it. And a young man with gold-rimmed glasses hauled me up.'

Hannah straightened at the description.

'If it wasn't for him ...' The woman took a breath to steady herself. 'I would have been among the ... the silent ones.' She wiped her eyes. The companions on either side put their arms around her.

'That sounds like the same man who saved my life,' said another woman sitting opposite with a bandaged arm. 'I believe his name is Karl. He was on the *Pacific*.'

Hannah swallowed a piece of orange whole. She coughed.

'I was trapped in the cabin. The ship had tilted so much that I couldn't open the door,' she continued. 'Water was seeping in. I climbed up to the top bunk, shouted and waved my hands through the porthole. Within minutes, this young man heard my cries. He appeared like an angel, reassured me, and alerted the rescue team, who cut open the porthole and got me out.'

Hannah could not hold back any longer. 'Karl, the man you are talking about,' she said, 'he's my fiancé.'

Everyone looked at her.

The woman from the trapped cabin crossed her hands over her heart. 'What a hero. He saved many lives,' she said. 'You must be very proud of him.'

'I am.' Hannah's smile wavered. Why hadn't Karl told her any of this?

The women dispersed after breakfast. Hannah showered and returned to her bed. She wrapped herself in a grey military blanket marked with the initials PP for Palestine Police. The sky grew overcast; there was a nip in the air. The thin cotton summer dress was unsuitable for late November, even in the more temperate Mediterranean climate. But for now, it was all that she had.

With nothing to do but wait, she wondered what explained Karl's silence. Perhaps he felt it would be inappropriate to seem as if he was bragging in the face of such tragedy? Or maybe he was still reeling after all the horrors he witnessed?

Questions swirled in her mind. As much as she told herself she was worrying unnecessarily, she couldn't dispel her doubts. Deep down, she still suspected that something else was behind his unusual behaviour.

Hannah's eyes grew heavy, tiredness creeping up on her again. She glanced around the hut to find at least half of the women were also resting. It seemed best for her to do the same.

She lay down, the threads of her thoughts loosening. She was beginning to drift off when someone burst into the hut.

'Quick!' Rachel called, beckoning the women from their beds. 'Come outside.'

Hannah sat up, alert at once. 'What is it?' She braced herself.

'They've recovered some of the luggage from the *Patria*.'

Hannah swung her feet to the floor and rushed to the entrance. Rachel pointed to a towering pile of suitcases, clothes, and assorted paraphernalia dumped in the dusty clearing. Women poured from the surrounding wooden huts. They jostled for position, argued, and rummaged through the salvage in search of their personal belongings.

Fabrics of blue, white, brown, green and red sailed overhead and spilled onto the ground. Two indignant women tugged at the arms of a burgundy dress, both claiming it was theirs. Hannah seized the moment to duck under the garment that strained between them. Fabric ripped above her head and shouts continued behind her. She stepped over an open suitcase, its contents spilling out, slipped past a woman examining a torn and sodden overcoat, and squeezed into a gap beside the pile.

Where to even begin in that unorganised mess? She made a slow circuit, looking above and below, prying at luggage handles similar to hers, trying to identify her suitcase.

She was on her second rotation when someone beside her threw a case back into the heap after determining it was not hers. Hannah grabbed the suitcase and took it to the outer perimeter, away from the crush to examine it further. She clicked open the metal hasps, lifted the lid and whooped to find among the effects a pair of shoes (the sensible ones), her wash bag, a warm cardigan, two spare dresses – soggy, but intact – and, most precious of all, the little photograph album containing the only picture she had of her late father. She stroked the water-stained cover but did not dare open the album for fear of tearing the pages.

Everything in her luggage was damp and musty. All her clothes would need a thorough wash. She could dry her shoes outside in the sunshine and the album on top of her suitcase inside the hut.

She repacked her belongings. Hers. It felt good to hold something that linked to her past and tied her to her identity. She could not wait to change out of the donated dress the brunette woman had found for her.

Out of the corner of her eye, she spotted the brunette woman crouching over an open valise and embracing a pink silk dress. Eyes squeezed shut, she pressed the fabric against her cheek before she carefully refolded it and closed the lid. Clutching its handle, she continued sifting through the pile until she came across a pair of black patent-leather heels. They looked suspiciously like the ones Hannah had abandoned on the *Patria* at the foot of the slanting staircase. But she could not be certain. The woman tried them on for size, examining them from all angles. She gave a nod of satisfaction, then strode back to her hut, suitcase in hand.

Hannah watched the brunette woman go. She made no move to stop her. She had recovered her sensible shoes. They would suffice for now.

CHAPTER 18

Hannah spent the rest of the morning sorting, washing, and laying out her belongings to dry. As she waited in the line at the entrance to their compound, her feet swam uncomfortably in her sodden shoes, but it was much better than walking barefoot on the uneven stone ground. Two *gaffirim* – members of the Jewish Auxiliary Police distinguished by their black sheepskin *kalpak* hats – stood guard. Any minute now, they would unlock the gate. She looked forward to seeing Karl, though disquiet tempered her anticipation given how withdrawn he had seemed yesterday. She steeled herself, certain more bad news lay ahead.

The gate swung open and the women poured out onto the path that ran down the centre of the camp. In the sunshine, it seemed less foreboding than when she had walked down it the night before. The men too spilled out of their compound. Karl spotted Hannah coming towards him and tentatively raised his hand in greeting. From his timid smile, he looked happy to see her, but his steps were measured. Hesitant even. He didn't rush towards her as she might have hoped.

'Hello,' he said on reaching her, with the same shyness she recalled from when they first met over eight months ago. His blue eyes lacked their usual lustre and were ringed with dark circles.

'Hello.' She waited for him to speak further.

Karl leaned in to hug her. He held her tight, as if she was his anchor and he dared not let go.

'How are you?' Hannah asked. 'How did you sleep?'

Karl drew back. 'I didn't. I couldn't stop thinking about ... everything.' He reached for her hand and they walked on in silence down the path towards the rear of the camp with all the other strolling couples. It reminded Hannah of a Sunday afternoon in Vienna's Prater Park, but for the encroaching barbed wire fences.

'How is your hut?' Hannah said, to break through Karl's quiet.

'Probably much the same as yours.'

'This morning at breakfast, two of my new roommates were talking about what you did.'

Karl went rigid. He studied her face. 'What did they tell you?'

'How you saved their lives.'

'Oh.' His features relaxed. 'That.'

'Why do you make it sound like it was nothing? It's incredibly brave.'

'I did what I had to do.' Karl's reply sounded more apologetic than humble.

'I had no idea until I heard those women talking about how they were rescued. Why didn't you mention it?'

Karl shrugged again. 'I hadn't had a chance yet.'

Hannah thought about the long hours when they had sat and waited together in the warehouse, the bus ride to Atlit. Had there really been no time for him to tell her? Maybe Hannah was being unfair. Karl had been tired, on the verge of collapse.

'I suppose I would have told you today,' Karl said, brushing the matter off like a speck of lint from his jacket.

'I'm proud of you.'

'Thank you.' Karl smiled. A mournful smile. 'That means a lot.'

They had reached the far end of the camp. They followed the path back towards the entrance.

He squeezed her hand. Tight. Like he was afraid she might let go.

'Karl,' she said. 'You know you can tell me anything.'

'Yes, of course I do,' he answered with careless ease.

'So, what are you keeping from me?'

'I don't know what you mean.' His gaze slid away.

Through the fence, they could see three British policemen sitting and smoking outside their barracks. Karl lowered his head. He released her hand and spun around, striding back the way they had come, his spine rigid. It was as if he feared the policemen. This was not her Karl, the man who had convinced her she could walk across a steel cable over open water to safety, and who had rescued passengers from certain death. He was acting completely out of character.

'Something is troubling you.' Hannah jogged to keep up with him. 'Please tell me what it is.'

Karl stopped. His shoulders drooped under an invisible weight. 'I can't tell you.'

'Why not?'

'I'm afraid that if I do, you won't want anything more to do with me.' He paused. 'I couldn't bear to lose you as well.'

Fear coiled in Hannah's stomach. 'Karl, if we are to share our lives, and I am to become your wife, you must be able to confide in me. Even if what you say will upset me, I'd rather you were honest. I don't want there to be any secrets between us.'

Hannah could not face being deceived again. Not after she had trusted Gerhard, her previous boyfriend, the man she thought she would marry. She had trusted him implicitly until he emigrated to the United States with his family, promising to help her and her mother get visas to join him. Three months later, all she got was a letter ending their relationship. His broken promises had cost her the chance to leave Vienna with her mother.

Karl remained silent, his eyes downcast.

'If you can't confide in me, how can we build a strong relationship and the foundation for a good marriage?' Hannah said. It felt as if their entire relationship balanced on a cable as precarious as the one she crossed to save herself from the *Patria*. 'If you tell me what is troubling you, I'll do my best to support you. I'll stay by your side. But if you can't, maybe our relationship is not strong enough. And if it isn't ... that's how you'll lose me.'

'I know you're right.' Karl looked up at her. 'It's tearing me apart. I feel like I can barely breathe.'

Hannah took his hand. 'I understand you're afraid, but whatever it is, let's face it together.'

Karl led her to the farthest corner they could venture, next to the barbed wire fence at the back, overlooking the open green plain beyond.

'I only managed to save a few people.' Karl spoke in a near whisper. Hannah leaned closer to hear him, her head touching his. 'I couldn't save them all. So many lost their lives, and it's my fault.'

'Oh, Karl. It's not your fault. You did the best you could. There are people who owe you their lives because of your bravery. It was impossible for you to save everyone.'

'But I am to blame.' Karl shut his eyes. 'For all of this.'

'Please don't torture yourself. I know you must have seen some terrible things. I understand, because I witnessed them too. When we were on the deck, I saw people fall into the water and drown. It's horrible to feel such helplessness when there is nothing you can do to save them. But I realise that what happened is not my fault, and neither was it yours.'

'But it is, you see. I played a role in this disaster.'

'That can't be right.'

Karl shook his head.

Goosebumps prickled Hannah's arms. 'How is any of this your fault?'

Karl took a shaky breath. 'A few days after we were transferred to the *Patria*, we discovered the British planned to deport us. We protested, held a hunger strike, wrote appeals. Some of us even tried to escape by swimming to shore. That's how Marcus got caught.'

'I remember you telling me all of this the night I joined you on the *Patria*.'

'But there is something else I didn't tell you. I couldn't because I was sworn to secrecy.' Karl swallowed hard. 'The Transport Committee, the *va'ad* were in contact with the Haganah on shore.'

'How is that even possible?' Hannah said, thinking how strict the British had been in isolating the *Patria*. They had attempted to cut off any means of communication between the passengers and the outside world. Mrs Hoyle confiscated the innocent letter Erika had written to Marcus upon discovering it in Hannah's pocket.

'There were people, a few good ones among the police and crew, who helped carry messages between the ship and shore.'

'Like Arthur?'

Karl nodded. 'And others.'

'What did the messages contain?'

'I'm not sure. I never saw or read any of them. The *va'ad* members must have destroyed them after reading.'

'So, how do you know about these messages?'

'Last week, a member of the Haganah came on board the *Patria* disguised as a worker, joining a small team brought in to fix the kitchen oven.' Karl continued with a seemingly unrelated story, as if he had not heard Hannah's question. 'I think the leader of the *va'ad* must have spoken to him first, but he had to be careful because the British were suspicious and always watching him. If the police saw the leader talking with one of the workers, it would arouse their suspicions. He chose my friend HW to become the liaison and speak to the Haganah operative.'

Hannah had many questions but didn't want to interrupt now that he was opening up.

'I never saw the leader of the *va'ad* and the Haganah man conversing, or learn what they said to one another. I only know about this because HW confided in me. HW too had to be vigilant. There were always British policemen patrolling and standing guard near the kitchen. So HW came up with innovative ways to communicate with the Haganah man. They spoke to each other indirectly. HW enlisted the help of a girl from their group to pose as his girlfriend. They would walk down the passageway, past the kitchen where the man was fixing the oven. HW pretended he was speaking to the girl, but his words were really addressed to the man. The Haganah spoke without ever looking at HW, so the guards assumed he was talking to another worker.'

'That's clever.' She still did not understand Karl's involvement.

'HW was smart and resourceful. And he was such a good-hearted person.' Karl managed a brief smile, but it was tinged with sorrow. 'I only met him on the *Patria*, but in that short time we became close friends.'

Hannah noticed Karl used the word *was*; he spoke about HW in the past tense.

'HW asked me if I would be willing to do a small favour which might help stop our deportation. As soon as the British transferred all the *Atlantic* passengers, the *Patria* would depart from Haifa. We'd tried everything else and were desperate to stop the ship from leaving. So was the Haganah. Someone – the Haganah, I presume – came up with a plan: they would temporarily disable the ship to prevent it from sailing so the British would have to transfer all the passengers to land. That would buy more time to appeal against the deportation, or else the Haganah would find another way to keep us in Eretz Israel. The man from the Haganah needed to give HW something to carry out the plan—'

'What kind of thing?'

'HW wouldn't say. He said it was best I knew as little as possible so that if I was ever questioned, I could honestly say I did not know. He also did not reveal exactly what they were planning or when it would be carried out. All he asked me to do was to be part of a group of trustworthy people to accompany the girl posing as his girlfriend. We were to act as decoys while she took a bag from the Haganah man. I agreed.'

Karl looked at Hannah as if checking her reaction. She tried to maintain a blank expression. Her heart pounded in her chest.

Karl swallowed. 'We accompanied the girl, pretending to talk and banter as we walked down the passageway. When we reached the kitchen, the oven worker was taking a break, sitting on a pile of sandbags while eating his lunch. The girl stopped to speak to him. She pretended to flirt with him while we surrounded the man, asking him questions as if we were interested in his work. While doing so, the girl lifted the leather bag that held the man's lunch. As soon as she had it, we encircled her so that the guards did not notice that she was carrying anything. Undetected, we walked away. Later that same day, we escorted the girl once more to the kitchen and performed a similar routine while she replaced the bag. None of the guards realised what had taken place.'

Karl paced in a small circle. 'They only wanted to prevent the ship from sailing. They did not intend to sink it. No one was supposed to get hurt. HW would not have knowingly put anyone's lives in danger. Nor his own. His greatest dream was to live in Eretz Israel.

'When I saw HW running down the stairs in a panic, after the boom, I realised that whatever the original plan had been, it had gone wrong. That's when I realised that the Haganah man's sandwich bag must have contained a small explosive device.' He looked up at Hannah with pleading eyes. 'I thought I was doing something good ... that it would help stop our deportation. Instead, I put everyone in danger. I put you in danger. People lost their lives ...'

Karl let out a strangled breath as if he were suffocating. He sank to his knees. 'I promise I didn't know. Otherwise, I would have tried to dissuade them.'

Karl looked broken. Hannah crouched down and hugged him. 'You mustn't blame yourself. Even if you had known, and tried to stop them, it's unlikely you could have changed their minds. Like you said, all of you were desperate to prevent the deportation. It was not supposed to happen this way.'

'What a price,' he rasped. 'What a terrible price.'

'HW?' Hannah said.

Karl nodded slowly. 'He ran down to the cells where Marcus and the others were locked up. Apparently, a policeman was obediently standing guard, even as the ship was heeling over. HW wrestled the keys from him and released the men from the cells. He was last seen heading down to our sleeping quarters in the hold where some of the men were still trapped. He hasn't been seen since. No one could rescue the men from the hold.' His eyes reddened. 'Arthur drowned too. A good man who sacrificed his life trying to save others. He didn't deserve to go this way. None of them did.'

'But at least HW saved Marcus,' Hannah said.

Karl looked down. 'Marcus was last seen following HW down to the hold.' He pressed the pads of his fingers over his eyes. 'This morning I was asked to identify a personal item: a siddur with M

Levy written inside. It was found in Marcus's pocket. They recovered his body earlier today.'

'Oh, Karl. I'm sorry. I'm so sorry.'

'Marcus was my best friend from the age of four. He was more like my brother. We grew up together. I can't believe I'll never see him again. Never see his smile that lit up his whole face. Throughout the journey, he kept me strong. We dreamed together. He was so eager to live in Eretz Israel. He planned to ask Erika to marry him.'

Hannah's insides seized at the mention of Erika, who expected Marcus might propose and planned to accept.

'Marcus suggested we have a joint wedding on the kibbutz. Two friends marrying two friends, surrounded by everyone we loved. He painted such a vivid picture. I could see it in my mind's eye.' His gaze grew distant as if revisiting that scene. 'Both of you in flowing white dresses, wearing crowns in your hair made of wildflowers that we had picked. We would live side by side, have children, and work hard to create a flourishing kibbutz as our families grew. Instead ... he is to be buried today in Haifa. And I can't even go to his funeral.' He rested his head on Hannah's shoulder.

Hannah had no words of comfort to offer. She held him, thinking about Marcus and Erika. Now they would never have the chance of a life together.

So many losses. How much more could they bear?

Guards called for the detainees. Visiting time was already over for the day. Karl heaved himself up, slow and unwilling. He hugged Hannah once more. 'No one must ever find out,' Karl whispered. 'Promise me you won't mention a word to anyone.'

'I won't,' she said. 'But please don't blame yourself.'

'Nevertheless, I was still involved. The British have arrested members of the *va'ad* for questioning. I don't yet know what will happen to them. If they discover my involvement, they'll arrest me too.'

'I promise I will never speak of this.'

Hannah watched him pass through the barbed wire gate. He turned around once. A silent understanding.

As Hannah walked back to her hut, she felt not only the crushing weight of Karl's secret but also the heaviness of the losses. Arthur. HW. Marcus. So many others.

Karl would never be the same person he was before the tragedy, just as the Hannah that he had come to know during their detainment in Bratislava was not the same carefree girl from Vienna. Hannah too had become a different person. Someone who was less courageous, less trusting.

Then, among her dark thoughts, she found an unexpected measure of comfort. She was not mistaken about Karl. He was nothing like Gerhard. Nothing at all. Karl was loving and kind, honest and responsible, sensitive. Her only mistake had been contemplating ending their relationship out of the fear that she couldn't trust him.

Hannah now understood why Karl had been reluctant to confide in her and empathised with his decision to help HW. In the same position, she might have made the same choice. She did not blame him. But Hannah also recognised why Karl blamed himself because she carried similar shame and remorse. No matter what anyone said, she lived with constant guilt for having left her mother behind.

The next afternoon, when they met, the tension between them had lifted. Karl admitted he was relieved to have told her the truth, that he would not lose her as he feared. He had even slept for a few hours. Yet, his spirits were low. Karl was still grieving his friends and haunted by the disaster. He tensed each time he saw a British guard, even though the *va'ad* leaders had been released after being questioned by the authorities and were now held with them in Atlit. Karl was fatigued. Listless. He did not seem able to look forward or talk about the future. It did not help that they had no idea what the future would bring or how long they would be detained.

Karl told Hannah that the only thing that brought him comfort was the time he spent with her. Hannah felt the same. In the hours without Karl, she was aimless and lonely. Perhaps, with time, they would help each other heal. They would grow stronger. But she had no doubt that this disaster would leave an indelible scar.

Three days after their arrival in Atlit, during the meeting hour, news spread through the camp that as an exceptional act of mercy, after taking all circumstances into consideration and in particular the terrible experience undergone by survivors, they would be allowed to stay in Eretz Israel. For the time being, they would have to remain in Atlit, but their numbers would be deducted from the next immigration quota and in another few months they would be released.

The announcement brought the first spark of life back to Karl's face. Then he gazed up at the overcast sky beyond the barbed wire fence. 'So many losses.' His eyes brimmed with tears. 'What a heavy price we paid.'

Each day brought more grim news as bodies were recovered from the wreck. The final number was not yet certain, but over one hundred passengers were confirmed dead and at least a hundred more still missing.

Needless losses.

If only they had been granted permission to stay from the beginning.

And what of Lilly and her friends on the *Atlantic*? Would they also be allowed to remain in Eretz Israel? Days had passed since the disaster, and Hannah had heard nothing about the fate of those aboard the stripped-out ship. Were they still anchored outside the harbour? Hannah longed for them to join her in Atlit. Surely the

British could not send them away after what had happened to the *Patria*.

Chapter 19

1 December 1940
Haifa Port

A few steps. A gangway. The last barrier that separated the *Atlantic* passengers from the land of their hopes.

For five days, ever since the tugboat had towed their ship into the harbour, Lilly and her friends had fixated on that gangway. They envied the policemen who crossed indifferently between ship and shore. Lilly, Max, or Erika would approach each new guard to request news of their loved ones. Alexander, Isaak, or Stefan would ask for Hebrew newspapers. The answer was always no.

They spent their daylight hours on deck watching the quayside. Lilly kept searching for a glimpse of Eugen; Gisela for her sons. Perhaps they waited somewhere beyond the fences. The port workers continued their daily routines, ignoring the Atlantic's passengers as if they were invisible. Even when Alexander or Isaak called out to them, there was no response.

Waiting. Watching. Wondering.

The British had begun disembarking passengers. Four days ago the first group, women and children, had left the *Atlantic*. Lilly and the other women could have joined them, but after the *Patria* disaster, the Lifeboat Chevra had agreed they would not let themselves be separated from that point forward.

The friendly blond soldier returned to help with disembarkation, and the Lifeboat Chevra cornered him once again. This time, when he offered cigarettes around, the other men followed Isaak's lead in accepting one, and stowing them in their pockets. As Isaak advised: 'You never know when they might come in handy for bartering.'

They learned from the soldier that the group was to be sent to Atlit.

'Is that the same camp where the *Patria* survivors are being held?' Lilly asked.

'Yes,' the soldier said. 'For the time being.'

'And what is to happen to them eventually?' Alexander asked.

'In an act of mercy, the British government has granted them amnesty.'

Alexander arched a brow. 'You mean they will be allowed to stay?'

'Yes, indeed.' The soldier smiled.

The Lifeboat Chevra exchanged glances.

'Does that mean us too?' Isaak blurted out.

'I haven't been told anything official,' the soldier said. 'But I reckon it's quite possible you'll also benefit from this amnesty.'

The knot of dread inside Lilly eased.

'Do you have a list of survivors yet?' Max asked. His face looked haggard. Dark circles shadowed his eyes from sleepless nights worrying about his wife and baby son.

'I'm afraid I don't,' the soldier said. 'But you'll be transferred to Atlit before too long and hopefully find your family there.'

Max lowered his head, his shoulders sagging.

The following day, policemen ordered Alexander, Isaak, and Max to fetch their luggage. The policemen had selected a group of five hundred men for disembarkation. Alexander and Isaak protested, saying they could not leave Janka behind. Max hesitated too, insisting he was married.

'Are you sending us to Atlit?' he asked the policeman. 'That's where my wife and child might be.'

He shook his head. 'Acco.'

Max stepped back from the line. The policeman in charge relented, though he warned they'd face a longer wait.

The Lifeboat Chevra spent three more nights on the squalid ship. But today, their turn to disembark had finally arrived. They gathered their belongings and joined the queue of fifty or so on deck. Alexander led their small group with Gisela on his arm. Behind them came Janka and Isaak, who carried both his own case and Gisela's. Lilly and Erika followed, with Jenny, Stefan, and Max bringing up the rear.

Lilly looked down at the gangway where passengers were filing past a towering policeman stationed on the quayside below.

She gazed upward and felt the warm sun on her face, so different from the pale winter light of Europe. Though it was already December, the sky was a clear, deep blue. Sunlight danced on the harbour water. A gentle breeze carried the scent of salt air from the Mediterranean, oil and wet rope from the harbour, the sweetness of oranges stacked in crates, and wild herbs from the slopes of Mount Carmel rising before them. A perfect day for this most auspicious event.

Just a few steps to solid ground. Eretz Israel. A new life.

'This is it,' Erika said.

'Yes,' Lilly said. 'This is it.'

Erika squeezed her hand. It trembled. Hers did too.

Lilly took a deep breath, placed one foot on the gangway, then the other. As the wood creaked beneath their feet, the words of the *Hatikva* stirred in her mind.

Our hope will not be lost,
The ancient hope,
To return to the land of our fathers ...

And after almost three months on the water, a passage shadowed by danger and uncertainty, Lilly stepped onto solid, holy ground. She had come home. Her legs swayed as if she were still on the ship, but the land held steady beneath her. Dockworkers shouted to one another in Hebrew, Arabic, and English, their voices carrying across the quayside. After the close quarters of the Atlantic, the port felt unconfined. Unbounded. She paused, wanting to imprint the scene in her memory forever.

Isaak set down the two suitcases. Alexander and Gisela stopped to watch. Isaak's voice caught on the ancient words as he recited the blessing: *'shehecheyanu, v'kiy'manu, v'higiyanu laz'man hazeh.'* Blessed are You ... who has kept us alive, sustained us, and brought us to this moment.'

'Amen,' Lilly said, along with the others.

Isaak knelt down on the tarmacked path. As he bent to kiss the ground, Lilly's throat tightened, feeling the weight of all they had endured crystallise in this single, sacred act.

But before he could rise, the tall policeman gave Isaak a sharp kick and hauled him to his feet. 'Up you get, sonny. Stop dilly-dallying.'

Isaak looked up at the policeman's face, his eyes seeming to flicker in recognition. He opened his mouth, but before he could speak, the policeman rounded on Gisela.

'Get a move on!' he bellowed.

He wheeled on Lilly and Erika. 'And you, cloth-ears, did you not hear me?' The shove from behind was unexpected. Lilly stumbled forward. 'Get a move on.'

'Please,' Alexander said, arms raised in a gesture of submission. 'There is no need for this. We are moving.'

The officer's nostrils flared. 'I don't need you to tell me what there is and isn't a need for.' He swung the butt of his rifle in a vicious arc. The crack against the back of Alexander's legs sent him staggering.

A sharp intake of breath escaped Lilly. Behind her, someone let out a cry. Then silence. The entire group seemed to hold its breath, watching as Alexander steadied himself, jaw clenched, refusing to show any sign of pain, denying the policeman satisfaction.

Alexander took Gisela's arm and nodded reassuringly. Isaak picked up the suitcases. They followed the line of people down the path towards a warehouse. As they marched at a brisk pace, the policeman continued barking at the group, urging them to move faster. And Lilly was sure she heard Alexander mutter '*Arschloch*' under his breath.

Lilly had grown accustomed to the policemen's coldness, but the brutality left her shaken. What kind of welcome was this?

Chapter 20

Inspectors rifled through refugees' luggage, flinging aside their clothing, confiscating whatever they deemed contraband. The last time Lilly had experienced such a customs inspection had been in Vienna, before boarding the paddle steamer, and the inspectors had been the Gestapo. Lilly had not expected to go through such an ordeal again. Not here. Not from the British.

From Janka they took her precious books. For Erika it was photographs of her family. And despite Lilly's protests, the inspector forced her to hand over all her documents: letters from her mother and brother, a birthday card written by her late father, love letters from her late husband, Salo. The inspector thrust a receipt at her, which was nothing more than a small slip with a number scratched on it. He said she would get them back in due course. Lilly no longer knew what to believe.

As Lilly gathered her belongings from the wooden table, she glanced over to her right where Stefan was protesting the confiscation of his camera. On the roll of film inside it were the undeveloped photographs he had taken of Jenny and the Lifeboat Chevra on their arrival in Haifa. The official tossed him a receipt.

'Get a move on!'

Lilly jumped at a voice bellowing from behind. She spun around to see the towering policeman looming over Gisela, who stood to Lilly's left, refolding and repacking her clothes.

'Hurry up, granny. We haven't got all day.' He knocked a pile of Gisela's undergarments off the table.

Gisela bent with a groan to retrieve them, her face reddening. Lilly knelt to help her. The policeman brought down his baton and slammed it into the floor not five centimetres from Lilly's hand. 'Worry about your own luggage, busybody.'

He swiped Lilly's suitcase off the table, sending it crashing to the floor.

'Move along!' He ordered the next passenger to take Lilly's place at the table while Lilly scrambled to pick up her scattered belongings.

To the credit of the official who had been examining Gisela's luggage, he scurried to help her as soon as the towering policeman turned his back.

'I'm terribly sorry about all of this,' he said, his eyes flicking up to ensure the policeman had not spotted him.

The other officials seemed just as intimidated by the towering policeman. Well, once they left the port, she would never see him again.

A polite official approached her. 'Excuse me, madam, please come this way.'

Lilly stood with as much grace as she could muster, picked up her case and rucksack, and followed him across the vast warehouse to where another line of four policemen sat behind tables, questioning individual passengers. He directed her to an empty chair between Erika and Stefan.

A dark-haired officer with greying temples looked up from his clipboard. Holding a gold-tipped fountain pen in his right hand and a cigarette in his left, he indicated the empty chair.

'*Guten Morgen, Fräulein.*' To Lilly's surprise, he addressed her in fluent German.

'*Guten Morgen*.' Lilly wondered whether she should correct his assumption of *Fräulein* to *Frau*. She decided to let it go.

'Your name, please?'

'Lilly Simon.'

He wrote her name in careful script at the top of the form on his clipboard, adding female and Jewess for her religion without consultation.

'Age?'

'Twenty-three.'

'Nationality?'

'Austrian.'

'Place of birth?'

'Vienna.'

The officer signed his name at the bottom of the form and added the date. He set down his cigarette on an ashtray close to the edge of the table, already filled with five stubs. The tip glowed red, a grey wisp curled upwards and caught in her throat. She tilted her head away from the smoke, her gaze falling on Stefan, who was being questioned.

'I can't give you any information about the shipyards in Danzig,' he was saying.

'You can't or you won't?' the officer sneered. 'One might think you're still a good German at heart.'

'A good German?' Stefan spluttered. 'I'm a Jew, and the Germans persecuted me for it.'

'Then tell us what you know about the submarines that the Nazis are building in the Danzig shipyard.'

'*Fräulein* Simon?' Lilly's attention snapped back to the policeman across the table. He slid a rectangular tin case towards her, the size of a tobacco tin. He opened the lid with a soft click, revealing a pad soaked with black, oily ink. 'Your forefinger, please.'

The policeman took her tentatively extended finger, pressed it onto the cold ink and rolled it from side to side. Then he lifted the top page at the bottom right corner. As he pressed her finger to a marked square on the page below, she wondered why he had not simply asked for her signature. Did he think she was illiterate? She held back from asking, not wanting to risk causing any trouble – especially after witnessing what Stefan was going through.

He was pleading with his interrogator. 'I've already told you, I don't know anything about submarines or what the Nazis are doing in the Danzig shipyard. For the last few months we were there, we were confined to what was essentially a ghetto. I was not free to walk around Danzig, never mind the shipyard. If I knew anything, believe me, I'd be happy to tell you.'

'Thank you,' the policeman said to Lilly. 'That will be all. Please go back outside. A guard will direct you onto a bus with the rest of the women.'

'Where are you sending us?'

'The disinfection centre,' he said, shuffling his papers, not bothering to look up.

Was the policeman telling the truth?

Lilly bent to gather her luggage. What choice did she have?

She caught up with Erika, who had finished moments before her and was heading towards the warehouse exit.

'How was it?' Erika asked.

Lilly looked down at her ink-stained finger. Erika held out her own with a rueful smile. She leaned closer to Lilly. 'What was that policeman grilling Stefan about?'

'Get a move on, ladies!' called a well-built policewoman in a straw hat waiting by the door, her nasal voice interrupting their conversation. 'Stop that chit-chatting and board the bus.'

'Later,' Lilly said through the side of her mouth.

Two buses idled on the quayside road, each watched by four armed guards. The first was half-filled with men – she spotted Alexander, Isaak, and Max among them. Women were filing onto the second bus where Gisela, Janka, and Jenny had claimed seats in the back row. By the time Lilly and Erika boarded, nearly all the seats were filled.

Jenny jumped up. 'Did you see Stefan inside?'

'Yes, I did,' Lilly said.

'Why are they keeping him so long?'

'I'm not sure.' Lilly searched for a reassuring explanation. 'Maybe the policeman's German isn't very good and there is a language barrier.'

'But Stefan speaks quite good English.'

'Oh ... well then, I'm sure he'll be out soon.'

'Ladies, onto the bus!' the policewoman shouted outside to the last stragglers. 'You're holding up the line.'

'Do you know, they confiscated Stefan's camera?' Jenny continued.

'I saw,' Lilly said. 'They also took all my letters.'

'I'd understand if we were trying to smuggle in vast amounts of money, jewels, or art. But why seize such harmless personal items?' Jenny said.

Janka waved a scrap of paper. 'They took my books, telling me they would return them "in due course" and gave me this receipt.'

'Do you believe them?'

Janka rolled her eyes and shrugged.

The engine roared to life and the bus pulled away from the warehouse, leaving the men behind.

'And why the need to separate us?' Jenny said.

'Apparently they are taking us to a disinfection centre,' Erika said. 'Perhaps they have separate facilities for men and women.'

'Maybe.' Jenny narrowed her gaze. 'But I still don't like it.'

Lilly did not like it either. The snippets of conversation she had overheard troubled her. It was almost as if the policeman was insinuating that Stefan had knowledge of the inner workings of the Nazi war machine. No matter how much Stefan insisted he knew nothing, they did not seem to believe him. Did they have the ridiculous notion that he was a spy? Is that why they had confiscated his camera and their personal items?

Before she had time to work through her thoughts, the bus lurched to a halt.

'Right, everyone off,' one guard ordered. 'And take all your luggage with you.'

Lilly picked up her case and rucksack, dread creeping over her as she realised they had not yet left the port. Had they come this far only to be sent back?

Chapter 21

Water cascaded onto Lilly like a summer rain. She raised her face, letting it run through her hair and stream over her. She washed the last traces of the pungent delousing liquid from her hair, lathered every centimetre of her body, scrubbing away weeks at sea. The harsh carbolic soap stung her skin, its sharp, medicinal smell unlike the delicate lavender soap she had used in Vienna, yet even this seemed like luxury. This was Lilly's first real shower since leaving home. The first time she could wash with running water and in privacy rather than the makeshift attempts behind a blanket on the *Atlantic*. The muscles in her back loosened and her shoulders eased. She was sorry when it was time to step out and let the next woman have her turn.

Lilly wrapped herself in a towel. She felt clean, refreshed – and empty. Loneliness struck her anew. Lilly had made it to safety, but her husband was gone. Her father was gone. What of her mother? They hadn't been in contact for months.

A wave of emotion rose in her throat. Lilly swallowed it down and pressed the towel to her stinging eyes. It hurt too much to keep dwelling on the past. She comforted herself that soon she could send a letter to Mama. Soon she would see Eugen. Soon ... would she learn what had happened to Hannah?

Lilly shut down her thoughts and forced herself to concentrate only on the moment at hand. In the changing room she found her clothes folded on the bench. They were still damp from the steam disinfection process, but they were clean. A cheery banter flowed between the other women, but Lilly had no heart for it.

She dressed and went to a small side room where a nurse vaccinated her. Lilly felt unmoored without her suitcase and rucksack as she left the disinfection centre. Officials had taken their luggage to be sprayed with DDT, promising it would follow later.

'Wait for me!' Erika's voice rang out.

Lilly paused to let her friend catch up. Erika looked like she had just walked out of a beauty salon: styled hair, reddened lips and cheeks.

'Lipstick?' Lilly stared. 'How did you manage that?'

Erika opened her palm to reveal a small tube. 'I slipped it out of my wash bag before they took our luggage.'

'Very clever.' Lilly smiled. 'And you look lovely.'

Erika beamed and linked her arm through Lilly's.

They headed towards the bus. Two waited outside now – their own, and a second that hadn't been there before.

'Do you think that's the men's bus?'

Lilly glanced back. Two men she recognised from their group emerged from the building. 'Yes, it is.'

The guard standing by their bus motioned them to hurry. They quickened their pace and boarded, returning to their seats in the back row where Janka, Jenny and Gisela waited. Lilly took the window, Erika beside her.

'*Ach*! I feel like a new person,' Gisela said, by way of greeting.

'I can't remember having a better shower,' Janka said.

Erika adjusted an errant curl.

'All this primping for Marcus, I see,' Janka said. 'Your hair looks fine.'

'I want to look my best.'

'You look beautiful.' Jenny reached out and patted Erika's arm.

'Did you see that the men's bus is also here?' Lilly said.

'I did,' Jenny said, relief evident in her voice. 'At least it looks like we're all going to the same place.'

So far, the authorities seemed to be keeping their word. Though their initial experience leaving the ship and passing through customs had been unpleasant, that came down to a few nasty policemen who derived pleasure from intimidating others. Those sorts existed in bureaucracies the world over. Since leaving the customs warehouse, the soldiers who escorted them and the staff at the disinfection centre had been cordial, or at least civil. Not all of them were cut from the same cloth. Despite Lilly's momentary fear when ordered off the bus, the authorities had processed their group through immigration, and they were now about to set off for Atlit.

As they waited for the last few women to board, Lilly tried to imagine what Atlit was like. What would she find? *Who* would she find? Her arms prickled with goosebumps.

The bus started, and Erika squeezed her hand. Lilly squeezed back. Focus on the present, Lilly reminded herself. She gazed out of the window.

They drove away from the port, and Lilly caught a last glimpse of the *Atlantic*. She was grateful to the ship for having brought them safely to Haifa, but she would not miss that rusty old vessel.

The bus navigated a narrow, dusty port road congested with delivery lorries and carts heading to and from the docks. Up ahead, two camels plodded along the roadside.

Camels!

Lilly pressed closer to the window. Not behind zoo fences, but here, sharing the road. Laden with sacks, their spindly legs moved with a distinctive bobbing gait. An Arab handler walked alongside, guiding them with a stick. One of the animals swivelled its head as they passed, lips pulled back revealing yellowed teeth in an almost comical grimace. Lilly smiled. This land she had dreamed of: it was real. She was in Eretz Israel.

The bus turned onto a smooth-surfaced, wide boulevard lined on either side with modern white buildings extending two, three, even six storeys high, many with curved Bauhaus-style fronts. Parisian-style canopies stretched over the entrances of shops and cafés, shading them from the afternoon sunlight. A British military vehicle travelled ahead of them. They passed a few pedestrians on the pavement. A mother pushing a pram, a religious Jewish man with a beard and a black hat walking in one direction, an Arab man in a traditional white headdress in the other. A British policeman directing the traffic signalled for their bus to halt. Three soldiers crossed the road followed by a young couple walking arm in arm.

She saw street and shop signs written in English, Hebrew and Arabic. But what she did not see were signs saying that Jews were forbidden. The Jewish shops had no smashed windows or *Jude* painted on their fronts. No one was walking in fear. Not the British. Not the Arabs. Not the Jews.

She recalled the conversation on the *Atlantic* with the Lifeboat Chevra the night they sailed through the Bosphorus Strait towards Istanbul, passing the grand palaces and elegant hotels that lined its banks.

'I can hardly remember,' Lilly had said. 'Imagine being able to walk the street without fear of being attacked. To enter a shop with no signs forbidding you to enter. To sit in a café, stroll in the park, or visit the cinema.'

'Isn't that why you're on this ship, taking risks and accepting the difficulties?' Alexander had asked. 'I want a chance to live like a normal person in our own land. To never have to feel afraid just because I'm Jewish.' Then he nodded towards the laughing, dancing, carefree crowd. 'Soon that will be us in Eretz Israel.'

And here they were. It felt like a dream. 'Alexander was right.'

'Yes, he was,' Janka said, and Lilly realised she had spoken her thoughts out loud. Janka smiled broadly.

On reflection, every hardship, every risk of their journey had been worth it to reach Eretz Israel. She already loved her new home.

This city.

Her thoughts came alive with possibilities. Maybe, once they left the clearance camp (how long would it take for the British to clear them through the camp?), she could rent a small apartment in Haifa and find a job in one of the many stores on the city's main streets. From Haifa, she could take a bus to visit her brother on the kibbutz and her friends scattered around the north and centre. Perhaps it would only be a brief stay, until she decided where to make her home. Or perhaps she would settle in Haifa and meet someone new. Now, that was a thought: one she had not been able to countenance before ...

The bus wove out of the city centre, along the coastal road, heading southward. To the right, the sparse landscape was bordered by the shimmering blue ribbon of the Mediterranean. To her left were the lush green slopes of Mount Carmel with low stone houses dotting its foothills. Surrounded by the beauty of the land in every direction, Lilly wanted to capture every scene in her memory, like a photograph.

She thought about the letter she would write to her mother describing the beauty of Haifa and its surroundings. If only there were a way for her mother and Tante Rebecca to join her. There was nothing left for them in Vienna. The city did not even want them; it had made them outcasts. But here they could build a new life and be free.

The bus continued, curving inland, until the sea was no longer visible and the road narrowed. An identical bus followed them.

'I wonder if that's the men behind us?' Janka said.

Jenny swivelled around to look out of the back window. 'It could be.'

'How is that possible?' Erika said. 'We arrived well before them. They couldn't have finished that quickly.'

'Well, you know men,' Jenny said, trying to make a light-hearted joke, still facing the rear, looking for Stefan.

'Maybe,' Janka said, giving Erika a sidelong glance. 'It's because men don't spend ages doing their hair.' She winked, and the others laughed, including Erika, who laughed along.

'You wait.' Erika wagged a finger. 'One day soon you're going to meet someone, and then I'll be the one laughing at you fussing over your hair.'

Janka pressed her hands together in a gesture of prayer. 'From your mouth to God's ears.'

At the next junction, the bus made a right onto a dusty track, leaving the Carmel slopes behind.

Jenny looked behind again. 'The other bus is still following. It has to be the men.'

'Where on earth are they taking us?' Janka said. 'There is nothing here. It's like a road to nowhere.'

Lilly shifted in her seat and scanned the rugged landscape. All she could see in every direction was open countryside: patches of barren terrain, rough fields and sparse meadowland. No sign of a town, a building, a house. The bus slowed. Lilly wondered whether Atlit was literally a camp of tents. Not that she could spot a single one.

'Perhaps they are expecting us to build the camp,' Gisela said. 'After all, aren't you young people supposed to be pioneers?'

'Alexander would love that,' Janka said. 'He'd be in his element knocking together wooden buildings and consider it practice before moving to the kibbutz.' She grinned. 'And what about you, Gisela, are you also going to become a pioneer?'

'I'll be the project manager.' Gisela chuckled. 'I can sit on a chair and direct the rest of you. With a proper cup of coffee, of course.'

'I can be your assistant.' Jenny raised her hand. 'I'd be excellent at watching other people work. I don't mind making coffee and I'll even bring you a slice of home-made strudel.'

Gisela clapped her hands together. 'You're hired!' She touched Lilly's sleeve. 'And what about you, Lilly? Do you plan on becoming a pioneer, or would you rather join the management team?'

Lilly faced Gisela. She could not enter into her friends' levity. They had not noticed what she had seen.

'I …' Lilly began. The bus shuddered to a halt. 'I think we might have arrived.'

'More likely a punctured tire from this rocky road,' Janka continued, oblivious. 'Never mind the pioneering. It looks like we'll have to learn to change a bus tire first.' She leaned forward and peered out of the window. That was when she saw the barbed wire fence. The smile that had been playing on her lips dissolved. She took a slow breath. '*Was ist das*?'

A guard rose and grasped the door handle. The latch disengaged with a click, silencing the women, smothering their questions. The door creaked open. Three of the guards exited the bus.

The remaining guard strode through the aisle. 'Everyone off.'

The women rose, their movements cautious. Only the rustle of clothes broke the silence. Lilly and her friends were the last off. As they descended the vehicle, the men's bus pulled up alongside them.

'Move along,' ordered the guard standing beside the bus exit, pointing to the line of women trudging up a rocky path. Four guards in unfamiliar uniforms, wearing distinctive woollen fez-like hats, funnelled them through a reinforced barbed-wire gate. Lilly wondered what kind of guards these were – they looked different from the British personnel they had encountered so far.

Jenny made no move to follow. 'I'm waiting for my husband,' she said, her voice soft but determined. Lilly and the others paused too.

The guard blinked twice and opened his mouth, but before he could say a word, Stefan descended from the bus. Jenny hurried to his side. Isaak and Alexander were next. Max appeared in the doorway, gripping its frame as he stared at the imposing barbed-wire fences, eyes wide with terror.

'*Komm schon, Max,*' Alexander said, extending a hand. 'Everything will be all right.'

Max remained rooted to the spot.

'It's all right.' Stefan said, trying to coax him down. 'We'll go together.'

'This is a concentration camp.' Max's gaze was distant. 'The barbed wire fences. The watchtowers. This is exactly what it looked like in Dachau.'

A chill ran through Lilly. Her father had been sent to Dachau in the Kristallnacht round-ups. Released three months later, he returned home a broken man and never recovered. Soon after, he suffered a stroke that left him paralysed; a second left him bedridden. During their stop in Crete, Lilly had received a telegram from her brother letting her know their father had passed away the month before.

Max too had spent several months in Dachau. His father had perished there. Lilly remembered the first time she met Max and Alma, when they boarded the paddle steamer in Vienna. His shaven head and gaunt appearance attested to his recent release from the concentration camp. His expression was as haunted then as it was now.

If Max was right about this place, what awaited them inside? And if their loved ones had survived the *Patria* disaster, in what condition would they find them?

Lilly did not notice the two bus guards until they were standing over the group.

'What is the meaning of this?' said the guard from the women's bus. 'You were told to move along. Now move!'

'And that goes for you lot as well.' The men's guard raised his baton, pointing it at Max. 'Including you.'

Max crouched and covered his head with his hands. 'Don't hit,' he whimpered.

The *chevra* began talking over one another, mixing English and German.

'He is scared—' Isaak said.

'He was in Dachau—' Lilly said.

'He is afraid this is a concentration camp—' Alexander said.

'Is he right?' Janka asked.

'Quiet!' the guard shouted over them. He blew his whistle. 'Reuben!'

A guard in a woollen hat standing at the top of the now empty path looked around at the sound of his name.

'You speak these people's language, don't you?' the guard called.

'Yes, sir,' the guard said.

'Come down here at once and speak to them. I don't know what they're blabbering on about.'

Reuben, a slight man in his thirties, with high cheekbones and a dark moustache, took off down the hill.

'Speak to that one,' the guard said. 'He's refusing to get off the bus. Find out what his problem is and sort it out.'

Reuben approached Max. 'Shalom, my brother,' he began in Hebrew, before switching to German. 'What is the matter? Why don't you want to get off?'

'This is a ... concentration camp ... like Dachau,' Max choked, his hands wrapped over his head for protection. 'They will shave our heads, beat us, and torture us.'

'No, no. It is nothing like that.' Reuben put his hand on Max's arm. 'No one will shave your head or beat you. They will give you food, and a place to sleep after your long journey. You are in Eretz Israel now.'

Max raised his eyes, studying Reuben's face, as if determining whether he was telling the truth.

'Excuse me,' Isaak addressed Reuben. 'Are the survivors from the *Patria* here?'

'Yes, they are here,' Reuben said.

'Max's wife and baby son were on the ship. Do you have a list of names? Do you know whether they were rescued?'

'I'm sorry I don't have a list. But if they were rescued from the ship, they should be here.'

'Max,' Alexander said. 'You heard what the policeman said. They won't hurt us. Alma and Chaim might be here. You want to see them, don't you?'

Max nodded.

'Come, Max,' Alexander said. 'Don't be afraid. We're in Eretz Israel. We are safe now and we are all here with you.'

Max took Alexander's outstretched hand and stepped off the bus.

Chapter 22

1 December 1940
Atlit Camp

Max's eyes darted around as the *chevra* passed through the entrance overlooked by a watchtower. Despite Reuben's reassurances and the other Jewish guards' warm 'Shalom!', his face remained set in a grave expression.

'Please let them be here,' he prayed under his breath, over and over. 'Oh God, please let them be here.'

Lilly felt he spoke for her and Erika. They could no longer cling to false hope. The truth about their loved ones lay somewhere in this camp.

The *chevra* entered a long barrack, at the far end of which a British policeman sat registering the new arrivals. Most passengers, it seemed, had already been processed. Lilly and her friends joined the short queue.

They pressed close together. The admittance procedure required only giving their names and signing a large accounts book. In less than five minutes they exited the building through the door next to the registration table where the *gaffir*, Reuben, waited for them with the rest of their group. 'This way, please.'

Reuben escorted them through a timber gate into a compound enclosed by barbed wire fences over two metres high. Wooden huts with bright yellow-painted doors and windows were laid out diagonally in two rows, in blocks of four. He led them at a brisk pace down a rocky path that ran between the huts. Gisela struggled to keep up; Lilly and Erika steadied her on either side.

A few people lingered outside the first group of huts, familiar faces that Lilly recognised as passengers from the *Atlantic* who had arrived in the days before them. But as far as she could see, no one from the *Patria*.

They reached the second cluster of huts, where a female guard, a *gaffira*, waited in a doorway. Reuben stopped to greet her before addressing the group. 'Ladies, this is your hut.' He gestured at the door, inviting them to enter. 'Bracha here will help you get settled.' Then he pointed to the opposite cluster. 'And this, gentlemen, is yours. Please follow me.'

Jenny hung back, clinging to Stefan's arm. 'When can I see my husband again?'

'As soon as you have settled in,' Reuben said. 'You're not confined to your huts. You are free to walk around and mingle as much as you like.' He shook his finger. 'Only the sleeping quarters are separate. Strictly no men are allowed inside the women's huts and no women inside the men's.'

The tension left Jenny's face. 'Thank you.'

'*Willkommen*,' Bracha said to each woman as they entered the hut. She handed them two military-grey woollen blankets stamped with the initials 'PP' for Palestine Police and a set of cutlery. It looked as if they would stay in Atlit for some time.

The word for welcome seemed to be Bracha's only German. She continued in a blend of Hebrew, English, and hand signals. '*Bevakasha*. Beds. You.' With arms spread wide, she indicated the fifteen wooden slatted beds along either side of the hut. Lilly and her friends claimed five beds together. Erika on her left, Gisela on her right.

Though the accommodation was basic, this was comfort compared to the several weeks she had spent sleeping on the *Atlantic*'s crowded deck. They each had their own bed, with enough space to walk between them. And what a view from the window. Beyond another row of huts and the fence, green open countryside stretched towards the foothills of the Carmel mountain range.

'For how long will we be in Atlit?' Janka said in faltering Hebrew.

Bracha shrugged. 'Come. Let me show you the washing facilities.'

The women followed the *gaffira* as she led them about thirty seconds down the path to a low building with showers and toilets. The facilities were spartan, but clean.

'Excuse me,' Gisela said in her halting Hebrew as the group paused outside, waiting for several women queuing for the facilities. 'I have family here in Eretz Israel. My two sons. When will I be able to see them?'

Bracha shrugged. 'Sorry, I don't know yet.'

'My brother also lives here,' Lilly said in English. 'Is it possible for me to send him a letter?'

'You must all be hungry. I will bring you some lunch.' Bracha left them.

As Lilly made her way up the path, she wondered whether Bracha was being evasive, or if she truly did not have the answers. She surveyed her new surroundings. Past the men's huts and the reinforced fence enclosing their compound was a central path running the length of the camp. Beyond lay a barbed wire enclosure with huts that mirrored the layout of their own. She saw a few men gathered outside.

Ahead, another barbed wire fence ran down the centre, dividing the enclosure – men on one side, women on the other. The women must have glimpsed the *Atlantic* group walking past the huts, because they rushed to the fence and began shouting. They were calling out names. Among the voices, Lilly thought she heard her own.

She stopped. She heard it again. Gisela met her eyes. 'Go.'

Lilly tore across the clearing. Other women ran alongside her. Alerted by the calling, the men followed on their heels as if joining a spontaneous race. Hearing her name encouraged Lilly onwards. Voices echoed back and forth, cries of joy as people found their loved ones. She wove between the crowd at the fence, scanning the women gathered opposite, looking for a familiar face.

'Lilly!' A woman with caramel-coloured hair stood at the end of the line, waving. Lilly ran the length of the fence. Past the enclosure, across the path, and wire barrier, stood her cousin.

'Hannah!' Lilly called. 'You are here.' A flood of relief rose in her chest.

Hannah placed a hand over her mouth as if her feelings were about to overflow.

Lilly hugged herself. If only she could bridge the divide that separated them and embrace Hannah. But she was here. Hannah was alive.

'I was so worried about you,' Lilly said. 'They would not tell us anything.'

'I wished I could send you a message,' Hannah said. 'But I had no way.'

'Is Karl ...?'

'He's there.' She pointed to the men's enclosure. 'He saved my life.'

'Hannah!' A medley of voices surrounded Lilly as the *chevra* joined her.

Hannah waved to her friends.

'Alma!' Max called out, desperate. 'Is Alma here?'

'Wait. One minute.' Hannah held up a finger, rushed to the huts and disappeared. They waited. A minute passed. Max stood beside Lilly, his attention fixed on the direction Hannah had gone. Another minute went by.

Max clasped his hands together, breathing shakily. No one spoke. Lilly glanced from Max to the fence, searching for a sign of Hannah, and back to Max. He stared ahead, unblinking. He let out a sound like a cry from the depths. '*Gott sei Dank*!'

Hannah reappeared with her arm around Alma, supporting her as she limped to the fence. Alma held Chaim in her arms, her right leg wrapped in a bandage.

'Alma! Chaim!' Max shouted as they slowly approached the fence. 'My love, are you all right?'

'I injured my leg while trying to escape from the ship,' she said. 'They took me to hospital. I'll be fine.'

'And Chaim?'

'He is wonderful.' She glanced at Hannah. 'Thanks to Hannah's fiancé ... He saved both of us.' She held up the baby so Max could see him better. 'Say hello to your Abba.'

'Oh,' Max's tears flowed unchecked. 'Light of my life.'

Lilly watched the reunion with tears in her eyes.

'Look, Max,' Alma said. 'He is smiling at you.'

Max reached out his hands, wanting to hold his wife and son, but the fences kept them apart.

Erika was still smiling when she called over to Hannah, 'Marcus ...?' She gestured towards the men's enclosure. 'Is he there too?'

Hannah's smile faded. She lowered her gaze and shook her head. 'I am sorry.'

Erika whimpered. She grasped the barbed wire fence, oblivious to the blood seeping through her fingers. Lilly and Janka each put their arms around her. Alexander eased Erika's hands from the fence and dabbed them with a clean handkerchief. The others surrounded Erika and hugged her.

Hannah could only look on from the other side. Helpless.

Chapter 23

Heavy rain hammered against the corrugated roof of their hut on that first night in Atlit like the beat of a dozen uncoordinated drums. The noise kept Lilly awake, yet she found it comforting.

For the past few months, Lilly, Hannah and the *chevra* had slept in, or huddled around, their little lifeboat on the *Atlantic*'s cramped deck. On nights when it rained, they would grab their blankets, fumble in the dark for their possessions, and scramble for shelter on the crowded lower deck where there was so little room that they took turns standing or crouching. On other occasions, when storms tossed their fragile ship like driftwood, they would spend the night moving from one side of the deck to the other, as instructed, in an attempt to prevent the ship from capsizing. They would spend the next day drying out their sodden clothing and possessions.

Lilly shuddered when she thought about the worst storm in the Aegean Sea. The ship climbed the crests, then plunged into the troughs, waves crashing over the bow. One fierce wave engulfed Lilly and, for a few terrifying moments, she thought she had been thrown overboard and swept out to sea.

It was over twelve hours since Lilly stepped ashore. The bed still felt as if it was rocking and swaying, even though the ground beneath her was solid. She had a roof over her head, a bed to sleep in, and her suitcase, delivered earlier that evening, tucked beneath the bedframe. The bed might have been hard, the mattress thin, but it was not as uncomfortable as lying on a bench or deck where she could not shift without bumping into the person next to her. Here she lay in her bed with a pillow, covered by two thick blankets, warm and dry, while the winter downpour fed the earth.

It was more than comforting. It was glorious.

The dampness released a woody scent in the hut. Its smell took Lilly back to Vienna and their synagogue's wooden sukkah, its roof covered with evergreen branches, the walls decorated with paper chains and pictures. As children, Lilly, Eugen, and Hannah helped decorate that sukkah. During the festival of Sukkot, they shared communal meals with family and friends. Those days were as golden as the autumn leaves that adorned the trees. Back then, they assumed their lives in Vienna would be as predictable as the cycle of seasons. How wrong they were. Now, the only reminder of those times was a scent from her old land in her new one.

The sukkah, a temporary hut, had protected the children of Israel when they wandered in the desert for forty years after leaving Egypt before they entered the Promised Land.

Here she was, protected by a wooden hut, in the Promised Land. True, she was locked up, but apart from the barbed wire, Atlit did not seem too bad. Like a sukkah, it was only a temporary abode. She was safe, she had food and shelter, and Hannah was here with her. It could only be a matter of time until they were no longer divided by fences. And before long, they would be released to start their real lives in Eretz Israel.

The small glimpse she saw of Haifa that afternoon captured her imagination. Earlier that evening, she wrote a letter to Mama describing the city. She assured her mother she was well and together with Hannah.

She did not mention the *Patria*.

How close they had come to being expelled from Eretz Israel. On the *Atlantic*, they had been oblivious to the plan. Lilly could not get over that fact. How could the British have betrayed them, especially after promising they could land in Haifa?

Whatever caused the ship to capsize, it had nevertheless saved them. If not for that tragedy, the British would never have reversed their decision. Instead of being in Atlit tonight, they would all have been on the *Patria*, sailing to an unknown destination.

What would have happened if Lilly had been on the *Patria* when it sank? Would she have been as fortunate as Hannah and Karl, Alma and Chaim? Countless people on board the Patria had lost their lives, including Marcus.

After her initial reaction to learning Marcus had drowned, Erika put on a brave face. She told the others she would be fine and just needed some time alone. The *chevra* decided it best to leave her be for a little while.

They tiptoed around Erika, who spent the rest of the day sitting on her bed and staring into the distance. She did not join them for meals, saying that she was not hungry. The fragrant orange, the juicy baby cucumber, and the sweet marmalade sandwich, which Lilly, Gisela, and Janka saved her from supper, sat uneaten on the narrow wooden ledge beside the window.

But Erika was not all right. In the bed next to Lilly, she was curled in a fetal position. The pounding rain masked her stifled sobs.

Lilly understood – only too well.

It took her a long time to come to terms with Salo's death and learn to live with the pain of his loss. Then, just four weeks ago outside Heraklion harbour, a telegram from her brother brought news that their father had died. Like Erika, Lilly maintained her composure. She wandered around for days feeling lost, not knowing what to do or where to put herself. No one could comfort her. Not even Hannah. It was Isaak – who had become one of her closest friends during the voyage – that finally helped her through. He had stayed up through the night with her, encouraging her to talk about her father. When dawn broke, though the pain remained, it was not as overwhelming, and she learned to make space for it.

Lilly slipped out of her bed, sat beside Erika, and touched her arm. Erika startled, then sat up and leaned her head on Lilly's shoulder. 'I can't believe he's gone.'

Lilly wrapped her arm around Erika. 'I know.'

'I had finally made up my mind about Marcus. If he proposed, I was ready to accept and spend the rest of my life with him. And now ...' she threw up her hands. 'I am here. After all these months, and everything we have been through, I am here, but Marcus is gone. It's as if my dreams for the future died with him and I no longer have a future. I am all alone in this unfamiliar place.' Erika took a deep breath to steady herself. 'I'm sorry. I shouldn't put this on you. What I'm going through doesn't begin to compare. You lost your husband. Marcus and I weren't even engaged. But his loss still feels like a blow.'

'One person's pain can't be measured against another. There's no need to apologise. You shared something special with Marcus. It's all right to cry and mourn him.'

'He was so close to realising his dream of reaching Eretz Israel. So close that he could see the land. But in this terrible twist of fate, I am here. And he is gone. He was young, his whole life ahead of him. He never had the chance to live in Eretz. To marry. To have a family. It's so cruel ...' Erika's voice broke. 'I can't bear to think I will never see his sweet face again.'

Lilly rocked Erika as she cried and allowed herself to cry silent tears in the darkness. Erika's grief had reopened the scar of her own painful memories.

'What do I do now? How do I get through this? How do I move on?' Erika let out a shaky breath. 'How did you?'

'It took a long time. In those early days I was consumed with grief and didn't know how to go on living. If not for my mother and Hannah and my aunt, I don't know ... But their love and support helped pull me through.' Lilly hesitated. 'The truth is, I can't say I'm fully over it. Maybe I won't ever be. But I am learning to accept that Salo is gone. He would want me to move forward and live my life. So that's what I am trying to do. One day at a time. One foot in front of the other. And I promise you won't always feel this devastated. You will never forget Marcus, but in time you will learn to accept his loss and think about the future.'

'I can't imagine how.' Erika's voice threatened to break again. 'I feel so alone. If only my mother were here.'

'Oh, Erika.' Lilly drew her closer. She realised that Erika's distress was not just about Marcus. In the aftermath of Salo's death, at least Lilly had her mother, Hannah, and her aunt to support her. Before tonight, she had never found reason to be grateful for anything connected to Salo's death. Now she recognised this small mercy. 'Perhaps your mother can join you soon.'

Erika shook her head. 'My papa was sent to Dachau. Just like yours. My mama wanted me to take a place on the transport, but she would not go without Papa. In the few letters I received from Mama during my stay in Bratislava, her news about Papa was vague. Maybe he was still in the concentration camp and she genuinely didn't know his condition. Or perhaps she knew but wanted to wait until she heard I'd arrived in Eretz Israel, knowing that otherwise, I would have wanted to go back to be with her. I don't know what has become of them.'

Erika paused. She stared at her hands. 'When I left Vienna, I was young and innocent. That night on the train, I met your cousin

Hannah. I thought our journey would last just a few weeks. Never having been away on my own before, I treated it as an adventure. I was most excited to meet new people and find a boyfriend. I thought it would not take long until my father was released and my parents would join me.' She looked into the gloom. 'And here I am. I found a boyfriend. And I lost him. I'm not sure if my father is alive. Or when I'll see my mother again. If ever.'

'Don't say that. When this war ends, hopefully we'll be reunited again with our mothers.' Did Lilly believe what she was saying? She could not contemplate the alternative.

'When ...' Erika's voice came out flat. 'I don't even have Hannah. We went through everything together. The Slobodarna hostel, the transfer to the Patronka. I met Marcus when she met Karl. It's not the same, calling to Hannah across the fence.

'This situation is only temporary. We'll soon be back together with Hannah. Of that I'm sure. And in the meantime, I'm here for you. We all are. We have become like a family. And we love you.'

'Thank you,' Erika said. 'That means so much.' She sighed. 'Do you know what is so sad? I have nothing to remember Marcus by. Not even a photograph. Well, I had one that he gave me. I put it in my photograph album. And they confiscated that.'

'What you have of Marcus is in here.' Lilly gently touched Erika's heart. 'And no one can take that away from you.'

Erika squeezed her hand.

'Tell me about Marcus,' Lilly said, remembering Isaak's words when he asked her to talk about her father. 'Tell me about the day you met.'

'Marcus appeared like a ray of light on a dark, miserable day,' Erika began, her face softening with the memory. 'We had just arrived at the Patronka. It was the grimmest place imaginable. Hannah and I had left our friends behind. I was especially disappointed about leaving Alexander, who I'd been secretly fond of since the day we met. I didn't know if we'd ever see him, Janka or Isaak again. We ventured out of our sleeping quarters, a damp and drafty warehouse, to see what was outside. That was when we met Marcus and Karl. Marcus had a smile that lit up his handsome, freckled face, and he was so warm and friendly. They offered to show us around. I walked with Marcus, Hannah with Karl. From that day onwards we became friends and eventually, couples.'

Erika told her about their daily walks, their conversations, the stories Marcus shared.

Each time Erika paused, Lilly asked her another question, just as Isaak had done for her. She fought against her drooping eyelids, listening to Erika until she reached the end: the last time she saw Marcus, when his ship passed the *Atlantic*, leaving Tulcea, on its way to the Black Sea and he waved to her.

Silence. Outside, the rain had stopped, and the light was shifting to grey dawn. A bird called in the distance.

Erika wiped away a tear. 'It helped to talk about him. I think it was exactly what I needed.' She yawned. 'Thanks for staying up with me.'

'Will you be able to sleep now?'

Erika lay back and let her head sink onto her pillow.

'Good night,' Lilly whispered. There was no reply. The steady rhythm of Erika's breathing told Lilly she was already asleep.

Lilly returned to her bed, thinking about Isaak and how he listened throughout the night as she spoke about her father. Talking about him soothed her loss like a balm. Isaak had known exactly what she needed that night. He had understood her better than anyone else. Better than she understood herself. When the sky lightened to blue in the hour before dawn, she felt a sense of calm.

Lilly felt that same peace now. Erika too would heal in time and recover from her grief.

But alongside that peace, Lilly felt a mix of other emotions. Gratitude to Isaak for helping her and for teaching her, with a wisdom beyond his years, how to comfort Erika tonight. Relief that Hannah was alive and here in the camp. Love for her friends who had become like family.

And hope.

For tomorrow. For the future. For their new life in this new land.

Chapter 24

2 December 1940
Atlit Camp

Hours later, Lilly awoke to the sounds of her roommates rising, dressing, chatting as they opened the shutters to welcome the morning. Bright sunlight streamed in through the windows in seeming defiance of last night's storm. The vivid blue sky belonged to a summer day in mid-June, rather than a winter one in early December.

'Good morning, *mein Schatz*,' said Gisela, already dressed. She strode over to Lilly, her movements crisp and purposeful as she arranged her peacock scarf around her neck. 'How did you sleep?'

Lilly stretched out, unused to the luxury of having a real bed all to herself.

'I slept well,' Lilly said. 'At least for a few hours.'

'I heard you and Erika talking during the night,' Gisela said.

'I'm sorry. Did we disturb you?'

'No, not at all. The rain hammering on the roof kept waking me up and then I saw you.' She glanced across at Erika. 'How is she?'

'It's raw and painful for her right now. But she is learning how to accept it. You and I can both understand that.'

Gisela gave a grim nod. 'We'll all support Erika and show her a lot of love.'

At the sound of her name, Erika stirred and looked around at the still unfamiliar surroundings.

Lilly climbed out of her bed and crouched beside her. 'How are you feeling today?'

Erika sat up, reached for Lilly's hand and squeezed it. 'Thank you for being there for me last night.'

'I'm always here whenever you want to talk.'

Erika forced a brave smile as her eyes glistened.

Gisela joined them. 'There, there, *mein Schatz.*' She hugged her.

Janka and Jenny approached from the other side of her bed, each placing an arm around Erika.

'We're all here for you,' Janka said.

'And we love you,' Jenny added.

Erika sniffed and wiped her eyes. 'I'm so lucky to have you all.'

'You should try to eat a little something this morning,' said Gisela, always the practical mother among them. Lilly's gaze followed Gisela's to the untouched food on the ledge. Gisela grimaced. Lilly noticed the tiny bite marks in the baby cucumber and through the wax paper covering the sandwich. Too small to be human teeth.

'But these are old now.' Gisela shuddered. Using two fingers, she gingerly picked up the sandwich. Mouth open, Jenny retreated a step. Behind Erika's back, Janka shook her head vigorously as she brought her finger to her lips, warning Jenny not to scream. Wordlessly, Janka and Gisela cleared the rest of the food from the ledge.

'Do you want to get dressed and come with us to the washing facilities before they deliver breakfast?' Gisela said.

Erika nodded and rose shakily from the bed.

Lilly, Gisela, Erika, Janka, and Jenny left the hut together, arms linked, for the short walk to the washroom.

The sky may have forgotten the rain, but the earth had remembered. Lilly's shoe sank into the unpaved path; the red earth yielding like sticky dough. She heaved her foot free with an unladylike squelch.

'*Um Gottes Willen*,' Jenny said, as they struggled through the mire.

Gisela slid. Lilly and Erika caught her before she landed on her rear.

Janka could not suppress a snort. Soon they were all laughing – even Erika let out a giggle – as the five of them waded down the path.

After washing, Lilly tried as best as she could to clean her shoes. A pointless exercise. By the time they returned to their hut, their shoes were as mud-caked as before. She left them outside the door, lined up in a row with all the others.

Breakfast had already been fetched from the kitchen – crusty slices of bread with butter and marmalade, hot tea, milk, and fragrant oranges bursting with juice.

Lilly eyed a slice of creamy halva that no one had yet touched. She broke off a corner and popped it into her mouth, relishing the familiar flavour and texture: a mild nutty flavour, combined with the sweetness of honey and a hint of vanilla. She savoured the halva as it melted on her tongue. The taste transported her to her best friend Serena's dining room in Vienna, where halva always appeared as part of her mother's magnificent Shabbat dessert spread. After the Anschluss, Serena and her new husband had fled to London, and Serena's sister, Allegra, had joined Lilly's brother, Eugen, on an earlier transport to Eretz Israel. Eugen and Allegra had since married; Allegra was now her sister-in-law. Lilly could not wait to see them again. After taking another bite, she cut the slice into squares for her friends. 'You all have to try this!'

'Are you being serious?' Janka said. 'It looks like sawdust glued into a block.'

'Well, it tastes like heaven.' Lilly handed her a piece.

'I hope this isn't a practical joke.' Janka studied it warily. 'Like those sea biscuits on the ship. You remember that?'

'Only too well. We thought those biscuits were dusted with sugar, but discovered it was mould.'

Janka placed a hand to her throat. 'We nearly got poisoned.'

'*Ach*! Don't exaggerate.' Gisela chuckled. 'You're still here.'

'Only because Erika kept reminding us to scrape the mould off the biscuits or bread before we ate.'

Erika acknowledged the credit with a fleeting smile..

'Well, this is nothing like those disgusting sea biscuits. I promise you.' Lilly broke off pieces from the halva block and handed them to everyone sitting around the table.

Janka took a cautious bite. 'Oh. It's sweet.'

'Delicious,' Gisela agreed.

Lilly lifted a cup of milk in one hand and a piece of halva in the other. 'This truly is a land flowing with milk and honey.'

Janka raised her cup in a toast. 'To our future in the land of milk and honey.'

The others lifted their cups and they clinked them together.

'*L'chaim*!'

As soon as breakfast was cleared away, Lilly and her friends left the hut, slipping on their muddy shoes outside. Peals of children's laughter rang out close by. The moment they entered the men's enclosure, Lilly discovered its source. Isaak.

Surrounded by a semi-circle of young boys and girls, he plodded like an elephant, swinging his right arm like a trunk, much to the children's amusement.

There was no sign yet of Alma or Hannah on the other side of the fence, but Max was already waiting.

Lilly and the others stopped to watch Isaak. He saw them and waved.

'Isaak, make magic!' shouted a curly-haired four-year-old boy, just as he had often done on the *Atlantic* whenever Isaak gave the children one of his impromptu magic shows.

'All right.' Isaak pulled out a piece of brown paper from his pocket and folded it into a hand puppet. In the outstretched palm of his other hand, Isaak revealed a pebble. He shut his hand and shook it. He opened his palm again to reveal the pebble was gone. His hand puppet started to make munching sounds. 'What's in your mouth?' Isaak asked the puppet.

'Nothing,' it squeaked.

'*Ach so*?' Isaak tilted his head. 'Open wide.' He forced open the puppet's mouth, withdrew the pebble, and held it aloft. The children and their parents applauded.

'Bless him,' Gisela said, like a doting grandmother as she clapped along.

Lilly's heart felt inexplicably full.

Isaak took a quick bow and then strode over to join the women.

'Good morning!' He hugged his cousin, Janka. 'Can you believe it? Our first morning in Eretz and on dry land.'

'I don't know about *dry* land.' Janka grinned, pointing to their mud-encrusted shoes. They all laughed.

Isaak's expression became more sombre as he approached Erika. 'How are you feeling?'

Erika shrugged and tried to smile, but her expression remained mournful.

Isaak patted her arm. 'We are all here for you.'

Gisela pinched Isaak's cheek. 'Your show was so sweet,' she said.

Isaak gave a modest smile. 'I wanted to try and distract the children.' He hesitated. 'They need it now more than ever. Especially after what happened.' He grew more serious, lowering his voice. 'We just heard that a three-year-old boy from the Danzig group passed away from typhoid fever.'

Gisela closed her eyes briefly.

Lilly put a hand to her mouth. 'Does Jenny know?' she said, realising she was no longer beside them.

'I think she just found out.' He tipped his head to the left where she and Stefan huddled at the side of the hut, his arm around her shoulders.

Jenny and Stefan were from Danzig too and must have known the boy.

They had lost too many people during their journey. Even here, it seemed they could not escape the nightmare's shadow. When would it end?

Hannah appeared on the other side with Alma and Chaim. Despite the difficulty of shouting across the divide, by lunchtime Lilly understood the story of Hannah's transfer to the Patria and how she had survived its sinking. She learned how Karl had stayed on the ship, helping to save many passengers, including Alma and Chaim. When the ship tilted, and the cabin started filling with water, Alma scaled the bunk bed – now angled vertically – while cradling Chaim in her arms. She injured her leg in the process. Alma tried to climb out of the porthole, but the hole was too narrow for her to squeeze through. In desperation, she lifted baby Chaim up and held him through the opening, shouting for help until Karl found her. He took baby Chaim and remained by her side until the rescue team arrived with blowtorches to cut through the steel and free Alma.

Erika joined Lilly, wanting to learn what had happened to Marcus. Hannah described his escape attempt, imprisonment, and how, after his release, he had joined HW in an effort to free passengers trapped in the ship's hold.

'You can be very proud of Marcus,' Hannah called. 'He was a hero.'

'I am,' Erika said through her tears. 'But it doesn't bring him back.'

Erika's melancholy overshadowed their midday meal. Learning the details of Marcus's final moments had awakened painful new emotions. After they finished eating, Erika walked the compound perimeter, deep in conversation with Janka, Alexander, and Isaak. Lilly understood. Erika shared a history with them she was not a part of. They had spent months together at the Slobodarna hostel in Bratislava until Hannah and Erika's transfer to the Patronka, and had reunited aboard the Helios for the journey down the Danube.

Gisela had returned to their hut for an afternoon nap. Jenny and Stefan were off by themselves. Hannah had gone to meet Karl as it was visiting hour. Lilly stood alone, waiting for Hannah. She gave Max and Alma space as they conversed across the fence.

'Mind if I join you?' Lilly turned, surprised to find Isaak by her side.

'Of course you can,' she said, glad for his company.'

For a few moments they watched in silence as couples strolled hand in hand along the walkway between the fences, talking, laughing, embracing.

'There's something I can't quite figure out.'

Lilly looked at him and wavered. 'What do you mean?'

'The British have segregated the men and women from the *Patria* except for this one hour every afternoon. It's the only time Hannah and Karl can leave their enclosures and walk together between the fences. Meanwhile, they have confined our group to a smaller area but allow us to mingle freely. In the Patria compound, they must be in their huts at nightfall, whereas on our side, Stefan and Jenny go for evening walks. Yet, they completely separate us from the *Patria* survivors. No meetings, not even for an hour. You shout across the fence to reach Hannah. Max can't hug his wife or child. Who exactly are the British punishing?'

'That hadn't occurred to me.' Lilly surveyed the camp as if seeing it through new eyes. 'I suppose we're in a slightly better situation than those in the *Patria* enclosure. Like you say, we're all together. But what reason would the British have to punish any of us? We've done nothing wrong. And surely the *Patria* survivors have been through enough?'

Isaak rocked his head from side to side as if considering the matter further. 'It just seems strange.'

'I agree. Could it be that they didn't expect they would have to accommodate so many people here at such short notice? There are still more people to come from the *Atlantic*.'

'I suppose it's possible.'

'We've been here less than twenty-four hours. It might take them a little while to get everyone organised. I'm sure they will let us meet up properly with our friends and family in the other enclosure over the coming few days. After all, there's no reason for them not to.'

'Maybe.' He did not sound convinced.

Isaak had always been their optimist. But here, in the very place they had dreamed of reaching, he was becoming a sceptic. Now, she felt his doubts taking root in her own mind.

Chapter 25

5 December 1940
Atlit Camp

Although Lilly had stopped marvelling at being on dry land, she still awoke each morning thankful to be in Eretz Israel, grateful for her safety. Four days on, life in Atlit had settled into a routine. After breakfast, she sought out Hannah at the fence before attending the newly established Hebrew lessons, absorbing the words she would need for her future life. Lunch was at noon. During visiting hour, when Hannah met Karl, Lilly strolled around the compound with her friends. She met Hannah again before supper at half-past five. Bedtime was at nine.

Lilly no longer felt the need to feast on halva. A small piece sufficed now; there would be more the next day, at breakfast, at supper. Just as she knew, with a certainty about tomorrow she had never felt during those weeks at sea, that she would see her cousin each day. There was a mundanity to her routine but comfort in that mundanity.

Yet, Isaak's observation lingered, prickling at the back of her mind. The *Atlantic* passengers remained separated across the divide from the *Patria* passengers, with no indication of when they would be allowed to reunite. When they asked the *gaffirim*, they received only shrugs in response.

Since their arrival, the gates had opened only to let people in – never out. First came the trickle of remaining passengers from the *Atlantic*. But right before lunch, the trickle became a flood as five hundred men poured into their compound: the men from their ship who had originally been sent to Acco.

That afternoon, as Lilly walked the usual circuit with the *chevra*, they passed Max at the fence, calling across to Alma and baby Chaim on the *Patria* side.

'Just as well we didn't go to Acco,' Alexander said. 'We would have ended up here anyway.'

'Didn't the British say we were supposed to be in quarantine?' Isaak said. 'So much for that. We're practically living on top of each other.'

With their compound's population having increased by a third, over 1500 people crammed together, the men had been forced to double up. The huts, designed for around thirty, now accommodated fifty people or more. Conditions were still not as bad as on the ship. Nothing was as bad as that.

'Clearly, plans have changed,' Alexander said. 'Dov told me that Acco was quite pleasant, even though the camp was attached to a jail for security prisoners. He said it was clean and organised. They served good food, and the guards treated them well. They were close to the sea, and they could walk on the sand during the day, but a barbed wire fence kept them from the water.' Alexander shrugged. 'Compared to Acco, he thinks Atlit is run-down and a bit of a mess.'

Lilly looked through the fence where she caught sight of Hannah and Karl walking hand in hand down the promenade and thought there was nowhere else she would rather be.

'Were they sorry to leave?' Janka said.

'It seems so,' Alexander said. 'They were sure that they would be in Acco for some time. They had even started planting a vegetable garden. Then, without warning, the guards told them to pack because they were sending them somewhere else.'

'Why move them all of a sudden?' Erika asked.

'I don't think the guards gave them a reason,' Alexander replied.

'You mentioned that Acco was attached to a jail.' Isaak's brow furrowed. 'Makes me think that perhaps at first the British were concerned that we were a security risk. Especially the men. But after observing them in Acco for a few days, they saw they weren't a threat. Maybe now they are realising that all of us are just ordinary, law-abiding Jews who had to flee for our lives. Not the enemy. Not Germans.'

'They certainly treated me as if I were a security risk on arrival.' Stefan shook his head in exasperation. 'The British officer who questioned me practically accused me of being a spy. Can you believe they actually thought I would be able to supply them with information about submarine manufacturing in the Port of Danzig? As if I, a Jew, would know anything about the Nazis' plans. Just thinking about that interrogation again is giving me a headache. And I'm still waiting for them to return the camera they stole from me. Not a word yet about that.' Stefan pressed his hands on his temples.

Jenny studied her husband with concern. 'What's the matter?'

'Nothing at all.' Stefan patted her hand.

'You seem to be having a lot of headaches lately.'

'I'm probably still exhausted from the strenuous journey. Nothing to worry about.'

Stefan and Jenny stopped to talk in private as the rest continued their stroll. Gisela glanced back at them, then hastened to catch up with the *chevra*, taking Isaak's offered arm as they followed the rocky path behind the huts. They resumed their earlier discussion about the men's transfer.

'You make a good point, Isaak,' said Alexander. 'In which case, transferring the men back to join the rest of us seems an encouraging sign.'

'Let's hope so,' Lilly said. 'If only they would reorganise the camp so that families can be reunited. My throat is getting hoarse from all that shouting at Hannah. And Max must be desperate to hold little Chaim in his arms and hug Alma. It is frustrating that we can only see them from a distance.'

'I can't see how they can keep us in these overcrowded conditions for too long. It's going to be impossible to live like this.' Alexander's gaze swept the camp as if making calculations. 'I wonder whether they are planning on releasing the *Libertad* passengers soon. After all, that group has already been in Atlit for over four months. It must almost be time for them to leave. And once they are gone, there will be more room for the guards to reorganise the rest of us.'

'Hannah has a friend who was on the *Libertad*,' Lilly said. 'I should ask whether her friend knows anything.'

'Please do,' Alexander said. 'And let us know what she says. If we also have to stay here for a few months, so be it. As long as we have an idea of how long the wait will be. And providing they sort out this overcrowding.'

'And as long as we can also have visits from our families on the outside,' Gisela said. 'Or at least be in touch with them. I haven't heard a word from either of my sons since we arrived, and I have not been able to contact them. Whenever I ask the *gaffirim*, they just dismiss me with a wave of the hand or a click of the tongue.' Gisela's gaze dropped to her feet, her mouth downturned. 'I'm not sure my family even knows where I am.'

'Don't worry,' Isaak said. 'They'll discover where you are and find a way to get in touch.'

Gisela mustered a smile. 'I hope you're right. I have waited so long to see them. And now that we've reached Eretz Israel, and they are so close, it feels even more frustrating.'

Isaak faced Lilly. 'I suppose you haven't heard from your brother either?'

'No. I've asked the guards several times if I could send him a letter, and also one to my mother, but they just brush me off.' She sighed. 'Perhaps they'd be more helpful if I could at least offer to pay for the postage.'

Lilly found herself comparing the help they had received from Jewish communities along their journey with the silence here. Since their arrival, not one representative from the *Yishuv*, the Jewish community of Eretz Israel, had come to welcome them. Was it out of choice or were they prohibited from doing so? Did the British rule the land with such an iron fist that they would forbid them from having contact with the local population while they remained locked up in Atlit and if so, why?

The only contact they had with any of the local population was the *gaffirim*. Pleasant as they were, claiming to help, they provided little real assistance. But ultimately, they were employed by the British and had to abide by their orders.

Lilly could not make sense of the irrational situation. She had always assumed the British were fair and honourable. They were allies. Fighting for freedom. She could understand restrictions for quarantine. But what would be the harm in sending a simple letter to her mother and brother?

Isaak fished in his pocket and pulled out two cigarettes. 'Perhaps these will work as payment?' He looked at Alexander. 'What if we offer to barter with the *gaffirim* – fine British cigarettes for stamps?'

'Worth a try,' Alexander said, as he handed over his cigarette.

Despite Isaak's best attempts, the *gaffirim* remained noncommittal about trading cigarettes for stamps. On Friday afternoon, the letters Lilly had written to her mother and Eugen remained perched on the ledge beside her bed. They would try again on Sunday.

In the meantime, Lilly tried to put that disappointment aside. Tomorrow, Friday night, would mark the start of their first Shabbat in Atlit and the various groups had decided to gather for an *Oneg Shabbat*.

Happy chatter filled Lilly's hut as her roommates prepared. The gathering offered a break in the routine and gave them a reason to dress up. That in itself lifted their spirits.

Fresh from the shower, Lilly slipped into her navy dress and cinched a belt around her waist. The day had been mild – in Vienna this would be considered spring – but once the sun dropped, the wind would pick up and it would get chilly. She pulled on a cardigan.

Running a brush through her hair, Lilly reflected on her first few days in Atlit. Apart from her inability to reach the outside world and the fence that separated her from Hannah, life was fine. No, it was good.

While the *gaffirim* seldom provided answers, they were friendly. The British policemen kept to the perimeter, interacting little with detainees. When they did, they were polite. Strange as it seemed, she was beginning to see advantages to her stay in Atlit. The food was good and adequate, if unvaried. The camp gave her breathing room. No immediate pressure to find work or lodging, no worries about rent or food. It had cushioned her landing and given her time to learn Hebrew. In less than a week she had already made progress. By the time they were released, she hoped to be proficient enough to secure employment.

Haifa had left a lasting impression on Lilly with its wide boulevards, modern buildings, and stylish canopied shopfronts. She might apply for a job in a dress shop. The idea appealed to her. Lilly had worked in her father's luggage shop during school holidays. She had gained business knowledge too. She had often watched Papa poring over the books and placing stock orders. Lilly let her imagination flow. Once she had some experience, perhaps she would open her own shop and design and make all the clothes. She could already picture the window displaying three mannequins, each wearing an original piece from the season's collection. Above the canopy would hang an elegant sign. She would call the shop Shoshana: her Hebrew name.

'Would you like me to do your hair?' Erika's voice broke through Lilly's reverie. Lilly realised she was still running the brush through her damp hair.

Though grief had subdued Erika these past few days, she was trying to maintain a brave face. Her hair, as always, was immaculately styled, and she wore imitation pearl earrings, yet her eyes remained mournful.

'Thank you. I'd like that.' Lilly handed over her hairbrush, hoping it might comfort Erika. A born nurse, Erika was never happier than when helping others.

Lilly sat on the end of her bed, and Erika set to work, brushing, curling, and pinning Lilly's hair. She stepped back to study her work with an expression of intense concentration. 'Do you have any lipstick? I think it will be the finishing touch.'

Lilly rummaged through her wash bag and found a forgotten tube at the bottom. She had not touched it since leaving Vienna. Erika carefully applied the lipstick to Lilly's lips.

'There,' she said. 'You look beautiful.'

Lilly's heart warmed to see the beginnings of a smile on Erika's face.

Erika reached for the hand mirror on her bed and held it up.

Lilly stared. The curls Erika had styled made her brown hair appear glossier and the Mediterranean winter sun had added some colour to her cheeks. The face in the reflection was both familiar and unfamiliar. She was not the same Lilly. She could never return to who she had been before. Loss had left its scar. But she looked like a young woman in her early twenties with a life still ahead of her.

Erika watched her with an eager expression. 'What do you think?'

'I love it.' Lilly turned her head from side to side. 'I almost don't recognise myself.'

If only Mama could see her now. She would be so happy to see her dressed up. Lilly shut her eyes for a moment, taking a breath to compose herself. She rose and hugged Erika.

'*Shabbat shalom*, my dear friend.' Erika's voice hitched a fraction as she hugged Lilly tight.

'Stunning!' Janka said, approaching them. She looked from Lilly to Erika, and wrapped her arms around both of them. Janka too wore a light touch of lipstick. It was the first time Lilly had seen her wearing makeup. Her straight hair, grown to shoulder length during the journey, had been curled under and clipped to one side. Lilly assumed that was Erika's work too.

'You look gorgeous too,' Lilly said.

Janka's face lit up at the compliment.

'Oh!' Gisela said. 'Look at these three young beauties!'

'You are also looking smart,' Janka said.

Gisela had dressed up in a green two-piece suit, which set off her silk peacock feather scarf to perfection.

'Very elegant,' Lilly said.

'Why, thank you.' Gisela beamed, stroking her scarf.

The four of them had no one in particular to dress up for. But it was enough to dress up for themselves.

'I think it's almost time.' Gisela moved to the little table set up at the front of the hut and lit the two makeshift candles. She circled her hands over them three times as if drawing in the light, before covering her eyes and reciting the traditional blessing.

'Amen,' Lilly and the others responded.

'*Shabbat shalom*, my darlings.' Gisela kissed each of them.

Arms linked, they left the hut, flowing into the stream of people heading toward the paths. Lilly felt somehow lighter. More comfortable in her skin than she had been for a long time. The sky was gilded in copper and gold, and a light westerly breeze blew in from the sea. Voices and birdsong suffused the air.

The *chevra* found each other outside the men's hut and exchanged hugs and greetings. Jenny and Stefan were already together, his arm around her waist. Max had gone straight to the fence to see Alma and Chaim. As Alexander embraced Erika, he whispered something in her ear. Whatever he had said, the words seemed to offer her a measure of comfort. She nodded and her expression softened.

'*Shabbat shalom*,' Isaak said, briefly hugging Lilly. 'You look ... really lovely.' He gave her a shy smile.

'Thank you,' she said, warmth rising to her cheeks.

The rest of the chevra joined those gathered by the fence. Opposite stood women and men from the *Patria*; Hannah and Alma with baby Chaim on one side, Karl on the other.

Twelve days ago, when the *Atlantic* landed in Haifa, Lilly had expected that they were all about to part ways. Yet here they were, together in Eretz, though separated by the barbed-wire fences. They could not stand beside each other, but their voices embraced instead. No fences could trap their songs. Joined in harmony, they sang the words of *L'cha Dodi*. Come, my beloved, let us welcome Shabbat, and *Shalom Aleichem*, Peace Be Unto You.

Dusk was falling, the sky tinged with amethyst, as they broke into *Hatikva*. It occurred to Lilly that after two thousand years of exile – centuries of persecution, pogroms, forced dispersal, generation after generation searching for sanctuary – here she was, finally, standing on holy soil welcoming the Shabbat.

Lilly was no longer a second-class citizen, rejected, living in fear. Nor a refugee sailing the seas, fleeing for her life. She had come home. And though she was confined in this camp, that was only temporary. Soon she would be a free citizen in her new land. Free to live her life as she chose.

Before the song concluded, British guards moved through the crowd.

'Back to your barracks,' one commanded. 'All of you. Now.'

Lilly lingered as the crowd dispersed. Hannah waved from the other side.

'*Shabbat shalom*!' She blew Lilly a kiss. 'Maybe next week, we'll be sitting down together for the Friday night meal.'

And for a moment, Lilly allowed herself to believe in the possibility.

Chapter 26

8 December 1940
Atlit Camp

Sunday in Atlit began like any other day for Isaak. After *Shacharit* prayers and breakfast, the usual group of children sought him out, begging for magic tricks. Isaak obliged, of course. How could he refuse? These children had scant entertainment, formal schooling, or structure to their days. They wandered around the fenced enclosure with little to do, making toys out of old scraps, sticks and pebbles. Isaak's shows brightened their day. They did not mind seeing the same tricks again. Isaak had already exhausted the repertoire of magic tricks his papa had taught him, but the children reacted with as much enthusiasm as the first time he had performed them.

If only his papa could see him now. Isaak did his best to maintain a cheerful disposition and help others wherever he could, don his tefillin and pray, keep kosher and Shabbat, just as his papa had always taught him. Isaak hoped Papa would be proud of the young man he had become.

Not a day went by without Isaak thinking about his family, though he masked his concern. Everyone here feared for relatives left behind. Since arriving in Atlit, even as he tried to maintain his happy-go-lucky attitude, his worry deepened. His family had started down the Danube before him. They were supposed to have arrived in Eretz by now. Instead, he had arrived first. They were still out there, somewhere, unreachable. What had happened to them in the two months since his paddle steamer had passed them at Kladovo? Had they followed on another paddle steamer, or were they still stranded on the riverbank?

Isaak found it difficult to focus on the morning's Hebrew lesson. He listened to the teacher, but the words did not penetrate. His family weighed on his mind. Perhaps the initial euphoria of their arrival had worn off. The daily routine had grown stale. Yes, they were in Eretz, but were trapped behind barbed wire, watchtowers, and searchlights. They remained in a state of limbo. They were still not free. Worst of all, they had no contact with the outside world. Despite another attempt before Hebrew class to trade his cigarettes with the *Gaffirim* for stamps, the guards remained noncommittal. If only he could get stamps, he could write to Alexander and Janka's father, his uncle, and ask if there had been word of his family. At least then he'd be doing something, rather than sitting helplessly in this cage, waiting. And Lilly could finally write to her brother in Eretz and her mother back in Vienna.

That afternoon, as the *chevra* took their usual stroll around the enclosure, Isaak had to tell Lilly the guards had once more refused his request.

'Thank you for trying anyway.' Lilly remained stoic, but Isaak could tell she was disappointed. She paused at the fence. Isaak waited with her while the others continued. Max was in his usual spot calling across to Alma. Lilly's eyes followed Hannah and Karl as they walked together on the other side.

'I'm really sorry,' Isaak said.

'It's not your fault.'

'Maybe they'll soon introduce a visiting hour between us and the *Patria* passengers. Then you can meet up properly with Hannah,' Isaak said.

'I hope so. She's so near and yet so out of reach. For Max, I imagine it's even harder. How he must long to hold his baby and hug his wife.' She threw up her hands. 'I don't understand their rules. Why keep us apart? What would be the harm in letting me see my brother through the fence, or in sending a letter to him and my mother? Don't get me wrong, I'm grateful we're safe and in Eretz. But I'm concerned about my mother and my aunt. I don't know how they are faring, and they don't know where we are.' She hesitated. 'You must worry about your family too?'

'Yes,' he admitted.

'Do you think there's a possibility that somehow they overtook us during the journey and are already here in Eretz? Maybe we never heard about it.'

Isaak shook his head. 'If they had, they would be here with us in Atlit like the *Libertad* passengers.'

'I suppose so.' Lilly was pensive. 'The not knowing must be a constant worry.'

'It is.'

Despite their age gap and different life experiences, he had come to regard Lilly as his closest friend. He could not quite make sense of it, but somehow they understood one another.

They continued their circuit around to the back of the compound.

'You don't talk about your family much,' Lilly said.

He looked down. 'We're all in a similar situation. I don't want to burden anyone else with my worries.'

'Did you find it a burden when you sat up with me that night on the *Atlantic*, talking about my father after I'd learned he'd passed away?'

'No. Not at all. I was happy to do so.' He hoped he had not given her the wrong impression. 'I enjoyed listening to all the stories about your father. I like talking to you.'

'Then it goes both ways. You won't burden me if you talk about your family. I'm here to listen just the same.' She stopped walking and faced him. 'I like talking to you too.'

'Thank you,' he said. 'I appreciate it. Some days I feel hopeful. And some days it gets me down. I don't know why.'

'There's not always logic to our feelings.'

'No.' A smile tugged at his lips before he could stop it. 'I suppose not.'

'You know, I don't think you ever told me why you escaped Vienna by yourself and ended up living in Prague with Alexander and Janka.'

'Oh,' he said. 'That's quite a long story.'

Lilly took a seat on a boulder facing the open fields, framed by the Carmel mountain range. 'I have the time if you do.'

'All right.' He settled on a boulder opposite, running his fingers along a groove in the rock.

'Alexander once mentioned you were sixteen when you fled and arrived at their home with only one Reichsmark in your pocket.'

'Not quite.' Isaak grinned. 'I was seventeen, actually.' Alexander always treated him like a little brother. Perhaps he still saw Isaak as the sixteen-year-old boy who had visited with his family in the summer of 1937, not the young man who had fled Vienna a year later, or the twenty-year-old he was now. Isaak didn't mind. Not too much, anyway. 'But the part about one Reichsmark in my pocket is true.'

'Seventeen is still very young.'

Isaak shrugged.

'Why did you leave without your family?' Lilly asked. 'Did you have an argument with them?'

'Oh, God forbid!' Isaak said. 'No, nothing like that. I had no choice. I was at risk of being arrested. Like my father.'

Lilly leaned forward.

'That Thursday afternoon, 19 May 1938, we'd gone to shul for a family wedding. The weather was warm and sunny. Ordinarily, it would have been the perfect day for a large outdoor wedding, but of course that wasn't possible after the Anschluss. So the wedding was to be a quick one, held inside and attended by a few close family members.'

'Were Alexander and Janka there too?'

'No, this was a cousin from my mother's ... stepmother's side,' Isaak said. 'Because of the situation, weddings were taking place in the shul like an assembly line. We had to be cautious and use the side entrance. When we arrived, one couple was leaving; another went in just ahead of us. Apparently, the bride was from Vienna, her husband-to-be from Bratislava. They, like most of the couples, intended to flee the country straight after. My cousins too had planned to leave for Amsterdam that evening. While we waited for the previous wedding to finish, I was sitting on the back steps that led down to the basement, speaking to ... a relative.' Isaak shifted position on the boulder. 'A ... cousin.'

She was not exactly a cousin. She was the groom's sister. They had first met at the engagement party that winter, before all their lives changed. They were around the same age. With her sparkling brown eyes and full lips that curved into a bright smile, Isaak was smitten with her. She seemed to like him too. That day it had been her suggestion that they disappear off to the steps to talk before the wedding started. He could not recall what they had talked about. He only remembered that he had loved her company, her laughter, the silk dress she wore that hugged her curves.

From the stairs, they heard hushed *mazel tov* wishes for the couple who had just married as they left through the side exit. Any minute now, Isaak and the girl would have to join the rest of the family in the shul for the wedding. She had smiled at him, as if she was waiting for him to take the lead. It was the perfect opportunity for his first kiss. But as he leaned towards her, a crash echoed through the vestibule and the front doors burst open with a series of shouts. Sounds of panic and frantic screams followed.

Isaak and the girl froze. From where they sat, they could not see what was happening, but Isaak sensed danger. He grabbed her hand. They tore down the stairs into the basement.

'As my cousin and I were talking, we heard the other couple leaving. We were about to join our family when men burst through the front door,' Isaak said. 'Nazis.'

Lilly gasped. 'What did you do?'

'We ran downstairs into the basement.'

Isaak's eyes took a few seconds to adjust to the semi-darkness. A small window high on the wall let in a strip of late afternoon light.

From above came scraping across the floor, crying, and barked orders. The girl whimpered. Isaak gently hushed her. He led her past stacks of folding chairs and tables, stumbling over a metal bucket that clanged against the concrete. Isaak tensed and collected himself. They pushed deeper into the basement past storage crates to the back wall where a heavy velvet *parochet* hung from a ceiling rail. They pressed themselves flat against the plaster wall, shielded behind the curtain. Isaak took shallow breaths. The air was heavy with musty fabric, sharp camphor, and earthy dampness seeping through the cold walls.

Minutes passed in the darkness. Two, five, ten – Isaak lost track of time, each second stretched endlessly. Boots pounded down the stairs. Isaak reached for the girl's trembling hand and squeezed it. His palms grew sweaty. They held still as a pile of chairs crashed down and a torch beam swept the basement. Any time now, Isaak was sure the Nazis would notice movement behind the curtain or hear their laboured breathing. The metal bucket clattered and rolled across the floor.

A man swore. 'I'm not rummaging further through all this rubbish,' he said. 'There's no one down here.'

Footsteps tramped back up the stairs. Isaak exhaled.

'My cousin and I hid behind a *parochet* at the back of the basement.' Just retelling the story brought Isaak out in a sweat. He rubbed his palms on his trousers. 'Two men – Nazis – came down. I was sure we would be caught, but they barely looked around. Thinking there was no one down there, they left.'

'What did you do next?' Lilly said.

'We waited until the men above had stopped shouting and then came out from our hiding place. As we crept upstairs, we could hear muted crying.'

All that remained of his cousin's wedding party were the women, a few young boys, and elderly men, all gathered in the vestibule. The bride's mother and sisters were trying to comfort the inconsolable bride. Even the groom and his father were gone. The girl released Isaak's hand and ran into her mother's arms. Isaak's stepmother held his younger brother close, her face pale, stricken. Then she noticed Isaak walking down the narrow corridor towards the vestibule. Her eyes widened. She let go of Isaak's brother and rushed over to him.

'They arrested Papa along with all the men between the ages of sixteen and sixty,' she said in a hurried whisper. 'I thought they had taken you too. If they were to find you ...' Her fingers fumbled with the clasp of her elegant, black evening bag hanging from her wrist by a delicate gold chain. 'You must run away. Quick.'

'Where do I go?' Isaak said.

'I don't know. I don't know.' She covered her face with her hands, too distraught to provide the answers. 'Find a place to hide. Don't go home. And don't let them catch you.' She rummaged inside her bag, pulling out a silk handkerchief, a tube of lipstick and house keys, until she found a coin at the bottom. She pressed one Reichsmark into Isaak's hand. 'I'm sorry, this is all I have. I didn't think I would need money this afternoon. Papa had his wallet ...' She swallowed a cry. 'Find a way to get word to me. Let me know you're safe.' She hugged him fiercely. 'Now, go!'

Isaak closed his eyes briefly, remembering that last hug, that parting from his stepmother and brother.

'Did your cousin also have to escape?' Lilly asked, bringing him back to the present.

'No, she ...' He caught himself, a flush creeping up his neck. 'She ... stayed with her mother.'

Lilly tilted her head, a hint of understanding in her eyes. 'So where did you hide?'

Where was he to go? Were there men still waiting out front? They must have known that the wedding parties had been entering and leaving through the side entrance. If he left the building through that door, would they be waiting there to grab him? Isaak ran back down to the basement to collect his thoughts. If the Nazis had a list of the men who had entered the building, or if they interrogated his father, they would realise he was still hiding inside.

It was not safe for him to remain in the shul, and if his stepmother's fears were correct, as long as he stayed in his neighbourhood, he was in danger. But who did he know outside of Vienna? Only his uncle and aunt: Alexander and Janka's parents. And they lived in

Prague. How could he get there? He had never travelled on his own before. One Reichsmark was not enough to cover the train fare. The journey would cost at least seventeen Reichsmarks. Besides, he had no travel papers.

Isaak waited until the sliver of daylight through the basement window faded, shadows swallowing the last light. He climbed the rear service steps and pushed open the door. The creak seemed to bounce off the courtyard, but no one appeared. He slipped across the cobbled courtyard and scaled the back wall with the help of a dustbin, dropping into the alley beyond. He pressed close to the walls, creeping through Leopoldstadt's side streets until he reached the Nordbahnhof. At the entrance, he brushed off the jacket of his wedding suit and straightened his tie, praying his attire made him look more mature. Shoulders back, heart hammering, he strode across the polished stone floor of the station's grand entrance hall.

He approached the information counter and requested a timetable. The last train to Prague had already departed. The next train to Prague was scheduled for half past six the following morning. In the coffee house, Isaak picked up a discarded newspaper.

After a few minutes of observation, he joined a group of passengers, following them up the stairs and onto the platform without being stopped. But there was nowhere to hide for long before guards would become suspicious and start asking him questions. He waved to a departing train, pretending to say goodbye to someone and returned to the entrance hall. It was getting late, the passengers were thinning, the staff beginning to close parts of the building. He would have to find somewhere else to spend the night.

The only place Isaak could think of to find a measure of safety off the streets was the nearby Prater Park. Darting through the night, he hid in the undergrowth just off a main path. Alone in the dark, the events of the day hit him with full force. He worried about his father, feared being caught by the night watch and tensed at every sound: the low moaning of the wind, the rustle of small animals in the bushes. Although it was spring, the night was still cold. He was grateful for his wool jacket but still shivered through that sleepless night, thankful when the sun rose again.

Trying to ignore his growing hunger, he waited until quarter past six before joining the early morning commuters streaming into the station. He took up position once more behind a pillar, watching for a group of passengers he could blend into. He spotted a white-haired woman in a grey spring coat struggling up the stairs with her luggage. Without hesitation, he rushed over. 'Excuse me, *gnädige Frau*, may I carry your bags?'

She looked up at him, a relieved smile transforming her care-worn face. 'Thank you, young man, I would be much obliged.'

Isaak took the valise and basket, slowing his pace to match hers. The train would leave in minutes, but leaving her to struggle was unthinkable.

Surrounded by passengers hurrying past, they became invisible, just two more travellers in the morning rush. They reached the platform without drawing attention.

'Thank you for your help,' the woman said. 'The train to Prague leaves in less than two minutes. I was getting worried I might not get up the stairs in time and miss it.'

'I'm also going to Prague,' Isaak said.

The woman looked him up and down with her keen blue eyes. 'No luggage?'

'I ... ' Isaak paused. 'My parents have already gone ahead and taken my suitcase for me.'

She stared at him as if she could read through his excuse. Isaak did not know whether she meant to betray him. He kept his composure, his hands gripping her bags. 'In that case, would you mind helping me to the carriage with mine?'

'With pleasure, *gnädige Frau*.'

They found an empty six-seater compartment. She instructed him to put the small suitcase on the overhead luggage rack and the basket on the seat beside her. She indicated the seat opposite, and Isaak sat down. As their train departed the Nordbahnhof, the tension in his shoulders eased. But any relief he felt did not last long. Moments later, the conductor passed through the carriages calling, 'Tickets, please!'

Lilly was sitting at the edge of the boulder, her hands grasping its sides. 'And you had no ticket?'

'No ticket. No travel documents,' Isaak said. 'If they had caught me without a ticket, at the very least, the conductor would send me back to Vienna. At the very worst ...'

Isaak's eyes darted back and forth. The conductor was one carriage away. Isaak could try to run the length of the train, but the conductor would catch up with him eventually.

'Under the seat,' the elderly woman said, pointing to the floor.

Isaak looked at her, too stunned to move.

'Now!' she ordered.

Isaak dived under her seat. She draped her coat over the front and side of the seat, concealing him from view.

'Tickets, please!'

Isaak prayed as the conductor passed through their compartment, continued to the end of the train and came back again. He remained folded under her seat. Hours passed. The train stopped. Footsteps thudded through the carriage, a voice announcing in Czech, followed by German, 'Tickets and travel documents, please!'

Isaak hardly dared to breathe until the train started up again.

'We have crossed the border,' the woman whispered.

He was another step closer, but the danger had not yet passed. If he got off at the station in Prague, he would most likely be caught at the exit without a ticket. His only option would be to get off the train earlier.

'What time is it?' Isaak asked, his low voice muffled by the coat.

'Half past ten.'

The train was due to reach Prague at half past eleven. He would have to get off a short time before that. 'Can you please let me know when it is ten past eleven?'

The minutes ticked by slowly; his heart sped up.

The woman cleared her throat. 'It's ten past eleven.'

Isaak slipped out from under the seat. Outside the window he saw poplars and hedges lining the track and flat farmland beyond.

'Thank you for all your help,' he said.

The woman nodded. 'Go safely. And God protect you.'

Isaak edged his way to the last carriage. The train sped onwards towards Prague. His throat tightened; he could hardly swallow. He yanked off his tie and stuffed it in his pocket. He kept his eyes trained on the window, watching, waiting. His heart pounded in his ears. The train began to slow as the line gently curved in its approach to Běchovice, a village on the outskirts of Prague. This was his chance. Isaak placed his hand on the lever and pushed down. The door swung open to the clatter of wheels on the track. Wind whipped at his face. Isaak braced himself. He crouched low, pushed off, and leapt from the train. A jolt reverberated through his legs. He rolled down the grassy embankment, the air knocked out of him. For a few seconds he lay there. Stunned. The train continued down the track, the rumble fading away. Birds sang in the trees.

Isaak checked himself over. He ran his tongue over his teeth: all intact. A few bruises on his arms and legs and a more painful one on his hip, but he was otherwise unhurt. He picked himself up and brushed himself off. Shielded by the trees and hedges, he began walking, following the track to Prague. Three and a half hours later, on Friday afternoon, Isaak rang the bell of his uncle's house. Alexander's jaw dropped when he opened the door to find Isaak standing there, alone, in a wedding suit, tie tangling from his jacket pocket, his trousers dusty and torn.

Lilly shook her head. Speechless. Much like Alexander had been in that first instant. 'I … I …' She released a breath and found her voice. 'Did you contact your stepmother to let her know where you were?'

'My uncle called her straight away.'

Isaak's stepmother was as surprised as Alexander to learn that he had made it as far as Prague. By himself. She had assumed he would find somewhere close by to hide until it was safe to return home. In her distress, she had not made herself clear. But on reflection, she decided that if his uncle and aunt were happy to have him, it might be far safer for Isaak to stay there for the time being.

Days later, they learned that his father had been sent to Dachau. Mama did not want to take any further risks with Isaak, so he remained in Prague. Until that time, Isaak had not known his uncle's family all that well. He saw them once a year during the summer holidays. But his uncle and aunt took him in and cared for him like another son. They did their best to cater for his religious needs. Alexander and Janka treated him like their younger brother. His agnostic cousin even presented him with the pair of tefillin he had abandoned after his bar mitzvah.

Several months later, his resourceful mama secured three places on a transport to Eretz Israel for Isaak's father, younger brother, and herself. By securing the transport, she got Isaak's father released from Dachau on condition of their emigration. Meanwhile, in March 1939, the Nazis had invaded Prague. Isaak's uncle wanted

Alexander and Janka to leave, though he and Isaak's aunt could not; his aunt's elderly mother was too frail to travel and they would not abandon her. The decision was made. Isaak would travel with Alexander and Janka on transport for *chalutzim* to Eretz Israel, where Isaak and his parents would reunite.

'At least,' Isaak said, 'that had been the plan. That brief glimpse of them in Kladovo was the first time I had seen them in over two years.'

Lilly reached out her hand to him. Isaak took it in his. No words were needed.

'Isaak!'

His head snapped around. Alexander was sprinting towards them, his face flushed.

Isaak dropped Lilly's hand.

Alexander stopped short, breathing hard. His eyes darted from Isaak to Lilly and back. 'We need to talk.' His voice was tight, his expression unreadable. 'Now.'

'Of course.' Isaak blinked. 'Would you ... like to join us?'

'Alone.' Something in Alexander's eyes made Isaak's chest tighten.

Isaak stood. 'I'm sorry, Lilly. I ...'

He followed Alexander, glancing back at Lilly. She looked as confused as he felt.

Chapter 27

Isaak hurried after his cousin, struggling to keep up as Alexander barrelled ahead. Had Alexander heard bad news about Isaak's family? That would explain his grave expression. But surely Alexander would have taken him aside to break such news gently. Questions flooded Isaak's mind. His stomach churned.

Was Alexander angry with him for spending so much time with Lilly? Isaak knew Alexander had once harboured feelings for her, but his interest had since cooled and now he treated her like any other friend. Unless he was hiding his jealousy. If that was the case, Isaak would explain he had not meant to step on Alexander's toes. He would never do anything to hurt his cousin. Not that Lilly would ever look at Isaak in that way. He did not have his cousin's charisma. Besides, Lilly would consider him too young. They were friends. That was all. And he'd tell Alexander so.

Alexander reached their hut and waited by the door. He beckoned for Isaak to hurry. Isaak broke into a run. Why had Alexander brought him here, where others might witness his outburst? He could have taken Isaak to a secluded spot, behind the washroom, and punched him in the face. This was not about Lilly.

When Isaak reached him, breathing hard, Alexander patted his shoulder, as if offering preemptive comfort. Alexander's jaw was tense, but his eyes held no anger.

'We've received some news.' Alexander's voice quivered as he spoke. 'Devastating news. The British will not grant us amnesty.'

Isaak stared at him. 'What does that mean?'

'It means they won't allow us to remain in Eretz.'

'What?' Isaak felt the punch that Alexander had not thrown. 'They can't do that. After the *Patria* disaster, didn't the British decide, "in an act of mercy", to let us stay?'

'Not us.' Alexander took a shaky breath. He held open the door. 'Only the *Patria* passengers.'

The air was thick with cigarette smoke. All the other men from their hut were already there. Heads turned as they entered, then looked away again. They paced the creaking wooden floor or sat tense on their beds, ready to spring up. They looked like relatives in a hospital waiting room awaiting a surgeon's verdict. Max sat on the floor with his head in his hands, as if the patient had already died.

'Have you heard anything more?' Alexander said.

'Not yet,' Dov said, standing by the window, taking a drag of his cigarette.

'I don't understand,' Isaak said. 'We're all part of the same convoy. There were people from the *Atlantic* who were transferred to the *Patria* like Hannah and ...' He coughed, remembering Max.

'Apparently, there is an international maritime law that states that survivors of a shipwreck must be given shelter in the nearest port and be allowed to remain there,' Alexander said. 'However, it does not apply to those of us who were still on the *Atlantic* when the *Patria* sank.'

'It's not fair!' Isaak's voice rose. He knew he sounded more like a petulant sixteen-year-old than a twenty-year-old, but he was too wound up to stop himself.

'No, it isn't.' Alexander steered Isaak to his bed and sat beside him. 'But they don't care.'

Isaak's mind swam with questions. 'Can't we appeal? Why doesn't our Transport Committee speak to them?'

'Every member of the Transport Committee has resigned in protest.'

'No Transport Committee? Who will speak on our behalf? Do the women know yet? What about the *Patria* passengers? Where are they sending us?'

Alexander held up a hand to calm Isaak and slow his outpouring of questions.

'Fritz Haendel has agreed to represent us. He's speaking to the camp's commander right now trying to appeal on our behalf.'

'Fritz Haendel, the artist?'

Isaak had first met Fritz at the Slobodarna hostel in Bratislava, where he was part of another group from Prague. He was about ten years older than Isaak, and though they had little to do with one another, Isaak had always found him friendly. Once, in the Slobodarna's exercise yard, they'd had a brief conversation and discovered they had similar backgrounds: they had both been born in Vienna and ended up in Czechoslovakia. A talented artist, Fritz had recorded their experiences since Bratislava through his drawings and caricatures, many of which Isaak found amusing. Especially a caricature of Spiro, captain of the *Atlantic*, slumped in a chair, drunk – as he often was – a cigarette dangling from the corner of his mouth. Isaak had told Fritz the picture captured Spiro perfectly. Fritz smiled and thanked him.

'Yes. He's astute, level-headed, and speaks English well. If anyone can appeal to the commander's sympathy and convince him to intervene on our behalf, it's Fritz.' Alexander's jaw relaxed. 'When he returns, we will find out whether he was successful. The situation is serious, but we still have a chance. For that reason, we want to keep the matter to ourselves until we know more. No need to spread panic.'

The door opened. All eyes focused on Fritz as he stepped inside. At least twenty men from the surrounding huts piled in after him.

'I'm sorry.' Fritz dropped his gaze. 'The commander refuses to help us. He says the decision has been made and there's nothing more he can do. The man showed no sympathy, ignored my requests, and seemed unconcerned about our fate.'

'Did he tell you where they are transferring us?' Dov asked.

'No. All he would say was that they are sending us to a *better camp*. Whatever that means.' Fritz shook his head. 'He said we must have our cases packed and ready for collection by midnight when the guards will come to take them to a depot. We need to rise at five o'clock tomorrow morning and be ready for departure with one piece of hand luggage and two blankets each.'

The men stared at Fritz in stunned silence. Isaak felt the ground shift beneath him.

'What am I supposed to do?' Max's voice caught. 'Leave my wife and baby behind?'

A shadow crossed Fritz's face. 'I tried everything but nothing I said moved him. I'm sorry I let you all down.'

'It's not your fault,' Dov said, his voice flat. 'You tried.'

'Would you like me to go back and try again?'

'If I thought that would help, I'd say do it.' Dov shrugged. 'But you spoke to the commander for well over an hour.' Dov flung his cigarette stub out of the window and lit another. 'It seems there is nothing more you or anyone else can say that will change his mind.'

'I should go and spread the word through the camp.' Fritz took a step back. 'In the meantime, consider this further and discuss it amongst yourselves. When I come back, we'll talk more and decide our next steps.'

Shoulders slumped, Fritz walked to the door.

'What.' Isaak leapt from the bed and shouted after him. 'That's it?'

Alexander tugged his arm. Isaak ignored him and remained standing.

His hand on the door handle, Fritz turned to Isaak. 'I must let the others know before rumours spread.'

'You're just going to tell everyone to pack?'

'No. I'll tell them what the commander said,' he said in a measured tone. 'None of us expected this. We have to think it through carefully and then discuss it further.'

'There is no time to think and discuss. It's already after four o'clock. The guards will arrive at midnight to fetch our suitcases. We have to do something. Right now.'

Isaak looked around at the men, then back to Fritz. 'We all had to flee our homes. Some here have spent time in concentration camps.'

Max's head shot up.

'Many of us, including you, spent nine months detained in Bratislava in terrible conditions,' Isaak continued. 'We undertook a dangerous journey and risked our lives to reach Eretz. We even paid the British for the privilege. And they gave us their word.'

Men murmured in agreement.

'No other country would give us a visa. Where were we supposed to go? All we want is to live in peace and safety, without persecution. This is the only place we can call home. I'm not about to let them deport me. I'll do whatever it takes to remain in Eretz.'

'Isaak is right.' Max rose from the floor. 'We don't have the luxury of time for long discussions. My wife and baby son are here on the other side of the camp. I will not allow them to send me to who-knows-where for who knows how long! We have to act fast.'

Fritz touched Max's sleeve, then addressed Isaak, 'I agree with everything you have said. Now, what do you suggest we do?'

'I ... I don't know.' All eyes in the hut fell on Isaak. 'A protest?'

Fritz gave a wan smile. 'The Transport Committee already resigned in protest. I protested to the commander for over an hour. Even if we all march outside, I doubt it will do any good.' He shrugged. 'But we can try, if you like.'

'Then what about something larger than a protest?' Isaak grew desperate. 'We could fight them.'

'Fight who? The armed guards?' Fritz's brow furrowed. 'I don't think so. First, we have no weapons, nothing to defend ourselves with. We don't stand a chance. Second, there are women and children here. We can't risk them getting caught and injured in a skirmish. Third, how would it look if we resorted to violence?'

Isaak's cheeks coloured.

'And if we go down that route the British will consider us undesirable. We'll be playing into their hands, giving them every reason to deport us. We don't want to do that.'

Fritz was right. Isaak's suggestions had been rash, poorly thought out. Alexander came to stand beside Isaak and put an arm around him.

'It's good that you're trying to come up with solutions.' Fritz retraced his steps to the centre of the hut. 'The first one may not be the right one, but keep going. We will find a way to resist. Don't give up.'

Reuben, the *gaffir*, patrolling outside, peered through a window. '*Lo lazuz mimkomchem*!' he shouted. '*Lo lazuz mimkomchem*!'

Max leaned towards Alexander. 'What's he saying?' he whispered.

'Don't move from your places.'

Reuben wagged his finger for emphasis. 'Don't leave without showing resistance. The country's entire Jewish population will support you.'

Other *gaffirim* took up the call, their shouts reverberating through the men's compound.

'Well, it appears we have the support of the *gaffirim*,' Max said. That's something, at least.'

'Wait!' Alexander's eyes narrowed, then lit up. 'Perhaps that's the answer. What if we don't do anything at all?'

'I'm not sure I understand,' Fritz said.

'What if we don't pack, don't hand over our cases – and tomorrow morning when the guards say it's time to leave, we refuse to get out of bed?' Alexander's words sped up as his enthusiasm grew. 'Didn't you say the commander didn't seem to care either way? Well, if he can't be bothered with the hassle, maybe he's expecting us to resist. If the *gaffirim* are on our side, they aren't going to force us to move from our places. So if we don't cooperate, and the *gaffirim* don't cooperate, perhaps he'll call the whole thing off.'

Stefan, two beds along, sat straighter. 'So you're suggesting passive resistance?'

'Exactly.'

Stefan paused. 'That's not a bad idea.'

'It might not be enough to reverse the decision,' Fritz said. 'But it would cause a delay.'

'When the *gaffirim* change shifts, they could get word to the leaders of the *Yishuv*,' Dov said with growing enthusiasm. 'And when the leaders hear about this, I'm sure they'll take action. They'll appeal, arrange a large protest, or find another way to block our deportation. We need to buy time.'

'What's to stop the other guards from pulling us out of bed?' Max said.

'Hmm,' Dov said. 'Good point.'

'What if we all went to bed naked?' suggested a man who had joined them from a neighbouring hut.

The men tittered.

'I say,' said another, adopting his best impression of an upper-class English accent. 'That would give the guards rather a surprise in the morning when they throw back the covers.'

'A *big* surprise,' added his friend.

Raucous laughter erupted. Isaak felt his cheeks burn. He chuckled along with the others to conceal his embarrassment.

'Let's be serious,' Fritz said, once the guffaws had died down.

'I am being serious,' the first man said. 'The British are gentlemen. They won't force us out of bed if we're unclothed. And especially not the women.'

Alexander's mouth dropped open.

More nervous laughter.

'You know,' Dov said, 'it might just work. We have nothing to lose. Anything that will stop our deportation, or at least delay it until the Yishuv can come to our assistance, is worth a try. And above all, it makes a strong gesture of defiance.'

'It's a terrible idea,' said an older gentleman. Isaak remembered him from the deck of the *Atlantic*. Emil – Mr Pencil, as Janka called him – who had once tried to demonstrate to the girls how to fetch water from the sea, only to lose his bucket.

'All right,' Fritz said. 'Do you have a better suggestion?'

'I don't,' Emil said. 'Why do we need an act of defiance? I think we should just comply. After all, the commander said he's sending us to a better camp—'

'No!' they all shouted at once.

Aaron Zwergbaum stepped forward. A thoughtful man from their Prague group, he had kept a meticulous diary of their journey from the start. 'It would be shameful and cowardly to allow ourselves to be expelled from Eretz without resistance.'

Men nodded in assent.

'Shall we put it to the vote?' Fritz said. 'It's slightly crazy, but it's a good idea. I vote yes. What do you say?'

One by one, the men raised their hands, all except Emil, who stood with his arms folded, his expression twisted in disgust.

'I'll spread the word through the other men's huts. Let's hope most will agree. Fritz's gaze swept around the hut. 'Now, who is willing to break the news to the women?'

Just the thought of telling them, especially Gisela – or Lilly – left Isaak mortified.

Alexander raised his hand once more. 'I'll speak to my sister. And she can pass the word along.'

'Excellent,' he said. 'Now there's one more thing. The guards cannot find out what we're planning, or they'll attempt to stop us. So from here on, apart from Alexander speaking to his sister, we must only speak about this behind closed doors. So no one is to shout across to the *Patria* compound to let them know what we plan to do.' He focused on Max. 'I'm sorry. That means you cannot tell your wife either. Or give any hint you're saying goodbye.'

'I understand,' Max replied. 'I won't say a word. But I don't intend to leave so there's no reason to say goodbye.'

'That's the spirit.' Fritz smiled. 'If we can help it, none of us will be going anywhere.'

Isaak met Alexander's eyes. His cousin nodded. They had a plan.

Chapter 28

Tension gathered like storm clouds in the darkening sky. Rumours swirled in the wind; the *gaffirim*'s shouts, the first rumbles of thunder.

Lilly could not make sense of it. People clustered in groups. Whispers poured through the compound: Deportation. It could not be true. Lilly did not want to believe it.

As she stood by the fence, calling to Hannah, she stole discreet glances back towards the huts. Alexander and Isaak were still holed up inside. Fritz Haendel had joined them. Other men followed. No one had come out yet.

Lilly's heart thumped with dread but she maintained a pretense of calm and kept the rumours from Hannah.

'What are the *gaffirim* shouting about?' Hannah asked. Was her cousin growing suspicious?

Lilly shrugged. 'I have no idea.'

Alma sensed the ripple of unease. 'Do you know where Max is?' she asked. 'He disappeared earlier this afternoon and I haven't seen him since. That's not like him.'

'I'm not sure,' Lilly said. She felt guilty for lying, certain that Max was sequestered in the hut with the others.

'Is something the matter?'

'Hello, Alma, my love!' Max shouted from behind, running the short distance to the fence.

Lilly looked over her shoulder to see men streaming out of the door, Isaak and Alexander among them, heading off in different directions. Isaak caught her eye, as if wanting to speak, but he did not approach. Around the side of the men's hut, Alexander and Janka were locked in conversation, their heads pressed together.

'How's our little one doing?' Max said with what sounded like forced cheerfulness.

'He's a darling.' Alma held him up to Max in the fading light. 'Is everything all right? I wondered where you had got to.'

'Everything is fine. Just a ... hut meeting.'

He gave a quick, guilty glance in Lilly's direction.

'A hut meeting?' Alma said.

'Yes, about cleaning up. Things like that. You can imagine what it's like. So many men sharing the same living space. The *gaffirim* have ordered us to keep everything just so.'

'Ah! So that's what the shouting was about.' Alma laughed. 'The *gaffirot* expect the same from us. We've developed a cleaning rota amongst ourselves. I think you need us in there to get things organised.'

'We do indeed.'

Soon after, Janka joined them. She waved to Hannah, then whispered to Lilly. 'We need to speak privately. Right away. But say nothing to Hannah.'

'Hannah, I have to go.'

'A meeting too?'

'Er ...'

'Yes,' Max broke in. 'We all have to organise our huts.'

Janka gave Max a grateful look.

'Maybe it's because they are finally going to reorganise the camp,' Hannah said. 'Perhaps we'll soon be back together again.'

'I do hope so,' Lilly said.

'Well, I suppose I'd better go as well,' Hannah said. 'It's almost supper time. Let me know tomorrow if you hear anything more about us moving huts.'

Lilly blew her a kiss. 'I will.'

Hannah returned the gesture. 'See you in the morning.'

Lilly followed Janka back to the women's compound. 'I'll explain everything once we're inside,' she said in an undertone.

The other women were already waiting, perched on the ends of their beds. Janka secured the door, then faced her roommates. 'You may have heard rumours,' Janka said. 'I have just spoken to my brother, and he has asked me to pass on the news.'

'Please tell us this isn't true,' Gisela said, her voice breaking. 'They aren't planning to deport us?'

'Where are they sending us?' Jenny asked, her face taut and pale.

Janka took a steadying breath. 'The camp commander has ordered us to have our bags packed by midnight and to wake up tomorrow morning at five o'clock, ready for departure. All they have said is that it's a better camp. We haven't been told where they intend to send us.'

The women gasped.

So the rumours were true. After everything they had gone through, the risks, the hardships. For what – to be turned away and sent somewhere else?

'But my children and grandchildren are here ...' Gisela pulled out a handkerchief and covered her face.

Lilly's brother too. And Hannah.

The women were speaking at once. Soft sobs punctuated the turmoil. Lilly swallowed and tried to keep a grip on her emotions. She swayed on her feet, steadied herself against the bed, and sat.

'Wait,' Janka called above the commotion. 'Wait. Please let me finish. It may not yet happen. The men have come up with a plan to prevent our deportation. Or at least to stall it until the leadership of the Yishuv comes to our aid. The *gaffirim* are encouraging us to resist. We have the support of the country's Jewish population.'

Lilly lifted her gaze. 'What do they want us to do?'

'Passive resistance. Their idea is not to cooperate with the commander and guards. So we don't hand over our bags tonight. We won't even pack them. And tomorrow at five o'clock when they call for us to leave, none of us move. We stay in our beds.'

'We can do that, can't we?' Gisela glanced around the hut.

'Yes,' the women responded as one.

'Do you think it's enough?' Jenny said. 'Will the plan work?'

'That's not all. I'm not sure if all of you are going to like it.' Janka hesitated, her mouth twisted in discomfort. 'They want us to go to bed naked.'

The women giggled, embarrassed.

'Is that a joke?' Erika asked.

'I know it sounds crazy, but I'm serious,' Janka said. 'The men think that because the British guards are gentlemen, they will not dare pull us from our beds if they discover we're not wearing any clothes. The men plan to do the same. Well, most of them anyway. Some of the senior men, Emil among them, have raised objections. He thinks we ought to just comply.'

Erika tutted. 'Typical.'

'I understand this is an uncomfortable request,' Janka said. 'But what do you say? Are any of you willing to do it?'

The women looked at one another. No one answered.

Lilly considered the plan. Part of her wanted to resist. Part of her was mortified.

'Perhaps we could have a show of hands?' Janka said. She raised her own. 'I've already told Alexander I'm prepared to do so if it might stop our deportation.'

Erika's hand shot up. 'I'll join you.'

'Has Stefan agreed?' Jenny said.

'Yes,' Janka said. 'I believe almost everyone voted in favour.'

'Then I'll do it too.'

Lilly raised her hand. 'So will I.'

One by one, hands went up. Gisela hesitantly held hers halfway. 'Would it be all right if I keep on my underwear?' She gave a bashful smile. 'My large bloomers will still be enough to give the guards a heart attack.'

Janka grinned. She covered her mouth but a snort escaped, setting off the rest of the women. Soon the hut reverberated with laughter.

'All right,' Janka said, catching her breath. 'Gisela has permission to keep on her underwear.' Her expression grew more serious. 'There is one more thing. This stays between us. The guards might stop us if they find out. If you see anyone from the *Patria*, don't mention anything about the deportation or our plan. Is that understood?'

Once supper was over and Janka had spread the word, Lilly and her friends met the men for an evening walk.

'We're all agreed,' Janka whispered.

'Thank you,' Alexander said.

They walked in the darkness, the arc of the searchlights illuminating their path. The *gaffirim* acknowledged them as they passed. The *chevra* exchanged glances. Everyone knew what everyone else knew, but none of them could mention it. The weight of what was to come pressed down on them. Everything hinged on the next few hours.

Lilly tried to push the thoughts from her mind, but the question gnawed at her. Would their plan succeed? Would she still be in this compound tomorrow night, safe in the knowledge that Hannah was just on the other side of the fence?

At the entrance to the women's quarters, they hugged each other. Isaak seemed to hold Lilly slightly longer than usual before they prepared to part for the long night ahead. What were they supposed to say? What were the appropriate words? 'Good night' rang hollow against what was to come.

Then Alexander spoke, '*Chazak, chazak, v'nitchazek.*'

Be strong, be strong, and let us strengthen one another.

CHAPTER 29

An eerie silence settled over Atlit. Lilly checked her watch. It was only half past nine. How was that possible? Hours must have passed since the hands pointed to nine. The night had barely begun and already it had outstayed its welcome.

Half the women lay in their beds; naked under the covers. The rest complained of the cold as they undressed. Too agitated to lie down or sit still, Lilly paced – length, width, length again. She looked out of the window at the *gaffirim* on night shift patrolling the camp. She thought of Isaak, their earlier conversation, his hug before parting. Was it just reassurance, or something else? Of course it was nothing more. What was she thinking? She was older than him. And a widow. Yes, they were good friends. They were both also fearful of what was coming. His gesture offered reassurance, replacing the words neither could say. That was all.

She returned to her bed. Quarter to ten.

'You should get some sleep,' Gisela whispered, blankets tucked up to her chin. 'We have to be up early tomorrow.'

'For what? I don't intend to go anywhere. Do you?' Lilly said, her voice braver than she felt.

'You know what I mean.' Gisela gave a half-hearted smile. 'Lie down and relax. Even if you can't sleep.'

'I can't relax.' Lilly shifted from foot to foot.

'Then sit at least. I'm getting exhausted just watching you.'

Lilly dropped onto the bed and picked up her needle and thread. She resumed sewing the seam of her coat collar which she had deliberately unpicked earlier. The stitching gave her hands something to do. 'Aren't you nervous?'

'I'd be lying if I said no. We all are. But it does you no good to work yourself up like this.'

'Do you think this plan will work?'

Gisela's mouth pulled to one side as she considered the question. 'The men seem to think so. The *gaffirim* too.'

'And if it doesn't?'

'Let's not consider that yet.'

'I think it can succeed.' Janka climbed out of bed and wrapped a blanket around her body like a Roman toga. She came to sit beside Lilly. 'There's over one and a half thousand of us. That's a lot of people to move if we all resist. And don't forget, the *gaffirim* are on our side too. Without them, would the British even have enough manpower? Besides, do you think Alexander and the others from the group will give up so easily on their dreams of settling on a kibbutz? It's a good plan, Lilly. It can work. Especially since they don't know what we have in store for them.' Janka got to her feet, waved her hands about and wiggled her body in a hilarious interpretation of an ancient dance. In her enthusiasm, the blanket began to slip.

'Whoops. Careful there.' Erika giggled from the next bed.

Janka grabbed her blanket and hoisted it up before she lost it altogether. She sat back down, her face colouring as she secured it with a knot over her shoulder. Erika propped herself up on her elbow. 'And let's not forget Gisela's large bloomers which will give the guards a heart attack.'

'*Richtig*.' Gisela chuckled. 'They are my secret weapon.'

Janka clamped her hand over her mouth. She collapsed on Lilly's bed, shaking with laughter, and set off Lilly and Erika. Women around the hut shushed them, but each time Lilly and her friends looked at one another, it started them off again.

Janka gave an exaggerated sigh and wiped the tears from her eyes. 'You are all too much.'

'So says the crazy dancer.' Erika poked her arms from beneath the blankets and waved them around, imitating Janka. 'When's the next performance?'

Janka stuck her tongue out. 'Perhaps later.'

'Shh.' Gisela put a finger to her lips and pointed to Jenny fast asleep in the bed on her other side.

Lilly lowered her voice. 'How did she get to sleep that quickly on a night like this?'

'Because it's getting late and she's tired,' Gisela said.

Lilly had noticed Jenny's constant fatigue. She was always the first to go to sleep and took an afternoon nap most days. Her face was as pale as during her bouts of seasickness on the ship. Lilly hoped she was not coming down with something. The typhoid epidemic that had broken out on the *Atlantic* had continued to spread. Once this current deportation crisis had passed, Lilly decided she would have a quiet word, maybe suggest Jenny should get a checkup by one of the camp's doctors. Better yet, she'd ask Erika. As a volunteer nurse, she might have more insight.

'You girls should get to bed and do the same,' Gisela continued.

'Gisela's right,' said Janka, straightening from where she sprawled on Lilly's bed. 'We should get some sleep. We need to be alert for tomorrow.' She squeezed Lilly's shoulder. 'Try not to worry. Somehow, everything will work out.'

Lilly finished the last stitches on her collar and set aside her sewing. Around the hut, lamps went out one by one. She undressed and slipped beneath the blankets, wincing at the cold. Especially her feet. She missed her socks, which she wore every night. Curling into a fetal position, Lilly tucked her head under the covers and let her mind drift.

A truck engine rumbled in the distance. The unusual sound pulled Lilly from the edges of sleep. The camp lay at the end of the narrow road. No vehicle had a reason to drive this route, especially at night – unless they were heading for the camp. She lay still, her senses alert. The noise was getting louder. Closer. Tyres bounced over the rocks. Five seconds later, another jolt and crunch of stones, followed by the screech of a handbrake. An engine clattered, then fell silent, but the roar in the background intensified. This was not one truck. It was a convoy.

Army boots tramped along the path. Men were talking loudly. Someone whistled.

Lilly wrapped herself in a blanket, slipped out of bed and crept across the floor. She peered out of the window at the camp. The gates were not visible from her vantage point, but under the beam of the searchlight she saw dozens of armed soldiers patrolling the footpaths of their enclosure. Her insides churned. She ducked as a guard walked past, his eyes trained on the huts. Crouched below the windows, Lilly crawled back to bed.

'What did you see?' Janka whispered in the darkness.

'British soldiers,' Lilly said. 'Lots of them. And I don't see any of the *gaffirim*.'

Janka let out a long, drawn-out breath.

'They sound in high spirits, though,' Erika said. The noise had woken her too.

Around the hut, women stirred and whispered. The night rang with men's singing and laughter, and the faint strains of a violin playing what sounded like a Viennese folk song. Every sound seemed to go through Lilly's bones.

'What time is it?' Janka said.

Lilly squinted at her watch face. 'Quarter to twelve.'

'Let's see what they do at midnight.'

Ten to twelve.

Huddled beneath her blankets, Lilly listened to the voices outside.

Five to twelve.

'Remember,' Janka said in a hushed tone to all the women in the hut. 'No one is to say a word or follow any of their instructions.'

Twelve o'clock. Two minutes past. Five past.

Footsteps approached.

A knock at the door. A pause. Then the door creaked open.

'Good evening, ladies,' a man said, speaking in English. He turned on the light. Peering from beneath her blanket, Lilly saw his policeman's uniform.

'I am here to collect your suitcases.' He spoke in an official but respectful manner, projecting his voice without shouting.

None of the women moved.

'The camp commander has ordered you to pack your cases.' He hesitated, as if waiting for a response. 'If you have not yet done so, please do so now.'

Silence.

'May I remind you that you need to be up and ready to leave by five o'clock tomorrow morning.'

The hut remained still.

'So ...' The man strode through the hut, his boots tapping against the wooden floor. 'I'd highly suggest that you get up and pack your suitcases.'

A chill draught blew in from outside. He tramped back to the door.

'Well ...' he said after a short while. 'I suppose ... in the meantime ... I'll bid you all a goodnight.'

He exited the hut, shutting the door behind him.

Jenny groaned, shielding her eyes from the brightness. 'Does anyone mind if I turn out the lights?'

'Not at all,' Gisela said.

Jenny tottered over to the switch, plunging the hut into darkness once more. She staggered back to bed. 'Good night,' she mumbled.

Erika stared after her with a slight frown.

Janka lit her kerosene lamp, keeping the flame low. 'That seemed to go well, didn't it?'

'He gave up on us rather fast, didn't he?' Lilly said.

'Yes. I mean, he may have asked us to pack a few times, but he didn't try to force us,' Janka said. 'Our silence seemed to make him uneasy.'

'If that's enough to make him feel uncomfortable, can you imagine his reaction in the morning if he tries to get us out of bed and discovers we're naked?'

'He'll run for the hills.' Janka gestured to the window in the direction of the Carmel mountain range. 'Literally.'

'Will our resistance work?' Lilly said.

A slow smile spread across Janka's face. 'If this is anything to go by, it might.' She extinguished the lamp.

Chapter 30

'Good evening, all!' The policeman said. He snapped on the switch. Bright overhead lights illuminated the hut.

Isaak burrowed further under his blankets.

'May I please have your suitcases?'

No one stirred.

'If you haven't packed your cases yet, I suggest you do so now.'

No response.

The policeman moved deeper into the hut and slammed the door behind him.

'Don't forget,' he said, 'you're leaving at five o'clock. So please get up now, pack, and leave your luggage outside, in front of the hut, ready for collection.'

The policeman paused, as if expecting acknowledgement. None came.

'If you don't hand over your suitcases ...' he sing-songed, his voice rising in emphasis on the last word, 'they'll be left behind.'

The policeman tapped his foot. The noise reverberated in the silence.

'Have any of you packed already?' He walked down the aisle between the beds, every step controlled. 'Someone? Anyone? No one?' He let out a sharp breath. 'Righty-ho ...' He headed for the door. 'I suppose I'll see you all at five o'clock, then. Goodnight. Gentlemen.'

The door to their hut banged shut. Isaak listened to the policeman's receding footsteps and his knock on the neighbouring hut.

Perhaps the camp commander was hoping they would offer resistance and give him an excuse to call off this ridiculous action. And yet ... the politeness felt like a threat.

'So far, so good.' Alexander crossed the floor, switched off the light, and returned to bed. 'Round one to us, wouldn't you say?'

'That seemed too easy,' Max said

'He has to go through the motions and pass on his instructions,' Alexander said. 'But he sounded like he couldn't be bothered and quickly tired of trying to get a reaction out of us.'

'I hope you're right,' Max said. 'But his friendliness at the outset troubled me. We've seen this act before. They start off so cordial and polite, but it's bait and they trap us every time. I don't trust any of them. Why have they brought in so many reinforcements? And where have the *gaffirim* gone?'

'Hmm.'

'But this time at least we have a plan.' Isaak propped himself up on his elbow. 'We're one step ahead of them.'

'*Genau*!' Alexander pointed at him. 'We're going to cause such a headache for them when we refuse to get up in the morning. What are they going to do with hundreds of people lying naked in bed? Men and women.' He suppressed a laugh. 'We have to delay them long enough until the leaders of the Yishuv can come to our aid.' He lay down and pulled up the covers. 'Meanwhile, we ought to get a few hours of sleep so we're fresh for tomorrow morning.'

Isaak sank back on his pillow, listening to distant notes of a violin, drunken singing, and raucous laughter. With any luck, the British police would be too hungover in the morning and oversleep. In the next bed, Alexander tossed and turned. With tomorrow's uncertainty hanging over them, Isaak doubted anyone was sleeping easily, if they slept at all. Except perhaps for Stefan who was snoring softly.

It was just after one o'clock. Max stood silhouetted against the window, wrapped in a blanket, the wooden shutters open a crack. On the opposite side of the barbed wire lay the huts of the *Patria* women's compound where his wife and baby son slept, unaware he might be torn from them. Max ducked as the searchlight swept past, then rose again.

Two o'clock. Isaak was still wide awake. Each second brought them closer to an uncertain confrontation. Would their plan succeed? It was unfathomable that they were to be deported. Why had they been singled out? He understood why the British had granted the *Patria* survivors asylum. But what about the *Libertad* passengers in the opposite compound – why could they stay, but not the *Atlantic* passengers?

After this brief taste of Eretz, even in captivity, it would be unbearable to leave again. He prayed that in a few hours this crisis would be behind them and he could resume his daily routine: eating halva for breakfast and supper, performing magic tricks for the little ones, taking a daily stroll with Lilly.

Faced with being sent away, suddenly nothing seemed more appealing than a prolonged stay in Atlit. However long it took for them to be released from the camp, whether it be days, weeks, or months, he would appreciate that they were in Eretz and never again complain about the monotonous routine.

Isaak wondered how Lilly was faring. What about Janka, Gisela, Erika, and Jenny? Were any of them sleeping tonight?

Isaak reached for his watch.

'What's the time?' Alexander whispered.

'Quarter past three.'

'Less than two more hours to go.' Alexander sighed. 'Have you slept at all?'

'No,' Isaak said. 'You?'

'Me neither,' Alexander said. 'The sooner it comes, the sooner it's over. But I have to admit, my stomach is churning.'

Even Alexander. Isaak was not alone in his fear. At some point Isaak dozed off – he jolted awake to find it was already half past four. Thirty minutes to go: no getting back to sleep now. Outside, it was still dark. The soldiers' earlier merrymaking had ended. Apart from the footsteps of the routine patrol, all was quiet. Max remained by the window. Isaak folded his hands behind his head, watching the searchlight's beam trail across the ceiling.

Alexander rolled onto his side and faced Isaak. 'Are you awake?'

'Yes,' Isaak said. 'Did you manage to get any sleep?

'Five or ten minutes. Here and there. You?'

'Not much more than that.'

Alexander checked his watch. 'Ten to five.'

Max crouched below the window line and crawled back to bed.

'Did you see someone coming?' Alexander asked him.

'No,' Max said, diving under the covers. 'But I want to make sure I'm ready before they catch me unawares.'

Isaak stared at the watch face. Part of him wanted time to stop. Minute after minute ticked by.

Five minutes to five.

Three minutes.

One.

Isaak's heartbeat quickened.

Five o'clock.

He held his breath.

Five past five. Silence.

Ten past five. Their door remained closed.

'They did say five o'clock, didn't they?' Isaak said.

'Yes, absolutely,' Alexander said.

'Do you think they have forgotten about us?'

'More likely it's some kind of trick.' Alexander checked the time. 'Quarter past five. Perhaps they're waiting to see how long we'll stay in our beds before we get restless or hungry?'

'Or until we wet the bed.'

Alexander covered his face with his palm. Isaak immediately regretted his comment. He needed to learn to think more before he spoke. Then he realised Alexander was trying to stifle his laughter. '*Wunderbar*!'

'Shh.' Isaak went rigid. Was that a knock? He tapped his ear and pointed to the wall. They listened. Moments later came another knock, louder this time, followed by the sound of a muffled voice. Alexander nodded to Isaak. They would be next.

Isaak pulled his blanket over his head. His hands tingled. Then came the rap. Their door opened. Footsteps crossed the threshold. The policeman switched on the light. 'Good morning, all.'

Isaak recognised his voice as the same policeman who had visited them at midnight.

'Time to get up, gentlemen,' he said. 'May I please have your suitcases.'

No one moved.

'I take it you all packed your suitcases, as requested?' he said with an edge of sarcasm. 'Or maybe you were packing through the night, and that's why you're all tired this morning. Yes, that must be the reason.'

The door squeaked as he leaned against the frame.

'I'll give you one more chance. If you get up now, you'll still have time for breakfast.' He paused. 'But if you don't get up now, you won't eat. And if you don't hand over your suitcases – at once – they will be left behind.'

His footsteps struck the floor. 'Don't think I don't know what you're up to. I know you're all just pretending to sleep. You can hear me perfectly well.'

He ran a baton against the wooden legs of their beds; up the row of beds on the right side of the hut and then down the left side. Isaak felt the vibration through the bedframe as the policeman passed. He kept his eyes shut and remained still.

'Well, your little game isn't going to work,' the policeman continued. 'The trucks are already waiting outside. One way or the other, you're leaving.'

He strode to the entrance of the hut.

'I'll give you one last chance. Get up now, pack your cases, and then you can eat before you leave.'

He ground his heel against the wooden floor. 'I'm waiting. Are any of you getting up? This is your last chance.'

The door handle rattled in his hand. 'All right then,' he said in a low, too-calm tone. 'If that's what you want. Have it your own way.'

The door slammed; its force reverberated through the walls. The policeman's footsteps faded. He knocked on the neighbouring hut.

Isaak threw back his blanket and gulped air.

'What did he mean by that?' he asked.

Alexander shook his head, unsure.

Chapter 31

9 December 1940
Atlit Camp

It was far too quiet. Lilly had been awake all night, tension crushing her chest. Waiting, checking her watch, bracing herself for five o'clock. But now it was twenty past five and nothing moved.

'Why has no one come yet?'

Lilly, Erika and Janka lay in their beds, blankets up to their chins, ready to dive under the covers at any moment.

'Is it possible the commander has given up?' Erika said.

'If only,' Janka said. 'I don't think they'll give up that easily.'

'Unless the policemen got an eyeful of the men and fainted?' Erika said.

Janka grinned.

'And we didn't even bring out our secret weapon.' Erika giggled. 'Gisela's bloomers.'

'Don't.' Janka wagged a finger at Erika. She pressed her lips together, shoulders shaking. 'Don't start me off again. Not now.'

'Do you think we can get dressed yet?' Jenny called over.

'Not yet,' Janka said. 'It's still too early. We'll wait a while longer.'

Lilly slipped out of bed, wrapping herself in a blanket.

'Where are you going?' Janka said.

'To the window.'

'Be careful no one sees you.'

Dizzy from lack of sleep, Lilly swayed and steadied herself against the bed frame. She crept across the hut and parted the shutters just wide enough to see. Outside, stars dotted the black sky. The men's huts stood quiet. The searchlight swept across two policemen, but they were heading away from the men's compound towards the camp's entrance.

Lilly climbed back into bed.

'Did you see anything?' Janka said.

'Only two policemen on routine patrol.'

'Were any of the men outside?'

'No.'

Janka sat up. 'This makes no sense. The policeman who came into our hut at midnight said we all had to be up and ready to leave by five o'clock.'

'Maybe the crisis is over?' Erika said.

'Oh, I do hope so,' Gisela muttered. 'I want to stay here and be with my family.'

'Try not to worry,' Lilly said. 'One way or the other, we'll stop the deportation and you'll see them again soon.'

The door swung open. Before Lilly could hide beneath her blankets, the lights blazed on. Bracha, the *gaffira*, walked in.

'Good morning, ladies.' She shut the door behind her. 'You must get up now,' she said, her voice unnaturally loud, gesturing for the women to remain lying down.

'Yes, yes.' She shook her head. 'You must get up if you want to eat breakfast.' She waved her hands again and paused before opening the door. 'All right, I understand,' she said, as if she was having a two-way conversation. 'I will give you another few minutes to get ready and pack. I'll be back soon.' She gave them a tight smile, switched off the light, and eased the door shut.

'She knows what we're doing,' Lilly said. 'And she's trying to help us.'

'I wonder if someone's helping the men too,' Erika said.

'Yes, that has to be it,' Janka said. 'That must be why we haven't heard anything from their side yet. Now all we have to do is lie still and extend this delay until at least midday. With a bit of luck, by that time the *gaffirim* will get word to the leaders of the *Yishuv* and they'll come to our aid.'

'See, Gisela,' Lilly said, leaning towards her. 'The plan is working. Soon we'll see our families again.'

Gisela replied with an uncertain nod.

Ten past six. Almost an hour had passed since the policeman had left Isaak's hut. The muted grey sky, visible through the cracks in the shutters, was softening into a pale blue. The only sound from outside was birds chirping. Isaak and the others had stayed alert, but the policeman had not returned. Had he actually meant what he said: that they would have it their own way? Perhaps he had simply given up and had left them to lie in their beds.

Then it began. The crunch of boots swallowed the birdsong, steady and merciless.

Isaak's chest tightened. The chilling rhythm transported him back to Vienna. The night of the Anschluss. When Nazi troops marched into the city and trampled over their lives. He took a deep breath to calm himself. Vienna was far away. He was in Eretz Israel now. Here the policemen were gentlemen. Well, most of them, anyway. If he disregarded their reception at Haifa Port – but those must have been the exception to the rule; angry, perhaps humiliated, after the *Patria* disaster.

The footsteps grew louder, drew nearer, closing in.

Perhaps this was all for show. The guards at Atlit had treated them fairly. Up until now. These additional recruits only wanted to scare the men into getting out of bed. Nothing more. Isaak had nothing to fear.

Objects struck the walls of nearby huts. Men barked orders.

The police had to make a show of authority. Of course they did. They could not be seen to surrender without a fight to a bunch of uncooperative, unarmed Jewish refugees.

From the next-door hut came a crash. Wood cracked and splintered. Officers roared. Men cried out.

Isaak's breath came in short bursts.

Batons pounded on the walls. The bangs reverberated through their hut. The door flew open.

'Get up!' a police officer roared. 'Get up at once!'

All fifty men remained still and silent.

'You have two choices,' he said in a low, controlled voice. He paced down the aisle between the beds. 'Either you get up voluntarily. Or …' He pivoted. 'We will be compelled to use force.'

Under the blanket, Isaak barely breathed, each inhale a risk.

'This is your last chance,' he said from the doorway. 'You have been warned.'

He clicked his fingers. Several pairs of boots tramped into the hut.

'Right then,' he said. 'Begin.'

Startled gasps pierced the air. Before Isaak could peer out, a policeman wrenched off his blanket and flung it to the floor. A sharp intake of breath escaped Isaak's throat. Exposed and ashamed, he rolled onto his side, away from the door, trying to cover himself.

The policemen went down the rows until they had ripped off everyone's blankets.

'Get up at once!' the policeman bellowed.

No one moved.

'Carry on,' the policeman called to his men waiting at the back of the hut. They divided, four to either side.

Sharp kicks. A thud. A moan.

The policemen kicked the flimsy legs out from beneath the beds. One after the other, the frames collapsed, sending the wooden slats, straw mattresses, and men tumbling to the floor. At intervals, they swung their batons, swiping at arms, legs, buttocks. Moaning, the men curled up on the floor where they fell. But no one got up.

A cold pair of eyes stared down at Isaak as a burly policeman kicked away the bed legs. The bed collapsed beneath him, sending a jolt through Isaak's spine. He hunched on his side, the wind knocked out of him. The next bed collapsed. Alexander landed beside him and groaned as a baton struck his thigh.

The policemen continued until they had completed their wave of destruction and exited without a backward glance. Batons rained on the hut next door. 'Get up!' the police officer shouted. The cycle started again.

Alexander rubbed the red welt on his leg and rolled over to Isaak. 'Are you all right?'

'Just about,' Isaak said, his breathing steadier. 'How about you?'

'*Ja ja*.' He brushed away Isaak's concern. 'I'll be fine. *Arschlöcher*,' Alexander muttered. 'All of them.'

Isaak tugged at his blanket, caught under the broken bed base, and covered himself. 'What now?'

'We stay right where we are,' Alexander said.

'On the floor?'

'Right here. We need to hold out for another few hours.'

A shout and several thuds jolted Hannah awake. She opened her eyes and sat up. It was just after six o'clock. Darkness shrouded the hut. The other women were still fast asleep. Chaim whimpered beside Alma.

'There, there, my *schatzi*.' Alma stroked him. 'Mama is here.' She cradled Chaim and drew him close. He latched on, sucking with urgent hunger. She looked across to Hannah. 'Another nightmare?'

She often woke Alma crying out in the night, haunted by the *Patria*.

'I thought I heard shouting and banging—' There it was again. Loud voices. Crashes. 'Did you hear that?'

'Yes. What is it?' Alma said.

'That's what woke me a few moments ago,' Hannah said. 'So I wasn't dreaming.'

Was that someone shouting 'Get up'?

Alma's eyes narrowed. 'Who's making such a racket this early in the morning?'

Hannah knelt on her bed, opened the window and pressed against the wooden shutters. They remained shut. 'That's strange.' Hannah pushed harder. She struck the wood with the heel of her hand. 'They seem to be stuck.'

'They might have warped from the rain,' Alma said. 'Try another one.'

Hannah moved to the next window, opened it and pushed the shutters. 'This one won't open either.'

Hannah hurried to the door, turned the handle and pulled. It did not budge. She tugged it several more times. 'It's stuck.'

'Here, let me try.' Alma climbed out of bed with Chaim. She crossed the floor, handed the baby to Hannah, and yanked on the door. It would not move.

'It's locked.' In the dim light, Alma's eyes widened. She rattled the handle again. 'They've locked us in.'

Chapter 32

Sunlight sliced through cracks in the window shutters. It was after eight o'clock. The men had lain on the floor for over an hour, awaiting the next assault. None came. Silence stretched over the hut, taut with apprehension.

'Could it be over?' Isaak shifted amongst the splintered bed frame.

'It's possible.' Alexander rested on his elbow. 'Maybe that was their display of authority? Let's hope the commander has given up on enforcing the deportation order. For the time being, at least.'

'Do you think they were surprised when they ripped off our blankets?' Isaak said.

One side of Alexander's mouth lifted in a restrained grin. 'I doubt they were expecting to find us all naked. It must have insulted their gentlemanly sensibilities.'

'Such gentleman.' Max's voice, tight and bitter, came from Alexander's left. 'And so much for Reuben the *gaffir*'s reassurance that no one would beat us.'

Stefan pushed himself up to see Max better. 'Are you hurt?'

'No. But he looked at me with such hatred and threatened me with his baton …' Max shrank back as if the policeman was still standing over him.

'They didn't like us making fools of them,' Alexander said. 'That's why they had a tantrum and lashed out. But they can't really do anything else to us because we have done nothing to provoke them. And they won't want to touch us with their bare hands. Unless we get up of our own accord, they are powerless.'

'They have already crossed a line,' Stefan replied. 'Destroying our beds. The welt on your thigh. That is serious violence. If word were to get out British policemen attacked unarmed Jewish refugees, it could cause them serious embarrassment. We ought to complain to the commander as soon as possible.'

Isaak kicked a bed leg aside and shifted position. 'How do we know when it's safe to get up?'

'We still need to wait a while,' Alexander said. 'At least until after midday. By then the *gaffirim* should have got word to the leadership of the *Yishuv*. They'll enlist the help of the people, order a general strike, and block the roads so that the British can't transport us anywhere. The commander will have to inform Harold MacMichael, the British High Commissioner. No doubt he'll be furious. But left with no other choice, he'll have to report to the government in London. Hopefully, they'll reverse the deportation order and allow us to remain like they did the *Patria* survivors.'

'So you mean to say we'll miss breakfast this morning?' A hint of playfulness crept into Isaak's voice.

'I'm afraid so,' Alexander said. 'Pity, though. I'm starting to get hungry. I could do with a bit of halva right now.'

Isaak grabbed his rucksack and reached inside. 'Just as well I saved some then, wasn't it?' He withdrew a brown paper package and unfolded it to reveal a small block of halva.

Alexander grinned. 'Trust you to have some.'

'It's always good to be prepared,' Isaak said. 'My mama always used to say, "never travel without food." I'll remember how hungry I was when I escaped from Vienna. By the time I reached your home, I hadn't eaten for over twenty-four hours.'

Isaak broke the block into pieces, took a tiny bite for himself, offered one to Alexander, then passed the rest on to Max, Stefan, and a few of the other men lying close by. They ate every crumb.

'Thanks, Isaak.' Alexander stretched out. 'That should keep us going until lunch.'

'I've got a sandwich packed too, in case we have to miss lunch as well.'

Alexander snorted. 'Of course you do.'

Isaak's head shot up.

'What—' Alexander began and stopped.

The stomp of military boots echoed down the path.

They were returning.

The footsteps grew louder, nearer, then halted outside.

'Men, roll up your sleeves!' A policeman's voice rang out. 'We have an interesting job to do.'

Isaak edged closer to Alexander, searching his face for answers. Alexander shook his head.

Roars erupted. The troops charged into a neighbouring hut. They heard scuffling, then cries and howls.

The noise grew louder, spilling from the hut.

'Get back here, you!' a policeman bellowed.

Cries, shouts, and pounding feet rushed past their hut.

Beneath the window came the sound of a blow. A howl of pain. A thud as he fell.

Alexander flinched at the man's weakening moans. Cold swept through Isaak. He drew his blanket tighter around him. Close by, Max lay curled up, shaking, covering his head with his hands.

Then a scraping sound. Like a rolled-up rug, or a sack of potatoes, being dragged along the ground. The low moans faded, lost beneath the screams of other men.

Dread gripped Lilly as screams and crashes from the men's side tore through the silence. The women exchanged terrified glances, their faces pale and drawn in the shadows.

'*Mein Gott*!' Gisela said. 'What is happening?'

'It sounds like they're throwing luggage around,' Erika had said.

'That's not luggage,' Lilly said with certainty. 'It's wooden furniture cracking.' She knew the difference. During Kristallnacht she'd heard luggage thrown around her father's shop, furniture splintering when the mob ransacked her neighbours' home.

'Perhaps the police are trying to get the men up by overturning their beds?' Janka said.

'They wouldn't do something like that,' Erika said. 'Would they ...?'

Were they about to receive the same treatment? But after a few minutes, the crashing and splintering subsided. The police left. None of the men emerged and no one entered the women's compound. An eerie lull descended over the camp.

An hour passed. Nothing happened.

'It looks like the police have given up,' Janka said. 'The men's resistance must have worked. Any minute now someone will come to tell us it's over, I'm sure of it. Then we can get dressed.'

Another half hour ticked by. No one came. Instead, renewed sounds of terror reached their hut.

Lilly wrapped herself in a blanket and slid from her bed into a crouch. A terrible sense of déjà vu washed over her. Just like that November morning in Vienna when she was awoken by the sound of breaking glass.

'Be careful,' Janka said.

Lilly crept across the floor, below the window line. Shouts and screams continued to fill the air. She and Salo had stood helplessly by the window as rioters destroyed the Jewish-owned shops below

– including her father's. The police arrested two men from the building opposite while their wives looked on, their pleas ignored. The tumult rose through the stairwell as the mob ripped through the apartment below. They had knocked on every door, searching for shelter.

This could not be happening again. Not now. Not here.

She peered from the side of the window. The breath froze inside her.

'What do you see?' Janka said.

Lilly opened her mouth to speak but no words came, only a broken sound.

'What is it?' Erika said.

Lilly pointed a shaky finger at the window.

Janka and Erika scrambled from their beds to her side and let out thin gasps.

One by one, the men were being dragged from their huts, beaten and bloodied. Policemen grabbed each arm and hauled them up the path. Those who resisted were subdued with a kick or punch. Four men fled from a hut. Their desperate cries rang out as they ran naked in different directions pursued by police armed with long batons. Two policemen trapped a man near the women's enclosure. One struck him across the back of his head with the baton. He fell.

'Get up!' the second policeman shouted. He kicked him in the ribs. 'Get up, dammit!'

The man lay on the ground. Unconscious. Blood pooled beside him.

Lilly could not bear to watch. She could not tear herself away. Black dots clouded her vision. She saw Salo's face again. His beautiful face, beaten and bloody. Unrecognisable. Unable to talk. She cradled him in her arms as he faded away.

The policemen rolled the unconscious man in a blanket, picked him up, and dragged him off.

'*Um Gottes Willen*!' Janka cried. 'They are going to kill our boys!'

Chapter 33

Isaak's stomach churned as shouts and crashes erupted from the neighbouring hut. Screams of pain pierced the air. He swallowed the bitter taste of bile. Their hut would be next.

'Perhaps we should make a run for it?' Isaak said.

A few men lying nearby nodded.

Alexander's gaze flicked from door to windows, then back.

Heavy boots thundered past their hut. 'Grab him!' yelled a policeman.

Beyond the walls, a blunt weapon found its target. A man howled. A heavy thud – body meeting ground.

Alexander's jaw tightened. 'I don't know if we'd be any better off.'

'If we escape now, before they come, we might stand a chance,' Isaak said.

'Where can we run?' Max pressed against the wall, his eyes darting wildly. 'They have us caged in on all sides.'

'If we stay here we're also easy targets,' Isaak said. 'Listen to what's happening next door.'

'What if we run to the women's huts?' Stefan said. 'We could hide there.'

'If they find us, we may put the women in danger. We can't risk that,' Alexander said.

'No.' Stefan took off his glasses and rubbed his eyes. 'We can't.'

Isaak raised himself to the window.

'Careful!' Alexander said. 'Don't let them see you.'

Isaak scanned the scene before he crouched down.

'What do you see?' Alexander said.

'Police are dragging out men from the hut next door, some injured and bleeding.' Isaak took a shaky breath. 'I saw them giving chase to one man trying to run away. There are policemen posted at intervals along the path. They're holding long sticks.'

'The women's compound might be our only chance,' Stefan said. 'And if they attack, we'll defend the women.'

'Maybe.' Alexander let out a slow breath.

'Come on!' Isaak was already on his feet. 'What are we waiting for?'

Max hesitated. 'What about the police outside? They're ready to pounce.'

'We'll run in a zigzag,' Isaak said. 'There's no time. Let's go!'

The door flew open and policemen charged in, voices roaring, batons swinging. Isaak and the others stumbled back, but the wall blocked any retreat.

The policemen lashed out at anyone within reach. Wood clashed with bone.

Feral roars. Desperate cries.

Two policemen: a burly one with a boxer's nose, his oversized limbs straining against his uniform, and a younger, freckle-faced one with ginger hair, cornered them against the wall and lashed out with their batons.

Max cowered. Isaak dived to the floor. The ginger-haired one hit Stefan's arm. The burly one struck Alexander's hip. He doubled over with a groan.

'Look!' the ginger-haired policeman shouted. 'That one's getting away.'

In the fracas, Max seized his chance, crawling between the legs of policemen too busy swinging their batons to notice. The burly policeman charged through the hut, shoving men aside in pursuit of Max, who had since disappeared out of the door. With the ginger policeman's attention diverted, Stefan bolted. Before Isaak could follow, the policeman lunged. Isaak dived sideways. The baton missed and slammed into the wall. The policeman raised it again, but Alexander stepped forward. He shielded Isaak, ready to take the blow. The man hesitated. He dropped his hand, cocking his head, as if granting a moment's mercy.

Alexander pushed Isaak through the chaos towards the door. Howls surrounded them. The metallic smell of blood mingled with sweat.

'To the women's huts!' Alexander said.

One moment Isaak was blinking against the sunlight, the next darkness engulfed him. He thrashed, fumbling with the blanket thrown over his head. He freed himself, tossed it aside and sprinted after Alexander and Stefan, who had reached the entrance to the women's compound. Stefan tugged on the gate. Locked. He rattled the lock frantically, but it held fast.

They veered towards the rear of the camp. A policeman hidden out of sight swung his baton. Isaak sidestepped, but it still clipped his head, stinging. He kept running; his lungs burned.

Another policeman, waiting at the perimeter fence, cut them off. The three of them darted onto the path behind the huts.

Max and two others emerged from a gap between huts, a policeman in pursuit. He threw a blanket over the last man and dragged him to the ground.

Ahead, three policemen waited, batons raised. They wheeled around. Two more were closing in, batons ready.

Isaak's chest heaved as he and the others swerved into the next gap to the right. Straight into an ambush. Police surrounded them and ordered them to lie on the ground. Nine of them lay in a circle, face down, hands on their heads.

The commander dragged his left leg as he approached. Stefan howled as the commander's boot struck his shin.

'Get back into your hut and get dressed!' he ordered.

Alexander raised his head. 'All right.' He caught Isaak's eye. 'We will all go to our hut.'

'I'm giving you two minutes,' the commander said.

Alexander stood up and half-ran to their hut. From the entrance, he beckoned for the others to hurry. As soon as the last man was inside, Alexander slammed the door and pressed his back against it. 'Quick!' he said. 'Grab the broken beds. Let's block the door.'

Alexander wedged a bed slat under the handle. The men dragged splintered wood and mattresses across the floor, piling them against the door. A knock came less than thirty seconds later.

'Open up!' A policeman tried the handle. 'Open up at once.' He knocked harder, tried the handle a second time, groaning as he threw his weight against it. He followed up with a kick. 'Dammit! Those bastards have blocked it from the inside. Get over here and give me a hand.'

They hammered the door. The flimsy barricade shuddered. It wouldn't hold for long. Minutes. If they were lucky. Any hope of resisting until midday vanished. It was not even nine.

The door buckled inwards. The wedge snapped.

'That's it lads, keep going,' the policeman said as the men heaved.

The boards and mattresses propped in front of the door began to slide.

Alexander retreated to the left wall, away from the door. He beckoned the others. Isaak spotted his rucksack lying in the debris by the opposite wall and lunged for it.

'Isaak!' Alexander hissed. 'Get back here.'

A kick. A blow. A push.

The door surrendered another centimetre.

'Nearly there. Give it another hard shove.'

Isaak grabbed his rucksack.

The door burst open.

A policeman charged in, but the barricade stopped him short. His foot caught. He pitched forward and landed head first. He cried out.

Isaak froze.

Howling and swearing, the policeman struggled to his feet. He clutched his nose, blood spurting through his fingers. His eyes locked with Isaak's. 'Grab them!' he yelled.

A wall of policemen, at least two for every man in the hut, blocked his escape. He edged over to Alexander.

The police set upon them. Fists, batons, and boots struck flesh. Men crumpled to the floor, crying out.

'Come on, Hitler!' a policeman shouted as he smashed his fist into Alexander's face. Alexander sprawled backwards.

Isaak sprang to his cousin's aid, but a blow to the side of his head stopped him short. Colours blurred. Spots filled his vision. He didn't see the punch that followed. It slammed into his gut and drove the air from his lungs. Isaak collapsed to the floor, gasping for air.

A hand took hold of Isaak and helped him to his feet. 'I've got you.' Alexander pulled him from the hut, half-dragging him. Screams rang in Isaak's ears. It was only when a rush of cold air hit his face that Isaak realised the screams were his own.

A blanket landed over Isaak's shoulders and his vision gradually cleared. Blood streamed from Alexander's head. A policeman threw a blanket over him too and wrenched him away from Isaak.

'Doctor,' Alexander said, his voice faint. He swayed on his feet. 'We need a doctor.'

The policeman snarled. 'Shut up, you bloody Jew.' He pressed his baton under Alexander's chin, forcing his head upwards. 'This is your doctor.'

Two policemen dragging Max ahead glanced behind at the commotion. Their attention diverted, Max wrenched himself free from their grip and flung off his blanket.

'Oy!' one shouted. 'Get back here.'

Pursued by the policemen, Max raced toward the fence separating him from his wife and grasped the barbed wire.

'Alma!' The shout ripped from his throat. 'Alma!'

A baton crashed against his skull. Another struck his stomach.

Max crumpled to the ground.

One policeman landed a swift kick to his ribs. 'Get up!'

'Max!' Isaak yelled as the policeman kicked him a second time. Rough hands clamped onto Isaak's arms and hauled him away.

'Max!' Alma cried.

Was it his voice she and Hannah had heard through the commotion, or had they imagined it? For the past hour, shouts, screams, and thuds had seeped through their sealed hut.

Alma yanked the handle of the locked door. She pulled and tugged, but it would not yield. Alma ran to the first window and tried to force the shutters. She tried the second window and the third.

'Max!' She pounded against the shutters.

Hannah tried the windows on the other side. None of the shutters would budge.

Alma returned to the door, banging and kicking it. 'Let me out! I want to be with my husband.'

Her yells woke baby Chaim, but Alma did not notice. He flapped his arms and kicked his little legs, his cries growing more desperate. Hannah approached Alma's bed, lifted Chaim, and rocked him.

'Let me out.' Her knuckles were red and raw, her kicks growing weaker until she sank to the floor. 'I want to be with my husband.'

Outside, engines rumbled to life. Hannah sat beside Alma and placed Chaim in her arms. Alma hugged him close and drew him to her breast. Exhausted, she rested her head on Hannah's shoulder.

'Max.' Alma's voice was barely audible. 'Please don't leave me.'

CHAPTER 34

Two policemen gripped Isaak's arms and marched him up the path. Ahead, two more were dragging Alexander. He stumbled and fell. They yanked him up. At the camp's exit, policemen flanked each side of the fence. They grinned as they shouted taunts.

'Look at the bloody Jews!'

'Goodbye. And good riddance.'

'Enjoy your one-way ticket out of here. You won't be coming back.'

Shoves sent Isaak and Alexander through the gate. Blood ran into Isaak's eyes and mixed with his tears.

On the other side of the barbed wire fence stood the *gaffirim*, locked out of the camp, their heads bowed. To their right, a line of tarpaulin-covered lorries awaited, watched over by armed soldiers.

As they passed the *gaffirim*, Alexander shouted, his voice hoarse, 'How can you just stand there and not say anything?' The *gaffirim* stared at the ground. 'Brothers, please help us! Have mercy. Don't let them deport us from Eretz Israel.'

A rough hand from behind sent Alexander stumbling forward. 'All right, we've heard quite enough from you.'

The two policemen picked Alexander up by his arms and legs and tossed him into the back of a lorry, like a sack of grain.

Then Isaak found himself airborne. For an instant, nothing beneath him. He landed with a thump, his fall cushioned by the rucksack he'd managed to keep hold of. Four British soldiers stood at the corners of the lorry bed, rifles with fixed bayonets at the ready. They looked away, disgust plain on their faces. Isaak crawled across the lorry bed to sit beside Alexander, the rough fabric of the military blanket scratching against his skin.

Six other wounded and defeated men from their hut were already in the truck. More followed – Stefan and Dov among them – thrown into the back, accompanied by the slur, *bloody Jews*.

'You know, this reminds me a bit of how we left Danzig,' Stefan said. 'The Nazis forced us to take a last walk of shame through the city centre to reach the train station. Townspeople lined the street, spitting and hurling insults at us as we left the city of our birth. "*Saujude*!" "Go back to Palästina!"' His chest heaved. 'It was humiliating. Even so, I was grateful that Jenny and I had the opportunity to leave. We were returning to our ancestral homeland to start our lives over, free from hatred and persecution. I could become a teacher once again. Have a family ...' He shook his head. His dreams torn from his hands. 'But even here we aren't welcome and they send us away with insults. Only for the crime of being Jewish. Where are we supposed to go?' His voice choked. 'Where do we belong?'

Tears streamed down Alexander's face. Isaak had never seen his older cousin cry. He looked around the lorry filled with naked men wrapped in rough Palestine Police blankets. The men all sat and wept.

The engine spluttered to life. Policemen lifted the last man onto the lorry bed. This time with a little more care. Max, lying on a stretcher, semi-conscious, his face beaten and bloody.

'Alma,' he mumbled. 'Alma. Chaim.'

Isaak reached for Max's hand. 'You'll see them soon,' Isaak said to comfort him, though he knew his words were a lie.

With the rear tarpaulin secured, hiding them from view, the lorry rumbled away from Atlit.

Isaak had hidden from Nazis in a synagogue basement and fled his home in Vienna. He had been locked up for nine months in Bratislava. Suffered the worst privations on the Atlantic. Stranded at sea. But nothing – nothing – he had endured could compare. This was worse than all of that. This felt like the end.

The rich aroma of freshly brewed coffee permeated the apartment as Eugen followed its scent to the living room, where Leo Klein sat at the dining table with two cups at the ready.

'Good morning. How did you sleep?'

'Very well.' Eugen sat opposite him at the table. 'After the long journey down from the kibbutz yesterday, I really needed it. I didn't expect I'd need to make this journey so often. Good think you'd already moved from Tel Aviv to Haifa.'

'Since you're spending so much time in Haifa, why not consider moving here?' Leo winked. 'Your wife might get to see a bit more of you.'

Eugen laughed. 'But we enjoy living on the kibbutz.'

Remarkable to think that until a fortnight ago, Leo had been a complete stranger. Now he felt almost like family. They first met at Haifa Port, standing beside each other in the crowd, waiting for relatives arriving on the SS *Atlantic*. After two hours, Leo had approached to Eugen and asked whether he knew what time the passengers were supposed to disembark. Eugen recognised Leo's accent as Viennese, and they struck up a conversation. Eugen said he was waiting for his sister, Lilly, and his cousin, Hannah. Leo, for his mother, Gisela Klein. The two of them tried to figure out whether they had ever met in Vienna or had friends in common and discovered they had mutual acquaintances. They reminisced about their old hometown, spoke about their own journeys to Eretz Israel, and wondered whether Eugen's sister and cousin might have got to know Leo's mother on their long voyage.

Three more hours passed this way. It began to rain. The *Atlantic* had not yet entered the harbour, and it was unlikely that the passengers would disembark that day. Leo's wife and two children were at home, waiting to meet their grandmother for the first time. Leo's brother was up north, ready to travel down for the reunion once word came. Eugen had his own dilemma. His wife had remained on the kibbutz, expecting Eugen to bring Lilly back by late afternoon. Should he travel back that evening and make the long bus trip again the following morning or should he find a hotel? Leo settled it, inviting Eugen to stay in their home for the night.

Early the following morning, they returned to the port and watched in horror as the *Patria* capsized. Some of the *Atlantic* passengers had already been transferred onto that ship. Eugen and Leo spent two anxious days searching for information. They tried the harbourmaster, the Jewish Agency, the police station, local hospitals. They eventually found the name of Eugen's cousin, Hannah, on a registry of survivors, but there was no mention of Lilly or Gisela on any list of survivors, victims, or missing.

Eugen took a sip of coffee and gave an appreciative sigh. 'Thanks for having me once more. I'm sorry to keep imposing on you both.'

'We're happy to have you. At least someone is getting use out of my mother's room in the meantime.'

'Well, I hope they'll be released from Atlit soon.'

'Don't set your hopes too high,' Leo said. 'If in our meeting today with the Jewish Agency they can even help us arrange a visit to see them in Atlit, that would be a good start.'

Eugen took another sip, wondering about their chances.

A loud, steady wail rose from outside.

'What is that?' Eugen set down his cup. It clattered against the saucer.

Leo stiffened, eyes wide, listening. 'I think it's an air-raid siren.' He scraped his chair back. 'Let's go to the stairwell.'

They hurried out of the apartment as the haunting wail continued; the slamming of the neighbours' doors echoed through the stairwell.

'It could be the Italians again,' Leo said. 'I first heard a siren in early September before we moved here. That terrible air raid in Tel Aviv. Over a hundred people killed.'

'I remember reading about that in the newspaper,' Eugen said. 'Did you hear the explosions?'

'And how. Our apartment was less than a ten-minute walk from where the bombs landed. The entire building shook.' The blood drained from his face. 'Oh God, I hope my wife and children are somewhere safe. They went on an outing to the park with her parents this morning.'

'I'm sure they'll be fine.' Eugen patted Leo's shoulder. The siren had ended. He held still, listening for the rumble of bombers.

'I don't think it's an air-raid,' a woman in thickly-accented Hebrew called down from the floor above. 'When we had the other ones, the siren was a rising and falling wail. This sounded more like a steady pitch.'

'What is it then?' Leo called up to her.

'Curfew!' A man with a hearty, booming voice shouted in German from the floor below. 'British curfew.'

'Are you sure?' Leo said.

'Yes, they announced it on the wireless.'

'Why is there a curfew?'

'Who knows? Maybe some disturbance between the British and the Arabs or the Jews. Or all three.'

'How long will it last?' Eugen said.

'They didn't say,' the man said. 'A few hours, perhaps.'

'A few hours?' Eugen was relieved they were not about to be bombed by the Italians, but frustrated that they would miss their appointment at the Jewish Agency.

'It looks like you might have to stay another night.'

Eugen shifted. 'I don't want to put you to any more trouble.'

'No trouble at all.' Leo smiled, his relief plain at the false alarm. He opened the front door. 'We might as well sit inside while we wait. The coffee is still warm.'

Chapter 35

The men were gone. Their camp lay empty. Their screams still rang in Lilly's ears. Many women sobbed. Lilly was numb. She stared out of the window at the deserted compound, but all she could see were the images that played over and over in her mind.

A frail, old man, his hands pressed together, begging, 'At least let me die here,' while the police looked on, unmoved, and rounded him up with the rest of the men. The camp commander himself threw a man to the ground and kicked him. A young man, his head covered in blood, naked apart from a blanket, dragged by two policemen, clutching a violin to his chest. A bearded, white-haired man, half-dressed, cradling a Torah scroll, herded along the path. The senior policeman laughed at the elderly men, spirits broken, stumbling and falling as the police led them away. Wounded, desperate men shouted in German, Yiddish, Hebrew, crying for their children, pleading for help, for someone to tell the world what was happening. Then a single policeman broke down and abandoned his post. And yet, none of the *gaffirim* appeared, nor anyone from the *Patria* side of the camp. Not even when Max stood at the fence, screaming for Alma until he was knocked unconscious and carried off on a stretcher.

She could not believe the brutality she had witnessed. Would Max survive? What had happened to Stefan and Alexander? And Isaak.

He had shown such courage in trying to escape, though there was nowhere left to run. Was he hurt too?

This was not supposed to happen. Their passive resistance was meant to appeal to the sympathy and humanity of their police guards. But they did not appear to care. Did they even view the Jewish refugees as human?

'We should get back into our beds,' Janka said in a flat tone. 'We have to create a delay until help arrives.'

Lilly crawled under the covers, even though she knew it was pointless. Now that the men had gone, they stood little chance.

Bracha, the *gaffira*, reappeared and closed the door. 'I'm sorry.' She walked down the aisle, hands clasped together. 'The police are waiting outside. You need to get up, get dressed, and pack your suitcases.'

This time there were no gestures to contradict her words. She looked at the women lying in their beds, waiting for a response. Not one of them stirred.

'Please get up,' she said. 'It's no use. You saw what they did to the men. You don't want the same thing to happen to you.' She continued under her breath, 'you tried your best ... I also tried.' Her shoulders sagged. 'I wish I could do more.' She paused at the door. 'Look, if you agree to get up they might let you send letters to your families. Let me try.'

Five minutes later Bracha was back.

'They've agreed to let you send letters to your families. But then you have to comply and get ready to leave. I'll be back in ten minutes.'

Lilly dashed off three letters to her mother, Eugen and Hannah. She was sealing the last envelope when Bracha reappeared. She made her way around the hut collecting the women's missives. 'And now you all need to dress and pack.'

'We can't,' Janka said, acting as spokesperson for the women. 'If we continue to resist, there is still a chance we can stay.'

Bracha's face fell. Outside, a steady procession of footfalls passed the hut. The women were starting to leave. There was none of the struggle that had taken place in the men's camp. Perhaps they were too afraid to resist further. Or they knew they had lost.

Janka's attention snapped past Bracha to the row of beds. 'What are you doing?'

Lilly followed Janka's gaze. 'Please forgive me,' Jenny said, fully dressed. She gathered the last of her belongings and threw them into her suitcase. 'I have to go.'

'But … but …' Janka sat up stiffly. 'Why are you giving up so easily?'

'I don't mean to surrender. But they have already taken Stefan. I don't want to be separated from him.' Jenny stared down at the open suitcase on her bed. 'Please understand …'

Lilly understood. Wouldn't she have done the same if Salo were still with her?

'Don't give her a hard time,' Lilly said, her voice hollow. Hopeless. 'Let her go.'

'Lilly, please don't be angry with me.'

'I'm not angry.' Lilly shook her head. 'Not with you.'

Jenny approached Lilly and gave her an awkward hug. 'I'm sorry it ended like this.'

'We understand,' Gisela said as Jenny backed away. 'You must do what you think is best.'

Jenny embraced Gisela.

'Forgive me,' Jenny mumbled as she hoisted her rucksack and picked up her suitcase.'

'Jenny is right,' Bracha said. 'You should follow her example.'

'No.' Janka scowled. 'We are not leaving Eretz.'

'It's over,' Bracha said. 'There is nothing more I can do. The police are fast losing patience, with me, with you. Don't make this harder than it is.'

Bracha put her arm around Jenny and led her out of the hut.

Lilly pulled the blanket over her head and shut her eyes, trying to block out what she had seen through the window, but the images had seared themselves into her mind.

Shrieks and gasps filled the air. This time they were coming from inside the hut.

'Grab them!' a man was yelling.

Before Lilly could lift her head, a sudden jerk ripped her blanket away, leaving her exposed. She gasped, echoing the other women. Around the hut, policemen muttered 'Disgusting' as they yanked covers away. Batons thudded against the floor.

'Get up! Get out!'

Lilly grabbed for the blanket to cover herself. 'Not gentlemen after all,' she murmured.

A burly policeman reeking of sweat and stale alcohol leaned over her. 'What did you say, miss?' he said, his breath hot and heavy in her face.

Lilly glared at him and pressed the blanket over her nose and mouth. He straightened to his full height and slapped his baton against his palm. Lilly shrank back in fear. A self-satisfied smirk twisted his lips.

Two policemen burst through the doorway, dragging two women back inside. The women, draped only in blankets, screamed and struggled to break free. They must have attempted to run through the camp like the men had done.

The burly policeman strode to the end of Lilly's bed. 'Right, ladies,' he said, addressing the women in the hut. 'You have a choice. We can either do this the easy way. You can all get up and dressed at once and leave here like ladies or ...' He took his baton and ran it along the edge of Lilly's bed. She went cold. The sound evoked a chilling memory: a baton striking the rails as it advanced up the stairwell of her apartment in Vienna on the morning of Kristallnacht, coming ever closer to her and Salo. 'Well,' he continued, following the edge of Erika's bed and then Janka's. 'No doubt you saw what happened to your menfolk when they resisted. You wouldn't want the same thing to happen to you. Would you?'

'We are not leaving,' Janka said with a tremor in her voice.

'Oh, really?' With a swift kick, the officer knocked out the bed's end legs. The sudden impact sent Janka sprawling onto the floor. She cried out and pulled her blanket around her.

'Excuse me, sir,' Gisela said. 'I'm an elderly widow. I came here to be with my children. They are all I have.' With a trembling hand, she dabbed her eyes. 'Please let me stay. I won't be any trouble.'

The officer cocked his head and waved a dismissive hand. 'Just get dressed.'

'Please,' Gisela cried, 'can I see my children before I go?'

'Madam,' the policeman said, unmoved. 'Did you not hear what I said? Get dressed. And get a move on about it. You're leaving.'

'All right,' Lilly said. 'We'll do as you say.'

She felt the women staring at her.

The policeman smirked. 'I knew you'd come around.'

Lilly swallowed hard. 'But you need to give us more time to get dressed and pack our bags.'

'Do I now?' He pointed a finger at her, then looked around the hut. 'Ten minutes. And not a second more.' He marched to the door. 'If you're not ready when I come back, you'll go as you are, wrapped in blankets, without your luggage.'

The two policemen shoved the women into the hut, and all three left, the door slamming shut behind them.

Janka let out a long exhale. 'Well done, Lilly.'

Lilly shook her head. 'I don't know how much it will help.'

'Every minute we can cause further delay might make a difference.'

'We should put some clothes on and pack,' Erika said, slipping a dress over her head. 'Chances are, he'll be back in ten minutes. Just leave a few things out of your suitcase so that when they return, we can pretend we haven't finished packing and ask for a few extra minutes.'

Lilly rose from her bed and went over to Gisela and hugged her. 'I can't promise anything. But we'll do everything we can to stay.'

Gisela nodded through her tears.

The convoy of covered lorries left the gravel road leading from Atlit camp and veered left onto a smoother, paved one.

Alexander squinted between the tarpaulin sheets. 'I see the Carmel mountain range on our right. We must be heading towards Haifa.'

So far, they had sped along unimpeded. But no one had reason to travel down that road, unless they were heading to or from the camp. The Haifa-Tel Aviv coastal road was different: it was the main road connecting the two cities. A convoy of this size roaring towards Haifa was bound to attract attention. At least, that's what Isaak was counting on. When residents saw the convoy from their windows or balconies, they would alert the *Yishuv*, who would set up a roadblock before the convoy reached Haifa Port.

It was not too late. So long as they were still in Eretz Israel there was a chance to stop their deportation. As far as Isaak knew, the women had not yet left the camp. Perhaps they continued to resist. But time was running out.

Isaak prayed the women would not suffer the same violence as they had endured. He could not bear the thought of them hurting his cousin. Or Gisela. Would they be so callous as to harm an elderly woman? What about Lilly? Despite her inner strength and the resilience she had shown throughout their journey, she remained vulnerable. The police violence risked not only physical harm but also breaking her spirit. Lilly had already endured so much grief after losing her husband and father. Would she have to leave behind her brother and cousin, Hannah, too?

His eyes rested on Max lying on the stretcher, drifting in and out of consciousness. Would Max be forced into exile, leaving behind his wife and baby son? It was unfathomable. Too cruel to contemplate.

'Excuse me,' Isaak said to the soldier standing nearest to him and indicated Max. 'His wife and baby are still in the camp. He cannot leave them. We must take him back.'

'That is unfortunate,' the soldier said. 'I wish we could. But we don't have the authority to do so. We're only supposed to escort the convoy.'

'What if you say he needs urgent medical care?' Alexander said. 'I mean, look at him. He is badly injured. Can't you request to turn the convoy around so he can see a doctor?'

The soldier shook his head. 'Sorry, I can't. If the decision were mine to make, I would. But when we reach the port, why not have a word with one of the policemen? Maybe they can help you.'

Isaak and Alexander looked at each other, knowing it would be futile.

The engines growled and the convoy picked up speed.

Alexander peered out again.

'Have we reached Haifa yet?' Isaak asked.

'It looks like we're just on the outskirts.'

'Where are we now?' Isaak asked a few minutes later.

'I see the main street. That one we passed when we first arrived.'

And no one had tried to stop them? They had not slowed; not once.

'Hello, Jews!' Isaak shouted at the top of his lungs. 'Help us! *Acheinu*, help us!'

'Isaak, there is no point shouting,' Alexander said, broken. 'No one can hear you. There is no one out there.'

'What do you mean no one?'

'There is not a soul on the street. Not even a dog. The shops are shuttered. Haifa is a ghost town. No one is coming to help us.'

Chapter 36

Ten more minutes. That was all Lilly had bought. It was not enough.

The door burst open exactly ten minutes later.

'Time's up!' the burly policeman bellowed. Two more policemen followed on his heels.

'We have nearly finished packing.' Lilly kept her eyes on her suitcase. 'Please give us five more minutes.'

She made a display of folding a dress, lining up the sleeves, the edges, to make a perfect square. Erika refolded clothes on her bed, one item at a time. Janka sat cross-legged on the floor, next to her collapsed bed, moving clothes from her suitcase to her rucksack and back again. Gisela fumbled with a pair of bloomers, the fabric slipping from her grasp each time she tried to fold them.

'What you haven't packed stays behind.' The policeman snapped his fingers. His two assistants stalked around the hut, wrenching the suitcases from their hands and hurling them through the door.

'Everyone out. Now!'

It was over.

The policeman barred the exit with his broad frame, leaving only a narrow gap for the women to pass. 'Form an orderly line.' He tapped his baton against his palm. 'No more funny business. I won't hesitate to use this. Don't think I won't.'

He prodded them as they passed. One by one, they left the hut – Janka, Erika, Gisela, then Lilly. Their luggage lay scattered across the path. Lilly retrieved her suitcase and took Gisela's arm while Janka carried Gisela's case along with her own.

Policemen guarding the women from the front and rear marshalled them through the gate into the deserted men's camp towards the exit. They trudged up the path as if they were on a funeral march. Many women wept. Gisela's tears flowed. Behind them, policemen carried two women on stretchers. At the sight of the open gate, Erika and Janka broke down. Lilly remained dry-eyed. She watched herself walking out of the camp. After everything she had been through, how could this be the end? Her dreams buried.

Several women shouted at the policemen. Others called towards the *Patria* camp, begging for help. The policemen ignored them. No one appeared on the *Patria* side.

Hannah's hut stood with door and shutters closed. Still and silent.

'Hannah!' Lilly called. Her voice echoed, unanswered.

I could have been there, Lilly thought. I was supposed to be there.

If the woman in pink and her companion had not knocked her over, she would have crossed to the *Patria* with Hannah. If she had not given Hannah her place on the lighter. If the policeman on the *Atlantic* had not accused Lilly and Gisela of lying about their names, they would have boarded the first lighter that morning. If their lighter had reached the *Patria* just a few minutes earlier, or if the explosion had happened just a few minutes later.

If. If. If.

But she did not blame Hannah, nor the woman in the pink dress and her companion. They were not responsible for this deportation.

Lilly wished she could rage and scream like the other women at the cruelty of it all. But she could not bring herself to do so.

They reached the exit. Lilly looked back once more at the *Patria* huts. How would she cope without Hannah? When would she see her cousin again?

'Goodbye, Hannah,' she whispered.

Gisela squeezed her arm, rested her head against Lilly's shoulder, and they walked out of the gate.

Silent *gaffirim*, heads lowered, lined the fence.

A convoy of lorries, led by an armoured vehicle with a mounted machine gun, rumbled away from the camp. A cloud of dust, thick with diesel fumes, billowed behind them. Five more tarpaulin-covered lorries waited, engines idling, each guarded by armed soldiers. Were the British so afraid of unarmed women that they needed to escort them with this show of force?

A policeman directed them to the second lorry, herding them like cattle. The *gaffirim* hurried forward to assist. Wordlessly, they took their luggage and loaded it into the back of the lorry.

'Where were you when we needed your help inside?' Janka said.

A *gaffir* glanced at the policemen overseeing them, then turned to the women with red-rimmed eyes.

Two *gaffirim* helped Gisela up onto the lorry bed. Another offered Lilly his hand. She waved it away and climbed up.

They loaded twenty-five women, their luggage, and four soldiers inside before fastening the tarpaulin flap, hiding them from view. The engine roared, gears grinding as the lorry accelerated, snatching Lilly away from Hannah and Eugen, hurtling her into the unknown.

The door to Hannah's hut was unlocked just after midday, flooding the hut with daylight. Instead of the familiar face of one of the *gaffirot*, a freckle-faced, ginger-haired British policeman stood in the doorway.

'You can come out now,' he said. No apology or explanation for sealing them in all morning.

'Why did you lock us in?' Hannah asked.

'You can come out now,' he repeated. 'It's time for visiting hour.'

'We heard a terrible commotion earlier this morning,' Alma said, rocking Chaim in her arms. 'What was it?'

The policeman shifted his weight. 'A slight disturbance. Everything is all right and under control.'

Hannah felt a surge of dread. She looked at Alma; a fearful glance passed between them. With hesitant steps, they emerged from the hut. Hannah shielded her eyes against the bright sunlight.

An unnatural stillness hung over the camp. The wind howled, a mournful sound, rattling the barbed wire fence.

On the other side, no one stood by the fence calling to their relatives or wandered the compound. No sign of Lilly. No sign of Max.

The doors to the men's huts swung loose, creaking and slamming in the wind. Inside, the huts lay empty. Everyone had gone. All trace of them vanished, as if they had never been there at all.

'No. No,' Alma said, her voice little more than a breath. 'Where have they taken them?'

Hannah shook her head.

She jumped at the scuff of footsteps behind, and spun around.

The policeman cleared his throat. 'Sorry,' he said. 'I didn't mean to startle you. Are either of you Hannah Rosen?'

Hannah's stomach lurched. 'I ... I am.'

'I was asked to deliver this to you.' From his pocket, the man retrieved an envelope with Hannah's name written in Lilly's distinctive handwriting.

Chapter 37

9 December 1940
Haifa Port

The lorry slowed, its deep rumble dropping in pitch as it ground down through the gears with a jarring metallic crunch. The shudder sent the men lurching forward.

Alexander stared, unfocused. 'At least we can be proud that we resisted until the end.' His voice was hoarse. 'We did not leave Eretz Israel without a fight.'

'We haven't left yet,' Isaak said. 'This is not the end.'

Alexander shut his eyes and drew a breath. 'I don't think anyone will be able to save us now.'

'No one has come because they don't know what has happened,' Isaak said. 'The police must have locked up the *gaffirim* so they could not get the word out. And why was there not a single person on the streets in Haifa? The British police seem to be doing everything they can to make sure no one can stop this. But they can't hide it forever. Eventually the police will have to allow the *gaffirim* to leave Atlit, and word will get out.'

'By then it will be too late. We will have gone.'

'But there will be an outcry when people learn how the British expelled us. The *gaffirim* must have witnessed how violent the British were. They certainly saw our injuries as we left. The *Yishuv* and the people. Lilly's brother and Hannah. Gisela's sons. Alma. They will all fight for us.'

'Alma,' Max rasped through cracked lips. 'She will fight for me. Just like she fought when I was in Dachau.'

Alexander clasped Max's hand. 'Yes, she will.'

'The same way the British are sending us away, they can bring us back,' Isaak said. 'We too will fight to return to our homeland.'

'You are right.' Alexander straightened up. 'We will continue to fight. We can make appeals to return to Eretz Israel. This is our home, and the home of our ancestors, leaders like Joshua, Gideon, and King David.'

'Abraham, Isaak, and Jacob.'

'King Solomon, Deborah and Queen Esther,' Stefan added.

Alexander lifted his voice, 'We carry their strength and spirit within us.'

With a whine, the lorry ground to a stop.

Alexander adjusted his blanket, wrapping it around him like his ancient forefathers. 'We will walk out of here with our heads held high,' he said. 'We will not let them break us.'

A policeman flung back the lorry's tarpaulin. Isaak recognised him at once and groaned inwardly. It was the towering policeman they had encountered after the *Atlantic* docked. The one who had kicked Efraim for not loading the crates of potatoes fast enough. He kicked Isaak when he first stepped onto land and bent to kiss the holy ground. He hit Alexander on the backs of his legs with his rifle butt. Of course it had to be him to welcome them back to the port.

'Right you lot,' the policeman said. 'Everyone out.'

Isaak stretched his stiff limbs and hoisted his rucksack as the men struggled to their feet. The armed soldiers remained on guard and acknowledged each man as he stepped off the lorry.

'Remember,' Alexander said in an undertone. 'Hold your head high.'

Isaak and Alexander stepped down from the vehicle. Standing tall, Isaak looked straight ahead as they carried Max on a stretcher between them.

'Hurry up. We haven't got all day,' the policeman said.

He marched them across to a large shed, the entrance to which was guarded by armed policemen, like the one they'd been sent to when they first disembarked the *Atlantic*.

Alexander looked over his shoulder at Isaak, his brow furrowed. 'Do they mean to give us another customs inspection? For a group of naked men in blankets?'

'That would be ridiculous.' Isaak gave a hollow laugh. 'What is there left to examine?'

Inside, two plainclothes officials sat behind a long examination table, guarded from the front and side by armed police.

'Mrs Hoyle,' one of the officials said. The stout policewoman Isaak recognised from their arrival stepped forward.

'Yes, sir,' she replied and began directing the new arrivals to the table.

Once processed, the men were directed to a civil servant holding a clipboard in the opposite doorway. Armed policemen guarded the entrance to the quayside. A group of Red Cross nurses observed from the side. Isaak was not sure why they were there. They offered no first aid to the injured – they just kept staring at the men and giggling.

Heat rose to Isaak's neck. He dropped his gaze to the floor.

'Ignore them,' Alexander said. 'Keep your head up and stand tall.'

Heeding his advice, Isaak looked straight ahead. He rolled his shoulders back. His arms were tiring from holding Max's stretcher, but he did not loosen his grip.

At the front of the queue was Dr Paul Horetzky, who had been head of the Transport Committee on the *Atlantic*. Mrs Hoyle directed him to the official on the right. Like all the other young men, Dr Horetzky wore a blanket and carried no luggage. His only personal possession was a small money bag around his neck, holding the remaining money from the men in his group. After a brief examination, the officer tore the bag off him. For an instant, Dr Horetzky stood stunned and speechless before regaining his composure. 'May I have a receipt for that, please?'

The official did not reply.

'I'd like a receipt for that,' he repeated.

The official waved him away, but Dr Horetzky remained in his place. 'You have just taken my money without justification. At the very least, you can give me a receipt.'

The official nodded to the policeman standing guard who grabbed him by the arm and pushed him towards the exit. The official added the bag to a small pile of objects on the floor beside him without looking up.

This was not a customs inspection. It was theft.

'*Unglaublich*! Just when you think you've seen it all,' he muttered under his breath to Isaak. '*Scheisser*. All of them.'

Mrs Hoyle directed another man to the official on the left and Stefan, next in line, to the one on the right. Unlike Dr Horetzky, Stefan carried no money. Nothing for the official to take this time. Or so Isaak assumed.

The official reached forward and yanked the glasses from Stefan's face. Stefan pressed his hands to his eyes. 'Please!' His voice rose in panic. 'I am short-sighted. I need those glasses to see. Why have you confiscated them?'

The official stared at him, his expression unmoved.

'Please, can you give me back my glasses?' Stefan said. 'And while I'm here, what about my camera that you took from me when we first arrived?'

'Your camera?' A smile played at his lips.

'Yes, my camera.'

'Do you have a receipt?' the official asked.

'I do.'

'Can I see it?'

'I ... I ... don't have it with me,' Stefan stammered. 'It's still in Atlit.'

He shrugged. 'Oh, well. I can't do anything without a receipt.' He gave Stefan a dismissive wave and threw the glasses onto the pile. 'Next!' he called, with a gesture to Mrs Hoyle.

'Your turn,' she said to Alexander.

He walked a few awkward steps forward, still carrying his end of the stretcher. 'What should I do about—'

Mrs Hoyle gave him a withering look. 'Oh, for goodness' sake! Just put him on the floor.' She pointed to the space next to the table. 'Just don't forget to collect him when you've completed customs.'

Isaak thought he heard her say, 'Because we've got no use for him.'

They gently laid Max down.

'We'll be back as soon as we can,' Alexander said to Max.

Max managed a slight nod, wincing. 'Sorry for putting you through all this trouble.'

'You're not the trouble.'

'Hurry up over there. You're holding everyone up,' Mrs Hoyle said.

Behind them, the line continued to grow as the next lorryload arrived. Among them were several older men, dressed and carrying their suitcases. Poor men. Their suitcases probably contained the last items they had left in the world. No doubt the officials would enjoy pilfering their luggage.

As the towering policeman walked past, ordering them into a straight line, Mr Finkelstein, a frail, elderly man from Vienna, went down on his knees, and folded his hands in a gesture of entreaty. 'Please,' he pleaded in German. 'Let me die here in Palästina.'

The policeman paused. He stared down at the poor man kneeling on the floor, so desperate that he had resorted to begging, and his nose wrinkled in disgust as though the old man were dirt on his highly polished shoes. He drew back his foot and kicked him. Mr Finkelstein cried out in pain and crumpled. The policeman smirked and turned on his heel. Mrs Hoyle and the policeman stationed next to the table grinned at one another as if they found the sight amusing. The old men in front and behind Mr Finkelstein helped him to his feet, weeping silently. Isaak looked at Alexander, tears burning behind his eyes. Alexander's eyes glistened too.

'What are you still standing there for?' Mrs Hoyle said to Alexander. 'Come on. Move it.' Then she glared at Isaak. 'And you.' She indicated the official on the left.

Isaak approached the table. Beside him, the official tore Alexander's watch from his wrist.

'Why?' Alexander said, his jaw tight. The official placed it on the growing pile.

Isaak wrapped his blanket over his arm to hide his watch as Alexander continued to argue.

'Place your rucksack on the table and open it for me, please,' the official said.

He hardly waited for Isaak to open it before he plunged his hand inside. He withdrew Isaak's belongings and spread them across the table. The sandwich, a pair of underpants, his penknife, two cigarettes Isaak had saved for bartering, paper and pencil, the length of string he used for magic tricks, his siddur, tallit and tefillin. First to go was the penknife. The cigarettes followed. When the official snatched up his siddur and tallit, Isaak spoke up. 'That's a Hebrew prayer book and a prayer shawl. What use are those to you?'

'You can put the rest back in your bag.'

Isaak swept up his remaining belongings and stuffed them into his rucksack. He was relieved the man hadn't confiscated his tefillin too. He tucked his rucksack under his blanket before the official could give them a second thought.

'Sir, I understand the confiscation of my penknife and cigarettes. But the prayer book and shawl have special value to me.' He lowered the blanket from his arm to reveal his silver watch. 'This is worth more than those items.'

The official leaned across the table. 'What are you implying, lad?'

'Nothing. I just thought—'

'Trot along before I change my mind and confiscate your entire rucksack.' The man dismissed Isaak with a flick of the wrist and beckoned the towering policeman who was talking and laughing with Mrs Hoyle.

Isaak retreated and joined Alexander beside Max. Alexander greeted him with a furious shake of the head. What was left to say?

'Best you keep a close eye on those two young toughs,' the official said to the policeman. 'Make sure they don't try any funny business before they board the ship.'

The policeman loomed over them as they lifted Max's stretcher and walked across the shed to the opposite door. At the exit, the civil servant with the clipboard asked for their names, as well as Max's, and checked them against his list. Ahead, two large grey ships lay at anchor in the harbour.

'Second ship to the right,' said the man with the clipboard. 'The SS *Nieuw Zeeland*.'

The ship assignments seemed arbitrary. Irwin Kovac and Fritz Steiner from their Prague group, who had assumed control of the *Atlantic* and brought them from Crete to Cyprus, were mounting the gangway of the first ship, the *Johan de Witt*, straight ahead. Dov walked a few metres ahead of them towards the *Nieuw Zeeland* further along the quay.

Stefan lingered on the quayside, outside the shed. He only recognised Isaak and Alexander when they were less than two metres away.

'Sorry about your glasses,' Alexander said.

Stefan shrugged. 'What is there left to see anyway?'

'You can get a new pair when we arrive at our destination.'

'Wherever that is.' Stefan squinted at them, his face drawn and tired. 'Which ship did they assign you?'

'*Nieuw Zeeland*. And you?'

'Same.'

Stefan held onto the side of the stretcher and they walked together along the quayside to the ship. Isaak took deliberate steps, as if by doing so, he would imprint his feet into the earth and a trace of him would remain. He took deep breaths, filling his lungs with the air of the Holy Land, in the hope it would fortify him for the challenges that lay ahead.

This is not the end, he repeated to himself. We will return.

They trudged up the gangway.

Isaak paused at the top. 'One minute,' he said to Alexander. He gazed up at the slopes of Mount Carmel, etching them into his memory. Footsteps thundered up the gangway. 'Where do you think you're going?' the towering policeman said. 'The entrance to the ship is that way.'

'I wanted one last look at Haifa,' Isaak said. 'Until the next time.'

The policeman barked a laugh. 'Better make it a good look then because there won't be a next time. You're on a one-way ticket, lad. You won't ever be permitted to return.'

'I will return.' Isaak kept his voice steady. He pointed to the Union Jack fluttering on the harbour flagpole. 'And one day, our flag will fly from that flagpole.'

The policeman snarled. 'Not in your lifetime.'

'Yes, it will be in my lifetime,' Isaak said. 'But hopefully not in yours.'

The policeman's nostrils flared. He raised his hand. 'Why you—'

'What are you going to do? Hit me?' Isaak gestured to his blood-encrusted head and Max lying on the stretcher. 'We've already been hit. Or are you going to kill me?' Isaak swallowed hard, the image of Mr Finkelstein collapsing to the ground still fresh in his mind. 'Well, if you do, at least *I* will get to die here.' His eyes pricked. He looked away and stared into the sea's familiar depths. 'I'm leaving. For now. But I will return. And I hope you're gone when I do.'

Chapter 38

9 December 1940
Haifa Port

Midday had passed, but no one was coming to save them. The lorry raced onwards; nothing hindered its progress. Lilly peered through a gap in the tarpaulin and saw why. Haifa's streets were deserted, shops shuttered, no pedestrians in sight.

From the apartments above, a few people watched the convoy's progress from their balconies. If they had wanted to help, what could they do against armed soldiers? But did they even know what the British were transporting, hidden under the tarpaulins?

Less than ten minutes later the lorry juddered to a halt. The tarpaulin cover was yanked aside, and a towering policeman barked at them to get off. Lilly recognised him. He'd been there when they disembarked from the *Atlantic*. He was the one who had kicked Isaak and struck Alexander. Where were Isaak and Alexander now? Were they all to be sent to the same unknown place?

Gisela gripped Lilly's hand as they stepped off the drop-down tailboard. Gisela teetered, then steadied herself.

'This way please, *ladies*,' the policeman said. 'Get a move on. We haven't got all day, you know.'

He marched them towards a shed. Janka and Erika walked ahead, carrying Gisela's luggage.

Lilly and Gisela lagged behind. Lilly scanned her surroundings. The harbour looked nearly empty of workers. She considered running, but she would not get far with armed guards everywhere. Besides, she could not abandon Gisela. She allowed herself to be led into the shed where two officials sat at a long table. Another customs inspection. Lilly simmered. Had they not already gone through this process upon their arrival? Had these officials not taken precious and personal items from them? And since that inspection, they had been locked away behind barbed wire. How could they have accumulated any other possessions during that time?

Cries of protest rose as the officials confiscated items from each woman. Between the men, confiscated items rose to the height of the table. Clothing, watches, glasses, shoe brushes, a doctor's medical bag. A tallit. They were being robbed.

A middle-aged policewoman Lilly remembered from their previous inspection called Erika to the table. Erika's face fell as the man confiscated her pearl clip-on earrings, hairbrush, and a small first aid kit. The policewoman summoned Janka. As Lilly watched Janka hesitate, she glimpsed Jenny on the far side of the shed, heading for the exit. Jenny looked back and their eyes met, but they were too far apart to speak. Jenny raised a hand to wave as she was directed out of the shed.

'Next!'

The policewoman directed Lilly to the position Erika had just vacated.

'Please open your suitcase and rucksack, madam.'

He spilled her possessions across the table. Lilly stood speechless as he swiped a bar of soap, her sewing kit, and two pairs of silk stockings. Then his hand crept towards her photograph album. Not that. She lunged across the table, grabbed the album, and clutched it to her chest.

'Everything has been taken from me. Everything. But this you will not take.' She kept her voice steady. 'That album contains the only photos I have of my late husband and my late father.'

'Calm down. There's no need to get hysterical.' He tutted, as if she were a small child having a tantrum. 'Stop this fussing at once and I'll let you keep your album. All right? There's a good girl. You can pack the rest of your things.'

Lilly gathered her clothing and possessions, tossing them into her rucksack and suitcase.

'Move along now.'

She picked up her luggage, paused, and set it down again. 'Actually, while I'm here, I would like to know what you did with the personal letters you stole from me last time.'

'Madam, what are you insinuating?' he said. 'We aren't stealing anything.'

For a moment, his certainty made her doubt her own memory.

'If we supposedly took letters from you, it would have been for security concerns. They would have been properly catalogued, and you would have received a receipt.' He flashed a smug smile. 'I don't suppose you have a receipt.'

Lilly reached into her coat pocket. 'As a matter of fact, I do.' She waved the piece of paper at him.

'Oh.' His smile vanished. He blinked. 'Right, then.'

'Now give me back my letters.'

'Well, they are not here at present. As I mentioned before, they would have been catalogued. They will be sent to your onward destination.'

'Really?' Lilly said. 'And where would that be?'

'To ... er ... um.' He glanced around. 'I'm afraid I'm not at liberty to say. You will be informed in due course. And if you give me your receipt, we will of course endeavour to forward your letters.'

Lilly scoffed. 'I don't believe you.'

'Madam.' He folded his arms and glared at her. 'I don't like the tone you are taking with me.'

'And I don't like the way you are treating us.' Lilly slammed the receipt onto the table. The man jumped.

'Have we finished here?' Lilly said.

The man sat up straighter. 'We have finished.' He gave her a cold stare and tilted his head. 'Mrs Hoyle!' The policewoman stepped forward. 'Leave your bags there,' he said, pointing to a small pile against the wall. Lilly recognised Erika and Janka's suitcases among them.

'Why?' Lilly said.

The official turned away. 'Next!'

Mrs Hoyle seized Lilly's elbow. 'Leave your bags,' she echoed and steered her to the pile.

'Where are you taking me?' Lilly said as Mrs Hoyle marched her through the shed. Without responding, Mrs Hoyle pushed her into a side room where two women with crimson lipstick and hair styled in Victory Rolls patted down Erika and Janka.

The woman attending to Erika exchanged a glance with Mrs Hoyle, who shut the door behind her.

'Right, you can go now,' she said.

'But my watch,' Erika said. 'I'm a nurse and I need it—'

'We have finished.'

'Do I get a receipt?' Erika asked.

'We have finished. Go outside and fetch the rest of your belongings.'

'You can leave too,' the other woman said to Janka.

'What about my necklace?' Janka said.

'What about it?' she sneered.

Janka followed Erika out, leaving Lilly alone with the two women. Dolls disguising devils, she thought. Under her heavy coat, sweat ran down her back. Her gold wedding ring, sewn into the fur collar, felt like a weight. The same fear from Vienna's customs inspection had followed her to Haifa.

'Hands out to the side,' said the shorter of the two. The woman's eager hands patted the shoulders of Lilly's coat and plunged into the pockets. 'Coat off.'

With trembling fingers, Lilly let it drop to the floor. The woman ran her hands down Lilly's dress.

'Dress and shoes off,' she said without ceremony.

Lilly stared, unsure whether she had heard correctly. The woman flicked her hand sharply. Lilly pulled off one shoe, then the other, and slowly undid her buttons. Her cheeks burned under the woman's piercing gaze. She crossed her arms over her chest.

'Hands out to the side,' the woman said once more.

Lilly shut her eyes as she frisked and prodded her a third time. When she was finished, she stood back, assessing Lilly.

'Remove your wristwatch,' she said.

Lilly had watched Janka and Erika go through the same process. Arguing was pointless. These customs officials seemed determined to deprive the women of anything that made them feel like human beings. Lilly said goodbye to her watch.

'That's it. You can dress and leave.'

Lilly fumbled with the buttons of her dress and wrapped her mama's coat around her like an embrace. These people might have tried to strip her of everything, but she was more than what they could take from her.

Lilly returned to the main hall and met Janka, Erika, and Gisela at the luggage pile. At the exit, an official directed them to the second grey ship to the right, the SS *Nieuw Zeeland*.

As she walked along the quay, despair hit her. Lilly's legs felt numb and heavy; she could barely lift them. She leaned on Gisela. They passed the first ship, the *Johan de Witt*, a magnificent liner. Lilly's throat hurt from the screams she had repressed. Her eyes remained dry. Her heart enclosed in armour.

In the distance, a faint wail rose – like an air raid siren. It reminded her of the one she'd heard once during their delay outside Crete. The prospect of an air raid offered a strange comfort. Maybe a fleet of bombers would strike the harbour and destroy the ships. If she perished as well? What did it matter?

But nothing of the sort happened. They had reached their ship.

The all-clear siren sounded. A long steady note.

Eugen jumped up from his chair. 'About time too.' He helped Leo gather cups and plates and carry them into the kitchen. Eugen checked his watch yet again. During the four hours he and Leo had waited for the curfew to end, breakfast had become lunch with several cups of coffee in between. Their appointment at the Jewish Agency had long passed.

'Do you think someone might still see us today?' Eugen asked.

'We might stand a chance if we hurry,' Leo said.

They left the sink piled with dishes and rushed out of the apartment. Down the stairs, out of the building, and onto the street where crowds streamed from their homes. They crossed the road, passing clusters of people in animated discussion. They had walked less than twenty metres when a voice boomed. 'Hallo! Leo!'

Across the street, a stout older man waved his walking stick, his trousers held up by braces stretched over his ample belly.

'Do you know that man?' Eugen asked.

'Yes,' Leo said. 'He's my downstairs neighbour.'

Eugen followed him back.

'Young man,' Leo's neighbour said. 'Didn't you mention your mother had arrived recently on one of those ships and might be in Atlit?'

'That's right,' Leo said.

'There are rumours the British used the curfew to move refugees from Atlit to Haifa. They're deporting them.'

'What?' Leo stiffened. 'Did you hear which group of refugees it was?'

'Since the *Patria* passengers were granted permission to stay, it's probably the refugees from the other ship.'

Eugen caught Leo's arm. 'We should go straight to the port. Your mother and my sister might be among them.'

'You might be too late.' Leo's neighbour looked down, tapping his walking stick against the pavement. 'Most likely, the passengers have already boarded.'

Chapter 39

9 December 1940
SS Nieuw Zeeland, Haifa Harbour

Armed guards watched as Lilly followed Janka, Erika and Gisela up the narrow gangplank. The SS *Nieuw Zeeland* was a large steamer and first impressions suggested it would provide every modern comfort. Yet Lilly resented this ship for deporting them from their homeland and transporting them to an unknown destination she already disliked.

At the top of the gangway, she and Gisela paused for one last look at Mount Carmel. Would they ever return to Eretz Israel? The thought of *never* felt too vast, too unbearable to consider.

'We will return, won't we?' Lilly said.

Gisela sighed. 'We must believe we will. We must.'

They were leaving. There was nothing more Lilly could do. She shut her eyes, took a deep breath, and boarded the ship.

After an official registered their names, birthdates, and nationalities, a policeman escorted them along a wide, well-appointed passageway. Lilly's feet sank into the soft carpet runner that stretched down the centre of the hardwood floor. Soft electric lighting illuminated individual cabin doors of polished wood with brass fixtures.

Erika glanced over her shoulder at Lilly and Gisela, her eyebrows raised. 'Well, this is quite elegant, nothing like the *Atlantic*,' she said in a hushed voice. 'At least we'll be comfortable.'

Lilly nodded, but her head felt heavy. Exhaustion swept over her – the strain of the last two days, the restless night. Lilly welcomed the idea of a bed, crisp sheets, a quiet cabin. Sleep. That was all she wanted. Drift into oblivion, beyond thought, where pain could not follow.

Lilly willed the policeman to pause outside the next cabin, or the one after, or the one after that, to simply open a door, any door, usher her inside and let her collapse onto a bed. But he kept walking, leading them along the corridor and down a staircase.

As they descended, they passed two crew members from the Far East in impeccable white uniforms who eyed them with curiosity. One bowed his head slightly, his gaze sympathetic.

They descended a second staircase and arrived at the hold, where scuffed brown linoleum replaced the elegant polished hardwood, exposed pipes ran overhead, and the passageway was barely shoulder-width.

'I should have guessed it was too good to be true,' Janka muttered as the policeman herded them through a low bulkhead door and into a mess room, already packed with over a hundred women and children from Atlit. Some sat on benches at one of the six long tables grouped at either end of the room. The rest sat on the floor in between. Electric lights cast a harsh glare over the space. It had no portholes; only an overhead air shaft in the centre.

'These are your quarters,' the policeman said. 'You are to remain here until further notice.'

'What about going to the lavatory—' Janka began.

'You are strictly forbidden to leave without permission.' The policeman cut her off and left.

Janka's shoulders sagged. 'Well, isn't this marvelous? It's even more overcrowded down here than on the *Atlantic*.'

'Jenny might have saved places for us like she did on the *Atlantic*,' Erika said. It had been Jenny and Stefan who had discovered the lifeboat on deck which they shared with the *chevra*.

'Where is she?' Janka's eyes swept the room. 'I can't find her anywhere.'

'She has to be here.' Lilly scanned the crowd. Her heart raced. 'I saw her leaving the port shed while we were waiting for the customs inspection. Gisela, didn't you see her too?'

'I ... might have done.' Gisela blinked slowly. 'I can't remember.'

'I definitely saw her.' Lilly searched the compartment until her head spun. Jenny was not there. She turned to a young woman from Danzig who had shared their hut in Atlit. 'Have you seen Jenny?'

'I'm sorry, I haven't,' the woman replied. 'A few women from our group are missing. They must have been sent to the *Johan de Witt*.'

'What about the men?' Janka asked.

The woman's face fell. 'We haven't seen any of them since they were dragged out of Atlit. My husband among them. We don't know where they are. They may be on another part of the ship, but it's also possible they're on the *Johann de Witt*. There are rumours ...' Her brow furrowed. 'They may be sending our two ships to different destinations.'

'*Mein Gott*!' Janka said. 'That can't be true.'

'I hope it isn't. I'm so worried about my husband.'

What had happened to Jenny? Isaak? Alexander, Max, and Stefan?

They were in a downward spiral. How much more could they take?

They were a ship of lost immigrants. Deprived of all rights. Rootless.

What if Lilly had stayed in Vienna and never followed Hannah on this journey? What if, when that Nazi had pushed her down the stairs in her parents' apartment she had reached the bottom and not awoken? Lilly would never have known the pain of losing Salo and their baby. She would never have endured a dangerous journey only to be separated from all her loved ones, bound for an unknown place.

The air was suffocating. Women were murmuring, shifting in the tight space. Babies were fretting and crying. Her vision narrowed to a tunnel. She was falling. Falling into darkness. Falling without end …

'Lilly? Can you hear me?'

Lilly opened her eyes at the sound of her name and looked up to see Erika. Lilly found herself lying on the floor, her coat folded beneath her. Gisela crouched to her right, Janka to her left, each holding one of her hands.

'You're going to be all right,' Erika said. 'You blacked out for a moment. Probably the heat. It's stifling here. Especially in your heavy coat. You must be dehydrated too. We need to get you some water.'

Erika had slipped back into her nursing role. But Lilly knew it was more than heat or lack of water. Darkness had crept into the place where hope had lived. She felt hollow.

'A group of women are queuing to use the lavatory. I'll join them and try to fetch some water.'

'I'll come with you,' Gisela said. 'Difficult at my age to wait so long.'

'I will too.' Janka grimaced, lowering her voice. 'I think my monthlies have just started.'

'Oh no.' Erika rubbed Janka's arm before leaning over Lilly. 'Will you be all right for a few minutes on your own?'

Lilly nodded and closed her eyes. She was not all right, but she could not tell them. She was afraid of her own thoughts.

Almost immediately the three of them returned. 'Already back?' Her voice came out rough, catching on dry lips.

'We didn't get very far,' Erika said. 'A line of women tried to leave the hold, up the stairs, in the direction we came. A policeman waiting on the stairs sent everyone back. He refused to let us go, even though some of the women told him they were desperate.' Her eyes flashed. 'This is cruel.'

Gisela rummaged through her rucksack and pulled out a small foil package. 'This might help a bit.' She broke up a bar of chocolate and handed little pieces to Lilly, Erika, and Janka, each accepting gratefully. Gisela continued distributing the rest to a few of the crying children. Their mothers murmured thanks, relief crossing their faces. She saved the smallest crumb for herself.

Lilly rolled onto her side, still light-headed. Erika and Janka helped her to sit up, and she sucked on the piece of chocolate. If nothing else, it helped ease her hunger pangs.

Gisela put an arm around Lilly. 'You're not alone. At least the four of us are still together. Jenny might be somewhere else on the ship. We'll find her soon, and we'll find out what's happened to the men.'

Isaak threw the blanket off his shoulders and tied it around his waist. The compartment in the hold, crammed with over four hundred men, was getting hotter and stuffier. He sat on the floor wedged between Alexander and Stefan. Max lay on the stretcher beside them, conscious now, groaning from time to time from the pain in his ribs. A doctor from their group had treated the injured as best he could without proper supplies or even water. He bandaged many of the injured men including Alexander, Isaak and Max. Examining Max, he diagnosed either a bruised or cracked rib. Max would be in severe pain for at least a few days, but was likely to make a full recovery from his injuries. Another man from Vienna was not so fortunate. He had received such an extreme blow to the head that he risked losing his sight in one eye.

'This is getting ridiculous.' Alexander wiped the beads of sweat from his upper lip with the corner of his blanket. 'How long do they intend to keep us cooped up in this hold? We must have been down here for an hour at least.' Alexander lifted his wrist but his watch was gone. 'Isaak, how long has it been since we got here?'

'Nearly two hours. Do you think they have forgotten about us?'

'It seems that way. Don't they realise there are people here who need to use the toilet? And I'd like to wash the dried blood off my face.' Alexander got to his feet and shook the stiffness out of his legs. 'I'm fed up with this waiting. Since it doesn't look like anyone is coming back for us I'm going to find the washroom.' He tightened the blanket around himself, wove between the seated clusters of men, and stepped through the bulkhead door.

Less than a minute later, Alexander was back, clutching his face, swearing furiously under his breath.

'What happened?' Isaak said.

'That *arschloch*!' he said between clenched teeth. 'When I reached the stairs I met a sharp-faced policeman standing guard on the steps. He asked where I thought I was going. I told him I only wanted to visit the washroom to clean the blood off my face. Without any provocation, the brute flew into a rage and bellowed: "You'll go to the washroom when I say you can go! And not before!" Then he punched me on the side of my face and ordered me to return to my quarters.'

Isaak winced. 'How bad is it?'

Alexander rubbed his blazing ear and cheek. 'It stings, but I'll survive.'

'If this is how it begins, before we have even left the harbour, God help us,' Stefan glanced about. 'We're at the mercy of madmen!'

'There's something else.' Alexander frowned. 'On my way to the stairs, I passed another hold compartment. I managed to take a quick look through the doorway and saw it was full of women—'

'Jenny!' Stefan interjected. 'Is she there?'

'That's just it. I didn't see any of them. Not her, nor my sister, or Erika—'

'What about Lilly?' Isaak said.

'Not Lilly or Gisela either.'

'Is it possible you didn't notice them in the crowd?' Stefan said.

'I don't know.' He hesitated. 'I suppose so ...'

'Or perhaps they're in a different compartment,' Isaak said. 'Wasn't there a door before ours when we first entered the hold?'

'I can't remember.' Alexander said.

'I'm sure I saw one. Perhaps they're on the other side?' Isaak said.

'Maybe.' Alexander pressed his hand to his burning cheek.

Stefan went pale. 'Unless ... What if they've sent them on the other ship?'

Chapter 40

Lilly's throat burned with every breath. The air pressed hot and stale against her face.

Exhausted and dehydrated, she sat slumped on the floor with her three friends. Around them, the rest of the women did likewise, clutching their meagre belongings, waiting.

Her watch confiscated, Lilly had lost track of time. A while ago, ten or twenty minutes perhaps, Gisela had mentioned they'd been in the hold for an hour. Lilly had no idea how much time had passed since then and had no energy to ask.

She drifted in and out of a disturbed sleep. A cough shook her awake, then a baby's wail. The same questions pounded in her head. Where were they sending them? Where was Jenny? Where were the men? In her stupor, she clung to the fragile hope that as long as their ship remained in Haifa, the British might still reverse their decision. It was all she had left to hold on to.

She did not notice the policeman in the doorway until the hold stirred with activity, women rising to their feet.

'Where are we going?' Lilly asked.

'We're finally allowed to use the lavatory,' Gisela said. 'Just as well. I was in danger of flooding the ship.'

The corners of Lilly's mouth lifted, barely, at Gisela's attempt at a joke.

'Are you coming?' the older woman asked.

For hours, Lilly had ignored her bladder. She scrambled to her feet and joined Gisela at the back of the queue that stretched through the hold and out of the bulkhead door. As they moved forward one shuffled step at a time, words rippled down the line in hurried whispers, their eyes solemn, mouths tight.

Janka tapped Erika's shoulder. 'What are they saying?'

'Women at the front of the queue say they saw men in the next compartment. Many are wounded. Some look badly hurt.'

Janka placed a hand to her chest. 'I hope Alexander and Isaak are all right.'

Erika asked a question of the woman in front of her and glanced back. 'It seems there is a third compartment at the end. There are more women inside.'

'Maybe Jenny is there.' Lilly said.

'She must be,' Gisela said.

Lilly held onto hope of finding Jenny. But in what condition would they find the men?

The line inched forward. Lilly followed Gisela and stepped through the bulkhead door. They pressed against the wall to the right of the narrow passageway to make way for the women on the left already returning to the hold.

Ahead of them, Janka had reached the men's compartment. She stared through the open door and her features froze.

'Keep moving!' a guard's voice echoed down the passageway.

Lilly approached the compartment. A blur of men in blood-soaked bandages crowded the entrance, searching the women as they passed. Was that Alexander and Isaak, their heads wrapped in bandages? A hand reached for hers and pressed something against her fingers. She closed her fist over it. Before she could look up, the line had carried her past.

A tiny piece of paper nestled in her palm. Lilly slipped it into her pocket to check once she reached the privacy of a cubicle.

The line edged forward. Lilly reached the second women's compartment. Like their own, it was crowded with a hundred women or more. She searched for Jenny, but it was impossible to scan each face before she had to move on.

Lilly climbed the stairs, past a guard with an angular face and razor-edged nose. He rubbed the reddened knuckles of his right hand, as if he had recently thrown a punch. Was he soothing his hand or threatening them? Either way, Lilly skirted past him, head down, to avoid attracting his attention.

As she reached the upper deck, Erika entered the lavatories and gasped. When Lilly followed her inside, she understood why. A row of toilet cubicles stood open: no doors for privacy. But what good would complaining do? She used the facilities as quickly as possible, patted her pocket to check the paper was still there, and hurried out.

Lilly descended the stairs and made her way back along the passageway. She slowed outside the bulkhead door leading to the second women's compartment and peered into the room again. Inside the men's compartment, Stefan stood near the door, clutching a blanket around him, squinting as each woman passed, searching for a sign of Jenny. His eyes met Lilly's. She could only shake her head. Guilt pressed down on her. She should have persuaded Jenny to stay with them, shouldn't have let her go alone. But they were not allowed to exchange a single word. She had to leave him standing there, his face stricken, and return to her compartment.

Lilly stumbled over the bulkhead door's threshold. Her chest tightened and she gulped for breath in the stifling air. The ship's engine started, its noise throbbing in her ears.

How could this be real? Torn from their beds, beaten, robbed. Packed into the hold like cargo. No dignity to use the toilet without permission. Not even doors for privacy. And for what? The crime of wanting to escape persecution, save their lives, and live in their homeland.

Her mind was unspooling from the events of the past twenty-four hours. Yesterday afternoon, she had been sitting on a boulder in Atlit, talking to Isaak. In their optimism, they had assumed it would only be a matter of time until they were freed from the camp.

Lilly looked around for her friends. Neither they nor their belongings were where she had left them. Alarm cut through her until she spotted the three of them to her left, crouched beneath the middle table, heads bent close together, and her belongings safe beside them.

She sidestepped a mother holding her toddler, a woman curled on the floor using her rucksack as a pillow, and a grey-haired woman checking and re-checking her bag of paltry possessions. Lilly apologised to each.

Under the table she found her friends poring over a scrap of paper with a hastily scribbled note. As Lilly crouched down, her friends stiffened. Janka placed her hand over the paper, glanced up, and relaxed. She shifted on the floor to make space.

'I got this from Alexander.' Janka glanced around for guards before handing it to Lilly. 'He slipped it to me as I walked past.'

Lilly took it from her and read.

Don't worry. We're not as bad as we look. We'll be all right. Did they hurt you? Are you together with Erika, Lilly, Gisela and Jenny? Stefan worried about Jenny. Please send note next you pass.
Alexander

Lilly looked up at Janka.

'They are going to be all right,' Janka said, as if to reassure herself.

'He seems more concerned about us than for himself,' Lilly said.

'That's my brother for you.' Her lips lifted in quiet pride. 'Always putting others first.'

'But Jenny ...'

Janka's smile vanished. 'I don't think she's on the *Nieuw Zeeland*. When I looked in the other compartment, I couldn't see her. None of us did.'

'I saw Stefan standing in the doorway. He looked very worried,' Lilly said.

'Poor Stefan,' Janka said. 'She must be on the other ship.'

'This is all my fault,' Lilly said. 'I encouraged her to go. I told her I understood. I should have convinced her to stay.'

'No,' Gisela said. 'You mustn't blame yourself. She would have gone anyway. Even if you had tried to persuade her, she wouldn't have listened. She wanted to follow Stefan. None of us could have known they would put us on two different ships.'

'Gisela is right,' Janka said. 'We had no way of knowing. And if you are to blame, we are all to blame. None of us tried to stop her.'

'But I also saw her in the customs shed,' Lilly said. 'I should have—'

Gisela placed her hand over Lilly's. 'She was too far away for you to have spoken to her. There is nothing you could have done.'

'Is it possible they really will send us to different destinations?'

Janka lowered her head. 'I don't know.'

Erika hesitated. 'I overheard two women earlier. They were speculating the British might send us back to Europe.'

A chill ran through Lilly. The possibility hung between them.

'They wouldn't do that? They couldn't,' Janka said.

'I don't believe it's true,' Gisela said. 'Unless we hear otherwise, let's ignore those rumours and assume we're all being sent to the same place.'

Janka's fingers traced her brother's words. 'At least Alexander has found a way for us to communicate. Any excuse we can find to leave our compartment, we'll take it and send a message in reply.'

Lilly reached into her pocket. 'I think I got one too.'

'From Alexander?'

'I'm not sure.' Lilly unfolded the paper strip. 'Someone placed it in my hand, but I didn't get a chance to see who it was.'

Janka, Erika and Gisela leaned in as Lilly read the tiny words written in cursive Hebrew.

Chazak, chazak, v'nitchazek.
Isaak

Janka's eyes glistened. 'Let us be strong. Let us be strong. And let us strengthen one another.' Her voice faltered. 'That's my cousin for you. He's right. We will strengthen one another.'

Huddled beneath the table, the shrinking circle of friends held each other close.

At seven o'clock in the evening the ship shuddered beneath them. They were moving.

From the windowless hold, Lilly knew what this meant: they were leaving.

They were leaving the Holy Land.

The land they had struggled to reach.

Land of their hopes.

Lilly was leaving Hannah behind. Eugen. A place to call home.

Heading for the unknown.

And no one had come to save them.

Broken.

Eyes shut against the ache in her chest, Lilly clutched Isaak's note like a talisman, repeating the words he had written: *Let us be strong. Let us be strong. And let us strengthen one another.*

It was all she had to hold on to. All that kept her from spiralling into the darkness.

CHAPTER 41

There was no time for Lilly to grieve. Half an hour after the ship's departure, policemen entered carrying mess tins and cutlery. They asked for two volunteers per table to collect the evening meal from the kitchen one deck above. Janka got to her feet at once. Her fingers closed around the note in her pocket and she joined the group of women who followed the policemen out of the compartment. Janka was frowning when they returned a few minutes later, their arms laden with serving trays.

'They took us up the other staircase,' she whispered. 'So we didn't pass the men.'

'You'll get another chance when they let us use the toilet again,' Erika said.

'I also noticed a porthole in the kitchen. But it was too dark to see out.'

'I'll offer to volunteer tomorrow when it's light,' Erika said. 'And I'll try to take a look.'

Twenty women gathered around the table – Lilly, Gisela, Janka, and Erika, and sixteen others with whom they had shared a hut in Atlit.

'At least the food is more plentiful than on the *Atlantic*.' Erika filled her mess tin from the serving trays. 'I suppose that's something.'

Lilly looked at the offerings: cheese, sausages, bread, butter. Her mess tin remained empty.

'You're not eating?'

Lilly shrugged. 'It's not kosher.'

'Oh …' Erika's cheeks coloured. 'I'm sorry. I forgot.'

Gisela inclined her head and said in an undertone, 'Take the bread.' Two slices spread with butter were already stacked in Gisela's tin. 'You have to eat to keep up your strength. You can't starve. In our circumstances it's a greater mitzvah to eat and protect our lives.'

Lilly followed Gisela's advice and helped herself to a slice of bread. She nibbled a corner and set it down. She had no appetite.

Instead, Lilly cradled a cup of tea served in an enamel mug. She had not realised how thirsty she was. It was her first drink of the day. She was careful to take little sips and make the drink last. She had no idea when the guards would next let them use the toilets.

After supper was cleared away, the guards reappeared and piled a stack of hammocks in the corner. The guards ignored requests to wash or use the toilet, and complaints that there were not enough hammocks for every woman or enough space for everyone to stretch out and sleep.

A few women claimed hammocks, which they struggled to attach to the hooks hanging from the beams above. The rest lay down wherever they could find space. On the floor, on the tables and benches, or underneath them. Lilly settled beneath the table, Gisela beside her and Janka and Erika opposite, their feet touching.

Lilly covered herself with her blanket and threw it off. A tarpaulin cover sealed the air shaft during the night's blackout, trapping stagnant air and the acrid smell of unwashed bodies. Confined by the small space, she grew restless, but she had to lie still; the slightest movement would disturb those around her. The noise from the ship's engines was constant and oppressive. Lilly did not know how she would sleep.

Last night she had been in her wooden pallet bed in Atlit. How she missed that bed. She hadn't thought it possible, but their new sleeping conditions were worse than the *Atlantic*. More than the bed, she missed Hannah. How had her cousin reacted when she discovered that they were gone? Was Hannah thinking of her? She imagined standing at the barbed wire fence, her cousin opposite.

Goodnight, Hannah – she willed the words to reach her.

Lilly touched the note in her left pocket. Stay strong, she reminded herself, stay strong. Her hand moved to the note in her right pocket, her reply that she would try to slip to Isaak in the morning.

> *Thank you. Your words give me something to hold onto in this hopelessness.*
> *Lilly*

'Wakey wakey, rise and shine!' a male voice bellowed.

Lilly jolted awake, disoriented and drenched in sweat as if she had slept in a steam room. At some point exhaustion had claimed her.

The angular-faced policeman with the reddened knuckles stood at the compartment entrance. 'Get a move on, ladies. Up, up!' He clapped his hands. 'Time for your wash and brush up.'

Women yawned and groaned.

'It's half-past four in the morning,' one said.

Lilly rubbed her eyes. What sort of time was this?

'If you want to wash and use the toilet, you'd better get up now.' He grinned. 'Or else, you'll have to wait for tonight.'

The message swept through the room – women translating for those who didn't understand – and in moments everyone was on her feet.

'There you go.' He gave a satisfied smile. 'That's more like it. Bring your towels and wash bags. Let's get moving.'

Lilly joined the line filing through the passageway and was disappointed to find another policeman blocking the entrance to the men's compartment, rousing them in a similar fashion. She would not be able to pass her note to Isaak.

The washroom on the deck above was next to the lavatories. Four long rows of basins filled the space. Lilly's eyes brushed past them and went immediately to the porthole on the far wall, but at this hour it showed only darkness.

The basins were crammed close together. Lilly squeezed in at a spare one, uncomfortable undressing so publicly with little personal space. She flinched each time the naked bodies of the women on either side accidentally brushed against her own. But after sweating through the night, the cool water felt refreshing on her skin. Until a shout startled her.

'Hurry up!'

Lilly snapped her head around to find the policeman standing in the doorway. Still lathered in soap, Lilly grabbed her towel and wrapped it around herself.

'Sergeant Tait.'

The angular-faced policeman straightened. 'Yes, sir.'

Another policeman with a dark moustache and a hard gleam in his eyes joined him. They spoke briefly and Sergeant Tait nodded before turning back to the women. 'You need to leave the washroom,' he said. 'It's the men's turn now.'

Instead of giving the women a few minutes' privacy to dress, the two policemen lounged against the doorjambs. They ogled the women scrambling to cover themselves, exchanging comments and laughing. Lilly juggled her underwear and clothes under her towel, dressing as fast as she could.

In her rush to the door, Lilly nearly collided with Janka. Furious and tight-lipped, Janka pushed past the policemen blocking the exit, forging a path that Lilly followed. The policemen sniggered behind their backs.

'Have they no shame?' Janka seethed as they stepped into the dim passageway: a disorganised queue of women waiting for the lavatory and men for the washroom.

'How dare they stand there and watch us like that.' Lilly clenched her teeth. 'I'd just started to feel clean. I didn't even wash off the soap properly.'

A spindly policeman with a pockmarked face standing at the toilet door waved Janka forward. She stepped inside and froze. '*Was ist das*?' She backed out again.

'What's wrong?' Lilly said.

Her mouth parted in stunned disbelief.

'If you've finished, please stand aside,' the policeman said.

'This has to be ... a mistake,' Janka managed, her voice quivering.

'What kind of mistake?' The policeman tilted his head with feigned innocence.

'There are ... men in there.'

'Oh, I see. Well, they have to answer the call of nature too, you know. Now, did you want to go in, or not? Because you're holding up the line.'

The queue behind Lilly and Janka had grown: men and women. Some hopped from foot to foot; others crossed their legs or hunched forward clutching their stomachs.

The policeman waved at Lilly to enter. She remained anchored to the spot. 'Can't we go at separate times?'

The policeman huffed and gestured for the two men behind them to enter. 'If you don't want to go now, you can wait until this evening.'

'Could we please speak to a superior about this?' Janka said.

He responded with a sardonic smile, then shouted, 'Sir!' towards the washroom. 'These ladies would like to speak to you.'

The moustached policeman turned, interest flickering across his face. He unpeeled himself from his vantage point at the door-frame and ambled over. 'Yes. How can I help you?'

'Are you the officer in charge?' Lilly said.

'Indeed, I am.' He drew his shoulders back, preening. 'I am in command here.'

'Well, Kommandant.' Lilly paused. 'We have a slight problem.'

'Oh, yes?' He cocked his head. 'What might that be?'

'The lavatories!' Janka said. 'There are men in there.'

'I see.' The Kommandant folded his arms, and waited for Janka to continue.

'How do you expect us ... to use it ... at the same time?' Janka stammered. 'There's not even ... d–doors. We have to see the m–men ... doing their things.'

The Kommandant smirked. 'Well, now. This is all we have available for you.' He shrugged. 'So you can either like it or lump it.' He spun around and returned to his position at the washroom door.

'What's it to be ladies?' the spindly one said.

Lilly entered the lavatories after Janka, shoulders hunched, one hand tenting her eyes, gaze fixed on the floor. She selected the farthest one available. She walked out, face burning with shame. Degraded. Her fists clenched at her sides.

At least she had not encountered any of her friends in the lavatory. One small mercy. She descended the stairs. Isaak and Alexander ascended toward her, heads bandaged, wrapped in blankets. As they passed, her hand met Isaak's. She slipped her note into his palm.

Chapter 42

The volunteers served breakfast soon after Lilly returned to the hold. Porridge, fresh white bread, butter and marmalade, sausages, and tea. More food than they had received in three days on the *Atlantic*.

The women ate in silence.

Spoons scraped against mess tins. Tea was poured and sipped. Someone reached for bread. Another for the butter. No one met anyone's gaze.

Lilly took only tea and porridge, dragging the spoon through the thick mixture. Janka, sitting opposite, slathered marmalade on her bread. Erika's hands trembled. Her cutlery clattered against her tin. Gisela stared at the pile of bread on her plate. Lilly's skin still crawled from the washroom, the policemen's laughter, the lavatories, the humiliation.

At the next table, a woman slammed her cup on the surface. 'They shouldn't be allowed to treat us like this. It's inhuman!' She jabbed her fork in the air, sausage still speared on the tines. 'I bet prisoners are entitled to better treatment.'

Her words broke the silence. Around the tables, voices rose.

'She's correct.' Janka put down her slice. 'We can't tolerate this.'

'It's not right. It's not decent.' Gisela shook her head. 'We ought to complain.'

'We already tried that,' Janka replied. 'They ignored our complaints. They don't care.'

'We should ask to speak to a superior officer,' Erika said.

'Apparently, the policeman we spoke to is the most superior,' Lilly said. 'He's the Kommandant.'

'Which one is the Kommandant?' Gisela asked.

'The moustached one.' Lilly shuddered at the memory of his eyes watching from the doorway of the washroom.

Gisela's eyebrows rose. 'He's the one in charge? He looks more like a member of the pirate crew from the *Atlantic*. Heaven help us.'

'What are we going to do?' Erika said.

'What can we do? They have us trapped and subject to their whims. We're as good as prisoners.' Janka slumped forward, resting her chin on her hands. 'All we have are two bad choices. Either we suffer the indignity or we don't go.'

Sergeant Tait entered the compartment. 'Ladies! Breakfast is over. Volunteers, clear the tables, take the serving pots back to the kitchen and do the washing up.'

Lilly pushed her half-eaten bowl of porridge aside.

'In addition,' he said, raising his voice above the clatter of trays and cutlery, 'please put your watches forward by one hour.'

'Where are you sending us?' the woman from the next table demanded.

Sergeant Tait left without replying.

Lilly exchanged looks with her friends. 'What direction is that?'

'Not Europe, that's for sure,' Janka said.

Gisela sighed. 'One small mercy we can be grateful for, I suppose.'

A breakfast volunteer brought back information from the galley she had overheard from its crew. The news swept through the group: they had reached Port Said. Egypt.

'I wonder where we will wind up,' Erika said.

'It might be another British colony. If only we had a map.' Janka shut her eyes and traced her index finger along an imaginary route. 'Now, which one might be east or south of Egypt?' Janka said.

'South Africa?' Lilly said.

'It's a possibility,' Janka said.

'Or India?' Gisela said.

'Hmm.' Janka frowned.

'Australia, perhaps?' Erika said.

'Now there's a thought,' Janka said. 'Do the British still send their convicts there? Because they're treating us like criminals.'

At lunch Lilly made sure to volunteer. It was worth it just to escape the humid, stuffy hold. She also hoped to find out more about their destination from the galley crew. Under the guards' watch, Lilly climbed the stairs to the galley. Before she had a chance to strike up a conversation with any of the staff, a mess cook handed her a large serving tray to carry down to her table.

Lunch was as plentiful as the previous meals and included meat, vegetables, and dessert. Lilly took only the mashed potatoes and overcooked spinach. The canned peaches for dessert were a welcome treat.

Afterwards, she ascended to the galley to wash the large pots. She took her time over the task. They had entered the Suez Canal. Through the porthole, the canal's turquoise water bordered a sloped embankment and beyond, barren desert stretched to the horizon, broken only by patches of sparse vegetation. It was her first glimpse of daylight in twenty-four hours, her first view outside. The sun shone. The sky was clear. Her eyes drank in the endless blue. But the view was bittersweet. Unlike their voyage on the *Atlantic*, this ship was taking them further away from Eretz Israel. Once, her ancestors had escaped slavery in Egypt and crossed the Red Sea as free people, heading for the Promised Land. Now they were crossing in the wrong direction – from the Promised Land back to Egypt. From freedom into captivity. Not from despair to hope, but from hope to despair.

At a shout to hurry up, Lilly finished the pots and returned reluctantly to the hold. Gisela was napping. Janka and Erika waited to hear what she'd learned. Lilly had little new information beyond describing the view from the porthole, which she was sharing when a lanky policeman with a rust-coloured moustache appeared in the compartment.

'May I please have your attention,' he said.

'What now?' Janka muttered.

'All women with children are to be reassigned to cabins on the deck above. Please collect your belongings at once and assemble by the left-hand staircase.' He paused. 'I'll need volunteers to help with the move.

Janka's hand shot up. Lilly and Erika joined her. Any excuse to get out of the hold for a while.

The policeman assigned Lilly to a young mother who carried her baby in one arm and led her toddler with her free hand. Lilly followed, hauling their luggage up the stairs.

The Kommandant waited on the deck above, but instead of organising the move, he ogled the women as they formed a queue. And when the first woman in line asked which was her cabin, the Kommandant waved her question away.

'Hargreaves!' the Kommandant shouted.

The lanky policeman with the rust-coloured moustache ran up the stairs two at a time and straightened as he reached his superior. 'Yes, sir.' His pale blue eyes blinked under the Kommandant's stare.

'Sort out these women and assign them to the cabins.'

'Yes, sir. Very good, sir,' Hargreaves said to the Kommandant's back as he strolled off along the passageway.

Hargreaves' stance eased with his departure. 'Well, then.' He looked along the line of women and children, his expression softening. 'Let's get you all settled, shall we?'

Lilly felt a touch of envy when Hargreaves showed the young mother and another woman with a three-year-old daughter into a small cabin. She understood the hold was unsuitable for small children and the move gave everyone more room, but she wished the guards had allocated all of them to cabins with bunks and portholes. Like this one.

Lilly followed the women into the cabin and set down the baggage.

'Well then ...' Hargreaves said, hovering in the doorway before taking a step back. 'I suppose I'd better let you get settled.'

'Sir,' Lilly said. 'Would it be all right if I stayed in the cabin for an hour to help them unpack?'

Hargreaves paused and looked up and down the passageway before answering. 'I dare say that would be acceptable.'

Once Lilly had helped the two mothers settle in, she had undisturbed time to look out of the porthole. At this stretch, the canal widened into a broad lake. White sand beaches lined the shore, fringed by palms, with expensive-looking cars parked nearby. People swam and sunbathed. It looked like a spa resort.

Confined to the hold, it was easy to forget that life went on. Even in wartime. What was happening out there in the world? What news of the war? How was her family – her mama in particular? Lilly hoped the letter she had given to Bracha, the *gaffira*, in Atlit would reach her. After months with no news, she would be frantic with worry. How long and from where would Lilly next write to her?

An hour passed all too soon. Lilly left the cabin, returned to the hold, and joined her friends in their place on the floor. The hold was less crowded now, but after the bright cabin, it felt heavier and more suffocating.

Erika, though, appeared brighter. 'You'll never guess what?' she said. 'I asked that policeman, Hargreaves, about volunteering in the infirmary, and he said they could do with extra staff. So I'll be working there from tomorrow.'

Lilly managed a smile at Erika's news. 'You'll be happy to get back to nursing.'

'Yes, I will. And I'll get out of this horrible compartment for a few hours.' Erika lifted her head towards the air shaft above and inhaled deeply.

Janka looked up from a notebook, where she'd been writing in tiny characters. 'I wish there were something I could do to volunteer.'

'If I see Hargreaves again, I'll ask,' Erika said. 'He seems more decent than the others we have encountered so far. Better than the Kommandant.'

'Well, that's not much of a standard.' Janka twirled her pencil between her fingers. 'It doesn't take much to be better than the Kommandant.'

'What are you writing?' Lilly asked. 'Another note to Alexander?'

'No. A diary. I want to write everything down that has happened to us since we left Prague before I forget the details. When we were on the *Atlantic*, I saw Franci Berger from our Prague group writing one. It didn't seem so important to me at the time because I thought we'd soon be in Eretz and could forget about that nightmare journey. But now I feel it's more essential to keep a record. Maybe as evidence.' She waved the notebook for emphasis. 'I don't think people would believe half of what we've been through. And the awful experience this morning was about the final straw.'

That evening at supper, after another degrading visit to the lavatories, they talked about the Kommandant again.

'Why can't the Kommandant make separate times for us to visit the facilities?' Janka said. 'It's so embarrassing.'

'Or hang a curtain, at least, so we don't have to see the "beautiful sights,"' Erika said.

'Beautiful sights.' Janka snorted.

'And how does he expect an old woman like me to go to the lavatory just twice a day?' Gisela said. 'I had awful stomach cramps all afternoon.'

'Oh, Gisela, I didn't realise.' Lilly placed her hand over Gisela's. 'Why didn't you say something?'

'I didn't want to worry you. Anyway, what could you do? While you were upstairs helping the mothers, a few women begged the policeman on duty for permission to go. He called the Kommandant, who refused outright and said the toilets were locked until this evening.' Gisela pulled her lips back in visible discomfort. She lowered her voice, 'One older lady was suffering from diarrhoea. The Kommandant didn't care.'

'Poor woman,' Erika said. 'What did she do?'

Gisela's hands fluttered in distress. 'What could she do?'

Lilly grimaced and saw her reaction mirrored in her friends' expressions.

'The Kommandant seems to find amusement in our discomfort.' Erika's voice hardened.

'And he struts about with as much self-importance as if he was the King of England himself.' Janka said.

'If he were anything like King George, he would have a semblance of dignity,' Lilly said. 'Our Georgi would not know what dignity meant if it slapped him in the face.'

'Our Georgi.' Erika giggled. 'That's a good one.'

Janka's smile faded. 'In all seriousness, "Our Georgi" strikes me as a depraved character. It's almost as if he's looking for ways to humiliate us. I don't think we should give him any more satisfaction. In future, when we go to the washroom or the lavatories, we should hold our heads high.'

'You're right,' Erika said. 'We shouldn't let them see we are embarrassed.'

'I agree. And yet, why should we have to put up with this treatment?' Lilly thumped her cup onto the table. 'At the very least, we should be entitled to privacy and a shred of respect. As that woman on the next table said earlier, they wouldn't be allowed to treat prisoners like this.'

Janka threw up her hands. 'What else can we do? We tried complaining to him and that other policeman, and it got us nowhere.'

'I don't know.' Lilly rested her chin on her hand and thought for a few moments. 'What if we find a way to undermine him?'

'Oh, I like the sound of this.' Janka leaned forward. 'How would we do that?'

'Perhaps we could speak to another policeman. One who is more sympathetic towards us. He could be the one to persuade the Kommandant so it seems like it comes from him, rather than us. And he could suggest the policeman wait outside to give us privacy when we wash, add a curtain in front of the lavatories, and not restrict the times when we're allowed to use the toilets.'

'Subtle. Clever,' Janka said. 'Now we just have to find one.'

'Maybe Hargreaves?' Erika said. 'I'll try to start planting the idea tomorrow, when I begin working in the infirmary.'

'Yes. ' Janka's smile was a quiet rebellion. 'Do it.'

That night, Lilly's despair didn't weigh quite as heavily. Their soft plans of defiance helped, as did the relative calm without the constant crying of infants. But mostly it was the brief note slipped into her hand on her way back from the toilets. She unfolded it beneath the table.

Don't give up hope. Never give up hope.
Somehow we will return to Eretz.
Isaak

Chapter 43

11 December 1940
SS Nieuw Zeeland, The Red Sea

Another morning. Another wake-up call. Another day trapped in the ship's hold. Each day melting into the next.

After a broken night's sleep, bathed in sweat, Lilly washed, refreshed by the cool water. She still detested the communal bathing, but she was learning to wash, dry, and dress faster, without giving Georgi too much time to stare.

Lilly followed Janka's suggestion to hold her head high and conceal her embarrassment while she waited in the queue for the toilets. All the same, she covered her eyes when she entered.

On her return to the hold, Lilly crossed paths on the staircase with Alexander, Max, Stefan, and Isaak. Again they were among the last in line. Perhaps it was deliberate to ensure they did not visit the toilets at the same time as the women. A thoughtful gesture, saving them all from even greater mortification. But it might have been out of necessity. Alexander helped Max as they climbed the stairs. Max gritted his teeth and grunted with every step, still in pain. Stefan looked unwell. He gripped the railing, his skin ashen, his face tight with discomfort. They passed without speaking, but Lilly managed to slip a note to Isaak.

It's hard to hold onto hope. But I'm trying. Your words give me strength.
Where are they sending us? Have you heard anything?

Lilly entered her compartment. The heat hit her like a blast furnace. The temperature seemed to rise daily. Her cotton dress clung to her back; the relief she had felt while washing in the cool water was already fading.

Janka pulled Lilly aside before she reached the table. She looked tense.

'As I left the washroom, I overheard a conversation between Georgi and a woman from the other compartment,' Janka said. 'He asked if she was married. When she told Georgi yes, that her husband was on the other ship, at first he looked disappointed. Then he broke into a smile. A cruel smile. His eyes remained as cold as glass. He told the woman it's unlikely she'll ever see her husband again because the *Johan de Witt* is heading for a different destination.'

'What!' Lilly said. 'Does that mean those rumours we heard the night we boarded are true?'

Janka's shoulders rose and fell, heavy with doubt. 'I'm not convinced Georgi was telling her the truth. Perhaps he was manipulating her, playing a cruel game. I wouldn't put it past him. Either way, the poor woman crumpled, saying over and over: "It can't be true. It can't be true." Her reaction appeared to amuse him.'

'So does that mean Jenny—'

'I don't know.'

'I passed Stefan on the stairs this morning,' Lilly said. 'He looks in a bad way.'

'Poor man. He must be sick with worry. I'd be too if Alexander and Isaak were on the other ship. But maybe he's just unwell. So many people are coming down with upset stomachs. This policy of only allowing us to go to the toilet twice a day isn't helping either.'

'No, it isn't.' Lilly let out a long breath. 'I'm worried about Gisela too. She also had stomach cramps yesterday. But you know she doesn't like to make a fuss.' She paused, noticing Gisela waving at them from the table.

'Later,' Janka said. 'Let's have breakfast. Best not to mention this to anyone. Let's hope it isn't true.'

They took their seats at the table where Gisela waited. Erika's place was empty. She had left for her first shift in the infirmary earlier that morning, before the rest were awake.

After breakfast, Janka remained at the table to write in her diary. Gisela dozed. Lilly spent the remainder of the morning bored and frustrated. There was nothing to occupy her, nowhere to go, no room to walk. Her hands were restless. The heat dulled her thoughts. She sat listlessly waiting for Erika. For the next meal. For anything to break the monotony.

They were sitting down for lunch when Erika stepped through the bulkhead door. There was a lightness to her steps Lilly hadn't seen in some time.

'I have so much to tell you.' On one side of a mess tin, Erika heaped tinned corned beef, mashed potatoes, and tinned carrots. On the other she added a generous portion of steamed pudding with raisins – curiously called spotted dick by the galley crew – and smothered it with lumpy custard. She smiled sheepishly. 'I'm starving. I didn't have time to eat breakfast before my shift.'

'Well?' Gisela said after Erika had taken a few bites. 'Tell us about your morning?'

'I won't lie, it was challenging,' Erika said. 'The infirmary's in a shabby double cabin. It's overflowing with people. We hardly have any medication. There's a terrible outbreak of diarrhoea. Not helped by these cramped living conditions and the toilet restrictions. But having said that, it's good to be back doing the job I love.'

A hint of contentment softened Erika's face; her eyes bright, no longer mournful. She looked more like her old self, the spirited Erika Lilly remembered from the beginning of their voyage on the *Atlantic*. Before she lost Marcus. Working at what she loved, caring for others, appeared to have a healing effect on her.

'After days stuck in the hold, feeling worthless with nothing to do, it's good to have a purpose again,' Erika continued. 'Another bonus is the infirmary has a porthole. That small thing, seeing daylight, makes all the difference. This morning, while looking after patients, I caught a glimpse as we came through the end of the Suez Canal. I saw a bustling port with many ships and some warehouses or factory buildings.'

'Did you ask any other members of the medical staff if they know our destination?' Janka asked.

'I did. But most of the doctors and nurses are our people. None of them know,' 'I have some other news, though.' Erika smiled. 'I saw Inspector Hargreaves. He came to the infirmary just before I finished my shift, to find out how I was getting on. I didn't manage to discuss the situation with the washroom and toilets, but he mentioned he has a couple of other jobs to fill. Someone to do a bit of sewing, mending and alterations to uniforms. And another person for some copy typing work.'

The word *sewing* caught Lilly's attention.

'And?' Janka said.

'I told him I know two women who would be ideal for the positions.' Erika looked from Janka to Lilly. 'If you're interested, the jobs are yours. He'll be waiting for you to start straight after lunch.'

'I can do the typing,' Janka said. 'I used to type my father's business letters all the time. It was a German typewriter, not an English one, but how different can it be? I'll type whatever he wants. Even the whole telephone book or a dictionary from A to Z.' Janka glanced at the airshaft. 'Anything to get out of this suffocating hold for a while.'

'I'd like to do the sewing and altering,' Lilly said. 'Thank you so much.'

'You did well, Erika,' Gisela said.

'Would you like me to find out if there's a job for you too?'

Gisela gave a soft chuckle. 'Oh, I don't think so. I'm retired. But if you can find another way to get me out of this hold, I'd appreciate it.'

'If I can find a way ...' Erika said.

'I know you would if you could.' Gisela stroked her cheek.

The tailor's room occupied a converted cabin one level up, past the washroom and toilets, a few doors away from the infirmary.

'I appreciate you helping us out,' Inspector Hargreaves said, as he ushered Lilly inside.

She hesitated in the doorway. Was it a mistake for her to help after everything this police force had done? This was not like Erika's work, nursing the sick, helping her own people. Lilly would be helping them.

'Miss, this way, please.' Inspector Hargreaves had walked to the far end of the cabin where a table sat underneath the porthole, flooding the area with natural light. A Singer sewing machine, similar to the one she had used in Vienna, was already set up and threaded. A nostalgic, magnetic pull drew her in.

Inspector Hargreaves pointed to a canvas hamper tucked to the right of the table. 'The items needing repair are stacked in here. Each item has a tag detailing the repair or alteration required. The new nursing assistant who started today assures me you are a proficient seamstress, so I assume you are familiar with how this machine works?'

Lilly nodded, gazing at the sewing machine, as if reuniting with a close friend after a long absence.

'You should find all the other tools and supplies you might require, such as needles and thread, scissors, pins and buttons, in that wooden sewing box beside it.' Hargreaves gestured to the left side of the room. 'Once you have finished with each item, please fold and stack it here.'

Lilly followed his gesture to the narrow wall shelf.

'It should all be quite self-explanatory. Do you have any further questions?' Hargreaves said.

'No, Inspector,' Lilly said. 'I think I understand.'

'Very good.' He marched to the exit, resting his hand on the door frame. 'Right then, I'll let you get on with it. I'll be back at five o'clock.'

Once Hargreaves had left, Lilly reached out to the sewing machine. She touched the handwheel and rotated it back and forth, watching the needle rise and fall. She had not used a machine since leaving Vienna. How she had missed sewing. Lilly leaned over the table and peered through the porthole at the blue sea, rippling in the sunlight. She looked around at the little tailor's room. She was alone. Alone. In a space of her own for the next few hours.

No, it was not wrong for Lilly to do this work. They had sent her on this ship against her will. The conditions over the past three days had been inhumane. Now she had a chance for a few hours' reprieve. She had been right to accept it.

Lilly took the first item out of the hamper, sat at the table, and read the tag. Her first task was to take up the hem by an inch on a pair of trousers. After she had measured and pinned, Lilly laid the trousers on the plate beneath the needle and lowered the presser foot to hold the fabric in place. She set her foot onto the treadle and rocked it into motion, calling up the rhythmic clack of the needle mechanism, an old, familiar song.

The machine's rhythm drew Lilly's thoughts inward, connecting her to memories and parts of herself she had locked away.

Lilly was back in Vienna, in the small apartment where she had lived with Salo. She was sewing curtains at the table while he sat beside her, reading the newspaper. Salo's joy as he helped her to hang them on the curtain rods above each window. The pride on her papa's face, in the days he was still sharp and agile, when he came upstairs from the shop to see her work. 'Isn't your wife talented?'

Salo beamed at Lilly. 'I'm the luckiest man in Vienna to have such a talented and beautiful wife.'

Hannah's excitement at trying on the new dresses Lilly had made for her before leaving Vienna.

Mama's approving smile after Lilly tried on the dresses she had made before her own departure. 'You will look so stylish on your voyage to Eretz Israel.' Back when the two of them had envisioned a voyage on a liner.

Lilly did not hear anyone enter the tailor's room. She did not notice him until he was leaning over her left shoulder. Lilly gave a start and looked up to see Georgi's face inches from her own. Close enough to feel his hot breath on her skin. Close enough to smell the alcohol on his breath.

Chapter 44

'Very nice,' Georgi said.

He edged closer, his hand stroking the shirt Lilly was working on. She stiffened.

'Very nice work, indeed.'

'Th-thank … y-you.' She wanted to angle herself away, but the sewing machine pinned her in place.

'Where did you learn to sew like this?'

'In Vienna.'

'Ah! Vienna,' he repeated. 'What is your name, my dear?'

'L-Lilly.'

'That's a nice name. And are you married, Lilly?'

'I … I'm …'

'Sir?' A sharp voice cut through from the passageway.

Georgi jumped back. Lilly exhaled at the sight of Hargreaves taking quick strides through the cabin. 'Is everything in order?'

Georgi straightened himself like a thief with his hand caught in the till. 'All in order, Hargreaves. I came to inspect the work of your new seamstress.'

'No need to trouble yourself, sir,' Hargreaves said. 'I know how busy you are. I can take over from here.'

'Very good.' Georgi held his head erect, shooting Hargreaves a venomous look. 'As you were.' He strode out of the tailor's room as if nothing untoward had happened.

'Miss …' Hargreaves began. He hesitated, at a loss for words. He stopped several feet away, at the shelf of completed items. 'How did you get on this afternoon?'

'I … just have one more piece to alter.' Lilly held up the shirt. Her hands trembled.

Hargreaves picked up the stack of folded uniforms from the completed shelf. 'And these are all finished?'

'Yes, Inspector.'

He read the instruction tag on a pair of trousers and unfolded them, examining the alterations. He repeated the process with the shirt beneath it. 'Excellent work.'

'Thank you, Inspector.'

'Besides that last piece, there's another hamper waiting for repairs. Perhaps you could come back tomorrow?'

Was Lilly expected to comply or could she refuse? 'I suppose I could.'

She had enjoyed sewing, and although she was eager to have an excuse to leave the hold again, could she risk another encounter with Georgi?

'Thank you, miss, that would be much appreciated.' He glanced at the entrance. 'I assume such painstaking work as yours needs concentration. It would be … acceptable for you to lock the door while you are working. And I can knock three times at the end of your shift.'

'Thank you, Inspector.' Lilly rose from her seat and followed Hargreaves to the exit. He ushered her out first, located the correct key on his overloaded bunch, and locked the door.

He accompanied Lilly as far as the staircase. 'Er, miss, perhaps tomorrow you could come straight after breakfast?'

'All right.'

He smiled faintly and lowered his voice. 'Rumour has it you might be able to go up on deck for a little while in the afternoon.' He tapped his nose before resuming his formal posture. 'Well then, until tomorrow.'

Lilly descended the stairs caught in a knot of conflicting feelings. The few hours away from the confines of the hold had made her feel freer. Weightless. Reconnected with herself. But Georgi had tainted the experience. Then there was the news she carried – important, if it turned out to be true.

The heat and dense air gripped Lilly as soon as she entered the compartment. But here were her friends, and their presence offered shelter. They waved from the table, waiting for the evening meal.

'How was your first afternoon at work as a seamstress?' Janka said as Lilly took her seat to join them.

'I did repairs and alterations on uniforms.'

'How was it?' Erika asked.

'Good.'

Lilly could not bring herself to mention Georgi. She knew she had done nothing wrong, yet the episode left her uncomfortable. Embarrassed even. She wanted to cast it from her mind, not dwell on it. 'I enjoyed working on a sewing machine again.' She looked across the table at Erika. 'Thank you for recommending me. It was also nice being out of the hold for a few hours in a cabin with a porthole.'

'What could you see?' Gisela asked.

'I'd imagine the same view as I had,' Janka said. 'Sea, sea, and more sea.'

'What colour is the Red Sea?' Gisela said.

'It's blue,' Janka said. 'As blue as the Black Sea and the Mediterranean. Although at sunset the water looked like rose gold.'

'I miss having a window.' Gisela looked wistful. Her eyes were hollow. 'It's amazing the difference a bit of natural daylight can make.'

'You may also have a chance for some daylight soon.' Lilly dropped her voice. 'I heard we might be allowed out onto the deck for a bit tomorrow afternoon.'

Erika raised her eyebrows. 'Who said that?'

'Hargreaves.'

'Ha!' Janka said. 'I'll believe it when I see it.'

Lilly shrugged. 'So how was your afternoon as a typist?'

'Well, as I was telling Gisela and Erika, I was typing letters and reports from handwritten notes. I had hoped I might find information about our intended destination, but no such luck. It took me a while to get used to the English typewriter after using a German one.' Janka laughed. 'I discovered that Z and Y are in swapped positions. So, until I got the hang of it, duty became dutz, yesterday became zesterday, and yes became zes. I suppose I must have done a satisfactory job because Hargreaves asked if I could continue tomorrow.'

The next morning, Lilly sewed without interruption, the entrance to the tailor's room locked. Hargreaves said nothing further about going on deck, leaving Lilly to think that nothing would come of it. But after lunch, as they resigned themselves to another monotonous afternoon in the hold, Sergeant Tait entered their compartment. 'Ladies, your attention please,' he said. 'You're now allowed up on the promenade deck until four o'clock. If you would like to take advantage of this opportunity, please make your way up the left-hand stairs in an orderly fashion.'

A fresh wave of energy swept through the compartment. The women rose at once, chattering as they filed out.

'Lilly, you were right.' Erika smiled.

'They are probably letting us out now because they think we no longer pose a threat,' Janka said. 'We're now far from any port and so less likely to blow up the ship.'

Erika rolled her eyes in mock exasperation.

'Just be grateful we're getting out for some fresh air at long last,' Gisela said as Lilly helped her to her feet. 'I don't care what their reasoning is.'

'Don't get me wrong, I am grateful.' Janka shut her notebook and slipped it into her rucksack. 'But that might be why they didn't let us out before.'

'That seems unlikely,' Erika said. 'What would have stopped us doing something from the hold? Not that we would have,' she added. 'Even if we had wanted to, we don't have weapons of any kind after their search in Haifa. Not even first aid scissors, or a hairbrush—'

'Or a pair of silk stockings.' Janka hoisted her rucksack.

'Why are you taking your rucksack?' Erika said. 'We're only going onto the deck for a few hours, not leaving.'

'Because of what happened in Haifa,' Janka said. 'I'm not letting the policemen take any more of our possessions while we're out.'

'Good thinking.' Lilly followed Janka's example. Erika and Gisela did the same, as did many of the women leaving the hold.

The ascent from the hold to the upper deck was slow going, a steady stream of women heading up the same narrow route. The climb up four flights of stairs challenged Gisela, who had hardly moved from the hold for three days. She was breathless by the time they reached the landing, but as Lilly and Erika helped her through the weathertight door, Gisela beamed, her eyes crinkling at the corners.

'Gisela!' called a familiar voice.

Lilly blinked in the bright sunlight and saw Isaak bounding over to meet them, Alexander a step behind. Both wore only blankets and bandages. Lilly's heart lifted at the sight of them.

'My darlings!' Gisela's words caught on a snatched inhale and she hugged them. 'How I've missed you both.'

'We missed you too,' Isaak said.

Gisela reached up and stroked Isaak's cheek, her gaze moving to the blood-stained bandage and his black eye. 'What did they do to you?'

'It looks worse than it is.'

Alexander hugged his sister, then Erika and Lilly. Isaak embraced them too.

'How have you been?' Isaak said as he pulled back from Lilly, his eyes still resting on her, so much unspoken.

'Where are Max and Stefan?' Janka asked.

'They are resting in the shade near the top of the staircase on the other side,' Alexander said. 'We just got here ourselves. It was quite an effort to climb all those stairs, especially for Max. He has a bruised or broken rib.' Alexander took Gisela's arm. 'Would you also like to sit?'

'I wouldn't mind,' Gisela said, still catching her breath.

Alexander led the way around the corner, where the ship's superstructure offered shade from the intense heat. Isaak accompanied them until he stopped short and broke away to peer over the railings.

'Look who I found,' Alexander said as they approached Max and Stefan. Max sat with his back against the wall, his head resting on a folded blanket. He gave them a weak smile. His head was bandaged, purple and blue bruises darkening beneath his eyes. His chest was strapped with bandages too. Stefan sat beside him, his face pale, eyes sunken.

Lilly crouched opposite Max. 'How are you feeling?'

'I've felt better,' he said. 'I've also felt worse. But my wounds will heal in time.'

Lilly nodded.

'And you?'

'What can I say? It isn't easy.'

'I know,' he said. 'I know.'

Isaak hurried back before Lilly could exchange a word with Stefan. 'We're travelling in a convoy with naval ships.' He squatted beside Stefan and smiled. 'And I saw the *Johan de Witt* a short way behind us.'

'See?' Alexander placed a hand on Stefan's arm. 'We're all heading in the same direction. You'll see Jenny again soon.'

Relief crossed Stefan's face. 'Thank God,' he said in a voice much weaker than Lilly remembered.

Erika leaned forward. 'Stefan, what's wrong?'

'I haven't been feeling well,' he said. 'Stomach issues. The toilet restrictions don't help.'

'No, they don't,' Erika said. 'I've been volunteering in the infirmary. The medical staff have made several complaints. I also mentioned it to a more sympathetic policeman, but to no effect so far. Perhaps you should come to the infirmary and let the doctor examine you.'

'Maybe being outside the hold in the fresh air will help me feel better. I'll see how I go.'

They settled on the deck in a circle, the way they had often done on the *Atlantic*, and took turns sharing what had happened since Atlit. The Lifeboat Chevra, reunited. But as Lilly looked around the circle, she noticed the absence of those missing: Hannah, Alma, and Jenny. The atmosphere on deck was not the same as on the *Atlantic*. Passengers were more subdued, beaten, weary. The hope that had sustained them through their journey lay abandoned in Eretz.

The *Nieuw Zeeland* had none of the crush they had experienced on the *Atlantic*'s deck. The passengers strolled the length and width, but under constant observation by the policemen – including Georgi. He seemed to pay particular attention to the young women. Lilly wedged herself between Isaak and Gisela, her back to the policemen, determined to stay out of Georgi's line of sight.

'Does anyone fancy a short walk around the deck?' Alexander said after they had been talking for an hour. 'I need to stretch my legs before they send us back into the crowded hold. This might be our only chance.'

'I'll come,' Janka said.

Erika and Isaak stood. Lilly got up as well.

'What about you, Gisela?' Lilly said.

'I'll get enough walking going back down those four flights. I'm happy to stay here with Max and Stefan.'

Lilly set off on a circuit of the deck with the other four. They stopped at the railings and looked at the ships: one vessel leading them and four behind, including the *Johan de Witt* carrying Jenny. Lilly was reassured that at least they were travelling together.

They continued walking around the deck, stopping to look at a small swimming pool, a remnant from the days when the Dutch ship was a smart passenger liner, before its requisition by the British government. How different this might have been if they were passengers on holiday instead of refugees being deported, strolling freely with no guards observing their every move.

Alexander carried on ahead with Janka and Erika as Isaak and Lilly fell behind.

'Thank you for your notes,' Lilly said when they were alone. 'They've been a comfort.'

Isaak looked down, almost embarrassed. 'I'm glad they helped. Your notes meant a lot to me too.'

'Your words were the only thing that kept me from sinking into despair.'

He hesitated. 'Surely they're not the only thing?'

She shook her head. 'I feel like every ounce of hope I had is gone.' She leaned against the railings. Isaak joined her.

'I've lost so much,' Lilly said. 'My husband. My father. My mother and aunt are trapped in Vienna. Hannah is somewhere I can't reach her. I have no home, no family with me. They've taken away the one thing I dreamed of – a new start in our land. And the way they treat us on this ship ...' She briefly covered her face with her hands. 'What's the point anymore?'

'I understand,' Isaak said. 'I'm worried about my family too. I'm devastated about what happened. Angry at the lies, the beatings, the way they're still treating us.' His passion rose, then steadied. 'But I haven't lost hope.'

Lilly studied him. His eyes held hers, unwavering. 'How can you still have hope after everything we have been through?'

'How can I not?' he said. 'What if right now Hannah, Eugen, and Alma have launched an appeal for our return? What if our situation is being debated in the Houses of Parliament in London? What if my parents and brother managed to board a ship and are waiting for me right now in Eretz Israel?'

She turned to the sea. The sea that had tossed them about, threatening their lives. The sea that had carried them to safety, brought them home, carried them away. Ally one day, adversary the next.

'Do you really think you'll never see Hannah or your brother again?' he continued.

'I don't know. I just don't know.'

'How can they keep us away from Eretz Israel forever?'

'But they said we can never return. Even once the war ends.'

'They said a lot of things like if we paid for the crossing from Cyprus we'd be allowed to land in Haifa.'

The reminder stung.

'Think of Gisela. Wrenched from the chance of a reunion with her sons. Can you tell her there's no hope of seeing them again?'

'No,' Lilly said in a small voice.

'If we give up, then there is no hope,' Isaak said, his tone measured but firm. 'We might as well accept every insult, every blow.' He faced her. 'But if we refuse to surrender, if we appeal and protest and fight for our right to return, then there's hope. They can't keep us away forever.'

Lilly blinked hard.

'We're not the first of our people to be exiled,' Isaak said. 'After the Babylonians destroyed the Temple, our ancestors wept by the rivers of Babylon. After the Romans destroyed the Second Temple, they carried our people as slaves to Rome. Through Crusades and Inquisitions and pogroms, we endured. We're still here.' His voice softened. 'We too have suffered, yet we reached the shore of Eretz Israel. We stood on the land, even if only for a brief time. If we don't give up, I believe we will return.'

A flicker stirred in Lilly: like the strike of a match against its box. A pause. Anticipation. Possibility.

'You truly believe it?'

'I do,' he said. 'And I won't give up.'

A pressure swelled in Lilly's chest, lodging in her throat until she could barely breathe. Then it broke as a sob.

'Hold on, Lilly,' Isaak said. He held her while she cried. 'Hold on. Don't give up hope.'

Within her despair, a spark. The match caught. Bruised and broken, she lifted herself once again. No, it was not the end. It would not have been better if she had never risen from the bottom of those stairs in her parents' apartment two years ago in Vienna. If she had not got up, she would not be here now, held by someone who refused to let her give up.

Chapter 45

13 December 1940
SS Nieuw Zeeland, The Red Sea

As Lilly and Janka emerged onto the promenade deck just after sunrise, with Gisela between them, Alexander and Isaak were already waiting by the companionway door.

'Isn't this better than being stuck in the hold all day?' Alexander said.

It was better. Earlier, Sergeant Tait had informed them they would be permitted on deck in the morning and afternoon, but they had to return to the hold for meals. No one knew whether this would continue beyond today. Lilly and Janka had grabbed their bags immediately. Only Erika stayed behind to sleep after her night shift.

Alexander's gaze moved past them to the door. 'Where's Erika?'

'She's catching up on sleep after a night shift,' Janka said.

'Oh.' He looked away briefly.

'But she said she'll come up in the afternoon,' Janka added.

Alexander nodded and led the way, Janka falling into step with him. 'Are we sitting in the same place as yesterday?'

'Yes, Max is already there, waiting for us.'

Lilly and Isaak followed with Gisela, who was catching her breath.

'What about Stefan?' Lilly said.

'He wanted to stay in the hold. He thinks he'll feel better after a few more hours of undisturbed sleep.'

'How are you feeling today, Max?' Gisela said as they reached him.

'Slowly, slowly,' he said. The outer edges of the bruises around his eyes were fading from blue to green.

They settled into a circle. Alexander and Isaak adjusted their blankets and lowered themselves to the deck.

'*Uff*!' Alexander fanned himself with the edge of his blanket. 'It's already getting hot out here!'

'I still prefer this to the stifling hold,' Janka said.

'But at least in the hold we don't have to stay wrapped up in blankets,' Alexander said. 'Which seem to have picked up lice in the hold. We saw them on the hammocks too. I squashed two this morning.'

Janka wrinkled her nose and edged back a fraction. 'What do you wear instead?'

He looked down. 'We don't have anything else to wear.'

Janka's eyes widened. 'You mean ... you go around in your Adam's clothing?

'Well, what are we supposed to do? We don't have any fig leaves handy. Apparently our suitcases have been loaded onto the ship but they won't give us access. So in the meantime we have no clothes. Not that the policemen care.' He winked at his sister. 'Maybe you could lend us some.'

'And what would you do with a skirt and blouse?' Janka chuckled.

Alexander shrugged.

Lilly glanced from Alexander to Isaak to Max. It could not have been pleasant wrapped in thick, prickly woollen blankets as the temperature rose by the day. And now lice.

'I wish I could sew some for you,' Lilly said. 'I have access to a sewing machine in the tailor's room. If only I could find some fabric.'

Alexander gave a lopsided grin. 'We wouldn't need much in this heat. Some swimming trunks ought to do it. Like them.' He tilted his head at the railings behind Lilly. 'They look comfortable enough.'

Lilly glanced back and saw two young women sunbathing in skimpy swimsuits. That wasn't all. Georgi was crouched beside the young women, talking and laughing. Lilly's stomach turned. His hand stroked the shoulder of the young brunette, no older than eighteen or nineteen. Worse still, she seemed to enjoy his attention and accepted the piece of chocolate he broke off for her.

Janka stared too.'What on earth are they thinking? Not even for a whole box of Demel chocolates tied with a silk ribbon would I consent to that. *Pfui*! With Georgi, of all people.'

'Georgi?' Alexander said.

'The Kommandant,' Janka said. 'We nicknamed him Georgi.'

'*Ach so*!' Isaak said. 'We call him the mad dog.'

'That's also a fitting name,' Janka said. 'He's mad all right.'

'Indeed.' Alexander and Isaak exchanged a look. Lilly sensed they'd also had an unpleasant encounter with the Kommandant. Neither elaborated. Lilly did not mention her own experience either.

'Actually,' Alexander said, 'about the clothes. Could you ask the women to bring whatever they can spare when we come back this afternoon? Anything at all.'

'Whatever for?' Janka said.

Alexander's eyes glinted. 'You'll see.'

Lilly could not imagine what Alexander had in mind.

The next morning, after breakfast, the policeman's voice echoed through the hold: 'Everyone on deck, no exceptions.' Lilly climbed the stairs with Janka and Gisela, and a reluctant Erika who had hoped to catch up on sleep.

As they reached the promenade deck, Lilly wiped the perspiration from her forehead. She lowered her hand. She blinked. Blinked again.

'What on earth—' Janka's voice rose an octave.

'Good morning!' Alexander stood before them wearing a tie knotted with effortless elegance at his neck – and nothing else but Janka's skirt. Isaak, beside him, wore Janka's blouse and his blanket tied around his waist like a sarong.

Lilly stared speechless.

'What is this, a Purim carnival?' A smile played at Gisela's mouth.

Lilly looked from one side of the deck to the other. Men were promenading in skirts, silky slips, and women's underwear. One man wore a blouse tucked into a pair of puffy ski trousers. Another, a blanket sarong and a brassiere.

Across the deck, Emil stood watching them, arms folded, with the expression of a man who had predicted exactly this sort of nonsense.

Janka snorted.

A man strolled past in a pair of enormous bloomers. Erika's eyes went wide. She gasped. 'Gisela? Are they ...?'

Gisela's shoulders shook. 'They're not mine.' She doubled over and clutched her sides.

Erika dissolved into giggles. Tears rolled down Lilly's cheeks. Alexander and Isaak were laughing too.

'I ... have to ... sit down,' Gisela said.

Alexander and Isaak put their arms around her, and the three stumbled around the corner. Lilly, Janka and Erika staggered after them, unable to look at one another without howling. When they reached Max, Janka collapsed on the deck. 'I can't breathe!'

Max had joined in the fun, his blanket tied like a skirt. He pressed a hand to his bandaged ribs, caught between laughter and pain.

Alexander sat down carefully, holding down the hem of the skirt. Janka gave him a look. He shrugged. 'I'm wearing it in the traditional Scottish style.'

'You've stretched my skirt.' She looked around at the others. 'Good grief. Why are you all dressed like this?'

'We thought it might get the policemen's attention,' Alexander said.

'It looks like you have succeeded,' Janka said.

The policemen were laughing among themselves. Georgi pointed to a man whose slip caught in the breeze, billowing up. The man tugged it down hastily. A young policeman turned away, his fist pressed against his mouth, his back heaving. Even Sergeant Tait's mouth twitched.

'Perhaps now they will realise how ridiculous this situation is and let us access our luggage and retrieve our clothes.'

'I wouldn't hold your breath,' Janka said.

'At least it gave everyone a reason to laugh.'

'On that, you certainly succeeded,' Erika said. 'I don't remember the last time I laughed so hard.'

Alexander smiled at her. 'I think we all needed that.'

'We did.' She returned his smile.

'Perhaps if we keep parading, it will help attract the policemen's attention,' he said. 'Would you care to take a walk?'

'Well, I—'

Alexander winked. 'Or are you embarrassed to be seen with me dressed like this?'

'No.' Erika's cheeks coloured.

'Yes, you are. Go on, admit it.'

'I didn't say that.' She covered her mouth, trying to compose herself.

'You didn't have to.' He adjusted his tie. 'Admit it, you're embarrassed to be seen with me.'

Laughter rippled through the group.

'I'm not,' Erika insisted.

'Oh, yes you are!'

Erika pressed her lips together, though her eyes still danced with amusement.

'I was going to say I needed a rest after my night shift.' She got to her feet. 'But I'll accept the invitation to go for a walk. Even if you're dressed like that.' Her smile widened. 'I'm not embarrassed to be seen with you.'

Alexander stood up and stopped short.

'What's wrong? Have you now lost your nerve?' Erika grinned, enjoying her chance to tease Alexander. He stared past her. Erika glanced over her shoulder to see what had caught Alexander's attention.

'Oh.' She stepped aside. A man in a smart white uniform stood before them.

An insignia adorned his shoulder, and his peaked officer's cap bore the prominent crown of the KPM logo – Koninklijke Paketvaart-Maatschappij, the Dutch shipping line.

He inclined his head. 'My apologies Fräulein, I didn't mean to startle you.' He spoke in German with a Dutch accent. Then he addressed the men. 'Allow me to introduce myself. I am the captain of this ship. I regret you were put in the position of boarding the *Nieuw Zeeland* without adequate clothing. It is most unfortunate. I understand you encountered some difficulties fleeing your countries. Something we understand well since the Nazi invasion of our homeland.' He spoke with none of the brusqueness of the British policemen, his expression sympathetic. 'Perhaps I might be of assistance. I can see you are in need of clothing. Might I offer you sailor uniforms? They will be cooler than the blankets – and perhaps more appropriate than your current attire.' He could not hide his smile.

'Thank you,' Alexander said. 'That would be much appreciated.'

'Very good.' He inclined his head. 'If you would like to come with me, our crew members will help to get you outfitted.'

Half an hour later, the men who had boarded the ship in blankets reappeared on the deck. They wore loose-cut cream shirts in cotton drill and matching trousers instead of their outlandish outfits, though they were still barefoot. As Alexander approached the *chevra,* he spread his arms wide.

Gisela's eyes twinkled. '*Ach*! Such stylish young men. As if you are about to visit the opera.'

Gisela might have been exaggerating. But the change in clothes made a marked difference in their bearing. Alexander and Isaak had removed their bandages. Isaak wore his cap again and seemed to stand taller. Max looked more like himself, not quite better, but on the mend.

'Why, thank you.' Alexander placed a hand on his chest and gave a theatrical bow. 'It feels much more comfortable than a blanket. Or my sister's skirt.'

Janka shook her head as she accepted the folded garment he handed her and stuffed it into her rucksack.

'Georgi appeared none too pleased, though,' Alexander said. 'When he saw us heading back to the deck in proper clothing he protested to the captain. He told him that some of his possessions were lost on the *Patria*, not to mention his close friend and colleague, Arthur. He asked the captain why he had given us clothes and reminded him he was the officer in charge. The captain looked at him and replied calmly, "As captain of the ship, I am in charge of everyone on it." That shut Georgi up.'

Erika appraised him. 'That looks much better.'

'So,' Alexander said. 'What about that walk now? Admit it, you're less embarrassed to be seen with me now.'

'All right.' Erika threw her head back and laughed. 'I admit it.'

'Ha! I knew it,' he said.

They strolled off together, heads close in conversation.

Lilly watched them and smiled.

Chapter 46

That night, Lilly lay on the deck and looked up at the stars glittering in the velvet sky. She inhaled the fresh night air, and listened to the lap and sigh of water against the hull. It was like slipping back into a rhythm.

With each passing day, the heat in the hold intensified. More than unbearable, it had become a danger to life. Earlier that evening, a man with a weak heart fainted from the heat. That must have led to the policemen's decision to allow them to sleep on deck. At first, the policemen allowed only the older people to come up, but soon after they lowered the age requirement, and then lowered it again. By eleven o'clock, they announced everyone should sleep on deck.

It reminded Lilly of the days on the *Atlantic* when the *chevra* had slept in and around the lifeboat. Almost, but not quite, because here on the *Nieuw Zeeland*, the police segregated the men and women on either side of the deck.

Obviously, the rules did not apply to Georgi, who did what he liked, flirting with women who flirted back. Especially the two young women – girls really – whom he had given chocolate to the day before.

'They should be ashamed of themselves,' Janka muttered as the girls laughed at one of Georgi's jokes. 'And for what, a piece of chocolate?'

Gisela tutted. 'How were they brought up?'

'How quickly they forget what these policemen did to us in Atlit and how they still treat us.' Janka kept her voice low. 'Georgi. Of all people. I'm going to have a quiet word with those girls tomorrow when he's not around.'

'Is it wise to get involved?' Erika said.

'Yes. He's trouble.'

'No more than the rest of them.'

'There's something about him that strikes me as dangerous.'

Lilly listened without commenting. She thought back to the tailor's room, Georgi's face inches from hers, his hand stroking the shirt she had been sewing. Nothing happened. Hargreaves had seen to that. But she'd felt trapped, and noticed the tension between the two men, the way Georgi bristled at Hargreaves' interference.

Georgi aside, it was wonderful to sleep in the open air. Lilly slept better that night than any other since they had boarded the ship. But they still had to return to their compartment for all meals. After a night spent in the open, the contrast could not have been more marked. The filthy, overcrowded hold was like a sealed oven and stank of old sweat and dust.

Was it any wonder sickness had run rampant? Almost everyone had suffered stomach cramps and diarrhoea. Others had come down with a fever. And when Erika joined them for breakfast after her night shift, they learned Stefan had gone to the infirmary.

'How is he feeling?' Lilly asked.

'He's getting lots of rest and we're doing our utmost to take care of him,' Erika said, her tone measured. 'Hopefully, he'll begin to recover in the coming days.'

She smiled, but her mouth was too tight, as if masking her concern.

'Let's go back up to the deck,' Erika said, changing the subject. Lilly decided against probing further.

Back on the promenade deck, the *chevra* settled in their regular spot. Erika lay down to catch up on her sleep, her head resting on her folded blanket. Alexander sat beside her while she slept, speaking in low tones with Max. Gisela sat in the shade, chatting to some of the older ladies. Janka was writing in her diary, chuckling to herself. Lilly imagined she was describing the previous morning's 'fancy dress' scene.

'Shall we take a walk?' Isaak suggested.

'I'd like that.' She got to her feet.

The ship swayed gently underfoot as they strolled along the deck. The sea was the roughest it had been since they had left Haifa. They stopped to look over the railings. Though the waves were not high enough to reach the deck, salt spray refreshed Lilly's face. Ahead and behind, the other ships in their convoy were still following the same course. Her thoughts drifted to Jenny. How was she faring alone on the *Johan de Witt*? Poor Stefan was so worried about her. Lilly wondered whether his strained nerves had made him ill.

'If we were on the *Atlantic* now, this ship would be swaying wildly from side to side.' Isaak's words drew her back from her thoughts.

'And we'd have a member of the Haganah on the bridge with a megaphone, ordering us to move to the right, then to the left, to keep the ship balanced.'

'Those were the days,' he said. 'Do you remember the night of that storm just before we reached Crete when we thought the ship was about to capsize?'

'How could I forget?' That night a wave crashed over the deck, dragging Lilly into a breathless tumble, and she hit her head. Isaak had been there for her that night too. He was the one who had pulled her out.

'And look how strong this ship is,' he said, before Lilly could find the words to express her gratitude again. 'Just a gentle rock. Not enough to make us feel seasick.'

'And yet, I would give anything to be back on that rickety ship, heading towards Eretz Israel, rather than on this strong ship heading to the unknown.'

Isaak gave her a wistful smile. 'Me too.'

Walking in easy silence, they started another circuit around the deck. Children splashed in the swimming pool. The crew permitted them to use it, and their shouts of joy carried across the water. They had just begun their third lap when Isaak cried out, 'Ow!'

'What's wrong?'

He winced, hopping from foot to foot. 'The deck is so hot, it's burning my feet.' He broke into a run, shouting over his shoulder, 'Let's go back into the shade.'

Lilly hurried after him back to their place to find Inspector Hargreaves hovering close by. 'Ah, just the person I was looking for,' he said. 'May I ask for your help with another sewing job?' He cleared his throat. 'Um ... undergarments.'

'Yes, I'd be happy to help.'

'Much appreciated, miss. You did such a good job last time.'

'Thank you. When would you like me to start?'

'Could you come to the tailor's room straight after lunch? And would any of your companions be interested in assisting you? It's quite a big job.' He looked from Janka to Gisela, who were reading an extract from Janka's diary and laughing together.

'I'm not all that good at sewing,' Janka said.

'I could teach you?' Lilly said.

Janka tipped her head from side to side. 'Can I think about it?'

'Maybe I could come and help you,' Gisela said. 'It might be good to keep occupied for a few hours.'

Janka slumped down at the table beside her friends. 'They told me to mind my own business.' Her face flushed with indignation. She'd approached the two girls who had been flirting with Georgi, hoping to warn them off.

Gisela shook her head, commiserating with Janka. 'What did you expect?'

'Don't they realise their behaviour is so irresponsible? How can they be so naïve? Georgi is not to be trusted.'

'Sometimes people won't listen to advice. They have to learn from their own mistakes,' Gisela said.

'Well, if their mistakes land them in the infirmary with some disease, I'll have words with them then,' Erika said.

'You don't really think …?' Lilly said.

Erika raised her eyebrows, and Lilly wondered what she'd encountered working in the infirmaries, first on the *Atlantic* and now here.

'Even if they didn't like my interference, they didn't have to be so rude to me.' Janka stirred her lumpy custard and pushed it aside. 'The taller one said I was only bothered because I was jealous and that the Kommandant would never look at someone as ugly as me.'

'Oh!' Lilly, Erika, and Gisela exclaimed at once.

'What a nasty comment,' Lilly said. 'Nothing could be further from the truth. Apart from which, you're too good for the likes of that vile man.'

'You are beautiful inside and out,' Erika said.

Gisela patted her hand. 'Don't take it to heart. They are just foolish, immature girls. And you are a beautiful, intelligent young woman. Don't let anyone ever tell you otherwise.'

'So, are you going to join us for some sewing this afternoon?' Lilly said. 'It might help you take your mind off things.'

Before Janka could answer, Sergeant Tait entered the compartment. 'Can I have your attention! I'm looking for volunteers this afternoon to give the hold a thorough clean. And there's a bonus.' He folded his arms with a self-satisfied smile. 'Whoever volunteers will be rewarded at the end with some delicious, refreshing ice cream.'

'Ice cream?' Janka murmured, staring at her discarded custard. She turned to Lilly. 'I think my mind is made up. Sorry, but the ice cream wins.' Janka raised her hand.

'Are you sure you want to spend the afternoon cleaning in the sweltering hold?' Lilly said.

'It won't be so bad once everyone has left,' Janka said. 'The work might help me burn off some of this anger. And it will be worth it for some ice cream.'

Inspector Hargreaves was already waiting in the tailor's room with a roll of cotton fabric and explained what they needed to do. Once he took his leave, Gisela looked out of the porthole. 'Isn't this lovely? Far more pleasant than the stuffy hold and better than the scorching heat on the deck.' She sat on a stool at the cutting table and spread out the fabric, setting herself up with scissors and pins from the sewing box. 'It's nice to do something productive too.'

They worked well as a team. Gisela cut and pinned the garments while Lilly sewed them on the machine, chatting as they worked. Lilly enjoyed Gisela's company and the security of her presence. With the heat, they'd left the door ajar to let air into the cabin. Although Lilly noticed Georgi peering around it a couple of times, he did not dare come in with Gisela there.

By four o'clock, when Inspector Hargreaves returned, they had worked through the fabric and produced a tidy pile of garments.

'Excellent work, ladies,' he said, looking through the finished pieces.

Gisela beamed. 'Excuse me, Inspector.' She pointed to the pile of offcuts. 'What will you do with those?'

'I have no use for them. I'll arrange for them to be disposed of.'

Gisela hesitated for a moment, 'May I keep them?'

He regarded her, bemused. 'Why, yes, of course. Though I don't know what you can do with those scraps.'

Lilly did not know either. The scraps were too thin and small to serve any purpose. Still, she helped Gisela fill her bag and stuffed the rest in her own rucksack.

'What do you want with all those *Fetzen*?' Lilly asked, as they ascended the stairs to the promenade deck.

'You never know,' Gisela said. 'They might come in useful.'

Lilly nodded, indulging her. Lilly was reminded of her grandmother, who had kept similar bags: one for fabric scraps, another for string, a third for buttons. All kept 'just in case' but almost never used.

On the deck they found Isaak, Alexander, Erika, and Max resting in the shade, but no sign of Janka. Ten minutes later she stormed onto the deck, crying with rage.

Alexander stood, grasped her shoulders, and searched her face. 'What happened?'

'They are liars!' she said between sobs. 'Every single one of them. I'll never trust them again.'

'Come and sit.' He helped her down. Janka's face was pale and glistened with sweat. She seemed on the verge of collapse.

'We spent hours in the heat cleaning the entire stupid hold. Tait had promised us ice cream at the end. It was long, hard, thirsty work, but we finally finished. We found him and asked for the ice cream he'd promised. "Were you so stupid as to believe I would keep my promise?" He smirked. I asked if we could at least have a glass of iced water, and he just laughed and walked away. Why did I volunteer? Why was I stupid enough to believe him?'

'Oh, Janka.' Alexander hugged her, stroking her back. 'You're not stupid. He was very cruel to trick you like that.'

'I am so thirsty. My head hurts. My tongue feels like it's sticking to the roof of my mouth.'

'Excuse me?' A crew member approached, cigarette in hand, speaking in a strong Australian accent. 'You need help?'

'She is very thirsty,' Alexander said.

'Let me bring you some water.'

He hurried away and returned minutes later with a tall glass of water, condensation beading on the outside. The water they usually drank was lukewarm. The policemen never let them have iced water, claiming it was harmful. Yet they seemed unconcerned about their welfare in every other respect.

Janka brought it to her lips and drank half in one long gulp. 'Thank you,' she said, breathless.

'You're welcome. The weather gets hotter the nearer we get to the equator. It's important to keep hydrated.'

'She's not only thirsty from the heat,' Alexander said. 'My sister cleaned the hold all afternoon, working herself to exhaustion. The policeman who called for volunteers would not give them a cold drink afterwards.'

The man shook his head in disgust. 'That isn't right. The way they treat you.'

'Sir,' Isaak said, 'you mentioned we were nearing the equator. Where exactly are we going?'

The question hung in the air. Around them, conversations trailed off. Fellow refugees nearby turned and drew closer to listen.

The man stubbed out his cigarette. 'Mauritius.'

Alexander raised an eyebrow. 'Mauritius?'

Lilly exchanged a look with Isaak. She had never heard the name.

'Where is that?' Lilly said.

'It's an island. A British colony,' he said. 'Off the east coast of Africa.'

'What?' Erika began, but a booming voice drowned her out.

'Don't you have duties to attend to?' It was Tait. He glared first at the empty glass in Janka's hand and then at the crew member. 'Move along and get back to your station.'

The crew member took the glass. He did not reply, but his expression held contempt before he walked away.

The policeman stared down at the *chevra*, as if he wanted to say more. Janka folded her arms, met his stare, and waited. After a long moment, he left them alone.

'Mauritius,' Alexander repeated, testing the unfamiliar name. 'I've barely heard of it.'

'I only remember that my father had a precious stamp in his collection that came from Mauritius,' Isaak said.

'Why would they send us there?' Lilly said.

'Maybe because it's so remote and no one has ever heard of it,' Max said.

'Do you think it's dangerous?' Janka said. 'Will it have wild animals roaming free?'

'I'm more concerned about diseases,' Erika said. 'Or whether they have proper medical facilities.'

'I wonder if they'll abandon us there,' Isaak said.

Gisela placed a hand over her heart and lowered her head. 'How will we ever get back? What if we're stuck there forever and I never see my family again?'

Lilly put her arm around Gisela.

'We'll find a way back,' Isaak said.

For the next few hours, Mauritius was all they could talk about. Lilly did not know how she felt. Their destination now had a name. But what did it mean for them? How long would they remain in Mauritius? How would she contact her family to let them know where she was? Would she ever see them again?

Part of her already disliked this unknown island, and yet she was curious to see this unfamiliar place.

After supper, Lilly stood by the railings, talking with Isaak.

'Is Gisela right? Might we be stuck there forever?' Lilly said.

'No, I don't believe it will be forever,' Isaak said.

'How will we let our families know where we are?'

'We'll write to them,' he said. 'If the place has stamps, there has to be a postal service.' He paused. 'We'll find a way through this.'

Lilly's eyes drifted over the deck. At Janka and Gisela, who had fallen asleep early – Janka exhausted from scrubbing the hold, Gisela drained by worry about her family. At Max, sitting on his own, deep in thought, no doubt thinking of his wife and child. Alexander and Erika were strolling around the deck together. And Georgi was back to flirting with the two girls.

Lilly faced the sea again. The full moon was rising above the horizon, glorious and serene. She and Isaak stood together and watched it climb.

Chapter 47

17 December1940
SS Johan de Witt, Aden

The convoy continued south, cutting through the Bab el-Mandeb Strait. To their left rose the arid, mountainous terrain of the Arabian peninsula, golden-brown and dusty beige. On their right, the Horn of Africa – rugged charcoal-grey mountains, sandy coastal plains, and shallow reefs that fringed the shore. The dramatic scenery passed Jenny by. Stefan would have pointed out every detail, explained the history. Without him by her side, she felt nothing.

Jenny's new friend, Gerda, had told her that the name Bab el-Mandeb meant *gate of tears*. A fitting name, Jenny thought. She had shed so many since boarding the *Johan de Witt*. Too late she realised she had been separated from all her friends, and worst of all, from her husband. When they had left Haifa, she had known neither their destination nor whether their two ships were bound for the same place. Jenny feared she might never see Stefan again.

At least she had Gerda. They had travelled on the same transport from Danzig and were acquainted with each other, but only on the *Johan de Witt* had they become close friends. Gerda, a few years younger than Jenny, was in her early thirties. Like Jenny, Gerda's husband was on the *Nieuw Zeeland*, or so she believed. She travelled with her delightful three-year-old daughter, Anni.

Gerda loved books and knew everything about everything. She did her best to keep Jenny's mind off her worries by regaling her throughout the voyage with anecdotes and fascinating facts. In that she reminded Jenny of Stefan. Gerda was one of the first to discover they were bound for Mauritius. She too was devastated to leave Eretz Israel. But Gerda was certain their two ships would end up at the same place; they would be together and they would be safe.

Jenny hoped Gerda was right, but she suffered during the journey from seasickness, cramps, restlessness, fatigue, the heat. Everything bothered her. She got nosebleeds, headaches, bouts of dizziness. Something was wrong. Most nights, after Gerda and the other women had fallen asleep, she lay awake, heart racing with fear. Many people on board their ship had fallen seriously ill with dysentery or typhoid. What if she had too? But she was too scared to tell anyone – not even Gerda – as though sharing it would make her illness real. As long as she concealed it, she could pretend nothing was the matter.

The heat was searing as they rounded the strait and entered the Gulf of Aden. Jenny sat in the shade with Gerda and Anni, barely able to move. From time to time, Gerda would carry Anni across to the railings to look out, then return to Jenny to describe the view: coral reefs, a convoy of British military ships, a distant lighthouse. Jenny's eyes flickered closed.

The rattle of the anchor chain jolted her awake; the ship had stopped moving, the sun lower in the sky. Disoriented, Jenny looked around. Had they arrived already?

'Jenny, come and look!' Gerda called from the railings, one hand holding her wide-brimmed straw hat against the wind, Anni balanced on her hip. Her ebullient tone hammered into Jenny's head.

Jenny liked her friend, but sometimes she could be too much. Too energetic.

'Jenny, quick!' Gerda bounded back. 'You won't want to miss this.'

Jenny got to her feet and, walking on rubbery legs, joined Gerda at the railings.

Gerda pointed to a port in the distance. 'There's the *Nieuw Zeeland*.'

Jenny's eyes locked onto Stefan's ship, which had stopped just outside the port's entrance. Too far to make out anyone on its deck.

Gerda beamed. 'See, our ships are still heading in the same direction, like I told you. Soon we'll all be together again. Anni and I with Otto, and you with Stefan.'

Jenny mustered a smile. 'Where are we?'

'A crew member told me this is Aden, a British colony.'

'Are we getting off here?'

'No. We have stopped to load fresh supplies,' she said. 'And they're also taking one of the ill patients from the infirmary to the local hospital.'

'Will they bring him back?'

She grew serious. 'I'm not sure.'

A pang of fear stirred in Jenny's stomach. What if they discovered she was ill? What if they took her off the ship to the hospital and left her there, alone?

Gerda gestured to the city beyond the harbour. Jenny glanced at the low white buildings, dwarfed by the dark grey, barren hills that loomed over the harbour. She kept her attention on the *Nieuw Zeeland*. If only they were close enough for her to see Stefan. Perhaps he too was looking out at her ship, hoping to catch a glimpse of her?

Gerda's chatter rang in her ears. The air seemed too thin, as if she couldn't draw a full breath. The view ahead grew misty and the land began to tilt from side to side. Or maybe it was their ship that was swaying.

'Jenny!' The voice sounded far away. Gerda set Anni down and grasped Jenny's arms, helping her sit. Jenny took a few shallow breaths, trying to steady herself. 'Are you all right? You looked as if you were about to faint.'

'It must be the heat,' Jenny said. 'I'm better now that I am sitting down.'

'Jenny, I think you ought to visit the doctor.'

'No, really, I'm fine now.'

'Be honest, you have not felt well since the start of this journey. You've been sick several times.'

'It's seasickness.'

Gerda shook her head. 'No one else is suffering from seasickness. The ship is stable. And you're pale and weak.'

'Please.' Jenny gripped Gerda's hand. 'Don't make me go to the doctor. What ... what if something is wrong with me?'

Gerda stroked the hair away from Jenny's face, the way she might have done to Anni.

'That's why you need to see a doctor,' Gerda said. 'Just in case something is wrong, so he can help you get better.'

'I'm scared.' Jenny's voice caught. 'I'm so scared.'

'I'll come with you,' Gerda said. 'Don't be afraid.'

She allowed Gerda to help her to her feet. Before leaving the deck, Jenny glanced back at the *Nieuw Zeeland*, one last time.

CHAPTER 48

17 December 1940
SS Nieuw Zeeland, Aden

Aden. Another shore they would ever view from a distance, like so many others they had passed on this endless journey: Tulcea, Istanbul, Crete, Limassol. Even Haifa, which they had glimpsed from the bus window on the way to their incarceration in Atlit. Standing with the *chevra* by the railings, Lilly gazed at the harbour and the port city spread before them.

'No wonder Britain rules the waves.' Alexander gestured at the fleet of British naval ships anchored in the bay: warships, tankers, troop ships, patrol vessels, motor launches. Bobbing closer to shore were a scattering of traditional dhows with their distinctive triangular lateen sails, and wooden rowing boats for fishing.

'Not just the waves but the city too.' Isaak pointed to a clock tower on a hill to the right, overlooking the town: a miniature Big Ben.

The city, or what little Lilly could see of it, surprised her with its orderly, European character with Eastern touches: a neat arc of low buildings tucked beneath striking grey hills, two and three storeys high, their white façades tinged amber from the setting sun. Arched windows and colonnades adorned several grander buildings:

shops and offices, perhaps, a bank or hotel. From that distance, it was difficult to discern details. On the coastal road, in front of the buildings, the occasional car drifted by.

It was nothing like she'd pictured a city in southern Arabia. Except for the heat and the barren landscape. A few trees clustered near the coastline, but otherwise nothing green relieved the stark terrain.

In sharp contrast to the ordered little town, rugged volcanic rocks rose steeply behind the buildings, their jagged contours glowing topaz, saffron and gold, shifting to soft purple as the day faded.

'I wonder who lives in Aden,' Lilly said.

'Many British people, I'd say, especially soldiers,' Alexander said. 'And Arabs and Indians, I suppose. Some must be fishermen, given all those boats.'

'I imagine traders too,' Isaak said. 'Aden lies at such a strategic point.'

'And a hot one!' Gisela dabbed her forehead with her handkerchief.

'You're not wrong there,' Janka fanned herself with her notebook. 'This must be the hottest city in the world. It's almost six o'clock in the evening, the sun is going down, and it's still warmer here than a typical summer's day in Prague.'

'And this is December!' Isaak said.

'If this is the temperature now, what is it like in the height of summer?' Gisela said.

'Isn't it strange to think that in Vienna it might be snowing already?' Erika said, her tone wistful.

Lilly found it hard to picture wintry Vienna in this heat. Winter had once held happy memories for her. Boots crunching as she strolled through the snow-covered avenues of the Prater, tobogganing on the hills, ice skating in the city's outdoor rink.

'Do you know, it was exactly this time last year I left Vienna. I remember the icy rain the night I boarded that train to Bratislava,' Erika said.

Alexander shook his head. 'Already a year since we left our hom es.Unbelievable.'

A year ago. Lilly remembered saying goodbye to Hannah. In the grim December days that followed, she waited in line outside the Central Office for Jewish Emigration, from morning to night in the bitter cold, attempting to get a place on the transport to Eretz Israel. The Brownshirts demeaned and assaulted them at will. She had watched them punch a young man in the face and kick over an elderly man. Lilly had not evaded humiliation either; a Brownshirt had forced her to her knees to clean the snow off his boots with her hands.

Those had been days of terror, when leaving her home felt like stepping into danger. The worry for her mama and aunt, still in Vienna, never left her. The heartbreak of her exile from Eretz Israel stayed with her. Her current situation was far from ideal and her future remained uncertain. But for now, at least, she was safe. She felt a wave of gratitude for Mama, Tante Rebecca, and Hannah for persuading her to leave Vienna and join this transport. Though the plan had not worked out as expected, Lilly realised she still had much to be thankful for.

She looked around at the *chevra*. A year ago she had not known any of them. A year on, they were as dear to her as family.

'Do you regret leaving Vienna?' Alexander asked Erika.

Erika was quiet for a moment. 'Despite everything, no, I don't think I do.' She looked up at him. 'I don't understand why things happened the way they did. But perhaps I'm where I'm supposed to be.'

Alexander's expression softened. 'Maybe we all are.'

Dusk settled over the harbour. Lights flickered on in the windows of the buildings, and the hills behind faded into shadow. The spindly policeman ushered them back to the hold for supper, announcing that while in port they would have to sleep below as well. Only older people would be allowed to spend the night on the deck.

Janka groaned and patted her brother's arm. 'I suppose I'll see you tomorrow then. If we don't boil to death during the night.'

Janka had spoken in jest, but that night, Lilly began to wonder if her words would come true. She spent hours tossing and turning in the suffocating heat, listening to the groans and restless movements around her, clothes soaked through, lying in a pool of sweat.

'Can't sleep either?' Janka said.

'Not a wink. If only they had let us sleep on deck with Gisela. I can barely breathe down here. And my clothes are glued to my body.'

'Me too.' Janka sat up, her hair plastered to her forehead, a damp patch of sweat on the front of her blouse. 'I need to wash. Even cold water on my face. Will you come with me to ask the guard?'

'I doubt he'll agree.' Lilly pushed herself up and pulled down her dress where it clung to her back. 'But I can't lie here anymore. I'll come with you.'

Lilly and Janka slipped out of their compartment, picking their way over sleeping bodies. The stairway stood empty. No guard. They exchanged glances. At the base of the stairs, Lilly paused, listening. Nothing. They climbed, each creak of the metal steps making Lilly flinch.

On the deck above, they froze. A guard sat slumped against the wall further down the passageway, head tilted back. A snore rattled from his throat. Lilly's heart pounded. She looked at Janka, who gestured toward the washroom.

They tiptoed forward, pressed to the wall. Each footfall seemed too loud. The guard snorted, shifted position. They tensed. Another snore. Janka reached the washroom, wrapped her fingers around the handle, and turned it slowly. It didn't budge. Locked.

Janka pulled back. She leaned close to Lilly's ear. 'Let's see if there's another.'

They crossed to the other side. No policeman here. They edged along the passageway. At the end of the row of cabins, where the passageway branched, another door. Lilly stopped and eased the handle around; it swung open. Inside, a proper bathroom with a bathtub. Lilly's eyes widened. Janka let out a breath. They looked at one another and crept inside. Lilly closed the door behind them, wincing as the spring latch clicked. They waited a few minutes but heard no footsteps pass. Silver moonlight slanted through the porthole and cast shadows over the room. They did not risk switching on a light, which might shine under the doorway.

'Do we dare take a bath?' Lilly whispered.

'We've come this far,' Janka said. She inserted the plug and turned on the tap to a slow, thin trickle that could not be heard from outside. 'You go first. I'll watch the door. Then we'll switch.'

Lilly climbed into the tub. The cool water was soothing. She sank beneath the surface and washed her hair. She lay there for a few minutes, letting the water ease the heat from her skin, before stepping out. Without a towel to dry herself, Lilly tugged her clothes on over her damp body. On that sweltering night, her wet hair felt refreshing as it dripped down her back, but by the time Janka had finished, it had dried again.

They stole out of the bathroom and along the passageway. At the stairs, they paused, listening. The guard still snored. They descended into the hold. Back in their compartment, they caught each other's eyes and grinned. Lilly lay down, cooler now. The harsh overhead lights blazed on, as they always did, but Lilly closed her eyes and waited for dawn.

CHAPTER 49

18 December 1940
SS Nieuw Zeeland, Aden

The Port of Aden looked different in daylight. The white buildings sharper, the volcanic hills stark against the pale blue sky.

Gisela emerged onto the promenade deck beside Lilly, handkerchief at her brow. '*Uff*! I don't know how you poor darlings slept down there last night. Taking a meal in the hold was bad enough.'

'We didn't,' Lilly said. 'Well, not much anyway.'

Janka winked. 'Until we found a way to cool down.'

Erika looked from Lilly to Janka. 'What did I miss while I was on shift?'

'Later.' Janka glanced at the guard and the other passengers within earshot. 'When we're not surrounded.'

Alexander and Isaak leaned against the railings looking towards Aden. To Lilly's surprise, Max stood with them.

'*Salaam*!' Isaak called as he waved to a passing fishing boat.

'Good morning.' Alexander grinned as they approached. 'Still alive, I see.'

'Just about,' Janka said.

'Us too,' Alexander said. 'It was hot as hell down there.'

'I heard they might let everyone sleep on the deck again tonight,' Erika said. 'At least one person fainted. It's too dangerous to keep us in the hold.'

'I hope you're right. Another night like that and you'll be treating me in the infirmary too,' Alexander said.

Max turned from the railing, one hand pressed to his ribs. 'How's Stefan doing?'

Erika shrugged. 'Much the same, unfortunately.'

'Is it anything serious?'

'It's hard to say. The doctors are monitoring him.' Erika managed a reassuring smile before giving her attention to Janka and Lilly. 'Now, tell us this little secret of yours.'

'What secret is this?' Alexander said.

'Well ...' Janka began. 'During the night, Lilly and I sneaked out of the compartment and had a cold bath.'

The *chevra* gaped as Janka and Lilly related their story.

'*Unglaublich*!' Alexander said. 'And that you didn't get caught either.'

'The heat had knocked the policemen out too,' Janka said.

'If you try again one night, and I'm not on shift, I'd like to come with you,' Erika said.

'So would I,' Gisela said. 'Though escaping from the deck will be harder with Georgi and the others patrolling.'

'Speaking of which, I haven't seen Georgi at all this morning,' Janka said. 'He didn't even come to leer at us in the washroom, which is unlike him. Has he decided to abandon ship in the port just like Spiro attempted on the *Atlantic*?'

Alexander laughed. 'No such luck—'

A loud crack split the air. Lilly jolted. The sound echoed. A flock of seabirds scattered overhead. She twisted around, pulse hammering, and scanned the deck. Her throat tightened. 'What was that?'

Alexander glanced skyward. ‘Georgi.’

‘What on earth is he doing?’ Janka asked.

‘Shooting seabirds,’ Isaak said.

‘Whatever for?’ Janka said.

‘Target practice? What do I know?’ Alexander raised his palms. ‘We heard the first shot just as we arrived on deck a few minutes before you. I thought we were under attack. Nearly scared me to death. Then we met that crew member who gave you water the other day, on deck for a cigarette break, and he explained what Georgi was doing.’

‘Poor birds,’ Erika said.

‘With a bit of luck, perhaps Georgi will decide to abandon ship and row off to the Port of Aden,’ Alexander said.

‘Like when Spiro tried to steal the lifeboat,’ Janka said.

‘Or when he tried to jump overboard,’ Isaak said. ‘And this time, Lilly, we won’t stop him. *Richtig*?’ He chuckled.

Lilly laughed. ‘This time we’ll help carry his bags and offer to row him there ourselves.’

‘We’ll all help,’ Alexander said. ‘And when we reach Aden, we should also stay there.’

‘What would you do in Aden?’ Janka asked. ‘You certainly couldn’t farm. From what I can see, there are no fields. Barely a tree.’

Alexander pointed to a passing boat. ‘We could fish.’ His gaze drifted. ‘And if we saved enough money we could buy one of those dhows and sail back to Eretz Israel.’

‘If only,’ Max said.

Gisela heaved a sigh.

Lilly felt a heaviness in her chest. That’s all any of them wanted: to return to the Promised Land.

Erika faced the others. ‘What do you think Mauritius looks like?’ Erika said.

Alexander shrugged. 'Something like this, perhaps.'

'Since it's an island, I imagine it looks flatter,' Janka said. 'A few trees near the coast and inland, very arid. Perhaps more sandy than volcanic grey rocks.'

'If it's near Africa, it might look more like a jungle,' Erika said.

'Do you think it has wild animals running around?' Janka's voice had that same edge it had when she'd last asked that question.

'It's a British colony, so I doubt it,' Isaak said.

Another shot rang out. Isaak tilted his head towards the bow. 'And if there's someone like Georgi there, he's probably already shot most of them.'

'A few more days and we'll find out,' Alexander said.

The mood shifted. As much as they tried to remain positive, even to make light of the situation at times, the sadness and fear always lingered close to the surface.

Gisela sighed again. 'My legs are getting tired. I'm going to sit.'

'Me too,' Max said.

Erika stifled a yawn. 'And I think it's time for me to catch up on some sleep.'

'I'll join you,' Alexander said. 'I barely slept last night.'

'Time to write my diary,' Janka said.

The *chevra* drifted back one by one to their usual spot in the shade until only Lilly and Isaak remained.

Another fishing boat was sailing out of the harbour. The fisherman wore a sarong-like cloth wrapped around his waist and a head wrap. The style reminded Lilly of how the men had worn their blankets until the Dutch crew gave them clothes. Two young boys sat opposite in white shirts and shorts, white caps on their heads. The boys looked around thirteen or fourteen. One was a bit taller than the other but otherwise identical – the same wide, dark eyes and bright smiles.

The two boys waved as the boat approached.

'*Salaam*!' Isaak called.

'*Shalom aleichem*!' they answered as one.

Isaak faced Lilly, raising his eyebrows. 'Did you hear that, too?'

'It sounded like Hebrew. Though it's hard to tell from up here.'

'So I didn't imagine it.' Isaak leaned over the railings. '*Aleichem shalom*.'

The boys' smiles widened.

Isaak shook his head in amazement. 'They seem to understand.'

Isaak raised a finger to tell them to wait. The older of the two boys leaned across to speak to the fisherman who immediately slowed his rowing.

'Quick!' Isaak pulled Lilly towards the staircase. 'Let's go down one level so we can talk to them without attracting too much attention.'

They clattered down the stairs. The boys had kept their eyes trained on the side of the ship and waved when Lilly and Isaak emerged below on the narrower shade deck.

'Jewish?' Isaak said in English, then switched to Hebrew. '*Yehudi*?'

The boys nodded. The fisherman's eyes darted around the ship.

'*Ken*,' said the older boy, responding in Hebrew.

'Brothers?' Isaak said.

He nodded and pointed to himself. 'Daniel.'

'Benzion,' said the younger one, who moved his finger from Lilly to Isaak. 'Married?

'Oh!' Isaak's laugh came out too loud. 'No ... er ... friends.' His hands moved uselessly as he stumbled on his words, speaking in a mixture of German and English. '*Chavera*.'

'*Chavera*,' Daniel echoed. He nudged Benzion and they chuckled.

'What did I say that's so funny? Did I say the wrong word for a friend?' Isaak's face reddened.

'I'm not sure,' Lilly said, though she remembered from her Hebrew lessons in Atlit that *chavera* could mean friend or girlfriend. She bit the inside of her cheek and focused on the boys.

Benzion batted his eyes at Daniel. '*Ayuni*.' Daniel nodded, and they giggled amongst themselves.

'What does that mean?' Isaak said, half to Lilly, and half to the boys.

Lilly shrugged. She was not familiar with the word either. Daniel waved the question away.

'I definitely need to learn more Hebrew,' Isaak said, under his breath.

'Are there Jewish people in Aden?' Lilly asked the boys.

'Yes,' Benzion said. 'Many.'

'How many?' Isaak said.

They conferred with each other.

'A few thousand,' Daniel said.

'A few thousand?' Isaak blinked. 'And you have a synagogue there?'

'Six, I think.'

'And Jewish schools?' Lilly asked.

'One for boys, one for girls.' Benzion put his finger to his lips with a mischievous smile.

Lilly grinned at Isaak. 'I think they're playing truant. Do your parents know where you are?'

Daniel's smile vanished. He placed a finger on his lips.

'How did you find out we are Jewish?' Isaak said.

'Someone told us a Jewish person from these ships was taken to hospital,' Daniel said. 'They said the ships were full of Jewish people from far away in Europe. Why are you travelling so far?'

'We had to escape because the Nazis don't like Jewish people. They want to hurt us.'

The boys looked mournful.

'I am so sad for you,' Benzion said. 'We will come back early tomorrow morning and bring you food from our mother.'

He consulted with Daniel. 'Bring a rope and we can—'

The boys startled at the crack. A spout of water shot up near the boat. The fisherman looked up at the ship and raised his hands, terrified. The boys raised their hands too.

'What are you doing next to the ship?' Georgi bellowed from above. 'Who are you talking to?'

Isaak pulled Lilly back out of sight.

The fisherman shook his head. 'F-f-fishing.'

'No fishing here!' Georgi said. 'Move away from the ship otherwise the next shot won't be a warning.'

The fisherman yanked at the oars, splashing water with every desperate pull to get away as fast as possible.

Isaak and Lilly pressed their backs against the wall beside the doorway.

'Bloody natives, no sense at all,' Georgi's voice carried down to them. 'Don't they realise there's a war on?'

Lilly's heart raced. 'What do we do?' she mouthed.

Isaak beckoned her to follow. They crept back through the door, crossed to the opposite passageway and up the stairs. At the top, Isaak peered around the corner. Nothing. He checked the other direction, then motioned to Lilly. They stepped out onto the promenade deck and kept walking, as casually as possible. Just two friends taking a walk. A guard passed without looking at them. They caught each other's eyes and laughed.

'That was a bit crazy,' Isaak said.

'They must have got such a fright when Georgi fired that shot,' Lilly said. 'Poor boys. They were so sweet.'

They leaned on the railing.

'How funny they thought we were married,' Isaak said.

She looked at him. He kept his gaze on the rowing boat, making a wide arc to distance itself from the ship.

'Yes, really funny.' The words came out too quickly.

Three years younger, his life was only beginning. She'd been married. Widowed. A chapter already closed. She stared down into the water. Isaak would never look at her like that. At least they had this.

They continued along the deck, watching the rowing boat enter the harbour.

'Do you think they'll come back tomorrow?' Lilly said.

'After what just happened, I doubt it.' Isaak blew out a breath. 'But you never know. We should wait for them tomorrow morning. Just in case.' He looked around. 'But where will we get a rope from? We can't exactly ask for one. Unless we can make one out of something. But what do we have that we could tie together to reach the water?'

'I can't think of anything either,' she said, her gaze sweeping the deck until it landed on the *chevra* dozing in the shade. Gisela sat up, rummaging in her bag.

'Unless ...' She stopped. 'I might have an idea.'

CHAPTER 50

19 December 1940
SS Nieuw Zeeland, Aden

Isaak lowered their improvised rope over the side of the ship from the shade deck to test its length. The line, made from thin strips of white cotton knotted together, stopped just above the waterline. 'That should do it.' He reeled it back up and smiled at Lilly. 'This was a brilliant idea of yours.'

'All thanks to Gisela,' Lilly said. 'She was the one who insisted on keeping all the *fetzen* leftover when we finished sewing, saying they might come in handy sometime. I couldn't imagine they'd ever be useful. But Gisela was right.'

'I suppose it proves it's true what they say.' Isaak coiled the line around his arm.

'What's that?'

'We should always listen to our elders. They usually know best.'

Lilly nodded. 'You're right. And Gisela is a wise woman.'

The heat was already rising. The port city teemed with activity: small dhows and large military vessels entering and exiting the harbour, fishing boats sailing back with their early morning catch. Fishermen called to each other in Arabic. The smell of salt water and fish hung in the air. Cars travelled on the coastal road beyond and a camel pulled a barrel on a cart. Lilly leaned against the railings, Isaak beside her, both watching the rowing boats leave the harbour. This time he didn't wave or call out '*Salaam.*' Not after yesterday.

'I wonder if the boys will return,' Lilly said.

Isaak shrugged. 'I don't know if they will dare after what happened yesterday. But you never know. And if they do, our rope is ready.'

'Who would have thought that we would find a Jewish community here in this small port city thousands of miles away.'

'It's remarkable. Then again, Aden is a major trading port and shipping crossroads. I suppose it makes perfect sense. I'm sorry that the British didn't decide to exile us here. At least we'd have a community around us, and shuls, and kosher food.'

'That's probably why they wouldn't send us here. They realise the community would try to help us.'

Isaak nodded grimly. 'It seems they are intent on sending us somewhere far away from everything and everyone so we'll be forgotten.'

Lilly gripped the railings, thinking of Hannah and Eugen. 'But our family and friends in Eretz Israel won't forget us.'

'No, they won't. I'm certain they'll keep trying to fight for our return.'

Isaak shaded his eyes, watching another rowing boat leaving the harbour. 'I don't believe it!' He leaned forward. 'It's them.'

'Are you sure? That doesn't look like the same boat from yesterday.'

'It's a different fisherman, but that's the two boys in the boat.'

Lilly peered closer. 'Oh yes, you're right. That is them. No doubt the fisherman from yesterday refused to take them a second time after Georgi fired at them.' She smiled. 'They are brave.'

'I've had an idea.' Isaak turned to her, eyes bright. 'What if we were to ask them to help us escape from this ship? They'll bring us to Aden. Maybe their parents or another Jewish family would agree to hide us for a while and help us find a way back to Eretz.'

Lilly straightened. 'How would we get off the ship? It's too high to jump, and our rope is far too weak to hold us.'

'We could tie a few blankets together and slide down onto their boat. They could cover us with the blankets and fishing nets as they row to shore.'

Lilly studied his face. 'Are you being serious?'

His eyes darted back and forth, calculating. The excitement melted from his face. 'I wish it were possible ...' He sighed. 'But I can't leave Alexander and Janka. And it would be impossible to bring them with us. If we disappeared they wouldn't know what had happened to us. They might even fear that we had fallen overboard and drowned.' He lowered his head. 'No. As much as I'd like to escape, I wouldn't do that to them.'

Isaak faced Lilly. 'But you could leave. I know how much you miss Hannah and want to see your brother again. His voice quieted. 'If you want to go, I'd understand. I'll help you.' He looked down at the rope in his hands. 'I'd ... I'd miss you, though.'

She opened her mouth, then closed it.

'What do you think?'

The rowing boat was now only a few metres away.

Isaak was offering her a way out. She could take it. But what if she got caught? Perhaps the community would help her return to Eretz Israel. But she would be on her own. Without papers, in wartime. She might be stuck in Aden indefinitely. Not only would she be separated from Hannah and Eugen, but also from the Lifeboat Chevra and Gisela. From Isaak.

Daniel waved while Benzion, the younger one, put his finger to his lips and shook his head in warning. Isaak lowered their rope. The fisherman cautiously rowed closer, his oars guiding the boat through the water without a splash.

'This is your chance,' Isaak whispered, 'if you want to take it.'

Lilly's gaze moved from Isaak to the boat below, the two boys with their faces tilted upward, watching them. Back to Isaak. She drew a breath. 'No. I can't leave either.'

Daniel secured a bundle to the bottom of their makeshift line. The boat slipped away as Isaak drew up the line and brought the bag, made from an old rice sack, over the railings. They waved to the boys who acknowledged their thanks as the fisherman headed towards the harbour.

Lilly watched the boat grow smaller.

Isaak opened the bag. Inside were ten flat pieces of bread dotted with what looked like black sesame seeds. There was also a little handwritten note. Isaak frowned at the writing. Lilly peered over his shoulder. 'It's Hebrew I think, but an unusual script.'

'More like *Rashi* script.' He mouthed them to himself, then sounded them out and translated.

> *To Isaak and Lilly. Some homemade food from our mother, as promised. This is Ka'adid bread. We hope you like it. It was lovely to meet you. We hope we meet again one day. Go in peace. Have a safe journey. Daniel and Benzion.*

'What a sweet gesture,' Lilly said.

'And a courageous one. Let's go back up to the deck and share their gift with the others.'

It was mid-afternoon when Gerda came to visit Jenny in the cramped infirmary. The doctor had ordered complete bed rest. Jenny drifted in and out of sleep, trying to shut out the sounds of the other patients' moans and coughs. She stared up at the ceiling, thinking about when life was tranquil, before she and Stefan had been forced to flee Danzig. She worried about what the future might bring on the unfamiliar island of Mauritius. Through the porthole on the other side of the cabin, the light shifted and changed. The hours blurred into one another.

'They brought Boris back to the ship from the hospital in Aden,' Gerda said, bringing her the latest news.

'Is he better?' Jenny asked.

'If they released him from the hospital, it must mean he's recovering.'

A shudder ran through the ship. 'What was that?'

'We're leaving Aden.'

Jenny raised her head off the pillow. 'And Stefan's ship?'

Gerda placed her hand over Jenny's. 'Don't worry. We're still travelling in convoy with the *Nieuw Zeeland*.'

Jenny lay down once more.

'Are you feeling better today?' Gerda asked.

'Perhaps a little,' Jenny said. 'The doctor says some of the symptoms were down to dehydration.' She paused. 'But I feel sick from time to time. I've had two more nosebleeds. The doctor still wants to keep me here under observation.' Jenny gripped Gerda's hand. 'You don't think there is something seriously wrong, and the doctor doesn't want to tell me?'

'I doubt it. You're looking better than when I first brought you into the infirmary.' Her voice brightened, but it sounded forced. 'Try not to worry. I'm sure you'll recover soon with more rest.'

But Gerda's eyes didn't meet hers, leaving Jenny to wonder which of them her friend was trying to convince.

Chapter 51

19 December 1940
SS Nieuw Zeeland, The Indian Ocean

The coastline of Aden receded like a mirage in the shimmering heat. Isaak welcomed the hint of an Indian Ocean breeze after the close air at the port's entrance. Yet a heaviness settled over him at leaving behind the kindness they had received. The *chevra* had loved the *Ka'adid* bread with its sprinkling of nigella seeds, a mild, nutty taste unlike anything they had tried before. Maybe it was not sadness so much as apprehension. They were now embarking on the last stretch of their voyage. Their destination was no longer a secret. In a week or so, they would land in Mauritius.

Isaak was relieved that Lilly had not accepted his suggestion to escape. He smiled at her as the wind blew errant strands of hair onto her face. She returned the smile, but there was sadness in her eyes. Perhaps she felt the same mixture of emotions as he did.

He had been reckless to suggest an escape without thinking it through. What would have happened if she had been caught and arrested? He'd never have forgiven himself.

Isaak wanted to believe her decision had something to do with him. But he knew better. More likely, she had feared getting caught. Or trapped on her own in Aden. Lilly was too sensible to take such a foolhardy risk. If she was hesitant to leave anyone, that would be Gisela, or the *chevra* in general.

After all, she had agreed quickly enough when he said it was funny that Daniel and Benzion had asked if they were married. Isaak regretted making that comment. Though what difference did it make anyway? Lilly would never look at him as anything more than a friend. No doubt she thought him too young for her. Too immature. Lilly was worldly, sophisticated. But even if she only regarded him as a friend, he would treasure that friendship. It would have to be enough.

Still, he wished he could broach the subject with her again.

But how ... What would he say?

'Do you remember when the brothers asked us if we were married? I worked out why they were laughing and nudging each other when I said you were my friend, my *chavera*. It's because *chavera* can also mean a girlfriend.'

Or: 'Do you recall when the brothers said the word *Ayuni* and giggled? A crew member told me what it meant. It's Arabic, not Hebrew. It means, my eye, but it's like calling someone my beloved—'

No! He would not dare say that.

Could he ask her: 'Would you ever think of us as more than friends?'

What if she didn't think of him that way and the question drove her away? But how would he ever know if he didn't speak up? Was it too soon to have such a conversation? Isaak cursed his lack of experience.

Do you remember ...?

He turned the words over in his mind, evaluated each one, rehearsed them.

Can I ask you something ...?

Perhaps that would be a better way to open the conversation.

'Isn't it strange?' Lilly said, jolting him from his thoughts. 'I almost feel sad to leave Aden. Like when we left Crete, even though we never set foot in either place.'

'Perhaps it's the kindness that you're sorry to leave behind,' Isaak said.

'Yes. You might be right.'

They stood in silence, watching Aden become a dot on the horizon, then disappear. Isaak's pulse quickened. Do it. Say it now.

Isaak cleared his throat. 'Do you remember—'

'Ladies and gentlemen!' Georgi hollered across the deck like a ringmaster about to announce the main act at the circus. 'May I have your attention.' He paused. The hum of conversation stopped. The rest of the *chevra* got up from their usual place in the shade and joined Isaak and Lilly by the railings. Isaak bit back his frustration. Georgi's interruption had stolen his chance.

'As you are no doubt aware,' Georgi continued, 'ever since you lot boarded the ship we've had a lice infestation ...'

Alexander leaned and murmured in Isaak's ear, 'And whose fault is that?' Isaak nodded. They'd first discovered the lice in the hammocks and in the seams of the British police blankets after being crammed in the hold. Georgi himself had restricted their access to the washrooms.

' ... This disgusting situation needs to be dealt with at once. Which is why I have decided it necessary for all passengers to have their hair cut and undergo a disinfection procedure.'

Murmurs of protest broke out among the women.

'He is not touching my hair.' Erika's hand flew to her pin curls.

'This is a direct order for everyone on board,' Georgi said, silencing the dissent. His eyes raked the crowded deck. 'We will start with the men. Ladies! You are to leave the deck at once and go down to the hold. You will be called when it is your turn.'

'Why is he making us go down into the hold in the heat of the day?' Janka whispered to Alexander.

'Probably because he wants us to get into our Adam's clothing.'

'*Na Wunderbar*!' Janka glanced skyward. 'Another madness has seized our Georgi.'

Alexander shrugged. 'I suppose it's necessary to get the lice out of our clothing and blankets.'

Isaak watched Lilly leave with Janka, Erika and Gisela, the four of them talking quietly. Georgi seemed to savour the moment as the women filed towards the exit. A smile, thin and unsettling, appeared on his face.

'Right then,' he said as soon as the last woman had left. 'Remove all your clothes and pile them up over there in the corner.' He pointed to the stern. 'Then form a line along the starboard railings.'

Around him, men slowly began to undress. Isaak did the same. His fingers fumbled with his shirt buttons. He added his clothes to the growing pile. Hunched over, he crossed his hands to shield himself as Georgi watched, his gaze moving over them, his thin smile widening. Isaak shuffled across the deck, taking his place beside Alexander and Max.

A team of policemen, clippers in hand, worked their way through the men, but Georgi handled the disinfection himself. Using a hand-pump he moved from man to man, from head to toe, conscientiously spraying them with Flit DDT. The chemical spray ran down their skin, sharp and acrid.

'Effective against vermin. Of every kind,' he said, savouring the words.

Isaak stiffened as his turn approached. With eyes shut and jaw clenched, he tried to detach from what was happening, to retreat somewhere inside himself where Georgi couldn't reach.

Georgi lingered at their backsides longer than anywhere else. 'It can be a hiding place for lice,' he said.

Alexander stood beside Isaak, his face flushed, jaw tight. Once Georgi had moved further down the line, he ground out, 'The biggest *Arschloch* is him.'

'And now,' Georgi said, reaching the end of the line. He smirked, enjoying himself more than any sane man should. He'd been waiting for this. The best part, saved for last. 'Turn around. Face the front.'

When it was over, the men stood silent, stunned. Max swiped away tears, head bent. 'I thought I'd left that nightmare behind,' he said. 'Back in Dachau.'

As for the pile of clothes and blankets in the corner, Georgi never glanced at them. They were of no interest.

Chapter 52

Sergeant Tait looked into the compartment. 'You are now permitted back on deck,' he said.

'Do we still need to have haircuts?' Erika called after him.

'Postponed. Until tomorrow. It's getting late,' he said, without looking back.

'At least that,' Lilly said as they left the hold and climbed the stairs.

'We should appeal,' Erika said. 'I don't want them touching my hair.'

Janka shrugged, palm upturned. 'I wonder how the men got on?'

Unease twisted in Lilly's stomach. An oppressive silence filled the space. The faint hum of chatter that trickled down from the promenade deck was missing. Usually, women's voices rose as they emerged, greeting the men on deck. Now, only silence. On reaching the landing, her nervousness spiked. She could hear muted gasps from the women ahead of them. As soon as she emerged onto the deck, she saw. She understood. The police had shorn every man's head. They looked like ... prisoners.

They rounded the corner and found the men sitting where they always gathered.

'*Um Gottes Willen*!' Janka gasped as she approached her brother. Stubbled head. Barely recognisable.

Alexander looked up at them, his face tight, eyes blazing. Beside him, Isaak sat with his cap pulled low, staring at the deck. And Max. He looked exactly the same as the first time Lilly met him, the day they boarded the paddle steamer after he was released from concentration camp. The same shaven head. The same haunted expression. Just like her father had looked.

Lilly stopped. Her hands dropped to her sides.

Gisela placed a hand to her mouth, shaking her head. Then she composed herself. She approached the men. To each, she placed her hands on their shoulders, and kissed their cheeks, whispering words of encouragement, the way a mother would.

Janka crouched between her brother and cousin, and hugged them both.

Erika's breath hitched. She knelt down and hugged Alexander. 'I'm so sorry.'

He pressed his hand against her back. 'It's just hair.' His voice was flat. 'It will grow again.'

Lilly wanted to approach them too, but she stood frozen.

'Lilly,' Gisela said. 'Do you have the *fetzen* that you used as a rope to haul up the bread in Aden?'

'It's in my rucksack.'

'Good. I need you to help me. Janka and Erika, you can help too.' Gisela led them away, out of the men's hearing. 'We'll make caps to cover the men's heads until their hair grows back.' She glanced back, her voice low. 'Some of them look terrible. We won't say that's why. We'll tell them it's for protection from the sun.'

Gisela brought out her sewing kit, distributed sewing needles and set the three of them to work.

Lilly's eyes blurred with tears, but her hands never faltered as she sewed.

The women's turn came the following morning. After they saw what Georgi had done to the men, their protests forced a concession: he would *only* cut their hair to their ears.

All the same, as hairdressers worked under Georgi's supervision, long tresses fell to the deck. Resentment hung in the air. Women cried out, complained.

With each rasp of the scissor blades through Lilly's hair, another piece of her humanity fell away. They had taken her freedom, her belongings, now this. How much more could they take?

Erika had come straight from her night shift for her haircut. Georgi made no exceptions. She stood, her eyes shut, silent as the glossy curls she had worked to maintain pooled around her feet. When it was done, she stepped over her hair without looking down and walked to the railings. She covered her face with her hands. Her body shook with sobs.

Alexander went to Erika at once and folded her into an embrace. The rest of the *chevra* gathered close: the men in their caps, the women with their cropped hair. Isaak and Max hugged Lilly, Janka, and Gisela.

'We're all in this together.' Gisela's voice was firm, though it wavered. 'And we'll get through this together too.'

'You're still beautiful,' Alexander said, holding her. 'Your hair will grow again soon.'

She shook her head. 'It's ... not ... that,' she said between sobs. 'I'm not crying about ... my hair.'

'What's wrong?'

Erika took a breath. 'It's Stefan.' She met Alexander's eyes, then the others.

'He has ... typhoid.'

Lilly went cold.

Alexander stiffened. The blood drained from his face. 'Will he …' Alexander began. 'I mean … is there …'

'He is very sick.' Erika answered the question he could not bear to ask. 'But we mustn't give up hope. We'll fight for him.' She looked from friend to friend. 'If you pray, please keep him in mind.' Her eyes settled on Alexander. 'Even if you never do, please pray for him now.'

Alexander nodded, blinking rapidly.

Two days later, Stefan's condition remained unchanged; no better, though at least stable. Each morning, Isaak donned his tefillin and prayed. When he finished, Alexander and the rest of the chevra clustered around him to recite a verse of *Tehillim*: 'I shall raise my eyes to the mountains, from where will my help come? … Behold the Guardian of Israel will neither slumber nor sleep.'

That afternoon, at half past two, the *Johan de Witt* signalled to the *Nieuw Zeeland*. Both ships stopped for the funeral of a passenger on board the *Johan de Witt*. The *chevra* stood by the railings, watching from afar, wondering – fearing – if it was someone they knew. Later that afternoon they mourned the death of one of their own, a sixty-eight-year-old woman, from heart disease and lung infection. At seven o'clock the morning after, the *Nieuw Zeeland* stopped again for a brief service while they buried the woman at sea. Gisela wept as they placed the board over the railings and the woman's body slid beneath the waves. The two women had first met on the *Atlantic*. They had been friends.

After the funeral, the chevra shuffled back to their usual spot. They sat in silence, their heads bowed. Lilly felt herself spiralling once more. An endless cycle of despair. Cast out to the farthest reaches of the earth, would they all die, forgotten?

It was Isaak who broke the silence. 'Do you know what I realised?' he said. 'Tomorrow night is the start of Chanukah.'

Alexander shrugged. 'What does it matter? We have nothing to celebrate.'

'On the contrary,' Isaak said. 'I think we all need a reason to celebrate. We should light the first candle of the menorah. We'll bring some light into this darkness.'

'I agree,' Lilly said.

'So do I,' Janka said. 'Tomorrow's also Christmas Eve. You think the policemen won't be celebrating? They'll be making merry and getting drunk like there's no tomorrow. They have taken so much from us already. We shouldn't let them take our festival too.'

Alexander was pensive, his jaw working. At last, he looked up. 'We'll ask for some candles.' A faint smile touched his lips. 'And we'll celebrate Chanukah.'

Chapter 53

24 December 1940
Atlit Camp

Hannah's eyelids drooped. She caught herself and jerked upright. Alma, sitting opposite, grinned at her. She nursed Chaim while taking notes. The two of them squeezed among the thirty women seated on benches around the rickety table at the front of the hut. Their makeshift classroom. The Hebrew teacher had been droning about verbs for over twenty minutes. The seven verb patterns. How to conjugate them in the past and present tense. Every morning, Hannah sat through these classes, yet instead of improving, the language only confused her more. Would she ever get the hang of Hebrew? Hannah picked up her pencil and forced her attention back to the teacher. But her eyes wandered to the washing strung from a line above her bed. In this drizzly weather, nothing dried. The whole hut smelled of dank laundry. Hers and everyone else's. Another forty minutes until lunch, then visiting hour when she would see Karl.

The door banged open and Hannah spun around. A thick-set British policeman, face ruddy from the cold, filled the doorway. The teacher broke off mid-sentence.

'Hannah Rosen,' the policeman said.

All eyes fell on Hannah. What did the policeman want with her?

He strode over to the table. 'Hannah Rosen,' he repeated. 'Please come with me.'

Hannah did not move. She had done nothing wrong. Unless this was about the hunger strike she had joined the day after Lilly was deported with the rest of the *Atlantic* passengers. But almost all the detainees had taken part. Why single her out? Or did this have something to do with the *Patria* disaster? Did they want to question her about what she knew? It could not be the start of another round of deportations ... could it?

'You have a visitor,' the policeman said.

'A visitor?' Hannah said.

Had they cancelled the deportation order? Perhaps Lilly had returned. There had been no word from her since that hurried note the freckle-faced policeman handed her hours after their departure. All Lilly wrote was the British were deporting them. She didn't know where. They had tried to resist without success. She'd write again as soon as possible and was sorry she hadn't been able to say goodbye.

'Well?' The policeman marched to the doorway, and glanced back. 'I haven't got all day. Are you coming?'

Hannah excused herself and followed the policeman out of the hut. Hurrying after him, her feet slipped on the muddy path. A bitter December wind blew through her thin cardigan. Rain hung in the air. She wrapped her arms around herself.

She rejoined the policeman as he continued right, away from the entrance, towards the camp's outer boundary. A trickle of detainees headed in the same direction. A cluster of them already stood at the wire fence, talking to visitors on the far side. Two policemen supervised. Another armed guard observed from the watchtower.

'You have ten minutes.'

Hannah approached the fence. She wedged herself into a gap between two women and scanned the faces on the other side – strangers, all strangers.

Halfway down the line, her breath caught. His skin was tanned from outdoor work; his wavy hair sun-bleached. He wore a worn woolly jumper, so different from the smart suits he wore in Vienna. But it was her cousin.

'Eugen.' Hannah reached out, then let her hand fall. The barbed wire stood between them.

'Hello, Hannah.'

'I don't believe it.' She stared at Eugen. It had been over two years since she had last seen him. 'How did you get here?'

Eugen gave a weary smile. 'On a very crowded bus from Haifa.'

'Lilly's gone,' Hannah said. 'They've deported her.'

He nodded, his expression heavy. 'I got a letter from her. She must have written it just before she left.'

'The rumours are they're being sent to Mauritius. I've never heard of it. Apparently it's an island off the coast of Africa.'

'I heard that too.' Eugen sighed. 'I tried to come and see you so many times, first at the port, then here. But it was impossible until now. I could not get permission. I was waiting for you both when your ship arrived.' His face darkened. 'The following morning, I watched the *Patria* capsize.'

'I was on the ship when it happened.' Hannah's voice dropped.

'The Jewish Agency eventually told us.' He studied her. 'Why didn't Lilly go with you?'

'She was supposed to join me, but someone else pushed in. Lilly swapped places with me at the last minute so I could board. The next morning, she was on the second lighter to leave the *Atlantic*. I saw and waved to her. Then ...' Hannah lowered her gaze. 'I transferred early to join my fiancé, Karl, who was already on the *Patria*. I don't know if you are aware I got engaged.'

He brightened. 'Yes, my mama wrote that you met someone in Bratislava and got engaged. Mazal tov! I'm so happy for you.'

'Thank you. I can't wait for you to meet Karl.' With a gesture toward the camp behind her, Hannah added, 'He's in the men's section.'

'It's wonderful to have some good news in the midst of everything. I have news too. Allegra and I are having a baby.'

'A baby! That is exciting. When is she due?'

'In four months.'

'Not long to go now. How is Allegra feeling?'

'Much better now that she's over the morning sickness.'

'Lilly will be an aunt for the first time.' Her voice trailed. 'She doesn't even know.'

'I'll write and tell her as soon as I get an address.'

'Five more minutes!' the policeman called.

Hannah still had so much she wanted to ask, to say. 'Tell me, what do you hear from your mother and mine?'

Eugen shook his head. 'The situation is becoming increasingly difficult. Far worse than when you left. They're managing as best they can. It's hard to tell what's really happening. The last letter I had was about a month ago. Their letters don't say much. There's censorship. They have to be careful what they write. Though, reading between the lines, I think a neighbour is helping them.'

'That must be Helga.'

He raised his eyebrows. 'We didn't have a neighbour called Helga. The only Helga I know is the one who lived above my father's shop. Her husband was a Nazi and her son in the Hitler Youth. It was Helga and her son who stood in the crowd on the street and laughed when my father and I were forced to scrub the pavement outside.'

'Yes,' Hannah said. 'That Helga.'

'How? Why?'

'I'll explain when I have more time. But Helga isn't quite who you think she is. She helped Lilly too.'

'One day, you'll tell me everything.' Eugen rubbed his face. New lines had formed at the corners of his eyes and on his forehead. 'I'm worried sick about our mothers and desperate to get them out of Vienna. But I can't find a way. I won't give up on Lilly either. Somehow, we'll get her back. Three days after the deportation, there were protest strikes all over the country. I took part in one in Haifa.'

'We held a hunger strike the following day.'

'But Lilly isn't aware of any of this. I hope she doesn't think we abandoned her.'

'She must realise we're fighting for her.'

'I hope so,' Eugen said. 'Tell me quickly. Did you meet someone called Gisela Klein aboard the ship?'

'Yes! Lilly and Gisela boarded the paddle steamer together in Vienna and became very close. We met when Lilly and I reunited on the *Atlantic*. Gisela looked after us all. And we cared for her.' The reminder brought Hannah back to that morning two weeks before, when she had walked outside with Alma to find the other side of the camp empty. Hannah looked down. 'She's gone as well.'

'Yes. I met her son at the port. We became friends. I'll tell him that you got to know Gisela and that she and Lilly are close and still together. I think it will bring him some comfort. At least his mother is not on her own.'

'Time's up!' the policeman called. 'End of visit.'

'Thank you for coming to see me. I can't tell you how much this means.'

'I'll visit again when I can,' he said. '*Chanukah sameach*.'

'*Chanukah sameach*.' The greeting rang hollow. Here she was in Eretz Israel, about to celebrate her first festival in the land. But she was imprisoned behind barbed wire. Lilly was on a ship to a remote island. Her mother and aunt were trapped in Nazi-occupied Vienna. There was not much to celebrate.

'Let's pray that next year we'll all celebrate Chanukah together. By then, we'll have a baby and hopefully you'll be married. I'll keep trying to find a transport to rescue our mothers, sending appeals to get Lilly back and get you out of here—'

'I said time's up! Detainees and visitors, please leave at once.'

'I need to go.' Hannah forced herself to step back from the fence.

'I won't give up on you,' Eugen called after her. 'Not on any of you.'

Chapter 54

24 December 1940
SS Johan De Witt, The Indian Ocean

Jenny's hands twisted in her lap, her gaze drifting to the porthole where the sun hung low over the water, while the doctor studied the notes on his desk.

'Well, Mrs Meyer.' He looked up. 'First, let me reassure you, there is nothing seriously wrong with you.'

The tension in Jenny's shoulders released. The breath left her in a rush.

'You were suffering from dehydration and heat exhaustion when you were first brought in.' He offered a gentle smile. 'But the explanation for the rest of your symptoms, I'm pleased to say, is a happy one.'

'I … I don't understand?'

'You're going to have a baby.'

Her hand flew to her mouth. A small sound escaped her.

'How?' she swallowed. 'How is that possible?' Heat rushed to her cheeks. She looked back down at her hands on her lap. 'My husband and I … we haven't … not since we departed Danzig. That was almost four months ago. And since then I have had some light bleeding.'

'May I ask when was the last time you observed any signs of bleeding?'

'Maybe a week or so after we left our home in Danzig. It was soon after we boarded the paddle steamer.'

'And nothing since?'

Jenny shook her head. 'I assumed it was because of the terrible conditions on board, the seasickness ... and I'm not always regular with my monthly cycle.'

'It is quite possible for a lady to experience a small amount of bleeding around the time the baby is conceived.'

Jenny's hand moved to her stomach. He paused; she looked up and nodded.

He continued, 'This occurs when the tiny embryo settles into the wall of the womb. We call this implantation. The bleeding tends to be light, as you described, and passes quickly. Sometimes it can be mistaken for the monthly cycle.' He smiled again. 'It appears, Mrs Meyer, that you are in your fourth month.'

'I've never reached this far before. Each time I miscarried by the third month.' She pressed her hands to her eyes, but tears spilled through her fingers.

'So far, everything is progressing as it should.'

'Thank you.' Her voice caught.

'Mrs Meyer, you have experienced an extremely difficult journey. I prescribe absolute rest from here on.' He rested his arms on the desk, clasping his hands together. 'I understand there is a party for your festival this evening?'

'Yes. We're having a Chanukah party. May I still go?'

'You can attend, but please don't exert yourself.'

'I won't. Thank you so much.' Jenny rose from her seat. 'And happy Christmas to you.'

He dipped his head. 'Many thanks. Let's hope the new year brings a swift end to this dreadful war.'

As Jenny left the doctor's cabin and closed the door behind her, Gerda paced back and forth in the passageway. 'What did the doctor say?' She studied Jenny's tearful face.

Jenny smiled through her tears. 'He said I'm expecting a baby. I'm about four months along.'

'Oh, Jenny,' Gerda hugged her. 'That is better news than I ever could have expected. I am so happy for you.'

Later that evening, Jenny and Gerda stood side by side in the ship's dining room to watch the lighting of the first candle on the menorah – candles the British commander had given them. Gerda held Anni in one arm, her other arm wrapped around Jenny. As Jenny watched the flicker of the flame, she thought of the new life growing within her. She could not wait to see Stefan again, to tell him that after ten years of marriage, they were having a baby. She wondered how he and the rest of the Lifeboat Chevra were faring on *Nieuw Zeeland*. Were they also lighting the Chanukah candles?

Raucous voices and laughter rose from below deck, the policemen's singing growing louder with each drink. But on the promenade deck above, melancholy settled over the *chevra*, sitting together in the darkness, each shout of laughter a reminder of all they were denied. They had nothing. Not even a single candle to mark the first night of Chanukah.

Alexander had asked Georgi for candles, but he refused. Other passengers had made the same request, but Georgi would not be swayed. He insisted the festival had already passed. Even when a rabbi showed him a calendar with the correct date, Georgi dismissed it. Lilly had approached Inspector Hargreaves. He shook his head, his expression apologetic. 'I'm sorry, there's nothing I can do. As much as I'd like to help, I can't override my superior.'

The week before, when the policemen cut their hair, Lilly had wondered how much more they could strip away. Now she had her answer.

Isaak lay on the deck, looking up at the star-filled sky. 'Do you know, this is kind of funny—'

'Funny?' Alexander broke in. 'That's not quite the word I would use to describe it. Miserable. Wretched. Gloomy, perhaps. Certainly not funny.'

'Over two thousand years ago, under the rule of the Greek Empire, the Hellenists tried to strip away our heritage.' Alexander opened his mouth and closed it. Isaak continued, 'They too persecuted us. We're living a similar experience to our ancestors who first introduced Chanukah.' Isaak propped himself up on his elbow. Alexander sat straighter. 'And where is the Greek Empire now?'

'Gone.' Lilly met Isaak's eyes. 'But we're still here.'

'Yes, we're still here. And more than two thousand years on, we're still celebrating the same festivals. Georgi might deny that it is Chanukah,' Isaak said. 'But he can't eradicate our festival. Neither can he stop us from celebrating.'

'I think he can,' Janka said. 'For one thing, we don't have any candles to light the menorah.'

'So we'll make do.' Isaak stood, his gaze lifting to the sky. 'We'll use a star in place of a candle. The policemen won't stop us. It's too noisy down there for them to hear us, and they're too drunk to care.' Isaak walked to the railings. Lilly, Alexander, Janka, Erika, Gisela, and Max followed. Isaak pointed to the stars above the Indian Ocean, thousands of miles from home, from everyone they loved, and he recited the blessings for lighting the menorah.

'Amen!' they responded as one.

They formed a circle, arms around each other, and sang the traditional Chanukah songs, concluding with *Maoz Tzur*.

'*Chanukah sameach*!' Alexander said. 'Next year in Jerusalem.'

'*Chanukah sameach*!' they answered. 'Next year in Jerusalem.'

Isaak leaned on the railings and gazed up at their celestial menorah. Lilly joined him.

'After candle lighting, my family and I used to play dreidel,' Isaak said.

'We did too.' Alexander looked at his sister. 'And you always used to cheat.'

Janka swatted his shoulder. 'I did not. You were just a sore loser.'

'I was not.' He grinned. 'Actually, I used to let you win.'

'On the first night we always had a family party,' Lilly said. 'Hannah and my aunt would be there ... and my mama made the most delicious potato latkes.'

'My mama used to make them too,' Erika said. 'Crispy on the outside, soft on the inside. The best I've ever tasted.'

Gisela sighed. 'Whoever would have thought by Chanukah I'd be halfway around the world on a ship again? I imagined sitting with my sons, my daughter-in-law, with my grandchildren on my knee. I'd play with them, give them *Chanukah gelt* ...'

'And I thought I'd be celebrating with Alma and Chaim. Our first Chanukah with our new son.'

Lilly put an arm around Gisela. Erika moved to her other side and did the same. Alexander and Isaak patted Max on the back.

'I've had an idea,' Janka said. She stood back from the railings. 'I've thought of a Chanukah gift for all of us.'

'Oh?' Alexander said. 'What's that?'

'While the policemen are too drunk to notice, we could go down to that cabin on the lower deck and have cold baths. What do you think?'

Erika giggled. 'I'm in.'

'Lilly,' Janka said. 'Will you join me again?'

'Of course.'

'Gisela?'

'Me do something as daring as that?' Gisela chuckled. 'Well, I suppose I could.'

Janka looked at Alexander, Isaak, and Max. 'We could take turns. Will you come too?'

'Why not?' Alexander gestured toward the stairs. 'Ladies first. We can stand guard outside and then we'll have a go.'

'We'll have to be careful going down the stairs,' Isaak said.

They filed onto the landing. Below, the policemen sang loudly and out of tune. Isaak leaned over the banister, looked down, and beckoned the others. They crept past the dining room where the policemen were celebrating and continued down to the deck below. On the lower deck, they headed for the unlocked cabin with the bathroom that Lilly and Janka had discovered. Gisela suppressed a smile. Her steps were lighter than usual.

Isaak stopped and held up a hand.

Alexander tilted his head in question.

Isaak pointed upwards. 'Someone's coming,' he whispered.

The singing was getting louder – one solitary voice. The clatter of footsteps grew closer. The lone drunken voice continued singing as he stumbled along the opposite passageway, banging on doors as he went. Georgi.

Janka beckoned. They tiptoed onwards to the bathroom. Lilly turned the handle and the seven of them rushed into the room. Lilly shut the door. Alexander and Isaak pressed their backs against it. They stood in the darkness, their breathing the only sound.

The singing stopped.

'Should we go back up the stairs?' Janka whispered.

'No,' Isaak said. 'Maybe he noticed us. He might be outside lying in wait.'

Another minute passed, tense and silent. They did not dare move.

A woman's scream sliced through the quiet.

'What was that?' Erika said.

Isaak cracked the door open and peered out.

The woman screamed again. Isaak and Alexander burst out of the cabin. Lilly, Janka, and Erika rushed after them, leaving Gisela and Max in the darkness. They ran along the passageway to where it branched, following the screams to the opposite corridor.

Shouts came from inside one of the women's cabins. Georgi's voice slurred. A brief scuffle. A yelp – Georgi's.

As Alexander reached for the handle, the door flew open, and Georgi tumbled out, his hands covering his head. Three women followed, slapping and cursing.

Alexander and Isaak grabbed him and locked his hands behind his back.

'Fetch the captain, policeman, someone!' Alexander said. 'Quick!'

Lilly, Janka, and Erika thundered up the stairs and split up. Lilly barged into the dining room where the policemen's party continued. She ignored Georgi's two girls sitting with Sergeant Tait; ignored the other men's stares.

'Miss?' Inspector Hargreaves said, looking up from his drink at a table near the entrance. 'Is everything all right?'

Lilly gasped for breath. 'You need to come.'

'Whatever is the matter?'

'There's a woman screaming from one of the cabins below.'

'Oh dear, oh dear. That doesn't sound good,' he said.

Hargreaves put down his glass and followed her out. They descended the stairs, Hargreaves taking them two at a time.

By the time they reached the women's cabin, the ship's captain and a crew member were already there. Lilly recognised him as the one who had brought Janka a cup of water on deck. They held Georgi between them. The women from the cabin continued to yell at him. Alexander and Isaak watched from the side.

'What the dickens is going on?' Hargreaves said.

'This man attempted to assault a woman,' the captain said. 'These young men were asleep in the hold. They heard the commotion and came to help. Thankfully, the women managed to fight him off and push him out of the cabin. These two held him until we arrived.'

'Is this true?' Hargreaves said.

The three women nodded. Alexander and Isaak did the same.

Georgi stared at Hargreaves, glassy-eyed.

'You are to be confined to your cabin for the duration of the voyage and relieved of your duties. Once we arrive in Mauritius, you will be handed over to the authorities.' Hargreaves turned to the women from the cabin. 'Ladies, I'm extremely sorry for any distress caused.'

Hargreaves addressed the captain and the crew member. 'Please assist me in taking him back to his cabin.'

Hargreaves and the captain each took an arm. Hargreaves inclined his head to Lilly. 'Thank you, miss.'

Georgi's legs buckled as they dragged him along the passageway. The Australian crew member followed behind. As he passed Janka, he caught her eye and the corner of his mouth lifted slightly.

'I think that's enough excitement for one night.' A smile played across Alexander's face. 'Let's skip the bath.'

They returned to the bathroom cabin. The door stood ajar. Inside, darkness and silence.

'Gisela? Max?' Lilly whispered.

No answer.

'Where could they have gone?' Erika said.

They climbed back to the promenade deck. Gisela and Max sat there, in their usual place, as if they had never left.

'How did you get back up here?' Lilly said.

'Us?' Gisela said with an air of innocence. 'We've been here all the time, haven't we, Max?'

Amusement flickered across his face. 'Indeed, we have.'

Gisela gave a mischievous wink, and they all burst out laughing.

By the following morning, word had spread through the ship. Georgi had been taken into custody and removed from his post. Inspector Hargreaves had been promoted to commandant in recognition of his quick thinking and actions.

The first change Lilly discovered when they visited the toilets was that a curtain had been erected between the men and women's sections.

'Better late than never,' Janka said.

Chapter 55

26 December 1940
SS Nieuw Zeeland, Mauritius

Dolphins leaped and dived alongside their ship as it cut through the water. Gulls circled in the sky above, a sure sign that they were approaching land.

Another shore. Lilly had never imagined her journey would end here, an ocean away from everyone and everything she had ever known. But Mauritius would be their home for now.

Lilly leant against the railings with the *chevra*. Waiting and watching, their questions and apprehensions unspoken. What awaited them here?

Shortly after four o'clock Isaak pointed to the horizon. 'I see land.'

A gentle breeze swept over them. Lilly shaded her eyes and made out two tiny dark peaks. They grew larger, their silvery summits catching the light, until they became a ridge of mountains surrounded by lush vegetation. Rich emerald surrounded by the sparkling turquoise waters of the Indian Ocean.

Lilly's breath caught.

The friendly Australian crew member paused beside them, cigarette in hand. 'Beautiful, isn't it?'

'What do they grow here?' Alexander said.

'Sugar cane and tobacco.' He gestured with his cigarette towards the verdant slopes. 'That's what makes it so green.'

In all their conversations about what awaited them – flat arid land, harsh rocky landscapes, untamed jungle – no one had imagined a magnificent island framed by mountains.

'I never dreamed it would look like this,' Janka said, her eyes trained on the scenery ahead, wide with wonder.

'It's like ... like a paradise,' Erika said.

They stood in silence as they drew nearer, transfixed by the island's unexpected splendour.

Soon a small town came into view with low buildings, even a car travelling on a road. The island's capital: Port Louis.

'It's not very big for a capital city,' Alexander said. 'But this is no uninhabited wilderness.'

'Do you think they have a hospital?' Erika said, glancing to where Stefan lay on a stretcher with the other seriously ill passengers, separated from the rest of the passengers by a bench. They had been carried up to the deck earlier that day in the hope that fresh air might help.

'They must do,' Alexander said.

'I hope it's a good one where Stefan can receive proper treatment and get better.'

'He will.' Alexander took her hand. She rested her head on his shoulder.

'Maybe it won't be so bad here after all,' Isaak said.

'It does look nice,' Gisela said. She forced a smile, stroking her silk peacock scarf. 'But it is far from our families.'

'And we're trapped here,' Max said.

'But only temporarily, until the war ends,' Isaak said. 'And it can't go on forever. It could be over in months. At least we'll be safe here in the meantime. We're so far from Europe.'

'But what happens afterwards?' Lilly said. 'The British say they'll never let us return to Eretz Israel.'

'We can appeal,' Isaak said. 'Especially since the *Patria* passengers were allowed to remain in Eretz.'

Max nodded. 'We should start writing letters to the British government, the *Yishuv*, and every other authority we can think of. I need to get back to Alma and Chaim. I can't leave them alone.'

'We'll do that as soon as we arrive,' Alexander said. 'If there's enough outcry the British may agree to let us return.'

'But what if they don't?' Janka said.

'There are other ways,' Isaak said. 'There always are. 'What if we took a ship to another destination, then travelled to Eretz Israel with new papers, different names? How will they know?'

'Have you forgotten that they have all our fingerprints?' Max said.

Isaak's shoulders dropped before his face lit up and his lips curled in a half-smile. 'A bit of sandpaper might solve that one.'

Alexander shook his head in amusement. 'Trust you to think of something like that.'

'One way or the other, this won't be forever.' Isaak studied the small town. 'Maybe we can find opportunities here. Work, start businesses, save some money. So eventually, when the war does end, we'll have the means to leave, pay for our journey, and establish ourselves in Eretz Israel.'

'I'm prepared to do anything,' Max said. 'Whatever it takes to support my wife and child and reunite with them as soon as possible. An office job, a driver, a farmer ...'

'There's plenty of cultivated land,' Alexander said, gazing at the wide stretches of vegetation. 'I can learn more about farming, so that when we move to a kibbutz, I'll have more expertise.'

'I can type and could get a job in an office,' Janka said. 'I quite like the idea of working at a newspaper.'

'I could continue my training at the hospital to become a qualified nurse,' Erika said.

'What about you, Lilly?' Isaak said.

'When we drove through the streets of Haifa on our way to Atlit, I had an idea ...' Lilly stopped and shook her head, hesitant to share further.

'Go on,' Gisela said. 'Tell us.'

'Yes,' Erika said. 'We want to hear.'

'Maybe it's a far-fetched idea,' Lilly said. 'But I thought perhaps I could open a little shop and sell dresses I have designed and made myself.'

'That sounds wonderful,' Gisela said. 'I could help with some sewing. I'll need a way to support myself while we're here and something to keep me occupied.'

'I'd love that! We make a good team, don't we?'

Gisela smiled. 'We do.'

'I could help you with sales,' Isaak said. 'The two of you will be too busy sewing to do everything.'

'You'd be excellent at that,' Alexander said.

In the golden light of the setting sun, as the ship drew closer to Mauritius, the friends formed a circle.

'This is only for a short time.' Alexander looked around the circle. 'We'll find a way back to Eretz. Somehow. Soon. Back to our home, our dreams, our families.'

They put their arms around each other. As they had done weeks ago in Haifa, before they realised their lives were about to take a different turn. Isaak stood beside Lilly, Gisela on her other side.

Isaak met her eyes. 'Are you afraid?'

'Yes, a little,' Lilly said.

'So am I,' Isaak said. 'But at least we'll be together.'

She thought back to Aden, to the question Alexander had asked Erika: Did she regret coming on the transport?

Lilly asked herself the same question. This was not the outcome she would have chosen. But maybe she was exactly where she was supposed to be.

This was not the end of the story.

Perhaps it was a new beginning.

Author's Note

Another Shore is based on true historical events that remained largely forgotten for decades. What began as research into a footnote of WWII and Holocaust history became something far more personal when I discovered, just as I was writing about the *Patria* disaster, that one of my paternal grandfather's first cousins and his wife were on board at the time of the explosion. Fortunately they survived.

Like *Wave After Wave*, the first book in this planned trilogy, the main characters are products of my imagination, but woven among their experiences are those of real people who endured this harrowing journey.

The refugees who were deported to Mauritius left behind diaries, testimonies, and drawings – fragments of memory scattered around the world. Over five years of research, I visited archives and museums including Atlit Detention Camp, Ghetto Fighters House, the British National Archives, the National Library of Israel, Haganah Historical Archives, and Yad Vashem. Online, I consulted sources including the Wiener Library and the United States Holocaust Memorial Museum.

Of particular value were conversations with those who made this difficult journey as children, and with descendants whose parents or grandparents had shared their experiences. From them I learned small details that had never been written down.

But perhaps most important were the written and oral testimonies, statements, and diaries of those who lived through these events. I am particularly indebted to the accounts of Isaac Adler, Dr Erwin Enoch, Alfred Heller, Dr Robert Hirsch, Ing. Erwin Kovac, Franci-Jehudith Lederer-Berger-Schlesinger, Karl Lenk, Ruth Sander-Steckl, Dr Erich Gershon Steiner, and Aaron Zwergbaum. I hope I have honoured their words. May their memories be for a blessing.

It would be many years before the full story of what happened to the Patria emerged. In 1957, Munya Mardor, the Haganah operative who had disguised himself as a worker repairing the kitchen oven, published a book revealing the truth: it was a Haganah operation gone catastrophically wrong.

The plan had been to plant a small explosive device to damage the ship and delay it in port for repairs, buying time for political intervention to cancel the deportation decree. The planners knew they had to avoid sinking an Allied ship because to do so would undermine the war effort as well as be used as a pretext by their enemies to condemn them as saboteurs of vessels essential for the war against Hitler. Above all, they did not want to endanger the refugees themselves.

The explosive was smuggled into the port in a sandbag, then transferred into a leather bag concealed among Mardor's lunch. Hans Wendel (HW) helped facilitate the transfer on board.

What went wrong? At the time of the explosion, the bulkhead doors were open. In modern ships, compartments below the waterline are separated by special watertight bulkheads designed so that flooding in one section won't sink the vessel. But the British had installed living quarters beyond permitted capacity in various parts of the *Patria*, making it impossible to seal off the affected areas.

The Haganah later conducted an investigation to determine why the ship sank so rapidly. The *Patria*'s hull, despite appearing sound, was in far worse condition than anyone realised. The rivets were corroded and could not withstand the pressure caused by the explosion. Due to the disintegration of the rivets, several panels tore away from the side of the ship simultaneously. Contrary to what was planned, large amounts of water poured in and caused the ship to capsize in under ten minutes. Over 260 people lost their lives, more than 200 of them Jewish refugees, along with British police, soldiers, and crew members. Approximately 170 were injured.

Almost none of the passengers knew at the time what had happened. Hans Wendel (HW), one of the leaders of the *chalutzim* on the ship, recruited trusted friends to act as decoys during the smuggling operation and helped set up the explosive device. In this novel, I made Karl one of those friends.

Hans Wendel was real, and his role was almost exactly as described in *Another Shore.* From testimonies of those near him in his final moments, we know that after the explosion, HW ran to the detention room to break down the door and release those who had been locked up by the British for attempting to escape. He was last seen going down to the hold to rescue those trapped there. His body was never recovered.

I tried to keep as closely as possible to the actual dates of events, with two exceptions made for pacing. First, the recovery of luggage from the *Patria* probably came a few days later than I've depicted. Second, the British government's decision to allow *Patria* survivors to remain was made between 27–28 November 1940, with news spreading around 2 December. I moved the timing slightly earlier so that when the Lifeboat Chevra passengers disembark from the *Atlantic* on 1 December, they're already aware of the amnesty granted to the *Patria* survivors – heightening the tragedy of their own deportation.

Many of the episodes and scenes throughout the story are based on diary accounts. The *Oneg Shabbat* in Atlit on Friday night, for example, comes from a diary entry by Egon Weiss, a survivor of the *Patria*. However, this gathering most likely took place within one of the men's huts in the *Patria* section of the compound, as the *Atlantic* passengers never mention it in their accounts. The guards likely would not have permitted such a gathering. I created this moment of connection across the fence knowing it was improbable – but not impossible, given that detainees regularly shouted to one another – and then increased the realism by having the guards quickly disperse it.

The *Atlantic* passengers conceived the plan for passive resistance amongst themselves in Atlit – going to bed naked, refusing to get up, refusing to pack. It was mainly the younger *chalutzim* who carried this out, as depicted in the novel, though there were older naysayers like the fictional Emil. At least one of the *gaffirim* (auxiliary police) did shout into the camp, as Aaron Zwergbaum recorded in his diary: 'No one decides to leave the land of our fathers and our national home voluntarily. We are encouraged in this decision by the *Gaffirim* patrolling outside, who shout: "*Lo lasus mimkomchem*" ("Don't move from your places")."

The brutal deportation from Atlit is based on a blend of accounts from different diaries, testimonies published anonymously by *gaffirim* shortly afterwards, and a haunting pencil drawing by Fritz Haendel. You can see a reproduction of it in the companion ebook to this novel.

Most of the policemen are fictitious, though many of the incidents they appear in are drawn from diary accounts – such as a policeman promising young women ice cream if they cleaned the hold of the *Nieuw Zeeland*, then admitting he lied. Several diaries mention a very tall policeman who kicked Mr Finkelstein in Haifa port. Mr Finkelstein was the elderly man who begged to be allowed to die in Eretz Israel. He died on board the Johan de Witt and was buried at sea. Mrs Hoyle is mentioned by name in an account I found in a file at the British National Archives. Inspector Hargreaves, the more sympathetic policeman, also appears in several accounts.

I'm not certain whether Georgi was the actual name of the commanding officer on the *Nieuw Zeeland*, but Franci-Jehudith Lederer-Berger-Schlesinger refers to him that way in her diary. I created the backstory of how his nickname might have originated. According to passenger statements, the commanding officer did attempt to molest a woman in her cabin one night. The women were able to offer resistance. He was caught, stripped of his position, and handed over to authorities on arrival in Mauritius.

Unfortunately, none of the diaries record the name of the kind Dutch captain of the *Nieuw Zeeland* who provided clothing for refugees who had boarded wearing only blankets.

The *Nieuw Zeeland* did stop in Aden on the way to Mauritius, and one passenger from the *Johan de Witt* was taken to hospital there for two days before being returned to the ship. But as far as I'm aware, members of the Adeni Jewish community were never able to make contact with the passengers. It's possible the British intentionally concealed that the hospitalised passenger was Jewish, and that the two ships just outside the harbour were filled with Jewish refugees. Had the local community known, they almost certainly would have wanted to help, as communities did previously in Istanbul, Crete, and Limassol.

The scene where the two boys meet Lilly and Isaak is fictitious, inspired partly by those other meetings between refugees and Jewish communities, and partly as a way to connect this story to one of my earlier novels, *Ayuni*. The boys, Benzion and Daniel, share the names of characters in that book – and in my imagination, they are their grandfathers as young boys.

If you're interested in reading more about the research and true story behind Another Shore, you can download the free companion ebook – *Forgotten Voices: The True Stories Behind Another Shore* – through my website: www.sarahansbacher.com

And if this story moved you, please consider leaving a review on Amazon or Goodreads. Your words will help ensure these voices aren't forgotten.

Acknowledgements

Although writing is often a solitary endeavour, bringing a book into the world requires a community. I am deeply grateful to the many people and institutions who helped me research and write this novel, and to those who shared their family stories so that these voices would not be forgotten.

Laura Karp – thank you for going over the manuscript again and again with unwavering enthusiasm, questioning everything, pushing me to fact-check and ensuring the story honoured those whose experiences we're telling. I cannot thank you enough, *ayuni*.

Lina Erez – thank you for another beautiful cover that perfectly captures the spirit of this story. It's always a pleasure to work with you.

To Kitty Schrott and Oscar Langsam, for graciously sharing your childhood memories of the journey to Mauritius. To Mickey Steiner, for sharing stories about your father, Fritz Steiner. To John Ponger, for telling me about your grandmother on the *Patria*. And to Dr Micha Werner, for recounting your childhood memories of visiting relatives who were survivors of the *Patria* disaster and were held in Atlit. Your personal stories brought history to life in ways no archive could.

Special thanks to Rabbi Moshe Silberhaft, the Travelling Rabbi, for your ongoing support and assistance with my research, and for helping bring this forgotten story to light.

To Marion Adler, for translating portions of Franci-Jehudith Lederer-Berger-Schlesinger's diary from German, revealing details I never would have discovered otherwise. To Carmela Shapira, for translating handwritten accounts by *gaffirim* who served in Atlit. To Hadassah Sabo Milner, for helping me obtain that rare book on the *Patria*, and for your affirming enthusiasm as an advance reader.

To Yael Kaufman of the Atlit Detention Camp Database and Anat Bratman-Elhalel of the Ghetto Fighters House Archive, for your invaluable research assistance. To Owen Griffiths, President of the Island Hebrew Congregation in Mauritius – those boat trips in Port Louis harbour gave me an entirely new perspective on the refugees' arrival. To Yanky Schleimer, for patiently answering my many random research questions, especially about transport and logistics.

For your encouragement, beta reading, and feedback: Elana Abraham, Claire Adler, Tom Gross, Nadine Stark, Ben Weiss, Michelle Wellins, and Rachel Woolfson.

To my father, Robert Schleimer, for your encouragement and support.

To Alon, Oren, and Itamar – thank you for your patience and enthusiasm throughout this journey.

Finally, to Shmuel – thank you for being my sounding board through every draft, for helping me work through plot tangles and technical details, and for your unwavering belief in this project. Your encouragement, wisdom, and love sustain me through every book and make everything possible.

Glossary

Key: **G** = German **H** = Hebrew

Acheinu - Our brothers (H)

Ach so! - Oh right! / Oh, I see! (G)

Ach quatsch! - Oh nonsense! (G)

Ayuni - My eyes – an Arabic term of endearment meaning 'my beloved'

Bevakasha - Please (H)

Chalutzim - Pioneers (H)

Chavera / Chevra - Friend or comrade (feminine form) or girlfriend / A group of friends (H)

Danke - Thank you (G)

Eretz - Land – short for Eretz Israel (H)

Erev Yom Kippur - The eve of the Day of Atonement (H)

Fetzen - A rag, scrap of fabric, used for cleaning or considered worthless (G)

Fräulein / Frau / Gnädige Frau - Miss / Mrs / Gracious lady (G)

Gaffir / Gaffira / Gaffirim - Jewish guard - male/female/plural male (H)

Genau - Exactly (G)

Gott sei Dank! - Thank God! (G)

Guten Morgen - Good morning (G)

Haganah - Defence organisation. Founded in 1920 to protect Jewish communities (H)

Chanukah / Chanukah sameach / Chanukah gelt - Eight-day Jewish Festival of Lights commemorating the rededication of the Second Temple (H) / "Happy Chanukah" (H) / small gifts of money traditionally given to children during Chanukah (H / G)

Hütte - Alpine hut or mountain shelter (G)

Irgun - The Irgun Zvai Leumi (National Military Organisation), operated from 1931–1948, known for its more militant approach than the Haganah (H)

Jude - Jew (G)

Kalpak - A tall felt or fur cap traditionally worn by the Gaffirim (Jewish guards)

Kibbutz - A collective community in Israel traditionally based on agriculture (H)

Komm schon - Come on (G)

Kosher - Food prepared according to Jewish dietary laws (H)

L'chaim - To life. A drinking toast (H)

Mazel tov / mazal tov - Congratulations! Ashkenazi and Sephardi/Modern Hebrew pronunciations respectively (H)

Mein Gott! - My God / Oh my God! (G)

Mitzvah - A commandment or good deed (H)

Parochet - The decorative curtain hanging in front of the Torah ark in a synagogue (H)

Pfui! - An exclamation of disgust (G)

Purim - A joyous festival commemorating the salvation of the Jewish people in ancient Persia (H)

Rashi - Rabbi Shlomo Yitzchaki (1040–1105), a medieval French rabbi who developed a distinctive Hebrew script and whose Torah commentaries are fundamental to Jewish study

Richtig - Right (G)

Shabbat / Oneg Shabbat / Shabbat Shalom - Sabbath / A social gathering on Shabbat / Shabbat peace - traditional greeting (H)

Schatzi / Mein Schatz - Darling / My darling (G)

Schon gut - All right (G)

Shacharit - Morning prayers (H)

Shalom / Shalom Aleichem / Aleichem shalom - Peace (hello or goodbye) / Peace be unto you (traditional greeting) / Unto you be peace (H)

Shema - A prayer said every day in the morning and evening prayer, before going to sleep and also before someone passes away (H)

Siddur - Prayer book (H)

Sukkah / Sukkot - A temporary hut / The seven-day Festival of Tabernacles commemorating the Israelites' desert wanderings (H)

Tallit / Tefillah / Tefillin - Prayer shawl / Prayer / Jewish Phylacteries worn by men at morning prayers (H)

Tehillim - Psalms (H)

Um Gottes Willen - For God's sake! (G)

Unglaublich - Unbelievable (G)

Va'ad - Committee or council (H)

Wie geht's - How are you doing? (G)

Was ist das - What is this? (G)

Willkommen - Welcome (G)

Wunderbar / Na wunderbar - Wonderful / Well, wonderful! Often sarcastic (G)

Yehudi - Jewish (H)

Yishuv - 'The settlement.' The Jewish community before the establishment of the State of Israel in 1948 (H)

About the Author

Sarah Ansbacher is the author of eight books, with her first published when she was just eighteen. Born in London, her storytelling draws from a deep interest in Jewish history, heritage, and culture, exploring themes of identity, resilience, and belonging.

Her current trilogy follows Jewish refugees who fled Nazi Europe via the Danube River in 1940 – a largely forgotten chapter of WWII history. The first two novels in the trilogy bring these true stories to life through extensive archival research.

Formerly at the Aden Jewish Heritage Museum, Sarah now focuses on writing and speaking about untold stories from Jewish history. She enjoys connecting with book clubs and readers. Visit her at www.sarahansbacher.com

ALSO BY SARAH ANSBACHER

Wave After Wave

Ayuni

Passage From Aden: Stories From A Little Museum In Tel Aviv

Made in United States
North Haven, CT
07 March 2026

89572973R00253